WHAT LIES BEYOND THE REALMS

ASHLEY R. O'DONOVAN

For Nicholas—
Because you would follow me into darkness any day.
I love you.

WHAT LIES BEYOND THE REALMS

CHAPTER
ONE

*S*omething's burning! I struggle to breathe as the sharp and pungent smell of smoke burns my nose. I feel like someone just blew sand in my eyes, which sting from the heat. I quickly survey my surroundings and realize the forest is on fire. Black trees burn and fall, and animals flee. I see the orange flames dance in the night sky, ash raining down on me like black confetti, sticking to my skin and coating my throat with soot. I attempt to run, but my bare feet are covered in a wet, sticky substance. Despite this, I continue running. The heat is intense, and I feel like my skin will melt off my face. I shield my face with my arms, but the smoke thickens and forces me to the ground. I crawl as fast as I can, gasping for air. My hands and knees become covered in the black, viscous substance on the ground as I crawl under the thick branches overhead, which seem to be bleeding or crying the sticky substance.

As I try to crawl in the direction the animals fled, I realize I had turned around. I can only see a few feet in front of me. I hear a loud snap overhead and quickly look up just in time to roll back as a black branch falls and fans flames across the forest floor. The fire quickly turns everything it touches to ash. In shock, I watch for a moment before a hand grabs my arm and pulls me away. I turn to see who it is.

My eyes burst open, and I awake from my nightmare to a far worse one—Samael, my stepbrother, is on top of me. His long, lean body is pressed against mine. His hand covers my mouth, and I feel his breath on my cheek as his shoulder-length brown hair brushes my arm.

"Oh, sweet sister, you looked fitful in sleep. I thought you would be delighted for me to wake you," he says while dragging his tongue across my cheek. His hot tongue glides across my face, the smell of smoke and liquor on his breath making me gag into his hand. As I look up at him, his eyes pierce through me with their malevolent darkness. Without warning, he abruptly peels away from me.

"What the . . ." he yells and looks down at Chepi, who's biting at his leg and growling something fierce.

"You're lucky I'm not in the mood," he says, looking back at me and then kicking Chepi off him. He turns and leaves the room, slamming the door behind him.

Samael is a corrupt and vile Sorcerer. Our age gap is not the only reason that he and I have never been close. He's thirty-five, and I just turned eighteen last month. His dad, King Silas, and my mother, Queen Macy, married when I was young after my father passed. Ever since, Samael has made it his life's mission to torture and humiliate me behind closed doors. My parents are blind to it—I don't know how, maybe he uses dark undetected magic on them—but everyone else in this realm knows he's evil. Even the animals sense it and stay away from him. As a Sorceress, I'm left completely vulnerable until the age of nineteen when I inherit my magic, which makes me easy prey for Samael. I've managed to survive this long by avoiding him as much as possible and hiding my fear. I refuse to give him the satisfaction of seeing how much he terrifies me. Just the thought of his touch makes my skin crawl and twits my stomach into knots. A shiver runs through my body, and Chepi comes over to lick my face.

Chepi is a Glyphie, a rare magical creature found in the Dream Forest of the Faery Realm in Nighthold. He was gifted to me by my father when I was just a little girl, and since then he has been my loyal companion and best friend. With his small black body covered in short and silky hair, Chepi may look like an ordinary dog, but his violet eyes and bat-like wings that can materialize at will set him apart. In addition to his flying ability, Chepi has another gift that not many know about, including my own mother. My father always warned me never to tell anyone that Chepi also has the gift of invisibility. When I hold him, he can make us both invisible for a short time, which has come in handy on more than one occasion, especially when I need to sneak around the castle grounds.

A knock at the door rouses me from bed, and Lili strolls in along with her usual scent of vanilla and lavender. I am suddenly surrounded by a flurry of activity as she orders servants around my bedchamber. My rooms are much larger than I need, but it's nice to have the space when I spend so much time in here. My bedchamber is adorned with delicate blue and beige throw rugs, softly laid upon the aged wood floor, providing a warm and welcoming ambiance. A grandiose bed, big enough for four people, rests in the center, its pristine white covers fluffed with a plethora of fluffy pillows, inviting me to nestle in. A quaint sitting area, complete with a table and two large cushioned chairs, their blue fabric stitched with delicate white flowers adding a touch of elegance and charm to my private haven. Next to the sitting area is a door that opens to a balcony with a beautiful view of the side gardens and forest just beyond. I have a spacious bathroom with a large claw-foot tub, a large closet, and a vanity with ample counter space.

Lili is charged with looking after me. She's my parents' most trusted servant and has taken care of me for as long as I can remember—even before my father passed and my mother remarried.

Lili is one of the few people I can rely on in this place. Despite her age, which I can only assume is somewhere around fifty, she shows no signs of slowing down. Her long black hair is always tied into a tight bun at the nape of her neck, giving her an air of elegance and power. I know that, like me, she is a Sorceress, but unlike me she has pledged her life to serve my family. Her loyalty and dedication are unwavering, and I don't know where I would be without her.

She looks at me with her soft hazel eyes. "Good morning, Princess Lyra—" She stops abruptly when she takes in my face, orders all the servants out of the room, and comes to sit on the edge of my bed. "You've had another premonition," she says.

I nod slowly, feeling the weight of exhaustion settling in from having a poor night's sleep. I raise my hand to wipe away the beads of sweat that have formed on my forehead.

Lili is the only one that knows about my nightmares, "premonitions" she calls them. They started happening about ten years ago, shortly after my father's passing. Lili calls them premonitions because sometimes what haunts me in my sleep becomes a reality. But sometimes they're just nightmares. This one felt rather ominous, and it's the second time I've had this nightmare. I recite the events of the dream to Lili, and a chill creeps up my spine.

"Did it look like the forest surrounding the castle?" Lili asks. I swallow hard and try to shake off the lingering dread from the nightmare. "It didn't look like any forest I've seen before."

Lili purses her lips then shakes her head as if she could shake away what I said. "Try not to fret over it for now. You have a busy day ahead. I've had a bath prepared for you and clothes laid out. I'll be back in a little while to do your hair. The king and queen are expecting an important visitor tonight at dinner and have requested your company. Your parents want me to prepare you for what is expected of you this evening." Lili brushes my sweaty, slick hair out of my face and gives me a reassuring smile before leaving the room.

I hurry into the bath and begin to wash my hair, wondering who could be joining us for dinner tonight. It's a rarity for my parents to invite me to dine with them, as they typically serve my meals to my room, leaving me to eat alone. Their sudden request for my company can only mean that some dignitary or noble from another realm is visiting, and they want to present a flawless, yet fake, image of our family. As the leaders of the Sorcerer Realm and the monarchs of Cloudrum, which encompasses the Lycan Realm, Sorcerer Realm, and Lamia Realm, they must maintain an appearance of strength and unity, even if it is a façade.

Across the Feral Sea is Nighthold, which is solely comprised of the Faery Realm and its numerous territories. The thought crosses my mind that perhaps a Faery will be attending dinner tonight. Despite never having met one in person, I can still recall the stories Samael used to tell me as a child about their razor-sharp teeth and their supposed penchant for preying on newly-powered Sorceresses during the night, draining them of their blood and magic. Although Mr. Drogo, my teacher, had merely laughed off my inquiries about it, I wouldn't dare ask my mother such a question.

My mother barely speaks to me. I know she loves me, but I've always thought she loved the idea of me more. She wants to raise the perfect princess to show off when people visit, but

5

she doesn't care to know me. She closely monitors my weight and makes sure I look the part. I can hear her now reminding me. She'll say, "Suck in your stomach, dear. Sit up straight. Don't speak unless spoken to." Looks have always been important to her—how I look, how she looks, how the family is perceived. As for my stepfather, Silas, he isn't very chatty. He's the one who insists I have a private teacher; he wants me to be well versed. Silas is the one who confines me, and that's why I often feel isolated and restricted. I can't set foot outside the castle grounds thanks to him. Despite reading about other realms and their magic in books and learning from my teachers, I've never seen them in person. Imagining a life beyond these walls is the only thing I can do.

I have a small circle I socialize with. Lili, who is basically my second mom, Mr. Drogo, my current teacher, Samael and his occasional follower, and obviously the castle staff, but none of them speak to me much besides Lili. I only get to speak to people outside the castle boundaries once every few weeks when I'm invited to a formal dinner, where I'm not allowed to speak unless spoken to. I talk to myself and Chepi more than anyone else most days. Even though he can't talk back, I know he understands me.

I finish washing up and throw on a casual light-purple gown that Lili left on the bed for me then go out on the balcony to get some fresh air and let Chepi out. He immediately runs toward the window and leaps through, his furry bat-like wings materializing as he disappears into the forest.

Must be nice to be able to fly away from this place. The thought of sitting through another formal twenty-course dinner is daunting. I wonder what poor exotic creatures were killed cruelly on the castle grounds this morning so my mother could impress her guests with another lavish dinner menu tonight.

"Come in here and let me start your hair before Mr. Drogo's lessons. I won't have time to do it tonight before dinner," Lili calls from my bedchamber, and I follow the sound of her voice to my vanity. I sit before its gilded mirror and watch her go to work on my hair.

My hair is long and wavy, falling just low enough to graze my hips, and it's a very light shade of blonde. My mother always says it's fitting for her daughter, who was born in the Tempest Moon District, to have hair the color of moonlight. My skin is rather fair, especially since I don't spend much time out in the sun. I'm aware of my physical attractiveness; my full lips and petite nose have been frequently complimented, and my mother always mentions my bright blue-green eyes, the color of the Feral Sea. While I am blessed with a curvy figure, complete with full breasts and shapely hips, I've often found that my looks attract unwanted attention. At times, I can't help but feel like it's more of a curse than a blessing.

Lili makes a long braid down my back, leaving a few short wavy pieces to fall around my face.

"Please don't mess up your hair before dinner. I'll leave a dress out for you to put on tonight after you meet with Mr. Drogo," she says while making finishing touches to the back of my hair.

"Who will be in attendance tonight? Who do I have to sit and look pretty for this time?" I roll my eyes in the mirror. I know it's not Lili's fault my life is like this.

"Her majesty didn't say, but she made it clear you needed to attend and mind your manners. Don't ask questions. Don't speak unless spoken to. If you're asked about your life here, keep your answers short." Lili smiles at me like she hasn't recited this to me a hundred times before. "Now, you're perfect. Go to your lessons before you're late. We both know

7

how Mr. Drogo can get crabby when kept waiting. I'll put out your clothes and jewelry. Try to have fun tonight. I'm sure it won't be all that bad."

"Thanks, and I'll try. Leave my window open for Chepi," I say to her on my way out the door.

I'm in fact late to meet Mr. Drogo in the library, and it seems he's in a particularly foul mood. His unkempt white hair resembles a tangled bird's nest perched atop his head, and his square-framed glasses rest on the tip of his long, pointed nose. His intense hazel eyes flit all over me, as if attempting to read my mind.

"You're late, Princess Lyra. Tardiness is not becoming of a princess."

He insists we go over the geography of Nighthold and the Faery Realm even though we've covered it in the past. There's another hour going over mannerisms of the Fae, and I'm thankful I have to end our lessons early to get ready for dinner.

I make it back to my room to find Lili left out a beautiful green gown. My mom will be pleased because it'll bring out the green in my eyes. She also left out my favorite necklace, a gold chain with a teardrop-shaped bloodstone. It's the last thing my father gave me before he died. When he gave it to me, he told me the stone would always protect me and give me strength when I needed it most. I didn't wear it for the longest time after he passed. Looking at it used to make me sad, but now when I'm feeling down I find myself seeking out the stone. Even now as I run my fingers over it, I feel a sense of calm. Not to mention the bloodstone itself is quite beautiful. It's a deep emerald with flakes of violet running through it that remind me of Chepi's eyes. I clasp it around my neck and move the gown off my bed over to my chair.

I still have some time before I have to get ready, so I try to lie on my bed carefully without messing up my hair. I'm still tired and feeling drained after having such restless sleep lately. Everything about the castle has seemed off these past couple weeks, and now having this nightmare twice makes me even more weary. Unease has started to fester in my chest, and I don't know what it means, but I want to get to the bottom of it.

Samael bursts through the door and is on top of me before I can even sit up. He has his hand around my throat.

"Listen, you little bitch, I don't want you at dinner tonight. Come up with an excuse and get out of it." He releases my neck then grabs my thigh and pinches it hard. "I wouldn't want to leave a mark somewhere visible." He grins at me with a cruel edge to his lips and winks. "Do you understand?"

"Yes, I understand, but I have to make an appearance or my mother will kill me. Lili already knows I'm well I can't lie to her now."

"You make an appearance, then you say you don't feel well and leave. I don't need you fucking up my plans. Do you understand, Lyra?" He pinches my thigh harder, and I know it's going to leave a bruise.

"Yes," I mutter.

"Good girl." He lets go of my leg and pats me on the head before leaving.

Now I really want to know who is coming to dinner tonight. Why doesn't Samael want me there? I know he'll make me regret it if I don't figure out a way out of dinner. If I go to my parents now and tell them I don't feel well, they won't care and will make me attend dinner anyway. If I wait until we're all seated and announce I don't feel well in front of company, they'll be forced to put on an act and let me leave without a fuss. I know this because appearances are everything to my mother, and it'd be inappropriate for her to force her sick daughter to stay at dinner and socialize with company.

Chepi swoops in through the window and flops onto his

back on the bed. I give him some belly rubs. "And where have you been all day, mister?"

He just rolls around panting.

I take my time getting ready for dinner, savoring the rare opportunity to dress up. My green dress hugs my curves in all the right places, accentuating my hourglass figure. It's a little more revealing than my usual attire, but I don't mind. I add a touch of pink to my lips and cheeks, wanting to look my best so I don't have to see another look of disapproval from my mother. As I glance at my reflection in the mirror, I notice that my braid has turned frizzy on top, and strands have come loose, thanks to Samael. With a sigh, I decide to undo the braid and let my hair fall in loose waves behind me. It's a more natural look and one that I prefer.

"Stay here. I'll bring you back dinner in a bit," I say to Chepi and head to the great dining hall.

As I enter the great hall, I'm struck by the breathtaking beauty of the room. It's decorated with exquisite detail tonight, just as it always is when used for entertaining. The vast space has towering vaulted ceilings and large gold mirrors that reflect the glowing light from the elaborate chandelier above. Paintings of enchanting landscapes within the Sorcerer Realm adorn the walls, transporting me to far-off lands with just a glance. The magnificent polished wood table, bedecked with black and gold dishes, sits at the center of the room, beckoning guests to dine in luxury. The ambient light from the chandelier casts the perfect glow over everything, creating an atmosphere of enchantment and wonder. The kitchen doors burst open, startling me as several servants spill out into the room with trays in their hands, and I scrunch my nose at the smell of sour milk cheese wafting off one of the trays. I take a drink of water then turn when I catch a man entering the room out of the corner of my eye.

As I turn to face him, I find myself momentarily stunned by his presence. Standing before me is a towering figure, broad-shouldered and undeniably attractive. His light, sun-kissed skin seems to glow in the ambient light, and his hair, as black as a raven's wing, is tousled in an effortlessly sexy way. His beard is a perfectly groomed stubble that complements his facial features well. But what draws me in are his beautiful, serene light-gray eyes, which seem to hold the secrets of the universe. He smirks at me, a knowing look in his eyes, and as he steps closer I can't help but be enveloped in his intoxicating scent. It's musky and earthy, like the first rain of the season, with a hint of sweetness that makes me want to breathe him in deeper.

He clears his throat. "Good evening. My name is Nyx."

I give him a nervous smile. "Forgive me . . . hello, Nyx. My name is Lyra."

"May I offer you a skull sweet?" says a servant holding a gold tray full of glasses filled with iridescent black liquid. Nyx takes a glass from the woman but keeps his eyes on me. The servant doesn't even bother offering me a glass since I'm forbidden from drinking alcohol. Nyx examines the contents of the glass carefully.

"What is a skull sweet exactly?"

I hold back a laugh as he sniffs the glass. "It's supposed to taste like wine. It's made from black grapes spelled to provide youth."

He looks like he is about to say something, but then more servants stream into the room in advance of my parents' arrival.

My mother looks beautiful as always. Her honey-blonde hair is piled high atop her head, wavy pieces hanging down to frame her slender face. She wears a splendid deep-purple gown with a gold crown. Her green eyes find me immediately, looking me up and down to make sure I look the part of her beautiful, poised princess. Silas is dressed to match her in a purple jacket with gold embroidering. Silas finds Nyx and ushers him away from me as they fall into conversation just out of my ears reach. Silas is average height for a man, but he looks short next to Nyx. He has a round belly and a full but clipped dark-gray beard that matches his curly mop of short gray hair. I wander over to my seat, surveying the room. There are a handful of people here I've never seen before.

My mother claps her hands, sending a gush of wind through the room, and all the candles burst to life. It's a sign for everyone to break away from conversation and find a seat at the table.

Samael finds his way next to me, and only years of hiding my emotions keeps me from visibly cringing. He gives me a good kick under the table, and I bite down on my lip to try to keep myself from flinching. His legs may be long and skinny, but they still pack a punch. I suck in a breath then take a drink of water, hoping no one noticed.

When I look up at Nyx, he's studying me from across the table, and I wonder if he saw me flinch. There's something dreamy and mysterious about this man. I know Samael will make me pay for it later, but I decide I'm going to stay at dinner a little while longer. I zone out while my mother gives some speech about the dinner courses planned for this evening. My eyes are inexplicably drawn to Nyx, as if there's a magnetic pull in my chest that makes me unable to look away. Our first course is brought out, and I frown at my bowl of conjure goulash. It's made from wattle brains, mixed vegetables, and red wine. I can't bring myself to eat it because I love the herd of wattle that graze the grounds. I move my spoon around in the bowl pretending to eat while eavesdropping.

Nyx is seated at the other side of the table next to Silas at the end. I strain to hear their conversation, only catching bits and pieces because of everyone else's talking. As I listen to Nyx, I can't help but notice how often he mentions Zomea, causing both of their faces to turn grim. Zomea is where we go in the afterlife, and I can't help but wonder why they are discussing it. The feeling in my chest intensifies, urging me to ask what's going on, but something holds me back. I want to stay longer and keep listening, but Samael kicks me again, and I almost drop my water goblet. I stand immediately.

"I'm sorry, but I must excuse myself. I'm not feeling well this evening."

"Oh, darling, I'm sorry. Please go rest. I'll have Lili bring you up dinner," my mother says in a sweet tone, but her eyes became hard stones for a moment.

"Thank you," I say then flash a smile at Nyx before taking my leave. As I walk away, I steal a final glance at him and notice his unwavering gaze fixed on me. Once I'm out of sight, I have the strangest feeling of dejection.

CHAPTER
TWO

I hurry back to my room where a plate of food is already waiting. It's a tomato tart with goat cheese, one of my favorite things to eat. I devour the tart, sharing with Chepi of course. I can't go to bed just yet. I can't escape this sense of foreboding. I need to know what Samael is up to and why he didn't want me at dinner.

"Are you up for a little spying tonight, boy?"

Chepi wags his tail in confirmation.

I change into tights and a tunic to be more comfortable but keep my bloodstone necklace on. My mother would probably incinerate my clothes on sight if she caught me wearing this in front of company, but luckily for me Chepi will make sure neither of us are visible. I pace my room for what feels like hours until I can no longer hear any noise in the distance. When I stick my head out into the hall, it sounds like all the dinner guests have finally retired. Time for me to go find Samael and see what he's up to.

I pick up Chepi and hold him tight to my chest.

"Okay, boy, it's time."

I glance at the mirror, and when I can't see us in the reflection I scurry into the hall. While Chepi has the gift of invisibility, I know he can't sustain it all night long without putting a significant strain on his body. I must hurry and make the most of our time. I rush down the stairs and across the castle. Samael has his very own wing on the ground floor furthest away from everyone else. I slow my pace when I reach the hall leading to Samael's private chambers. It's eerily quiet in this part of the castle. Samael doesn't even allow servants to enter his chambers.

I stop dead in my tracks when I hear Samael speaking to someone. I wish Chepi's gift included walking through walls. I put my ear to the door, and when I don't hear anything I quickly crack it open and slip inside. Once inside Samael's room, I'm immediately struck by its size. It's really three large rooms that he has combined to create a seamless and disturbing hall. Compared to this, my own room looks like a closet. I tiptoe against the wall, following the sound of his voice. It's dark in here, and only the light from the fireplace in the distance helps me not trip over anything. There are stacks of books everywhere and a long table cluttered with something on it that smells like death. I press my back to the wall and scurry past the table. I press my hand over my mouth to keep from gagging. The table is covered in body parts, not human body parts but some poor dissected creatures. Chepi buries his face in my armpit, and I hold him tighter. Samael is sick. He needs to be stopped.

"I need to get the Moon Grimoire," he says while pacing in front of the fireplace. Every family of Sorcerers has a Grimoire that's passed down generation after generation. It's how we learn spells and rituals. *The Moon Grimoire* belongs to my mother. It's called the Moon Grimoire because her family name is Moon. Before she married, she went by Macy Moon. I wonder what Samael could possibly want my family's grimoire for. He surely must have access to his own.

"When all of this is done, she'll belong to me. I need you to make sure they're ready," Samael says to someone, but I can't see who it is. They're sitting in a tall black chair, and they have their backs to me. I keep padding quietly along the wall trying to get closer. I just need to see who he's talking to. Chepi starts pawing at my arm, and it's my warning to get out of there before his magic wears off. I tiptoe quickly back to the far end of the room.

"You have my word, master."

It's a woman's voice I hear, startling me as I slip out the door. I race down the hall, turn the corner, and smack face-first into a firm chest.

Chepi jumps to the ground, and I look up to find Nyx smirking at me. He grabs my arms, steadying me gently.

"Are you alright?"

I clear my throat. "Yes, thank you. I didn't see you there."

"Clearly," he says, chuckling softly. "What are you doing wandering around the castle so late?" I brush my hands down my tunic. "This is my home. Shouldn't I be the one asking you what you're doing wandering around in the middle of the night?"

Nyx just laughed. "I take it you're feeling better then, Princess."

I'd almost forgotten I left dinner pretending to be ill hours earlier. "Yes, quite better, thank you. I must be going now, goodnight." I start to hurry away before he can ask me anything else.

"Goodnight, Princess," he says from behind me.

I don't turn back, but I can feel his eyes on me until I'm out of sight.

I feel breathless back in my room. My heart is racing. Not racing from Samael but racing from my encounter with Nyx. How does this man have such an effect on my body? I shake the thought away and crawl into bed with Chepi. I have no clue what woman Samael could've been talking to. The only woman at dinner other than me was my mother, and she would never call him master. Maybe one of the servants is doing his bidding for him. I need to know why he wants my family grimoire and who will belong to him. I'm also a bit suspicious of why Nyx was so close to Samael's wing of the castle so late at night. My mind is exhausted from spinning with the possibilities.

I toss and turn all night, plagued by strange dreams of unknown places. As I awaken, the image of Nyx's face lingers in my mind. My curiosity about the elusive man who Samael wanted me to stay away from intensifies, but I know no one here will share any information with me.

It's still early. The sun's not quite visible yet, but the soft-blue hues of this blue hour are present. I go onto the balcony for some fresh air to clear my head. Taking in deep breaths, I let the crisp air fill my nose with scents of fresh pine and chimney smoke. I love the fall air and the sound of the forest just before dawn. I pause to listen for the early morning birds chirping, but when I don't hear them the hair on the back of my neck stands up. I get the strangest feeling I'm being watched.

The gardens below catch my attention, and I nervously glance around until my eyes fall upon a figure standing below my window, gazing up at me. It's not just any man, but a Lycan, easily identified by his glowing light-blue eyes. He has a strong build and shoulder-length white-blond hair, and I can't help but wonder what he's doing outside in the cold, shirtless. I don't recall ever seeing him before, not even at last night's dinner. It's been a while since a Lycan visited the castle. I pinch my arm to make sure I'm not dreaming. The sharp pain tells me I'm awake. I quickly go back inside and lock my door, feeling awkward and uneasy about seeing the man outside watching me.

I have to meet with Mr. Drogo early this morning. The closer I get to my nineteenth birthday, the closer I get to finally inheriting my magic and the more he wants me to study.

Lili barges into my room, and I recognize her by her distinct scent before even looking up. Her presence distracts me from my thoughts for a moment. After quickly selecting a simple and comfortable light-blue gown, I let her take over and style my hair.

"Why are you so quiet this morning? What are you thinking about?" Lili's voice pulls me from my train of thought. Her hazel eyes meet mine in the mirror.

"There was a strange man outside my room this morning. I was letting Chepi out on the balcony, and he was near the garden just staring up at my room. Do you know who it could've been?"

"Their Majesties have requested I bring you to their chambers this morning once you're ready. I don't know what man you speak of, but maybe they'll have something to say about it."

Lili is never one to give much information. Seems I'm always kept in the dark about everything.

"Done. You look like a beautiful princess, ready for training," she says while patting my shoulders. She's always better at doing my hair than I am. Today she made several large braids then gathered them all in a tight bun at the nape of my neck.

"Now follow me. I'll take you to your parents. I believe they're having breakfast arranged for you in their chambers. I'll take Chepi downstairs and make sure he gets a good breakfast in the kitchens." She starts walking toward my parent's wing of the castle with Chepi in tow.

I wonder why my parents want to have breakfast with me this morning. This is very out of character for them. I usually have breakfast alone with Chepi. It's probably to chastise me for getting out of dinner last night.

I know I've reached my parents' wing of the castle when the hallways somehow become richer with color. Everything is a deep purple and gold. Elaborately stitched rugs extend down the halls, and I almost feel bad for walking on them. The walls have several stained-glass windows, and when the sun shines just right they make dreamy rainbows cascade about.

"I can go the rest of the way alone, Lili. Will you go feed Chepi? I know he's starving."

I pass by her and continue down the long hallway alone before she can object. I knock on the door to my parents' wing, and my mother lets me in. Her golden locks fall over her shoulders as she turns away from me. They do indeed have breakfast set up for just the three of us. The heady scent of wine slaps me in the face, and I look to where Silas is dunking pieces of biscuit into a goblet of deep red liquid.

"Come, dear, please take a seat. I know you must be hungry, and we have much to discuss." My mom takes her seat across from me at the table next to Silas.

"Good morning, Lyra," says my stepfather with a mouth full of food. Beads of wine dribble down his beard. I refrain from cringing.

"Good morning, Silas," I reply while loading my plate with fresh fruit and biscuits with jam. "So what do you wish to discuss with me?" I take a big bite of a biscuit.

"It's about your training," my mom replies. Her green eyes look to me then at my plate. "I think one biscuit is plenty darling. You wouldn't want to ruin your figure." She smiles at me, and I want to roll my eyes.

"Yes, mother." I give her my best fake smile. I've been put through training and lessons for as long as I can remember. Mr. Drogo is my current teacher, and we've mostly been focused on learning the history of the realms and their geography. I used to have another teacher, Mrs. Scampi. She taught me about herbs and making potions and casting spells until Silas decided it was too dangerous to learn such things without having any real magic yet.

"What about my training?" I ask.

"Up until now your training has been mostly academic, but starting today you're going to start physical training. I want you to know how to wield a blade and a bow and be able to defend yourself physically," says Silas. "Now, don't look so worried. We're only looking out for your best interest."

"I don't understand. I'll never need to fight. I'm a princess, not a warrior. I don't even have muscles. Why are you making me do this?"

"Enough, Lyra. Your father doesn't need to explain his reasons to you. You'll do as he says, and you'll not question it," says mother, silencing my protests, her green eyes cutting into me.

"He is not my father," I say before I can stop myself.

My mother visibly flinches. "Watch your mouth, young lady." She's got fury in her gaze.

"The first stage of your training begins after breakfast. I have brought Aidan the leader of the Lycan Realm here to train you. He'll stay at the castle, and you will train with him every day until he sees fit. Do you understand?" Silas says, sternly.

"Yes, I understand," I mutter

"Good. Now finish your breakfast then head down to the back courtyard. Aidan will meet you there." Mother seems to have regained her composure.

No longer hungry, I excuse myself and make my way to the courtyard.

CHAPTER

THREE

Aidan is already waiting for me when I reach the courtyard. He has a shirt on now, but it's tight and shows off his defined muscles. He's tall and broad. His white-blond hair is straight and glossy next to his face. His jaw is wide and strong, speckled with white stubble. His face shows a little bit of age, mostly around his eyes where wrinkles are slightly pronounced even when he's not smiling. Those pale blue eyes look at me now, but they aren't glowing like this morning in the forest.

"Um . . . Hi, I'm Lyra, and I was told to meet you here." I try to hide my vexation.

"Yes, hello again, Lyra," he says with a sly wink, as if he's referring to our earlier meeting when he was lurking outside my bedroom. "My name is Aidan, and your parents have asked me here to assist in training you in physical combat. And, from the looks of it, I have my work cut out for me." He smirks and takes in my less-than-impressive physical appearance.

"What's that supposed to mean?" A wave of warmth spreads across my cheeks.

"I mean no offense. It just doesn't look like you have very much muscle on your body. Although, I must say it's a nice body." An arrogant grin spreads across his face while eyeing me up and down.

If I wasn't flushed before, my face is now on fire and burning a million shades of red. I look around feeling awkward and slightly uncomfortable with the way his eyes linger over my body. I've never really held a conversation with a man like this before. My parents are overprotective and have always kept me trapped within the castle grounds. All of my previous teachers have been female except for Mr. Drogo, but he's a cranky old man and very professional. The only other male I talk to is Samael, and it's not by choice.

"Let's get started. Today I'm going to take it easy on you. We're going to learn some basic stretches and defensive stances."

The next few hours are excruciating. I thought my body was relatively fit—I mean, I do like to go jogging from time to time—but damn, my body feels dead after hours of stretching. I didn't know stretching could take such a toll on me.

I'll admit Aidan is attractive in his own way, for an older man. As he stretches, he removes his shirt to cool off, revealing his glistening, muscled stomach. It's a welcome distraction, but all day he's been finding ways to touch me, instructing me on how to extend my leg just so or suck in my core. It's a strange sensation, and I don't know how to feel about it. A part of me wants to cry out for help, to beg him. *Take me away from this wretched place, show me the world and free me from Samael's grasp.* But I don't know if Aidan is a good man or if he's working with Samael. I can't trust anyone here.

"I think that's enough for today. You'll be sore tomorrow, but after a week or so your body will start getting used to it, and every day you'll get a little bit stronger. Now meet me back here at sunrise. I want to get an early start. And, Lyra, maybe try to wear pants tomorrow, if you own any."

"Okay, I'll see you in the morning," I say before forcing my body to walk back up the hill toward the castle. I steal a look back at him when I reach the top of the hill, and he's still watching me. As I come to a stop, his gaze lingers up my body and meets my eyes. A sly grin spreads across his face, betraying that he has been checking me out this entire time. I chuckle and shake my head, feeling a mix of amusement and discomfort before hurrying toward the stairs.

It's only today that I realize how many stairs I have to walk up to get to my room. My thighs are burning, and my stomach is growling. I'm starving after a day out in the sun sweating.

As I walk down the hallway toward my room, a loud bang suddenly echoes through the corridor, causing me to stop in my tracks. I strain my ears and hear hushed whispers coming from the library. Curiosity gets the best of me, and I tiptoe closer to the door to eavesdrop. I peek around the corner just in time to see Samael strike my mother across the face. I throw my hand over my mouth to cover the gasp that escapes me. My mother does nothing. She's a powerful Sorceress; she's the queen of Cloudrum. How she can just let him get away with this? I don't understand. Samael kicks over a stack of books and turns toward me to leave the library. I run as fast as I can away from the corner before he can see me.

Once out of sight, I take my time walking back to my room. I'm stunned by what I just witnessed. My mother may not be the most loving mother, but I still care for her deeply, and the thought of Samael possibly abusing her all these years makes my stomach churn.

CHEPI IS ALREADY in my room waiting for me when I get back. He's sprawled out across my pillow on my bed.

"Hey, get your dirty butt off where I rest my face," I say.

He just rolls onto his back, pleading for a belly rub. I oblige him. Just as I'm settling back onto my bed, there's a knock at the door. I let out a sigh, dragging myself back up again to answer it. It's a servant from the kitchen, bringing me a dinner tray for yet another meal alone in my bedchamber.

Dinner tonight is another poor exotic bird soaked in pads of butter and covered in a sickeningly sweet marmalade. The scent alone sends a wave of nausea rumbling through my stomach. I pick up the glass of water and find a note tucked underneath it. It's a note from my mother.

Lyra,

Silas and I have important business to attend to and may be away for a few weeks. Samael is in charge while we are gone, and you are to continue training with Aidan and do whatever he says until we return.

Mom

Of course, she doesn't say where they're going or that she loves me or will miss me. My mother has always been distant, especially since she married Silas years ago after my father died. I love my mother, but a part of me also hates her and hates Silas. I hate that everything I do is dictated by them. I hate that I'm never allowed to leave the castle grounds in Tempest Moon. I hate that they don't know what Samael does to me. Or worse, they do and turn a blind eye to it. I can't believe my mother did nothing when Samael hit her. Something about Samael's darkness must scare her. At least with her out of town I won't have to worry about her. If my father were still alive, I know things would be different. I miss him so much, but I can't let myself dwell on it.

CHAPTER
FOUR

The next few weeks fly by. Everyday I'm so busy training from sunrise to sunset with Aidan that I barely have time to stuff my face with dinner before I pass out. My parents are still away, and I haven't seen Samael, thank the gods. Aidan and I are getting into a nice routine together. Every morning we begin with an hour of stretching, then we practice archery followed by my favorite part, sparring off against each other. He hasn't let me actually wield a sword or anything yet, but I'm learning to block and throw punches and kicks. I haven't landed any on him, but I'm getting pretty fast at dodging blows. My body is sore, and I'm using muscles I didn't even know could hurt, but I'm starting to enjoy it. I think I like Aidan. We've become almost friends, and we have even started to enjoy breakfast and dinner together in the dining room since my parents are away. I haven't seen Samael, and only the servants have been around to see to us.

"Hurry and eat your eggs. You need all the protein you can get. After breakfast, we're leaving on a little field trip. I've asked Lili to prepare a pack for you and take care of Chepi while we are away." Aidan's voice pulls me from my thoughts.

"What? Where are we going? How long will we be gone?" I try but fail at hiding my excitement.

"Just for a few days or so, and I'll tell you the rest on the way." He laughs, getting up from the table.

"Now that I'm finished, I'm going to gather my things. Meet me in the front hall in twenty minutes," he says before walking out.

I'm still in shock after he leaves. I've never left the castle before. I wonder if my parents approved of this field trip. I don't care if they did or didn't. I'm too excited to care. I'm actually going to get away from this place. Even if it's just for a few days, I'll take it. I might get to see the Shifting Forest, a magical forest in the Lycan Realm where plants are known to have minds of their own. My mind is racing when Lili walks in, looking at me with uneasy eyes.

"Lyra, I don't think this is a good idea. Prince Samael is in charge, and I don't think he would approve of you leaving the grounds at all, let alone with a Lycan."

"Samael may be in charge, but I haven't seen him since my parents left, and my parents said Aidan was in charge of me. I'm to train with him until they return. Now stop looking at me like that. Will you promise to take good care of Chepi and let him sleep in bed with you? He likes to cuddle, and he likes his belly rubs. Please don't let him out of your sight. I've never left him alone before." My words fumble out so fast, trying to keep up with all the directions my mind is going.

Her eyes soften. "You know I'll take good care of Chepi. Now, we don't have much time, so listen to me." She places her hands on my shoulders and makes eye contact with me. Her soft hazel eyes are full of concern. "I packed everything you'll need. It's being loaded on the horses now. I want you to be on your guard, Lyra. I don't know why Aidan is taking you away from the castle, and I feel uneasy about it. Please be careful. I know men like him, and I don't trust him. He's not your friend." She brings me in for a tight hug then releases me.

"Yes, yes, I will, Lili. Don't worry. Just take good care of Chepi, and I'll see you soon." I brush off her concerns while giving Chepi pets and kisses. "I'll be back soon, boy. Don't you worry. Lili here is going to give you lots of belly rubs and treats."

His ears perk up. I leave Chepi and Lili in the dining room and make my way to the front hall. Aidan is already there leaning against the wall waiting for me.

"I've had a couple horses prepared for us. Now let's get going," he says while opening the front door.

I follow after him and am immediately concerned when I see the two horses out front. I don't know how to tell him I can't ride a horse. I feel embarrassed, and my cheeks are already flushing with heat. I want to go on this field trip so bad . . . do I just try to get on the horse and pretend I can ride? Hope that I don't get bucked off on my ass in the first two minutes? He must notice my apprehension, because he stops and turns to me.

"What's wrong?"

"Well . . . umm . . . Aidan, I've never been on a horse before." I'm practically red in the face. *Please don't cancel the trip. Please don't cancel the trip.*

"Relax, Lyra, you can ride with me. Just give me a minute to transfer my bags onto your horse."

I breathe easier. "Okay thanks," I mutter, still feeling embarrassed.

I watch as he moves around the horses and repacks the saddle bags. Both horses are huge. One is a solid chocolate brown, and the other is the same color except for a white spot on its face. They've both got beautiful, thick, and shiny coats.

"What are their names?" I ask.

"Well, the stable boy says this one here carrying our packs is Sadye. She's a mellow girl, and that's why I've chosen her for you to ride. This boy here with the white spot over his eye is my horse from back home, and his name is Geri. Now we're all set. Come over here and stand by Geri," he instructs. "I'm going to help you get on. First, grab the pommel with both hands and steady yourself. Then I can climb on behind you." He places his hands on my hips, effortlessly lifting me onto Geri like I weigh nothing.

I squeeze the pommel tight, already feeling anxious about falling off, but Aidan gets on behind me right away and pulls me back close to him. I suck in a breath at his close contact.

"Are you comfortable?" he asks as the horses start to head down the dirt path leading away from the front of the castle.

"Yes, I'm alright," I say through gritted teeth. I'm hunched over with my ass in the air squeezing the pommel so tight my hands are already sore. I feel like I'm way too high on Geri. The last thing I want to do is fall off. I must look ridiculous because Aidan chuckles behind me.

"Come on, Cheeks. Lie back and relax. I won't let you fall." He pulls me back so I'm flush against his chest. His warmth seeps into me. I try to lean into him and relax a bit.

"Why did you just call me Cheeks?"

"Whenever you're around me those pink cheeks of yours always flush and make you look adorable . . . and now I'm learning your other cheeks are rather plump and nice too." He places his arm around my waist, tugging me back so my ass is tight against his front. I feel heat in my core at this new level of closeness.

Instead of acknowledging the nickname, I simply ask, "So are you going to tell me where we are going now?"

"I'm taking you to the Cinder territory where I'm from. The full moon is three days from now, and there's a festival called the Shifting Moon. I have to be there, and I figured it would be good for you to get away from the castle and have some real-life training. It's a little over two days' ride to get there, so we'll camp for two nights along the way."

"What is the Shifting Moon Festival?"

"Well, you know how you don't get your powers until you turn nineteen?"

"Yes."

"The Lycan don't shift into wolves until they turn sixteen and attend the Shifting Moon Festival. It's a blessing ceremony and a celebration representing their change into adulthood."

"Is it painful to shift into a wolf?"

"The first few times it is, but you get used to it pretty quickly."

For the next few hours, we ride on in silence. I'm mostly enjoying the surroundings and trying to get used to the fact that my legs are killing me from riding. We're still in the Tempest Moon territory, so everything looks pretty similar to the castle grounds. Tempest Moon is made up of a coniferous forest covering vast mountains, lots of mature pine trees that tower over everything as well as black and white spruce trees, and very little ground vegetation. The ground is littered with pine needles and pine cones. The air is crisp and fresh. Pine fills my nose, and the scent will always remind me of home. It's almost winter, and winters are long in the Tempest Moon district. We get lots of rain and snow, and even though it's been abnormally sunny the last couple weeks, there's still a chill in the air. If it wasn't for the warmth radiating off Aidan, I'd be pretty cold right now.

I must've dozed off at some point, because I'm jolted awake when I feel water on my face.

"Sorry I didn't mean to sleep on you." I feel a little awkward for using Aidan as my very own pillow and blanket.

"Don't worry about it. Riding all day takes a toll on you if you're not used to it. But now with the rain we'll stop and make camp soon. The sun is only a couple hours away from setting. I want to get closer to the river where we can rest, but I still didn't make it as far as I would've liked today. We'll have to ride harder tomorrow."

I just nod in return. I'm tired and hungry and cold. I wonder how the Lycan's strength compares to Samael's powers. Aidan and I are becoming fast friends, and I can't help but think maybe if I told him about Samael he could help me do something. Who am I kidding? Samael is the prince of the Sorcerer Realm. No one would make a move against him. Maybe Aidan alone couldn't kill Samael, but with an entire pack of Lycan behind him he could. I can try to convince all the Lycan to help me and get the packs to stand against Samael. It'd take a lot of convincing to get the Lycan to make a move on the prince. I don't think my feelings of foreboding would hold much weight in that conversation. I need to come up with something.

CHAPTER
FIVE

About an hour later we make it to the river, and I spend another thirty minutes feeling useless while Aidan tries to teach me how to set up our tent and build a fire. We share a meal of dried meat, nuts and cheese, but even out here by the fire I'm still shivering from the rain. The trees help a little to protect us, but it's still raining, and the fire is not thriving.

"Come on. Let's lie down in the tent. We have an early day tomorrow, and I don't like listening to your teeth chatter out here." Aidan gets up and extends a hand to me. I grab hold of his warm, calloused hand and let him lead me into the tent.

Once we get inside, I realize it's a tiny tent and there's only one makeshift bed on the ground off to the side. There's a pile of furs to sleep on top of and a few heavy wool blankets to cover us.

"Are we sharing this bed?" I try not to let the nervousness slip through in my voice.

"Yes, Cheeks. I need to keep you warm, and the best way I know how to do that is to share my body heat with you," he says while kicking off his boots and removing his clothes. I turn around so quick I almost trip over myself.

"Why are you getting naked?" I ask, alarmed.

"Calm down, Cheeks. I'm leaving my under shorts on. Skin-to-skin contact will keep you warm throughout the night. Now tell those pink cheeks to relax and get out of those wet clothes so I can get you warm before you get sick."

"Aidan, I'm a princess, and it's highly inappropriate for me to get naked with you in a tent." I'm still stunned and facing away from him when I hear him chuckle behind me.

"Oh, Princess, there's no one around for miles. Don't worry. It'll be our little secret."

I can't help but feel a bit uneasy, but the chill in the air is overwhelming, and all I want to do is get warm and go to sleep.

"Fine, but go lie down and cover your face with the blanket. I don't want you watching me undress."

He obliges, and I begin to peel off my wet clothes and lay them out next to the coals he brought in to warm the tent and dry our belongings. Once I'm left in just my white chemise, I walk over to the makeshift bed he's already lying in.

"Now I'm going to pull back the blankets and get in bed. Close your eyes . . . please." I try to sound stern.

"Yes, Cheeks, my lids are closed," he says and then chuckles softly.

I pull back the blankets, and sure enough his eyes are closed, but he opens them right away. I see the way he looks me up and down, then holds my gaze, his pale-blue eyes glowing fiercely in the dimly lit tent. I'm in stunned silence for a moment, still not believing he didn't obey my request, but it's freezing, and he can't stare at me if I'm under the covers. I hurry down onto the furs next to him and pull the blankets up to my chin. I turn onto my side so I'm facing away from him and not touching him at all, but I do feel heat emanating off his body, warming me.

"I can't believe you just did that."

"Relax, Lyra, I'm here to protect you. I won't let anything happen to you. You're safe with me."

I try to hide the discomfort in my voice and change the subject. "What exactly are you protecting me from? What lives out in these woods?"

"There are lots of creatures in these woods, but none of them will bother us. They can smell me, smell my Lycan blood, and most creatures fear Lycan. They wouldn't dare enter our tent."

Before I have a chance to respond, he brings his arm over me and presses his hand to my stomach pulling me back into him. I immediately go to move away, but his hold on me is strong, and I can't move.

"Lyra, let me hold you."

I can feel my heart rate increase, but it's not a good feeling. A knot forms in my stomach. Even though I like Aidan, I have never been with a man before, let alone slept next to one. The only male who's ever touched me is Samael, and it wasn't my choice. My skin crawls just thinking about it, and I can't help but think about Lili and how she told me to be on guard and that she didn't trust Aidan. If he wanted to have his way with me right now, there's nothing I could do. There's no one out here for miles. No one to hear me scream. The thought sends a tingling chill up my spine.

"I told you the full moon is only in a few days, but I don't think I told you that us Lycan get very aggressive and . . . hungry around the full moon. Especially at night, if you know what I mean."

I can feel his breath on the back of my ear.

34

"Please, Aidan, can we just sleep?" I try not to let him know I'm afraid, but he's a Lycan and can probably smell my fear.

"Yes, Cheeks, sleep. I've got you." He tucks his right arm underneath me and lets his hand fall over my breasts while his left hand is still pressed against my stomach holding me to him. I can feel his hard length pressed against my backside, but I don't feel turned on by Aidan right now. The knot that's formed in my stomach begins to churn, but he's warm. I have no choice right now but to play nice, so I let myself relax against him. If he wants to touch me, then so be it as long as it doesn't go any further.

The moment he feels me relax, he gives my left breast a squeeze. "Good girl. Now, sleep."

I wake up gasping for air, drenched in sweat. The nightmare is still fresh in my mind, and I can feel my heart racing. I sit up in bed, trying to calm my breathing, but my mind is in overdrive. Why do I keep having these dreams? What does it mean? Is it just a manifestation of my fear of Samael? Or is it something more? I shake my head, trying to push the thoughts away. I need to get some rest If I'm going to survive another day of riding with Aidan. I try to relax and sleep does find me again eventually.

"Wake up, Lyra. It's time to get ready to go." Aidan pats me on the ass before getting out of bed. Cool air shocks my body. I wake from one nightmare back to whatever this is. I don't know how I feel about Aidan after last night. I thought we were friends, but the way he acted didn't feel very friendly. It's hard to tell if I can trust him or not. Part of me wants to believe he's on my side, but Lili's warning about him makes me doubt his intentions. And yet I can't deny that I'm a little drawn to him. Maybe it's because he's the only one who seems to understand how trapped I feel in the castle. But can I really trust him with my safety and secrets? The thought gnaws at me as I try to make sense of my feelings, but I don't have time to dwell on it right now.

He packs up camp quickly, and we share some dried fruit and nuts for breakfast then continue our ride toward Cinder territory. We don't speak much, and we keep a fast pace all day, only stopping along the river for the horses to drink. It isn't raining today, but it's cold and muddy everywhere. The first snowfall could happen any day now.

It can't be much longer until we make camp. The sun begins its descent from the sky.

"How old are you?" I ask after a long stretch of silence.

"That's random. So quiet all day, and then you want to know my age."

"I was quiet all day because it's hard to hold a conversation when I'm being all jostled around, but now that we've slowed our pace I'm just wondering. I don't know much about you."

"I am almost eighty years old. I know I don't look much older than mid-forties in mortal years, but us Lycan age slower than mortals. We don't live nearly as long as the Fae or Lamia, but most of us live to be two to three hundred years old. Some-times even older."

I can't even fathom having a lifespan like that. To live for hundreds of years would be amazing. I also wonder if it would make you enjoy the little things less. I imagine that shorter lifespans probably correlate with your appreciation for life itself.

"And you are King of the Lycan?" I ask curiously.

"Yes, I am but we don't use the term king. There are many different packs of Lycan, and each pack has a pack leader, but I'm the leader of even the pack leaders. I look over the entire Lycan Realm. Just like Drew looks over the Lamia Realm."

I've never seen any Lamia. I've only overheard my parents talk about Drew before and how her eyes glow red. The Lamia are all female, but they must reproduce with mortal males, and they survive off of the blood of humans. At least that's what my teachers taught me at the castle.

I've always wondered why everyone is so segregated. Why do the different realms even exist? Surely there must be sexual affairs between races, but I've never heard of a Lycan marrying a Lamia or a Fae marrying a mortal. Why are there these pretenses that we all must stick to our own kind when it comes to marriage and children? It doesn't seem right to me. But what do I know?

"THIS LOOKS like a good spot to make camp. No fire tonight. It's already late, and I want to get the horses situated and the tent set up before dark. You can go wash up down at the creek while I set things up here. In your pack there should be some soap and clean washcloths." Aidan stops the horses and lifts me off Geri.

I head down the embankment toward the creek with my fresh clothes and soap in tow. I need a warm bath, but this will have to do. The creek is out of sight from camp, so I quickly remove my cloak, gown and chemise then fully submerge myself in the freezing water. I make quick work of washing my hair and all my important bits then hop out and throw on my chemise and cloak. I choose to forgo my gown because I don't want to get it wet, knowing I'll be taking it off as soon as I get in the tent anyways. I use my fingers to comb through my hair. The vanilla and lavender soap smells of Lili and makes me smile. I head back up the hill to find the tent ready for me.

I crawl inside. I don't see Aidan, so he must've gone to another part of the creek to wash himself. I quickly remove my shoes and cloak then get huddled under the covers. It's freezing, and my hair is wet, which probably wasn't the best idea, but I wanted to feel clean. Without the coals in here tonight it's going to be extra cold. I'm almost looking forward to Aidan's body heat so long as he doesn't try to get handsy with me.

I am in full shiver mode by the time Aidan makes it back to the tent. I'm facing away from him knowing he's probably going to undress before climbing in next to me. And he does just that. Gods, his body is warm. The Lycan blood just radiates heat, and it feels nice.

"Come here. You're freezing. Let me get you warmed up." He turns me to face him, and I comply. He collects all my wet hair and twirls it before resting it up above my head so the wetness isn't soaking into my back. Then he pulls me close to him, my face pressed into his chest and his chin resting atop my head. He uses his hands to tug my chemise up and strokes my back up and down every now and then, stroking down lower to cup my ass too.

"Better?"

I'm not going to lie. It is better. His body is so warm I practically melt into him, and I do feel safe with him wrapped around me—to an extent.

"Yes," I whisper.

"Gods, your body feels so soft. It is taking all my self-control not to turn you over and bury my cock inside you right now." He rubs his face against the top of my head. My thighs clinch together at his admission, and my heart rate speeds up.

"Aidan. I—"

"Sleep. I promise you're safe with me." He squeezes my backside and pulls me tighter to him. I close my eyes and obey. Sleep finds me before I have time to overthink the situation too much.

I wake to Aidan tossing my clothes at me.

"Get yourself together. We leave in ten. We can make it to

my home before dark if we hurry." He walks outside to give me some privacy.

My hair is dry, thank the gods, but it's all tangled and unruly. I try to comb it out the best I can then make two long braids. One goes down either side of my head. I pull on my gown then wrap my cloak around me, and I'm out of the tent ready to go. Aidan is there waiting by the horses and gives me a handful of nuts and dried fruit to eat while he breaks down camp. I'm grateful for the food, but I'm already missing a nice hot meal. I hope Chepi is getting his fill back home.

CHAPTER
SIX

Once again, we've kept up a quick pace all day. I'm exhausted by the time we get to Aidan's village. I've only snacked on a few pieces of dried meat for lunch, and my stomach is beginning to grumble.

The village is far from grand and not much of a village at all. This place makes the castle grounds look very grand. A variety of log cabins are spread out amongst the trees, and the trees...oh my gods. What the village lacks in grandeur, the trees make up for. I stare in awe, mesmerized by the fantastic sight before me. The giant tree trunks and twisting branches are a striking charcoal gray, while their egg-shaped leaves glow a brilliant midnight blue, deep and swirling like a tumultuous night sky. Amidst the typical pine trees, these midnight trees stand out even more, adding to their otherworldly charm.

People are gathered around several large fire pits roasting meat and chatting together. My stomach growls, and my mouth salivates at the smell of smoked meat filling the air. People turn to face us as we pass and give nods to Aidan, but no one approaches us. We continue down a winding, dirt path that is littered with midnight leaves until we reach a cobblestone fence and gate. Aidan jumps off Geri and opens the gate then proceeds to walk, pulling both the horses and me with him up the path.

"Is this where you live?"

"Yes, this is where I stay when I'm not traveling to other territories dealing with pack politics."

The narrow dirt path we're on is leading us to a barn and stables. Past the barn on top of a hill surrounded by trees is an aged log cabin with a large cobblestone fireplace. Another building sits further back behind the house, maybe a shed or guest house of sorts. Beyond that there are rolling hills as far as I can see in varying shades of blue, cobalt, and navy. They run in zigzags across the hillside. Once we make it to the barn, Aidan helps me dismount Geri, and a boy comes out to greet us.

"Hello, sir, glad to see you've returned safely," he says while bowing his head to Aidan and taking the reins.

"Lyra, this is Luke. Luke, this is Lyra."

"Hello Luke, it's a pleasure to meet you." I nod, unsure of how to act. I know he's a Lycan because he has those piercing light-blue eyes like Aidan and like all the Lycan, but he doesn't look much older than maybe fifteen. He has tan skin and fluffy, short brown hair growing wildly atop his head.

"The pleasure is mine, Lyra. Please let me unpack your bags for you. I have a fire going in the house, and I'll bring you both up some dinner after I settle the horses. I believe Marth is roasting clippers tonight." Luke nods at Aidan then disappears into the barn.

"Come, Cheeks. Let's get you cleaned up."

"What is all of that growing on the hills?" I ask, pointing beyond the house to the blue crops.

"It's wheat."

"I've never seen wheat grow like that before. It's blue."

"You'll find blue runs through the Lycan Realm in various ways. It has to do with our blood and the moon magic that allows us to shift into wolves. It's why our eyes glow light blue as well."

"It's like how the Sorcerers have black and white magic," I say.

"It is similar to that in a way. I cannot cast a spell as you can, but I do carry magic in my blood, and magic flows through these lands." Aidan places his hand on the small of my back and leads me up toward the cabin.

I step inside and take in my surroundings. The cabin is old and basic, lacking any sort of luxury or refinement. The large cobblestone fireplace dominates the space, taking up almost the entire wall to my left, and its crackling flames breathe life into the whole cabin. In front of the fireplace, a well-worn settee beckons, its red cushions inviting me to sink into them. To the left of the fireplace is a table and chairs and a tiny kitchen nook for food preparation. The cabin is made entirely of huge logs, and the ceiling is vaulted with large wooden beams cutting across its peak.

I follow Aidan down the hall to a single bedroom and bathroom. The bedroom is sparsely furnished, with one large bed made from the same logs as the rest of the cabin, covered in furs of varying shades of brown and black. The bathroom is equally basic, with a large tub in the center of the room and a bucket and mirror off in the corner. While lacking in any kind of luxury, at least I can take a warm bath and sleep in a real bed tonight. Aidan is already busy going back and forth, filling the tub with warm water from pails beside the fireplace. I can only imagine Luke must have left them there anticipating our arrival somehow.

"I'll let you take a bath and get cleaned up. Come out when

you're ready, and we can eat together and discuss tomorrow. I'll leave your bag Lili packed on the bed so you can get some clean clothes." Aidan heads back down the hall.

I close the bathroom door, strip my clothes off, and sink into the tub. The warm water feels delicious on my frost-bitten skin. There's a tray of soap next to the bath that smells of rosemary and mint. I grab it and get to work cleaning my skin and my hair from head to toe. Once I'm pleased with my complexion, I get out of the bath feeling all warm and minty fresh. I towel off and head into the bedroom. Laid out for me is one of my light-blue silky nightgowns and a pair of light-blue wool socks. Lili must've packed this for me, and Aidan didn't want to give it to me to dirty up at camp. It feels good to be warm and clean again. I get dressed and head to the dining table ready for whatever roasted clipper is.

Aidan is sitting at a table he must've pulled closer to the fireplace, waiting for me. He motions for me to take a seat across from him.

"We have roasted clipper with moon bread. What would you like to drink?"

"What are my options?" I reach for a glass.

"Water or something stronger." He starts filling his glass with a bottle of reddish amber liquid.

"I'll have whatever you're having." I raise an eyebrow, watching him down his glass.

"It's a type of whiskey fermented under the blood moon. We call it potato piss. Try it."

I hold up my glass, and Aidan fills it more than halfway full. I've never actually tried alcohol before, since it was forbidden to me at the castle, but Aidan doesn't know that. It smells acrid, but maybe it'll help me relax. I take a big gulp. It burns all the way down to my stomach, spreading heat across my body.

"What an awful name." I take another drink anyway.

"Yeah, well it does taste like piss. It'll put some hair on your chest and keep you warm in the winter." Aidan dishes food out on both of our plates. "I didn't take you for a whiskey drinker, Cheeks," Aidan says before shoveling chunks of meat in his mouth.

"What is clipper?" I push the pieces of meat around my plate.

"Fat black and white game birds. You'll see them all over the Cinder territory."

I decide to start eating the moon bread instead. It has a nutty flavor to it and is the same light-blue color of the Lycans' eyes. It's different than the overly decadent food I'm used to being served back in Tempest Moon.

I don't know how I feel about Aidan. He's nice to me and seems to care about training me well, and he got me away from the castle so I could live life a little. I just can't help the uneasy feeling I have in my gut. Is he really working for my parents? Can I blame him for making me get undressed to keep me warm? I didn't exactly hit him away when he touched me. I just let it happen, so maybe I can't hold it against him. He's a Lycan male after all, and Lycan are known to be very dominant and sexual. Maybe I can trust him and shouldn't hold his nature against him. He didn't force himself on me. I don't know what I'm trying to convince myself of right now. I pick up my cup and take a long gulp. It burns down to my core and instantly warms me up. It feels like a fire is burning deep in my stomach. Hopefully this potato piss will clear my head or at least let me get a good night's sleep without overthinking everything.

"Damn, Cheeks, slow down. Get some more food in your stomach before you top off that glass or I'll be carrying you to bed tonight," he says while handing me another piece of moon bread.

I do take a few more bites, but I'm suddenly not hungry. I'm feeling all sorts of flushed. I pull my wool socks off and refill my cup then toss myself onto the settee. I sink right into it, and I could fall asleep right here. This couch is perfectly worn to hug my body just right.

"I'm not that hungry anymore. What is it you want to talk to me about?" I remember he said he wanted to speak about tomorrow.

"I have to meet with a few pack leaders tomorrow to finalize plans for the festival. I'll be gone most of the day. Luke will drop something off to you for breakfast, but you can sleep in and relax. I want you to stay inside and wait for me to return. Don't go wandering off and getting into trouble. Can you manage?" he asks, coming to sit next to me with his own glass of potato piss.

"Of course I can manage. I'm used to being locked in places."

"First of all, you are not going to be locked in. I'm asking you for your safety to stay inside and rest until I return. Second, have you really been locked in a castle all your life? I thought those were just rumors." He sounds surprised.

"It's not becoming of a princess to wander, and it's not safe outside the castle boundaries for a girl with no power. Not exactly safe inside either," I say under my breath, but he doesn't miss a beat.

"What do you mean that it's not safe inside either?"

"Nothing . . . just can make you go stir crazy, you know." I try to brush it off like it's nothing by taking another long drink. "Why did you agree to train me? What's in it for you?"

"Times are hard for us Lycans, and it can't hurt having the king and queen owe me a favor." He winks at me, a devilish smile spreading across his face, but his eyes remain cold, not reflecting the humor of his expression.

Aidan's lips are surprisingly enticing, and despite the alcohol haze I can't help but fixate on them. I've never experienced a kiss before, and the idea of what he might do if I made the first move is both exciting and nerve-wracking. Would he tell my parents? Would he still continue to train me? The last few nights with him have been far from innocent, and the alcohol is making my inhibitions vanish. No wonder my parents keep the wine flowing at their dinner parties. I already feel a weird sense of confidence that wasn't there before.

For as long as I can remember, I've been taught to keep my head down and stay out of the way. Being passive and stoic has been my go-to for avoiding trouble, even if it means bottling up my emotions. The outside world might see me as calm and collected, but inside, I can be a screaming mess sometimes.

I was a bit of a wild child when I was little. My dad used to call me his little pixie. He said it meant cheerful and mischievous. The castle was a different place before he passed away. He brought warmth and light to our home, and his death felt like the sun had disappeared from our lives. Now, my mother and Silas seem to thrive in the cold emptiness that remains. I deeply miss him and often wonder what my life would be like if he was still here with us. I imagine traveling the world with him. He always encouraged me to feed the fire in my soul, the fire Samael has been slowly stifling out. Sometimes I don't know what happened to that girl, the girl with spirit, the dreamer with fire in her soul. Now I feel more like a domesticated horse letting people ride all over me.

"Aidan, can I ask you something?" I turn toward him and take the last swig from my glass then place it on the ground.

"I can already tell this is going to be good by the color of your cheeks. Yes, please ask me anything." He moves to face me, chuckling a bit.

"My cheeks are red from the alcohol and the fire in front of us, nothing more . . . just forget it." I'm already losing my nerve, and anger is heating my face too.

"Oh, relax, Cheeks. I must hear what's making you blush. Please tell me. I won't laugh." He looks at me now in all seriousness.

I lock eyes with him, and my insides feel like they're in disarray. *Should I say it? What if I mess up my words and sound like a fool?* I take a deep breath and gather my courage.

"I don't want to go my entire life without knowing what it feels like," I say, my voice shaking. "I've waited eighteen years, and I don't know when I'll have another chance like this. Aidan, would you...would you kiss me?" The silence that follows feels like an eternity, and I quickly try to clarify. "I mean, now. Please kiss me now."

He's staring into my eyes without a smile on his face. I'm ready to laugh it off and say I'm just kidding, but then he lifts his hand to my cheek and presses his lips against mine. My mind goes blank, and my body responds. His kiss is rough and not what I expected, but it feels good. His hands grip my face tightly, deepening the kiss with his tongue. I'm hesitant at first, but I open to him, and our tongues dance in a sensual rhythm. Just when I think it's over, he pulls back, his eyes locked on mine, holding my face in his hands. I can feel my lips tingling, and the taste of alcohol lingers on my tongue.

"You're going to be trouble, Cheeks," he says with a devilish smirk on his face.

I get up and refill my glass, then sink into the cushions and watch the fire. I can't help but think that life is short and I don't want to waste it. The life of a Sorceress isn't nearly as long as other beings. I will age much quicker than any Lycan or

Lamia or Faery. I'll be lucky if I live into my eighties, and even then I'll be old and frail.

Growing up in Tempest Moon, I was trapped in a life I didn't choose. My dad's death left me alone with a mother who was distant and indifferent, more concerned with appearances than my well-being. She married Silas, and suddenly I had a stepbrother, Samael, who made my life a living hell. Silas wasn't cruel to me, but his strictness was suffocating. I was forbidden from leaving the castle grounds, speaking to visitors, or attending meals with everyone else. I was isolated, with only my teachers, Samael, and sometimes his friends as company. It was a bleak existence, and if it weren't for Chepi I'd have no one to talk to. Lili was around, but her loyalty was to my parents, and I couldn't always trust her with my secrets. I often wondered if my mother knew about Samael's abuse. Seeing him strike her the other day filled me with dread; what if he hurt her too and she just turned a blind eye? The thought is unbearable.

As I feel the warmth of the alcohol spread through my body, I feel an urge to just let go and live life to its fullest. I am young and healthy, and I feel confident in my appearance, but I have been denied a life of my own for far too long. I want to experience everything that life has to offer. I want to explore all the realms, try different types of food, and learn to ride a horse. Most of all, I want to love and be loved by someone who sees me for who I am. I want to feed the fire in my soul, to feel and experience everything that I can while I am still young and full of life.

I know Aidan would never love me. He looks at me like I'm something he wants to play with, own even, but not love. But tonight I'm not looking for love, and I'm not saving my virginity for some prince charming, because the only prince I know is abhorrent. Aidan isn't evil. He may not care for me, but I don't think he'd want to hurt me. I also think sleeping with him could be a good time, and my parents would be furious if they found out. All the more reason to do it.

"Are you ready for bed? Looks like you're about to fall asleep over there." Aidan nudges me with his elbow. I take another sip from my glass.

"Yes, I am." I pull myself up off the couch and head to the bedroom.

Aidan follows me to the bedroom. He doesn't know it yet, but I don't plan to sleep just yet. I walk toward the bed then turn around to look at him. Instead of crawling beneath the blankets, I grab the bottom of my nightgown and pull it up over my head, then drop it on the ground, letting it pool near my feet. I'm completely naked now, and it may be dark out but the candles in here leave nothing to the imagination. My gaze meets his, and it's like starring into icy fire, burning with a fierce blue intensity.

"What are you doing?" he asks, his voice sounding a little hoarse.

This alcohol stuff is great because I'm not losing my nerve at all. I feel confident. I'm not going to shy away from his eyes. I want him to look at me. I want to be seen, and I want to know what it feels like to be wanted.

"What does it look like I'm doing?" I smile sweetly at him and bite my bottom lip.

"It looks like you're teasing a very hungry Lycan the night before the full moon, and the only reason I'm not inside of you right now is because I have eighty years of practicing restraint under my belt," he replies, and hearing him talk about being inside me makes my face warm and my thighs squeeze together.

"I'm not teasing you. I want you to take me. I want you

49

inside me, Aidan." I stare at him and see the animalistic look in his eyes staring back at me, taking in my words.

He takes a step toward me, keeping eye contact. "Have you ever been with a man, Cheeks? Not even just a man but a Lycan male?" His voice comes out low and guttural again.

"No, I haven't." My voice comes out smaller than I'd like.

"No, you haven't what, Cheeks? Been with a man? Or been with a Lycan?"

"I've never had sex with anyone before, okay? Is that what you want to hear?"

"If you want this, Cheeks, it's not going to be whatever fairytale you imagined in your head. I don't know how to make love. I only know how to fuck, and with the full moon coming I can't promise I'll take it easy on you. My blood is boiling just looking at you. This is your one out, because once I touch you I'm not going to stop until you're full of my seed." He takes another step closer.

I feel afraid for a moment, and my heart is racing so fast it feels like it might burst out of my chest, but I don't care. I want to feel him inside me, and I won't let fear hold me back. I don't know when I'll ever have this opportunity away from the castle again. Better Aidan then Samael or one of his friends.

"I want it," I whisper, and before I can take another breath he's right in front of me grasping me behind the legs and pushing me back on the bed. He takes off his shirt, and I can see his erection pressed against his pants. He follows my stare and gives me a self-satisfied smirk while dropping his pants to the floor, releasing his hard cock in a bounce. I stare at it and suddenly regret my decision. He's huge, and I don't think he's going to fit inside me. If he does, he's right that it's going to hurt.

He uses his knee to spread my legs. "Scoot back."

I do as he commands, and he never takes his eyes off

me. Just when I think he's going to get on top of me, he doesn't. He lies down next to me on his side. I look at him confused, but before I can speak he puts his finger to my mouth.

"Shhh. Just relax." He runs his finger back and forth across my bottom lip. "Open your mouth."

I do as he asks, and he puts his finger all the way in my mouth.

"Now suck."

I coat his finger with my tongue and suck on it thoroughly. He makes a deep groaning sound then takes his wet finger away from my mouth, gliding it down my body and pressing it inside me.

"Already wet for me, Cheeks." He breathes against my ear.

He curls his finger inside me and presses his thumb against my clit. A moan escapes my mouth. He moves his finger all the way out, then presses two fingers in and out slowly. My body answers to him by arching against his hand.

Then just as it's starting to feel really good, he pulls his hand away and sits up. He has a carnivorous look in his eye. He spits in his hand and rubs his cock with his slick saliva, then grabs my hips and flips me over, pulling me back to him. I reach out to catch myself as he slams his cock inside me. I feel an explosion of burning pain between my legs, and I can't help the scream that comes out of my mouth. He grabs the back of my head, fisting his hand in my hair and shoves my face into the pillows. He holds my waist in place with his other arm while he thrusts in and out of me, hard. I feel wetness on my thighs, and I know it has to be blood. I bite into the pillow and take it. He releases my head and grabs my ass with both hands, pulling himself all the way out, holding me in place, and slamming back into me hard. He's going faster and harder, and he has to be close. *Please let him be close.* I don't know how much more of this I can take. Finally, he slams into me one last time and moans. I feel his cock twitch inside of me, and I know he's coming in me. He stays there for a minute, breathing heavily, then pulls out of me and falls onto his back next to me.

I turn onto my side, unable to face him and pull my knees up to my stomach. My face is wet with tears, and it's burning down there. I know he said it was going to be rough, but I had no idea it'd be like this. I expected sex to feel pleasurable, but what I experienced was far from it. He doesn't say anything, and I can't bring myself to move. Finally, sleep finds me.

CHAPTER
SEVEN

Something's burning! The crackle and hiss of the fire overhead compels me to run faster. Viscous hot globs of ... blood, I think it's blood, rains down on me from the trees. I'm straining to see; the smoke and heat are burning my eyes. Everywhere I turn the flames fan up in front of me like they have a mind of their own. I try to wipe the sticky blood from my face, from my eyes. I drop to the ground choking on smoke. I squint to see anywhere I can go to get away from the fire. I put my arms out, digging my hands into the mucky earth, pushing with my feet and propelling my body forward. A hand grabs me by the arm and pulls hard. I kick out, panicked by the touch. A woman holds my arm. Her face is shadowed by a hood, and her hands are withered with age.

"You must choose, Lyra." Her voice sounds desperate and demanding.

I'm jolted awake by a noise to find Luke standing next to me.

"Sorry, miss, but I brought you breakfast, and when you didn't answer the door I wanted to make sure you were okay."

He looks down at me then at the blood on the blankets. His eyes widen. "Are you okay, Lyra?" His features soften, and he reaches down to touch my shoulder.

I pull the blankets up to my neck and sit up.

"Yes, I'm fine. Thank you for the breakfast. Can you leave it on the table for me? I'm not ready to get up just yet."

"Yes, of course." He eyes me and the blood then leaves the room. I hear him place the tray on the table then go out the front door, and I relax back onto the bed.

I have a throbbing headache, and a sense of regret hits me. Last night wasn't what I imagined for my first time. Aidan did warn me, and I knew what I was getting into, but I didn't expect it to be like this. The light in the room feels too bright, and I wonder if it's because of the excessive consumption of potato piss. I force myself to get out of bed and find my nightgown on the floor. I quickly slip it on and head out to the fire.

Breakfast is very interesting. I'm definitely no longer in Tempest Moon. Luckily for me, someone has taken the time to put labels on everything, Luke presumably. I don't know if I should be offended or not by the fact that Luke thinks I need my food to be labeled, but I'm grateful for it nonetheless. I'd be more grateful however if these labels included a description. The bowl with brown congealed jam reads wolpertinger jam. This would be helpful if I had any idea what wolpertinger is. The fluffy white buns look harmless enough, but they're called towarra buns. I have no idea what towarra is. I pick up a bun, cutting it in half and spreading the jam on top. It smells like a mix of campfire, nuts, and earthy mushrooms, not a sweet jam like I'd expect to be served back home. I take a bite, letting the flavors coat my tongue. The buns taste like a normal biscuit, except it's extra rich and buttery. The jam has a slightly salted earthy taste to it. It is surprisingly good. I wonder if wolpertinger is a type of mushroom. Maybe that is what's giving it an earthy taste. I finish off the buns and jam, laughing when I see that the bowl of apple slices is labeled as well, as if I wouldn't know what an apple is. The apples are divine, crisp and sweet. The apple skin is the same midnight blue as the leaves on some of the trees, and I wonder if those were a type of apple tree.

The fire is still roaring, and it looks like someone left a large bucket of warm water for me. Although I wish I had a warm bath to soak in, this will have to suffice for now. I feel dirty, and even after scrubbing every inch of my body with soap and warm washcloths the feeling just won't go away. I trudge back to the bedroom and find my things Lili packed all laid out on the desk. I slip on some fur-lined leggings and a long-sleeve cobalt-blue tunic to keep warm. I go to the bathroom and glance at my reflection. My hair is a mess of long, tangled waves and curls. I comb through it the best I can then leave it to fall behind my back.

I wish Lili was here. I wish I had someone to talk to about my dream. It was just like the last two, only this time I finally saw someone, a woman. I don't recognize her voice and can't make out her face. What must I choose? What could this mean? I rub at my chest trying to calm my anxious heart. I know Aidan told me to stay in the house until he returned, but I'm already feeling restless, and the last place I want to be today is in this bedroom alone. My mind is going to go crazy trying to decipher my nightmare, not to mention I can't get comfortable in this bed after last night. I slip on my boots and open the front door, thinking maybe I'll go explore a bit and see the horses.

I find Luke sitting on the front steps of the cabin eating an apple.

"Hi," I say, a bit surprised to find him here. Is he watching me? Did Aidan tell him to make sure I stayed in the cabin?

"Hello again, miss. Can I get you something?" He smiles up at me.

"Just call me Lyra please. What's there to do for fun around here?"

"Aidan told me he wanted you to stay in the cabin today, Lyra," he says, almost stuttering.

"Come on, Luke. He's going to be gone most of the day. We can be back before he is, and he'll never know I wasn't safe inside all day. Tonight's the festival. Aren't their preparations to be made? You don't have to watch me. I'm sure you have more important things to do." He doesn't look convinced, so I push. "Or are you prepared to hold me down in the cabin and keep me there by force? Because that's what it will take."

Now I have him. I see the realization crossing his face.

"Okay, but I'm not leaving you. Where would you like to go?"

I'm not sure because I haven't thought this far ahead. "How far away is the Shifting Forest from here?"

"I can't take you to the Shifting Forest, Lyra. It's way too dangerous, especially today."

I sigh in frustration. "Well, where can you take me? I don't know anything around here. All I know is I can't stay cooped up in that cabin all day. Not after last night." I say the last part to myself but understanding fills his face.

"There's a really great swimming hole about an hour walk from here. It'll be freezing this time of year but invigorating, and it's a nice little hike. I can pack lunch for us to take as well."

I laughed. "That sounds great. I'm all for invigoration."

"Ok. Wait here. Give me five minutes to make a pack then we can head out," he says, hurrying into the cabin.

I sit on the steps and tighten my bootlaces, making sure they're comfortable enough for our hike. It's a beautiful morning, with fields covered in frost and mist and streams of sunlight warming the ground. There's a chilly bite in the air, and the smell of chimney smoke adds to the winter ambiance. Although there's no snow on the ground this morning, it still feels like winter here. I lean back on the deck and take a deep breath of the crisp air.

"Who are you? And what are you doing?" a deep male voice asks, and then a boy appears.

Gods, my training has done nothing because I didn't even hear him approaching.

"Um . . . my name is Lyra, and I'm not doing anything. Who are you exactly?" I sit up, raising my eyebrows and waiting for an explanation.

"My name's Rhett. Is Luke around?" he asks, eyeing me up and down. Just then Luke comes out the front door.

"Hey Rhett, what's up?" He sounds surprised to see him.

"Nothing, man. I just thought you'd be helping set up for tonight, but I couldn't find you in town."

"Yeah, um sorry, this is Lyra. Aidan tasked me with watching her today, and we were just about to take a hike up to the old Mudhole. Want to join us?"

"Wait, old . . . Mudhole? What? I thought this was a swimming hole. When you said invigorating, mud didn't exactly come to mind," I say.

Rhett looks at me and starts to laugh. "Mudhole is just the name. The water is quite beautiful. Yeah, I'll join you guys, anything to avoid Marth. He's ordering everyone around town frantically to prepare the feast for tonight." He speaks in a deep, husky voice that belies his age. Rhett doesn't appear much older than me, but he exudes a mature, masculine vibe. With his jet-black hair, tan skin, sharp jawline, and piercing blue Lycan eyes, Rhett is undeniably attractive. He looks much more rugged and manly than Luke. Poor Luke still looks like a young boy who's not quite done going through puberty. His voice is still a little mousy at times.

"You ready?" Luke asks, looking at me.

I nod, and with that we start off down the dirt driveway together.

"So, Lyra, where are you from?" Rhett asks beside me.

"I'm from the Tempest Moon District. Aidan brought me here to see the festival, although I'm not quite sure why."

"The Tempest Moon. So are you a Sorceress then?" Rhett asks, beaming at me with a fat smile plastered across his face.

"Yes, I am. Well, I will be. I'm only eighteen, and we don't get our powers until we turn nineteen. So, I may be a Sorceress, but I don't have much to show for it yet."

Rhett laughs. "Don't worry. Luke here may be a Lycan, but he doesn't have much to show for it either." He grabs Luke around the neck and rubs his fist on the top of his head, messing his hair about.

"Hey, you won't be able to say that after tonight." Luke bats him away, laughing.

"Would either of you like to explain to me what exactly happens tonight?"

"Once a year when the full moon is at its fullest, we hold the Shifting Moon festival for one night only. Any Lycan who turned sixteen since the last festival will finally shift for the first time tonight along with gaining everything else that comes with being a Lycan. Like how you get your powers when you turn nineteen, it's similar to that. Before we turn sixteen and attend our first festival, we're just regular mortals. The Lycan blood within us hasn't awoken yet," says Rhett.

"I understand all of that, but what happens at the festival?"

"Packs from all over have been arriving all week in anticipation of the festival. Every Lycan attends, no matter their age, and that's why you'll see lots of tents set up all around the village. The real festivities start at sunset. Marth prepares a huge feast in the big hall. We all eat together and visit with other packs we haven't seen for a long time. We just catch up and enjoy good company and good food. Then after dinner they have a huge bonfire built outside the dining hall. Everyone enjoys beer and whiskey while the elders take turns telling stories about the newest members about to make their first shift. People dance and play music. It's like a big party under the moon. Then at midnight we all bear witness to the first shift the new Lycans make."

"I've never seen a Lycan in wolf form before," I tell them.

"Would you like to now?" Rhett gives me a cheeky smile, and I can see all of his perfectly straight white teeth. He is handsome.

"Yes, please." I give him a sweet smile in return.

"As you wish." Rhett ducks behind some trees, and then he emerges in slow motion. The first thing I behold is an enormous black paw, as though crafted by nature itself to embody strength and power. My gaze ascends to a jaw full of razor-sharp teeth and penetrating light-blue eyes that seem to exude a commanding presence. Rhett is even more imposing and majestic than I had imagined, with shaggy fur that's the deepest shade of black.

"Show off," Luke mutters, rolling his eyes.

I let out the breath I hadn't realized I was holding in. Rhett comes right up to me in his wolf form.

"Can I pet him?" I ask Luke.

Luke laughs. "Oh, I'm sure he'll love that."

I reach for him with both hands and pet his ears and his face while looking him in the eye.

"You are so beautiful and . . . terrifying," I whisper while smiling at him.

We keep a fast pace, Rhett running along ahead of us in his

wolf form. The hike is charming. Most of the trees have lost a lot of their leaves since winter is encroaching. The birds are chirping, and I can hear the sound of a river in the distance. The air smells of damp moss and rainwater. I'm not cold anymore because all the hiking is keeping me warm, but I'm sure my nose and cheeks are still pink from the chill in the air.

Finally, we come around a bend at the top of a hill, and the trees thin out a bit. At first all I see is Rhett in front of us with his naked, tan ass in our faces.

He looks back to us. "Come on. Don't be a chicken."

He jumps, falling out of sight.

I run forward to the edge of the cliff, and a breathtaking swimming hole comes into view. The water is a serene and inviting emerald green, and the shores below are strewn with tiny colorful rocks of all shades. Even the same enchanting midnight trees from the village are here. Luke is already at the edge, tossing his pack down onto the rocky beach below. Even though the water is going to be freezing, I can't wait to dive in and immerse myself in the beauty of this place.

I kick off my boots and take off all of my clothes except for my chemise, which I'm thankful I decided to wear under my tunic. It barely falls to my thigh, but it's better than going naked. I toss my clothes down next to the pack, then I look to Luke who's blushing and trying not to make eye contact with me.

"Have you never seen a half-naked woman before?"

"Nope this would be a first," he mutters.

I laugh. "Well, don't just stand there. Hurry up."

I get a little bit of a running start then jump off the cliff into the water below.

60

CHAPTER
EIGHT

The water is freezing. It feels like tiny needle pricks all over my skin. I surface with a gasp, and Rhett is right there to grab me.

"Are you okay?" He holds out an arm so I can steady myself in the water. It's too deep to stand, so I hold his arm and kick my feet to stay afloat.

"I think so. Just wow. Didn't expect it to be this cold." I laugh, holding back a shiver.

"Yeah, it's cold for me, and I always run warm, so I imagine you're out of your mind freezing right now." Rhett laughs again.

There's a splash next to us, and Luke surfaces.

"Invigorating, right?" He has a huge smile plastered across his face, and I know he's cold too.

"Yes, very," I say. I smile at them. I'm hardly able to contain how happy my heart feels in this moment. I've never been able to do something like this before, just casually have fun with friends. I've never been able to have friends. It's a new feeling, but one I hope to have more often.

"Okay, fuck this. I'm going to go build a fire and unpack lunch. I brought towels for us. When you guys are ready to get out, I'll leave them on a rock for you," he says between chattering his teeth and starts to swim toward shore.

"If you're too cold, you can follow Luke, or if you're feeling a little more adventurous you can hang onto my back and I'll swim us behind the waterfall. It opens up into a huge cave. It's worth seeing. Plus, my body heat will keep you warm." Rhett smiles and gives me a playful wink.

"Ever the gentleman you are. Yes, turn around and take me to the cave, wolf."

I wrap my arms around his neck and let my body press against his back. My legs come up behind us, kicking along with his. He's deliciously warm, and it helps to slow my breathing. I hadn't realized I was practically hyperventilating from the cold.

The waterfall is small but large enough to hide the cave opening behind it. I hold my breath for a moment as we duck under the falls. I wipe the water from my eyes and wrap my legs around Rhett's waist. It's now shallow enough for Rhett to stand and hold us up, but I can't quite reach the bottom yet. The cave is enormous. The walls are slick and covered in light green moss. At the roof of the cave is a tiny opening. I pause, taking in the magnificent view of the treetops swaying in the winter breeze. A rainbow of orange, blue, and green leaves dance and blow off the trees, some of them tumbling into the cave. I watch in awe as they gradually slow their descent, twirling and glistening in the soft, buttery beam of sunlight. The leaves finally come to rest on the calm water that surrounds me, creating a serene and peaceful ambiance. Rhett walks us straight over to the beam of sunlight and stops beneath it. I let my feet fall to the rocks and release him now that I can reach the bottom. The sunlight spreads across my face. I tilt my head back and close my eyes, calling the warmth to me. The water is surprisingly tolerable here in the cave.

I bring my face back up to look at Rhett, who's staring at me.

"The sun feels nice."

"So you think I'm beautiful and terrifying," he teases.

"Are you trying to flirt with me?" I tease back, giving him a flirtatious smile.

"Can I ask you something?" he says, the seriousness back in his voice.

"Sure, what is it?" I look up, meeting his eyes.

"What are you doing with Aidan? Are you two a thing?"

A laugh escapes me. "Oh, gods no. My parents hired him to train me. I don't know why he brought me here. I think he took pity on me because I've never been allowed to travel anywhere before."

Rhett doesn't look convinced.

"Aidan doesn't take pity on anyone, and he doesn't do anything without a reason. Just be careful around him, okay?"

"Okay, I will." I smile and nod, but unease fills my gut.

We share a brief look while he raises his hand and tucks my hair back behind my ear.

"You're the beautiful one, Lyra. I'm sure after your nineteenth birthday when you inherit your powers, you'll be the terrifying one too." He smiles, but it doesn't reach his eyes. "Aidan doesn't deserve you. He's not—he's not good. Don't give yourself to him, whatever you do. Stay for the festival then go back home. Don't linger around here. It's not safe for you."

"Believe me, I learned the hard way what kind of male Aidan is. I won't linger. I promise."

WE SWAM TO shore and found our towels waiting for us. Rhett, ever the gentleman, hands me my towel and doesn't even let his gaze linger on my mostly naked body. I wrap myself in the towel's warmth and plop down on a rock next to Luke by the fire.

"What's for lunch? I'm starving." I nudge Luke with my elbow.

"Wolpertinger pies. It's not much, but we don't want to fill up before the feast tonight anyways."

We all start to dig in. The pie is delicious. It's got the same spiced, earthy flavor as the jam I had at breakfast. For Lycans, they certainly don't eat as much meat as I thought they would.

"Is wolpertinger a local mushroom?" I ask.

Luke practically spits out his food at the question. "No, it's a type of rabbit."

"Who in their right mind makes rabbit jam?" I exclaim.

"Marth is quite the innovative cook; he makes all sorts of creations to make food last longer around here. He likes to utilize every part of the creature as well so nothing is wasted," Rhett says.

"I feel bad now eating a cute, little, furry bunny. But it is rather good though."

"Wolpertingers are anything but cute. Don't feel bad," Rhett says.

"Yeah, they're not cute. They have red eyes with fangs and black antlers. They reproduce like crazy too. The Shifting Forest is stock full of them," Luke says.

It's quiet for a time. There's just the sounds of us chewing and the fire crackling with life.

"Lyra, can I ask you what happened last night?" Luke says softly, looking at me.

"What do you mean?" Rhett asks, pie crumbs falling from his mouth.

I turn to Rhett. "Do you get more aggressive and—I don't know—horny when it's around the full moon?"

"Everything we feel is more heightened around the full moon. But you're not going to feel more aggressive unless you are already aggressive in nature, if that makes sense. It's like we have more heightened senses. More extreme moods," Rhett explains. "What happened last night?"

"It's nothing. Nothing happened."

"Lyra, there was a lot of blood on the bed this morning, and you didn't look well when I woke you up," Luke says.

"Did that bastard hurt you?" Rhett asks between gritted teeth.

I look between the two of them, unsure of what to say. I feel embarrassed. Aidan only gave me what I asked for, didn't he?

"He didn't do anything I didn't ask for. I drank too much, and we had sex. It was my first time, and that's why the blood was there. It didn't mean anything. He didn't hurt me, so please don't say anything," I beg.

They don't look convinced. They look at each other and nod in understanding.

Dying to change the subject, I ask Luke, "Are you nervous for tonight? For your first shift?"

"Nah, I can't wait. I've been looking forward to this day for as long as I can remember."

"Do you think there will be any more of that moon bread at the feast tonight?" I ask before taking another bite of my meat pie.

"How do you know about moon bread?" asks Rhett.

They're both staring at me, and I have no idea why their faces have turned so serious. "Luke left it for Aidan and I last night and I ate it with dinner."

"I didn't leave you any bread last night. I dropped off the roast clipper, and that was it," Luke says.

"Are you sure it was moon bread?" Rhett asks.

"It was light blue and had a nutty flavor to it," I say. I'm losing my patience with them and don't understand what the big deal is about the bread.

Rhett shakes his head slowly, running a hand through his hair. "Lyra, it wasn't the alcohol that made you give up your virginity last night. Aidan is a reckless motherfucker."

"What are you talking about?" I ask.

Luke cuts in before Rhett can respond. "Moon bread is magical bread made from the blue wheat you see covering the rolling hills past Aidan's cabin. It's fermented on the full moon and can make anyone who's not a Lycan go mad if they eat it."

"I don't understand. I didn't go mad. Why would Aidan give it to me? And what does it have to do with my virginity?"

"Some Lycans enjoy the moon bread because it lowers inhibitions in a way that alcohol alone can't achieve. With alcohol, you may get drunk, do something foolish, and be more vulnerable to being taken advantage of. However, the moon bread can make you believe that your actions are your own idea," Rhett says.

I shake my head in disbelief. Aidan drugged me so that he'd have no trouble getting me to have sex. For my first time being with a man, I was tricked and used. Now nothing could ever change that. I hung my head a little, lost.

"I hate to say it, but we have to head back soon. I don't want Aidan knowing we took you out today," Luke says, pulling me from my thoughts.

"Whatever you do, Lyra, just be on your guard around him, and don't eat anymore moon bread," Rhett says, getting to his feet.

We gather up our things and get presentable, then start the

hike back down to Aidan's cabin. Halfway through the hike, Rhett bids us farewell, saying he'll see us later tonight and something else about helping his mom before the festival. He shifts into his wolf form and takes off. Luke and I hike mostly in silence until we reached the cabin driveway.

We both freeze as we catch sight of Aidan sitting on the steps, watching us. His expression is tense, his body language is defensive, and I can tell that something is bothering him. It takes a tap on my back from Luke to get me moving again. I feel a wave of anxiety wash over me as I realize how angry Aidan looks. I'm afraid of what kind of trouble he's going to unleash on Luke for breaking the rules.

"Aidan we—"

"Go get ready for tonight. I'll deal with you later," he says to Luke.

Luke gives me a look that reminds me of a puppy being scolded by its master. I give him a slight smile and nod to tell him it's fine, then he leaves us.

"Inside. Now." Aidan's tone is anything but joking. I hurry up the steps, and once inside I turn around to face him. He slams the door.

"I told you not to leave this goddamn cabin today, Lyra," he yells, looking down at me.

I try to defuse the situation with Aidan. "We didn't go into town. No one saw us. It's over now, and I was safe the whole time. So please just calm down." But I can feel the tension in my own voice as I respond to him. Despite my efforts to sound calm, my voice gets louder and more agitated in return.

"Bedroom. Now," he growls.

I'm ready to protest, but he grabs my arm and drags me toward the bedroom.

"Take off your clothes," he demands.

"Aidan, please." My voice cracks, and a surge of panic washes over me.

"Take off your fucking clothes now."

He grabs my tunic and rips it down the middle with both hands. My breasts break loose, and I use all my strength to push him away, but he just grabs my wrist and shoves me back on the bed, hard. Fear takes hold of me, and I frantically kick out, trying to distance myself from him. He clutches my ankles, seizing me. He gets a grip on my pants and pulls them down around my ankles. Dread creeps up my spine.

"Please don't. Aidan, I'm sorry," I plead, tears running down my cheeks.

"You want to act like a little bitch and disobey me, Cheeks, then I'm going to show you who the boss is right now." His voice is low and menacing, and I can tell he isn't trying to mask his dark side anymore. He pulls me to the edge of the bed. My ass hits against him and my legs go up in the air. I try to kick him away again, but he catches my legs and rips my boots off. *He rips them off with claws.* Sharp claws protrude from his fingertips. He pulls my leggings the rest of the way off, licking his lips and revealing that his teeth are now replaced with sharp canines. He pulls his pants down then grabs me by the throat. There's a feral look in his eyes, and he thrusts into me. I cry out in pain. He's holding my legs to his chest while slamming into me over and over again. It's burning, and I'm crying harder now. My heart is racing, and my mind goes blank with disbelief as I struggle to grasp what is happening to me.

"Aidan, please. You don't have to do this," I mutter between sobs.

He grabs a pillow and puts it over my face, snarling. "Stop crying, Lyra. It's time to grow up and respect the people in charge."

I stare into the pillow, trying to think of anything else to get through this moment. He grabs my breast with his hand and squeezes hard.

"You like when I fuck you like this, don't you?"

I don't know how long this goes on because at some point I just black out while crying into the pillow. I wake up when Aidan removes the pillow from my face. With one hand he grabs me by the hair, pulling my face right to his cock. I try to turn away, but he takes his other hand and squeezes my jaw, forcing it open. He pushes his dick in my mouth and comes— salty, warm, and thick fluid in my throat.

"Swallow it," he says, still holding my jaw open, pressing his claws in.

I gag and choke down what he released in my mouth. Then he pulls out and pushes me back on the bed.

"You're lucky I took your mouth. Next time it'll be your ass, and I don't think you will enjoy it as much," he says with an evil smile on his face.

I lie there tears streaming down my face, seized by shock. I hear him fill the bath with buckets of warm water.

"Go take a bath. You're filthy. I want you to look good tonight. I'll lay your clothes out on the bed. Now cheer up, Cheeks. You know you enjoyed that."

CHAPTER
NINE

I'm lying in the bath, trying to soothe my burning skin and stop my trembling hands. I've cried all my tears, but the pain won't go away. My fingers clutch at my necklace, the cool bloodstone doing nothing to relieve the churning in my gut. I feel like my body is shutting down. I can't process what just happened. My stomach lurches, and I vomit onto the floor. The dry heaves are violent and unrelenting. I try to catch my breath, but my heart is racing, and my chest feels tight. My mind keeps replaying the events over and over, and it's too much to bear.

When I look down at my body, it doesn't feel like it's mine anymore. The only visible evidence of what happened is a little bit of blood in the water and a dark bruise developing on my breast, but I feel like what happened covers me everywhere.

No amount of scrubbing can wash away the shame and fear. I need to get out and face the world, but every inch of me is screaming for the safety of the bath. I force myself to stand up, the world spinning around me, and I know that I'll never forget this moment, no matter how hard I try to escape it. I feel so dirty, filthy, and used. My body convulses with a gut-wrenching heave, and I can't help but cry. I need to be clean, but no amount of scrubbing will make it go away. The past has wrapped around me like a snake, suffocating me. I don't know how I'll ever recover from this, but I know one thing for sure. My life will never be the same.

I towel off, trying to rub away the feelings of shame and disgust that still linger on my skin. I comb out my hair, trying to distract myself from the thoughts swirling in my mind. I pick up the clothes Aidan left for me in the bedroom, grateful for the distraction. The crimson dress is stunning, but as I slip it on the smell of red currants and gooseberries fills my nostrils, making me feel sick. I know I'll be itching all night; my skin never agrees with brush berries. The neckline is cut lower than anything I wore in Tempest Moon, but it's a welcome change. I'm sick of hiding my body behind heavy velvet and itchy wool.

Despite the beauty of the dress, I'm freezing, and I know the cold will only serve to bury the pain that I'm not yet ready to face. I pull on my boots and sit down, trying to calm my racing heart. I take deep breaths, telling myself it's going to be okay, that I just have to get though the next couple of days, and then I'll be back home. I can't let this asshole break me. I pep talk myself for a few more minutes, the weight of what happened still heavy on my shoulders.

Once I'm satisfied that I can steady my hands and my breathing, I leave the bedroom to meet Aidan. As I walk, I try to push down the sickening feeling in my stomach and focus on the present, telling myself that I'm stronger than this and that I won't let him win.

～

As I walk down the hall, Aidan is waiting for me by the fireplace. He's dressed formally, wearing gray pants and a white tunic with white furs draped over his shoulders. The sight of him causes a familiar sickening feeling to flare up in the pit of my stomach. My heart races, and my palms begin to sweat. I remind myself that I'm a princess, a Sorceress, and the daughter of Euric Lewis, one of the most powerful kings to ever rule over Cloudrum. I'll cower to no one, not even this monster.

But despite my resolve, the feeling of disgust doesn't go away. I force myself to look Aidan in the eye, but it's a struggle to keep my composure. I can feel the bile rising in my throat, threatening to choke me. I take a deep breath, steeling myself for what's to come. It stops here and now. I won't let this man take advantage of me again.

I walk straight to the front door, trying to ignore the pounding of my heart and the tremble in my legs. The weight of everything that's happened bears down on me, threatening to crush me. But I know that I have to be strong, that I can't let him see my fear. I'm determined to get through this, to show him that I won't be broken.

"Can we go now, please?"

"Yes, Cheeks, we can go," he says. The sound of his voice and him calling me that triggers me. I bite my cheek until the metallic taste of blood touches my tongue. *I will not let him get under my skin.* I repeat this in my head until my jaw loosens, and I follow after him out the front door. The sun has just set, and it's not quite dark yet. He takes me to the stables, and we ride Geri together toward town. Aidan must feel the hate radiating off me, but he says nothing. Thankfully we reached the hall in the center of town after only a few minutes of riding.

There are Lycan walking around everywhere in human

form. There's a huge bonfire set up outside the hall entrance. It's not lit yet, but it's taller than me and as wide as a carriage. As I approach the bonfire, I notice benches scattered around and beautiful blue and white flowers tied together and strewn overhead. Laughter from the dining hall echoes in the background as more people arrive, and the excitement in the air is palpable. Aidan offers me a hand, and I reluctantly let him lead me into the large hall, which may not be fancy, but it feels warm and welcoming.

Most everyone is having a great time, clinking glasses together, and their elevated voices ring out across the hall. The celebratory atmosphere is infectious. The room is lined with rectangular wood tables, with one smaller table placed at the head of the hall going the opposite direction. The floor is covered in the most unusual fur rugs, dyed the deepest shade of blue. The tables are adorned with linens in the same deep blue as the fur rugs, and huge platters full of food are arranged on top of them. My senses are overwhelmed by the aroma of spiced meat and rich caramel.

I see whole roast clippers, wolpertinger pies, towarra buns, and about a dozen other dishes I don't recognize.

Aidan walks me to the table at the head of the room and pulls out a chair for me. I sit down, and he sits next to me, unfortunately. Everyone is dressed formally in bright colors and draped in rich furs. However, this doesn't seem like a formal sit-down dinner. No one pays any attention to us. People are standing and sitting scattered all around the room talking, eating, and drinking. There are enough bodies here to make me forgot about the cold and feel like it's a warm summer evening. I see Rhett across the room. He's in conversation with a couple who could be his parents. They're all laughing and seem to be enjoying each other's company. This is so at odds with what I'm used to seeing at the dinner parties back home. I haven't spotted Luke yet, and I hope Aidan didn't get to him while I was bathing.

I soon realize I'm sitting at the table for all the pack leaders. Every time someone sits at our table, Aidan introduces me, but I've already forgotten everyone's name because I'm too distracted looking for Luke. The man next to me is the only one I remember because he won't stop asking me questions.

"So, Princess Lyra, how are you liking it here in Cinder territory so far?" Zog asks. Zog is a pack leader, and his pack resides deep within the Shifting Forest. He's very tall and muscular with a similar build to Aidan, only he has short brown hair and a full beard. His breath stinks of onions, and he kind of gives me the creeps.

"It's very nice. Thanks for asking." I stay charming even though I cringe at the thought of this place. I never thought I'd be excited to go back to Tempest Moon.

"Would you care for some potato piss or a hot claw, Princess? I see you're not drinking anything." Zog leans closer to me.

"Hot claw please." The gods know I need it. He brings me a large mug. It smells of apples and honey with hints of vanilla. "What is in a hot claw?" I ask.

"It's hot cider spiked with potato piss. Too sweet for my liking." He holds his glass up. "To you, Princess." His voice is toneless and makes my skin crawl.

"Umm . . . thanks." I smile and take a long drink. I feel it travel all the way down, warming my insides. At least alcohol is allowed here. It'll make this night easier to bear. I'm not exactly hungry, but I pick at a roll and a few pieces of clipper trying to pass the time.

It's dark now, and everyone's been eating and chatting for a couple hours. I've had to listen to Zog tell me stories of hunting monsters that live in the Shifting Forest. He has a lot to say about spider wraiths and how they only recently started to plague these lands. While it's interesting to learn about the Shifting Forest, I just don't want to learn about it from him. I'm so relieved when Aidan stands and announces it's time to gather outside and light the bonfire.

When I stand to go outside, I have to catch myself for a moment. I'm fully feeling the effects of the hot claw now. I guess I should slow down or I won't be able to stand outside until midnight. Plus, I know Luke is excited, and I want to be there to see him shift and support him. I still haven't seen him, which is worrisome, but there are a lot of people here. I could've just missed him.

Everyone gathers outside around the fire pit and Marth, a rather round older-looking gentleman with a gray scruffy beard, lights the fire. The fire is gigantic and lights up the entire village center once it gets going. The sound of sizzling pops and cracks can be heard every now and then over the music and chatter. The air is thick and smells of smoke and pine.

Aidan has been in deep discussions with other pack leaders, so I make my way around the groups of people talking and laughing and try to find a familiar face. Finally, I see Rhett. He seems to spot me at the same time and comes over, embracing me in a big hug. I have to bite my cheek again to keep from breaking down and telling him everything right then.

"Hey, have you seen Luke?" I say instead, trying not to sound worried. I don't want to give away anything that happened earlier. Better Rhett doesn't know.

"No, I haven't, but I'm sure he's just preparing for tonight. He's probably nervous for his first shift." He looks at me, furrowing his eyebrows. "Come dance with me." He pulls me over in front of a lady singing next to a man playing guitar. It's a slow song, and a few other couples are swaying around us. I wrap my arms around his neck and let him take the lead.

"Is this your way of trying to distract me so I don't worry?" I say into his shoulder.

"Yes, is that obvious?"

I feel him smile.

"Tonight is supposed to be a happy night. It's exciting. It's something we celebrate every year, and there's rarely ever any outsiders. Consider yourself lucky to attend." He laughs, lightening the mood. He breaks away from me, taking my hand. "Come with me. I want you to meet someone."

We weave through small clusters of people drinking and talking and stop next to a large tree away from the fire and crowds.

"Wait here. I'll be right back," he says.

"Okay." I smile and nod.

He goes over to a group of men and talks for a moment then heads back toward me with another man next to him. Rhett is tall, but this guy is really tall, like well over six feet. He has short, black-gray hair and a strong jaw with gray-speckled stubble covering it. He has the same pale-blue eyes as all the Lycan.

"Lyra, this is Larc. He's my pack leader," Rhett says as he moves in front of me.

"Pleasure to meet you, Larc." I extend my hand, and he takes it, giving me a broad smile.

"The pleasure is mine, Princess Lyra."

"Just Lyra please." I smile. His hand is warm, and his touch gentle but strong.

"So how long have you and Rhett known each other?"

Larc elbows Rhett in the shoulder. "This guy I've known since he was born."

"And how long have you been his pack leader?" I asked, honestly curious.

"Well, when we're born, we're assigned a pack, but your true bond develops more after you go through the shifting, and that's when you are duty bound to your pack leader— until he dies that is. Then his second in command would take over the pack, and you would be bound to him," Larc says, shifting his weight.

"What do you mean by duty bound? What if you don't like the pack leader you're assigned to?"

Rhett laughs and Larc continues, "Well you don't really have a choice unfortunately. Once you're duty bound to a pack leader, there's no getting out of it unless the pack leader dies. If the pack leader makes a command everyone in the pack must follow it. There is no choice. It's like our blood answers to the leader. I know it's a lot of power for someone to have over others, but we don't abuse it."

"What if you asked everyone in your pack to jump off a cliff? Would they do that?"

"Yes, they'd have no choice, but don't worry. No one's going to do that, and if one of us did we'd have to answer to all the other pack leaders and face judgment," Larc clarifies.

"How many pack leaders are there?"

"Seven if you include me," Larc says.

"Is there anyone ranked above the pack leader? I thought Aidan had told me he was in charge of the Lycan Realm. Is he just another pack leader?"

Rhett and Larc exchange a disgruntled look, and I get the feeling neither of them care for Aidan much.

"Aidan is in charge of the Lycan Realm. You could say he is the pack leader of the pack leaders," Larc says.

"What if something were to happen to Aidan? Does he have a second in command?"

"Not exactly. A higher power would have to come into play to find a replacement for Aidan," Larc says.

By the hard look that passes between the two males, I get the feeling I should change the subject.

"Are you Luke's pack leader as well?"

"No, Luke has been assigned to Zog's pack. After tonight he will be relocating to the Shifting Forest with his pack." Larc doesn't look pleased.

"Come. Let me refill your drink and find us a spot to sit by the fire. The stories are about to start," Rhett says, taking my hand and nodding goodbye to Larc.

"It was nice meeting you." I smile at Larc and follow Rhett toward the fire.

"Likewise, Princess." Larc gives a wave and disappears into the crowd.

CHAPTER

TEN

While sitting by the fire listening to the stories, I learn there are three Lycans being celebrated tonight that have all turned sixteen since the last festival. Two males and one female will be shifting for the first time later this evening. All three are from different packs, and their pack leaders each stand up one at a time and tell a few stories about their soon-to-be newest member.

Zog is the first to stand. He speaks about Luke, and I learn that Luke is a skilled hunter, and that's why fate placed him with Zog's pack to help keep the monsters at bay in the Shifting Forest. Luke also has a little brother named Chandler. He's expected to make the shift next year, and he'll also be joining Zog's pack. It's hard to imagine Luke as a skilled hunter. He seems so sweet and innocent, so young. I can't imagine him facing off against anything that dwells in the Shifting Forest.

Next up is a woman pack leader named Nicoletta. She's stunning. Tall and slender with straight black hair falling to her waist and pale skin that contrasts her blue eyes. She has a beautiful but wicked smile, and something about her rubs me the wrong way. Yuri is joining her pack tonight. She speaks about the boy, but I don't know if he's here or what he looks like. I do learn that he has great potential because he is a skilled healer.

Lastly, a stocky older man with gray hair and a thick gray beard named Phelan speaks. He talks about the girl Lycan who's named Dawn. Dawn is a tracker, and Phelan is most pleased to have her in his pack. His pack territory borders the black forest, and her tracking skills will come in handy when people go missing. Often visitors who have to travel through the black forest go missing, and a tracker is usually hired and paid well to find them—dead or alive.

After all the pack leaders are finished speaking, there's several toasts and cheers for the three newest Lycans making the shifts tonight. Marth announces from somewhere in the crowd that it's almost midnight.

I realize I haven't seen Aidan since Rhett pulled me away to dance earlier. I wonder where he is. It doesn't seem like him to not keep tabs on me all night.

Everyone migrates away from the fire to the forest edge where there's a wooden stage set up with four wooden chairs atop it. I wonder who the fourth chair is for. This must be where they bring out the Lycan and make them shift in front of everyone. It seems kind of cruel to me to have everyone watch something that's rather intimate and scary. It's their first time shifting, and they have to do it in front of all these prying eyes. I guess it's just natural to them. I appear to be the only non-Lycan here tonight, so I'm probably the only one who's never witnessed a shift like this anyways.

"I've been looking all over for you." I jump at Aidan's whispers. He's come up behind me, putting an arm around my waist. I have to remind myself not to jerk away from him.

"I have a special seat for you," he says.

My heart sinks as he pulls me toward the stage. I know what he's going to do, and I hate it. The fourth chair. The one reserved for the special guest. The last thing I want is to be the center of attention. I can feel the eyes of the crowd on me, watching me as I make my way to the seat. I try to ignore them, but I can feel my face growing hot and my palms starting to sweat.

Aidan guides me to the chair, pulling it to the side of the stage so that I'm facing the three empty chairs in front of me. At least I don't have to look out at the sea of faces. I feel exposed and vulnerable up here. I take a deep breath, trying to steady myself, but my heart is still racing.

Aidan hands me a glass of potato piss before turning to address the crowd. I take a sip, trying to calm my nerves, but it only makes me feel more nauseous. I wish I could just disappear, be anywhere but here. But I know I have to be strong, and I want to show my support for Luke.

"Tonight, for the first time in many years, we have a special guest. A non-Lycan here to be a part of our festivities. For those of you who have not had the pleasure of meeting her yet, this is Princess Lyra Lewis from Tempest Moon."

I glance to my right and smile, giving a quick wave to the audience. I down my glass in one long drink then place it on the ground next to me.

"I think it's time we bring out our other special guests for this evening. Let's welcome Dawn, Luke, and Yuri to the stage," Aidan says.

Nicolette, Zog, and Phelan emerge from the forest to my left. Each of them drags what I assume is the newest member of their pack with them. Only I can't see Dawn, Luke, or Yuri because they have brown sacs over their heads. The three kids are stumbling as they reach the stage.

They must be drunk, and I wonder why they are hooded. Is this normal practice? They are each placed by their pack leader in the three wooden chairs in front of me, which face out toward the crowd. Their arms and legs are tied to their chairs. A hush falls over the crowd, and I feel thick tension in the air.

"As you can see, tonight we're going to be doing things a little bit differently," Aidan says, his voice cutting through the silence with a harsh tone. My eyes quickly go to his as a sense of panic fills me. Not just panic though...I feel unwell. My limbs are suddenly too heavy for me to hold up, and my vision narrows.

Aidan comes close to me and leans down so his face is right up against my left cheek.

"Sorry, Cheeks, this is the deal I made with your parents. It'll all be over soon." He pats the top of my head. I want to protest, but I can't speak. A sense of dread courses through my body, settling heavy on my chest. Goosebumps spread over me, coating my skin. What is Aidan going to do to me and to these poor kids? How could my mother make a deal with this animal, this rapist? I'm not surprised Silas would make deals with such a man—he did raise Samael after all, but my mother... For a moment I think I might vomit. It's then I see an older woman on the stage. She looks oddly familiar, but I don't think I've met her before. She's talking to Aidan and the other three pack leaders, but when she makes eye contact with me, I see she's not a Lycan because her eyes are black. She's a Sorceress. She has four huge scars across one side of her face, and I wonder if a Lycan clawed her in the past. My mind is racing, but I can't make my thoughts clear. Aidan must've drugged my drink or this Sorceress put a spell on me. Then I realize, *Luke*. Oh my gods, Luke is not drunk. He must be drugged or put under a spell like me.

I hear people talking in the crowd, but I can't make out what anyone is saying, although it sounds hostile.

"Attention everyone, I have consulted thoroughly with your pack leaders, and I assure you the actions I am about to take tonight are for the betterment of our Lycan community and our future. I expect full compliance from each and every one of you. You will heed my words and follow the instructions of your pack masters. Let it be known that any interference during the ceremony will not be tolerated." Aidan's voice echoes across the crowd and an uncomfortable silence falls over everyone.

I no longer see Nicolette, Zog, or Phelan. The Sorceress is gone too. Cold hands clamp down on my shoulders. I try to look up at whoever is touching me, but my head is wobbly.

"You're going to make history tonight, my sweet Lyra." The old hoarse voice of a woman fills my head with a familiar sound. I know it's the Sorceress standing behind me, touching me.

I see the body of a female. Dawn must be nearest to me. Aidan approaches her first and removes the bag from her head. Curly black hair falls down her back. She has a gag in her mouth, and her head sways like she's intoxicated. Her eyes don't look drugged, and they don't look afraid. She looks pissed. If looks could kill, she'd be throwing daggers at Aidan right now. He just smiles and pats her on the head then removes the hood next to her to reveal Yuri.

Yuri is a large male. Bigger than both Dawn and Luke, he practically towers above them. For this reason, I can only assume they put extra care into his drugged cocktail because he's very out of it. He has spiky dark-brown hair atop his head. He's gagged and doesn't even make eye contact with Aidan or anyone in the crowd. His eyes keep rolling back in his head, and there are sweat beads dripping down his face.

Aidan removes the last hood, and my heart sinks as I see Luke, who looks terrified. His eyes are wide and bloodshot, darting around the crowd and then landing on me. We make eye contact, and I hold his gaze. I try to apologize with my eyes. This is all my fault for coming here. He just stares back at me, and I feel so utterly helpless to do anything. Tears begin running down my face, and I hold back a sob. What's happening? What is Aidan going to do to these poor kids? To me?

Aidan turns toward the crowd.

"Remember what I'm doing tonight is for all of you. For your future," he says.

I watch in horror as Aidan's face twists and contorts. His jaw cracks and elongates, his lips curling back to reveal razor-sharp teeth. His mouth froths and drips as he snarls in rage. His clothes tear away as a dense coat of scruffy white fur slowly covers his once-human form. I am filled with disgust as I witness his limbs snap and rearrange, becoming more beast-like with each passing moment. His eyes burn with a supernatural blue light, but there's a hollowness in them, a lifelessness that betrays his evil and deranged nature. I compare him to Rhett, who embodies grace and power as a wolf, but Aidan is nothing like him. Aidan is a monster, the monster that violated me, the monster that my mother foolishly trusted with a deal.

I don't realize I'm trying to get up until I feel the Sorceress's hands tighten on my shoulders. The dread in my chest is suffocating. I can't calm my racing heart, and I need to move. Aidan walks a slow circle around the three chairs in front of me. Each paw hits the stage heavy with purpose. My heart beats faster against my chest, and my pulse echoes in my ears. For too long that's all I hear—Aidan's slow steps and my racing heartbeat. I don't think anyone knows what the hell is happening. The audience is quiet except for a few little murmurs I can't make out. He jumps up, placing his front two paws on top of Dawn's lap. He digs his nails in, and I see little drops of blood pool around his paws and slowly drip onto the wood below. Everyone is hushed, and I swear I hear drops of blood hit the stage. His paws flex, and I think he's going to jump off of her, but instead his maw opens wide and thick, and his sharp teeth sink into Dawn's throat, blood misting across his white fur. It's silent. Just the complete, utter silence of stunned shock. Then a gurgling noise escapes Dawn. Someone in the crowd screams. I focus on Dawn and her eyes, which want to say something, but Aidan's jaw clamps down. With that one bite, he almost severs her head completely. It falls to the side, dangling at a terrible angle as her lifeless eyes stare into an invisible abyss. Her last words never take form.

Roars break out in the crowd. My vision falters. I hear commotion to my right, but everything is happening too fast. Aidan does the same thing to Yuri, only Yuri is a lot larger than Dawn, and Aidan's bite only severs part of his neck. He's still alive, convulsing and making a wet gurgling sound as blood sprays out onto the stage and into the crowd, which is full of his family and friends. Aidan's white fur is now drenched with blood dripping down his chest. The metallic smell fills my nose. I lean forward and vomit on my feet before the Sorceress hauls me back in place, lifting my head to the horrific scene unfolding before me. Why is no one stopping him? There's commotion in the crowd, but no one takes the stage. I try to form the words. I try to yell out for someone to help, but the drugs are drowning me inside. I know if Aidan made the order, then everyone is powerless against him. I scream out again, but I don't know if the sound actually leaves my mouth or not.

My eyes find Luke. Luke looks so young, innocent, and absolutely terrified. Intense fear tears into my chest. I don't realize I'm screaming until the Sorceress places her hand over my mouth. There are tears streaming down Luke's face, and I start to wobble my chair side to side. It's all my body can do to move. I bite down on the old woman's hand, and she slaps me hard, sending stars shooting through my vision. Luke is watching Aidan approach him. I know there's nothing I can do to save him.

"Luke, look at me." His eyes dart to me. "I'm here. I'm with you. Just look at me." Aidan jumps up and bites Luke's throat. I hold his gaze as his head falls to the side and the life leaves his eyes.

I sob, and my body shakes violently. The Sorceress is gone, and I try to stand but fall out of my chair onto my side. My face hits the stage hard, and I almost black out from the impact. I see the Sorceress place a glass next to Dawn's severed head, filling it with her blood. She does the same to Yuri and Luke. I can't hear anything, and I know my body is in shock and trying to recover from whatever drugs I was given. I'm clawing at the wood with my arms and pushing with my legs, trying to make my way across the stage like a fish out of water. I want to get away from this horrific scene, but everything seems to be happening in slow motion. I can't get my body to move fast enough.

Aidan is back in his human form, and I feel a fleeting sense of relief. But as he pulls me into his lap and cradles me like a baby, my heart sinks. I try to fight him off, but my limbs are like jelly, and I'm powerless to resist. He runs his hands through my hair, and I can feel the terror building inside me.

Suddenly, the Sorceress appears in front of me, and I know that things are about to get much worse. She grabs my jaw with her withered hand, and I can feel her rough fingers against my skin. I try to pull away, but it's useless. She motions to pour the glass of blood into my mouth, and I feel a surge of panic. This is Luke's blood spilling down on me. I can't breathe, and the metallic taste is overwhelming.

I try to turn my head and spit in her face, but she slaps me hard, and my vision goes spotted. I'm choking on warm blood, and I can't take it anymore. She pours the whole fucking glass down my throat while speaking in a language I don't understand. I feel like I'm going to die. My throat is on fire, and I can't breathe. I need air, but there's none to be found.

The Sorceress finally removes the empty glass from my face, and I try to suck in a breath. But before I can, she leans into my face and puts her mouth to mine. The smell of rot fills me, and I can feel my stomach turning. And then...blackness.

CHAPTER
ELEVEN

Something's burning! I choke on the thick smoke that fills the air. Panic sets in as I frantically search for an escape from the raging inferno. Dropping to the ground, I extend my arms, grasping at the muddy earth and pushing with my legs to propel myself forward. My vision is obscured by a shower of blood that rains down from the trees, coating my face and blinding me. I pause to wipe my eyes, and just as I do a hand grabs me, pulling me violently. I react out of instinct, kicking and flailing, panicked by the sudden touch. I am relieved to see a hooded woman holding my arm. Her face is shadowed, but I can see that her hands are wrinkled and weathered with age.

"You must choose, Lyra." Her voice sounds desperate and demanding.

"Choose what? I don't understand?" I cough, choking on the smoke. "Please, tell me what you mean." Panic fills my voice.

"You are the key; you have all the power. You just need to unlock it," she says quietly.

"The key to what? I don't have any powers."

"You're running out of time. Choose or it will be decided for you, and you will destroy us all."

～

My head bounces against something hard, and I wake up to find I'm in the back of a carriage. Aidan is next to me, and it appears to be daytime. Outside the window I can see the ground covered in snow.

"What's going on? Where are we? My head is killing me." I look over at Aidan, squinting because it's too bright. He pulls the window curtain up, blocking out the winter sunlight, and I blink a couple times while trying to focus my vision.

"Finally, you're awake, Cheeks. You've been out for two days. We should be arriving back at your castle by nightfall."

Suddenly, it all comes slamming into me like a storm in summer, and I remember the festival. I remember Luke's eyes, the look he gave me when Aidan bit into his throat and his life faded away. My eyes swell with tears, and my stomach turns sour. Nausea creeps up my throat. I turn to Aidan.

"You," I practically spit at him. Vengeance hangs heavy in my voice. I'm sobbing, and I start hitting him hard in the chest with both hands. "You killed them. You killed Luke. How could you?" I swing my fist at his chest and face. He grabs my hands and pulls me close to him.

"Lyra, stop. Calm down, and I'll explain everything to you." His voice is stern, and his grip on me is tight. I don't want him anywhere near me, let alone touching me. I try to pull free, but he's much stronger than I am. It takes me a couple minutes to focus and slow my breathing. I'll kill Aidan if it's the last thing I ever do. I'll kill this man for what he did. In the meantime, I need to get it together and hear what he has to say. I'll be home

89

soon, and I can plot my vengeance there. Breathe. Once the tears stop running down my face and my body stops shaking, Aidan releases me. I slide away from him to the other end of the carriage bench.

"I had to do what I did. Do you think I enjoy killing my own kind?"

"No one has to do anything. You had a choice. You always have a choice, and you killed them."

"I had no choice. Maybe one day you'll understand that to be the truth."

"My parents are going to have you killed when I tell them what you did."

"I'm sorry, Lyra dear. I don't think you remember the entirety of the night, but I was only executing your parents' wishes." My blood boils at his smirk, and I can feel the strain behind my eyes. I clench my fists at my sides.

"My parents would never kill innocents like that," I spit back.

"The king and queen do not stay the king and queen by bestowing peace on everyone in Cloudrum. Maybe you'd know that if you ever left the castle."

"Why? Why did you do it? What's in it for you?"

"Oh, Cheeks, you're so worried about what I did and why I did it. Have you ever asked yourself what it means?" He wears a stupid, wicked smirk on his face.

I hadn't asked myself what it means. He must see the concern flash across my face at the realization.

"Yes, think about that Cheeks."

Aidan's right. I don't care what he gets out of it. I need to know what it means for me. Why would my parents make a deal with him? Why would they force the Lycan blood down my throat? Am I going to turn into a Lycan on the next full moon? My heart starts to race in my chest. What has he done to me.

Suddenly the carriage comes to an abrupt stop, and I have to slam my feet down to keep from flying forward off the bench. Before I can say anything, the Sorceress from that night climbs into the carriage across from us. Her black eyes and the claw marks across her face are just as unsettling now as they were that night.

"What are you doing here?" Aidan asks, his voice sounding alarmed. I know her presence is a surprise to him too. Now with a clear mind I can really see her. She looks old. She's at the end of her life and has to be in her eighties or nineties at least. She has light-olive skin and a thin, withered face with black eyes and light-gray hair plaited atop her head. I try not to focus on the scars across her face, but I can't help but wonder what kind of monster put them there and what kind of monster she must be to have defeated it.

"Quiet. There's no time. You need to listen to me now." There's a sharp edge in her voice.

Aidan and I both stare at her in alarmed silence. I want to jump across the carriage and strangle her, but something inside me tells me I need to listen to her.

"The king and queen are dead. Samael is going to take the throne. He cannot know what we did, or he will use her in all the wrong ways. When you arrive at the castle, play nice with Samael, and if he asks where you've been tell him you've been training Lyra as was ordered by the king and queen. That's all."

My breath catches as it hits me. My parents are dead. My parents are gone. Samael is going to take the throne.

"How...how did they die?" My voice breaks.

"It's still under investigation, and the castle is in lockdown. You'll be allowed in, but no one else is being allowed out until the investigation is complete."

"What are you going to do to keep her from talking?" Aidan asks the Sorceress, looking at me.

"Lyra will not talk. She doesn't want anymore attention from Samael than she already has. Isn't that right, Lyra?"

My eyes widen. What does she know? How does she know?

"Who are you?"

"That's for me to know, girl," she replies sharply, then looks to Aidan. "There will be a funeral in one week's time. I will see you then, and we can discuss future plans. Until then, be on your guard, and don't trust anyone in that castle. Lyra, I'll find you when I can, and all will be revealed in time." She looks at Aidan as though his life depends on doing what she says then disappears out the carriage door.

With Aidan's cruel words still ringing in my ears, I turn away from him and curl up in a ball, my body wracked with sobs. My heart aches with a profound sense of loss. My parents, the only family I've ever known, are gone, leaving me alone and vulnerable in a world that's suddenly turned dark and treacherous. Samael's grip on the kingdom grows stronger every day, and I fear what will happen if I don't find a way to stop him. And then there's Luke, sweet Luke, who was taken from me in the most horrific way possible. I can't believe he's really gone, and the thought of never seeing him again is too much on top of everything else.

Aidan's presence next to me is suffocating, and I can feel his cold gaze boring into my back. If what he says is true, then everything I thought I knew about my parents is a lie. My mind reels with the implications of this new knowledge, and I'm left feeling lost and helpless. I cry until there are no more tears left, until my throat is raw and my eyes are swollen shut. And yet the pain lingers, a constant ache in my chest that I feel will never truly go away.

"Lyra, it's time to collect yourself. It won't be much longer now before we reach the castle," Aidan says.

If I'm not mistaken, I'd say he almost sounds like he feels bad for me, but then I remember he caused this. For all I know he had something to do with my parents' deaths as well. I've been unconscious for two days. I don't know anything and can't trust anyone.

"Don't speak to me," I tell him through clenched teeth. I see his jaw flex, but he doesn't respond. We sit in silence for the rest of the ride, and although I have a feeling I should press him for information, I just can't bring myself to care. We pull up in front of the castle, and guards are there to greet us. I don't even look at Aidan as a guard escorts me to my room.

The castle has a different feel, one that's colder and eerily quiet. The guards who helped me out of the carriage accompany me all the way to my room, which has never happened before, sending shivers down my spine. As I enter the room, the guards shut the door, and I hear a click that echoes through the silent chamber. Panic sets in as I realize that the door is locked from the outside, and my heart starts to race. Chepi is nowhere to be seen, and I wonder if he's safe. I hope Lili is taking care of him and keeping him out of harm's way.

Trying to calm my nerves, I head to the bathroom to clean up. At least there's one positive thing about being back at the castle, and that's the modern plumbing. I fill the tub with hot water and step in, wincing as the water burns my skin. The scalding sensation is a welcome one that distracts me from the pain eating away inside me. I scrub my body and hair until my skin is raw, wishing that I could wash away my worries just as easily.

After my bath, I dry off and slip into a nightgown before crawling into bed. I pull the covers up over my head, trying to muffle my sobs as I let the tears flow freely. Sleep eventually finds me, providing a brief escape from the harsh reality of my situation.

CHAPTER

TWELVE

Almost a week has passed since the tragic events that shattered my life. Each day blends into the next as I go through the motions, trying to keep my mind from dwelling on the horrors I've witnessed. But no matter how hard I try to distract myself, I can't escape the nightmares that haunt me every night. They come in different forms, but the pain, fear, and helplessness all make me feel the same. I sometimes wake with the metallic taste of blood in my throat, and I panic all over again remembering being forced to drink my friends blood.

The worst of these nightmares is the one that feels more like a memory than a dream. The one where I see the hooded woman and hear her cryptic words. Her message still echoes in my mind, leaving me with more questions than answers. What choice does she speak of? What power does she believe I possess? And most importantly, what is the key?

Sleep hasn't brought me back to that burning forest since the carriage ride, but sometimes I wish it would. I would rather speak to the hooded woman and try to get answers than see the life fade from Luke's eyes again.

As I try to make sense of it all, the reality of my situation continues to weigh heavily on me. The castle is eerily quiet, and the air feels thick with tension. I'm being watched and guarded at all times, making me feel trapped and alone, but I'm thankful I have Chepi.

After my first night home, Lili is finally allowed to come see me and bring me food. Chepi is well, thank the gods. He's been licking my face and waking me from my nightmares most nights. Lili isn't able to share much with me, but I shared with her all the horrors of the shifting moon festival. I haven't been allowed to leave my room, Samael's orders, but Lili has been bringing me all my meals and making sure I'm taken care of.

Lili comes in to wake me, even though I've been stuck awake for hours. Her familiar smell of lavender and vanilla warms my heart.

"Lyra, hun, I brought you and Chepi some breakfast," she says softly, sitting on the edge of my bed.

I sit up and eat a slice of toast while feeding Chepi my bacon. "No point in you being locked up all day too." I push open the window beside my bed so he can fly out. Lili sits across from me on the bed. Her soft eyes study me.

"How are you feeling today?"

"I'm okay, Lili." I try to sound convincing.

I'm not okay. I've barely slept. My head won't stop aching, and I feel desperate. I'm desperate for anything to lessen these feelings in my chest, which feels tight. I wish I had access to whiskey, wine, anything to make me feel less of this hell I am currently residing in.

"Have you had another premonition?" Lili asks.

"Not that I'm aware of. I've had nightmares, but none are like the one in the burning forest."

"I've been sneaking into the library at night searching for any references that may help you." Her words send a jolt of worry through me. "Lili, you can't do that. If Samael were to catch you . . . gods only know what he would do. Have you found anything?"

"I have. But, Lyra, I don't like it, and I don't know what it means. I found it in one of your father's journals. I didn't want to take the entire journal, so I ripped the page out."

"What are you waiting for? Let me see it," I exclaimed.

"Before I give it to you, I just want you to know whatever this is, whatever it means, we'll get through it. I'm here for you okay." Her words make me feel uneasy. I'm almost afraid to read the journal entry, but I take the page from her anyways.

I visited Zomea today and finally figured out how it will work. All of my work hasn't been for nothing. What I thought was impossible has been hidden right before me this entire time. He shared the prophecy with me, and it was then I knew. I know it will be her.

One born of Fae and Sorcerer blood must consume blood of the Lycan and Lamia before their powers manifest. Blood of all the realms must live inside her. To successfully unlock the bridge to Zomea, three innocent Lycan must die at the hand of the one they trust before the first shift under the full moon. A single Lamia must choose to end her life prematurely, giving her blood willingly under the light of the blood moon. Only then may the key unlock the bridge.

I read the page over three times. What was my father doing? How did he visit Zomea, the afterlife?

"Lili, this cannot be about me. I wasn't born with Fae blood." I get off the bed, feeling the need to move, to pace.

"I know, Lyra, but the Lycan ceremony is exactly the same. I knew your father, and he was a very secretive man, brilliant but secretive. I don't know what this means, but it has to be about you somehow. Or your mother believed it was about you."

"What do you know about Zomea? Is it possible the burning forest from my dream is in Zomea?" I ask her while running my hands through my hair.

"I don't know much about Zomea, but it would make sense. You did say it was a forest like nothing you've ever seen before. So it's possible?" Lili says.

A servant knocks on the door. Lili gets up and exchanges a few hushed words with him.

"Today's the day you know, right?" Lili speaks softly, like I might break at her words.

I move to sit at my vanity and stare at the mirror, trying to tame my hair. This is the day of my parents' funeral, and I don't know what to feel. Part of me wants to scream with anger and pain, to throw things and lash out at everyone around me. But another part of me just feels hollow, empty, and numb. How do you mourn the loss of people you were never close to? People who used you, sold you out to some dark and twisted bargain? People who never cared about your feelings or your trauma, who only saw you as a pawn, as a key, in some dangerous game of power?

My mother, the one who gave birth to me, the one who was supposed to love and protect me, was the worst of them all. I still remember the way she treated me, the way she belittled me and made me feel small. The way she changed after my father died, and now she's gone, and part of me wants to celebrate, to dance on her grave. But another part of me just feels... nothing. It's like I'm watching everything happen from a distance, like I'm not really here at all.

I take a deep breath, trying to push away the emotions that threaten to consume me. I know I have to be strong, to put on a brave face for the sake of appearances. But it's hard. So damn hard.

"I know the funeral is today, Lili. Don't worry about me. I can handle it...as long as you help me do my hair." I give her a light laugh and half smile while meeting her eyes in the mirror, hoping to cut the tension in the air.

"People from all over have been arriving all week to attend the funeral. I'm sure that's why Samael has kept you in your chamber. He's just making sure you're safe. Can you blame him after losing your parents? You're all he has."

I try not to let the utter disdain for Samael show on my face. "Don't make excuses for him, Lili. Samael is vile and evil. I don't trust a damn thing about him."

"Lyra, I know you're upset, but you can't speak about him like that. He's your king now. You must show him respect, no matter how you might feel. We'll figure all of this out about Zomea, your father, the nightmare. I promise I'll help you, but in the meantime just obey Samael and stay out of trouble please." She touches my cheek as if to soothe me, but I flinch. "I'm sorry, Lyra." She gives me a pleading smile. "It may cheer you up to know the good-looking man you had dinner with a few weeks back is here for the funeral."

My heart jumps for a split second. I'd almost forgotten about Nyx with everything that's happened. It feels like a lifetime ago that I was swooning over that dreamy man. A fluttering sensation returns to my chest at the mere mention of his name. I don't know what it is, but something on a cellular level draws me to him. Probably something I should be more afraid of. But my heart warms at the thought of seeing him again. I don't know why.

"You mean Nyx?" I asked.

"I don't know his name, but if that's the name of the

gentleman you attended dinner with before your training with Aidan began, then yes. Now try to rest for a bit and take a bath. I'll be back in a few hours to help you get ready for the funeral." Lili gives me a small smile and leaves.

I hear the lock click on my door behind her. Even Lili is drinking up whatever shit Samael is filling her head with. She may be trying to help me, but in the end I know she'll always put her duty to the king first. Even if he's despicable.

I take a bath and wash my hair, then I wrap my big white comforter around myself to keep warm and go sit on the balcony. It may be freezing outside, but it's better than being caged in my room all day.

I am consumed by thoughts of the mysterious old Sorceress. I long to know her name, and I can't shake the feeling that she is familiar to me in some way. I wonder how she could have known about Samael and what the disturbing ceremony with the Lycans might mean for me. Every time I think about it, I feel a mix of sadness and fear. I am heartbroken for the Lycans who were senselessly murdered, but I am also filled with dread about the unknown power that now possibly courses through my veins. I can't shake the feeling that there is some truth to the prophecy written by my father, and the idea that it might be about me is both bewildering and terrifying. With my parents gone, I can't help but wonder who else might know about it.

A woman in the gardens catches my attention. She is tall, slender, and wearing a long, flowing black gown. Even though her face is shrouded by a black veil, I can sense that she is not human. Her movements are unnaturally graceful, like she is gliding across the ground without taking any steps. I try to get a better look at her, but when she turns to face me I freeze. Her red eyes glow ominously under the veil, and I feel a cold shiver run down my spine. I stumble back into my room, the sound of the balcony door slamming shut behind me echoing through the chamber. It is then that I realize what she is— a Lamia.

This Lamia must be one of the higher-ups to come here for my parents' funeral. It's possible that she is even Drew, the feared head of the Lamia Realm. Although I've never met her, rumors of her cruelty have reached my ears. The thought of Chepi flying among these unknown creatures fills me with unease. I can only wonder what other creatures have come to pay their respects and may be lurking around the castle grounds.

It's getting late, and Lili should be here by now to help me get ready. I feel a little anxious. What could be keeping her? I pace my room and try to calm my anxiety when a knock sounds at my door. It's followed by another knock. Why are they not just coming in?

"Hello, Princess Lyra, are you there?" It's the muffled voice of a woman, one I can't quite place.

"Yes, you may come in," I reply, slightly annoyed.

"Sorry, Princess, but I don't have the key. I was only sent to tell you that your presence will not be required at the ceremony today," she says, sheepishly.

"What?" I hurry to the door, banging on it.

"I'm sorry, Princess. I do not wish to upset you. Please forgive me." Her voice is merely a whisper now.

"Please get the key. You must let me out. I have to attend the funeral. Get Lili please. She'll let me out."

"I'm sorry," she whispers then hurries away. Her steps grow quieter as she leaves.

There must be a guard outside my room. Samael wouldn't leave me locked in here unattended. I bang on the door over and over, pleading with whomever is out there to open the door, but no one responds. Eventually I exhaust myself and sink to the floor crying. Samael can't keep me locked in here forever. I am already going stir crazy.

I cry until my eyes burn and my face feels puffy. I have no one. The realization of this really sets in over the next few hours while I just lie here on the floor. Samael is evil, and everyone here will follow him blindly. Lili's not on my side. Aidan's no friend of mine. My parents are dead. I have no one. Chepi is all I have, and he can't even talk back to me. I don't know what Samael is going to do with me, but I know it can't be anything good. Maybe he knows about the Lycan ceremony and plans to use me somehow like the Sorceress had said. Maybe she'll free me from this place. My thoughts go from desperate to hopeless until I fall asleep on the ground.

A gray wolf is all of a sudden on top of me, licking my face. His pale-blue eyes glow into mine. Then it's no longer a wolf on top of me—it's Luke. He's shaking me.

"Wake up, Lyra. Wake up!" he pleads. I stare at him in confusion because I am awake. "Wake up now, Lyra. Leave the castle. You must hurry." Luke sounds panicked. He shakes me again. "Run."

I open my eyes to find I'm still lying on the floor in front of my bedroom door with my cheek pressed to the hardwood. That was an odd dream. Luke was here, and it felt so vivid. I wonder how long I was out for. It's dark outside, so it must be late. Shit. I fell asleep without leaving the window open for Chepi. I jump up to open it when my door flies open, just missing me. I turn to come face-to-face with Samael.

"How dare you lock me in here all week. How dare you forbid me from going to our parent's funeral!" I yell into his face. His eyes glow black with fury. I've never spoken against him before, and I regret my words immediately when his eyes land on mine.

102

Samael backhands me so hard I fall back and hit the ground. I bring my hands to my face in shock. He follows me down to the ground, and before I can block him he brings his fist down on my face again. This time I taste blood, and then I see black.

CHAPTER
THIRTEEN

I open my eyes, and I'm still in my room, but my hands are bound behind my back with rope. My shirt is ripped open, and I'm on full display. Samael is sitting next to me looking down at me, stroking my hair.

"Oh, sweet Lyra, I'm glad you're finally awake. I didn't want you to miss anything." His voice is toneless.

"What are you doing, Samael? Untie me please." My voice quivers, and my head aches.

"Untie you? Now why would I do that, my little bird?" Samael clicks his tongue.

"Please," I plead. "What do you want from me?" My voice is hoarse. I feel something smooth gliding up my leg and look down to find a giant black snake slithering up my body. He comes all the way up until he's resting on my chest. "No, please. You don't have to do this. I'll do whatever you want."

Samael continues to pet my hair like I'm a dog. "Don't fret, little sister. His bite will only make it so you can't fight me. You'll still feel everything I do to you." He speaks gently like he's soothing a child. I look him in the eye and spit in his face. A mix of saliva and blood splatters his cheeks. He uncovers a handkerchief from his jacket and wipes the moisture from his face with a deliberate gesture. His eyes fix upon me, radiating an evil that could plunge the world into darkness.

"That you'll regret. I'll make sure of it. You have a little bit of fight in you tonight, Lyra. What's gotten into you? I thought you enjoyed our nights together. Has the Lycan blood already started taking effect?" he asks. His voice sounds more collected now.

"What Lycan blood?" I try to keep stoic.

"Tsk, tsk, little sister. You think I don't know what that bitch of a Sorceress is trying to do." His voice is calm, but his eyes are vicious. "Enough small talk. Bite her."

Before I can even squirm on the floor, the snake strikes. His fangs sink into my chest, then release, but the damage is done. His venom wreaks havoc on my body. I can feel blisters forming where his fangs penetrated my skin, and my entire chest is burning. My limbs feel heavy, and I feel like my body is on fire, but I can't move.

"Don't worry, Lyra. It won't be long now." Samael pats my head.

I try to say something back, but a slurred sound escapes my lips, and he gives me a pitying look.

"Shh, don't try to speak. It'll only make it worse." He puts a finger to my lips in emphasis. "I know you let that Lycan filth fuck you. Now you must be cleansed, and you must be punished." He lets his façade slip a bit, and anger shows through in his sharp tone.

He runs his hand across my left breast, pinching my nipple. He whispers something under his breath, and his fingers pulse with electricity and shock my flesh. I try to squirm, but my body betrays me. I don't even flinch at the pain. The snake's venom has taken full effect.

"Yep, you're ready," he says while getting to his feet. Once he's standing over me, he gives me a wicked smile then kicks me hard in the ribs. All I can do is suck in a sharp breath and stare at him. He kicks me again in the same spot, and a gargled scream starts in my throat, but it dies before it can leave my mouth. I feel tears running down my cheeks. I know he's broken a rib, but I can't do anything. I close my eyes and try to imagine being anywhere but here.

"No, you don't. I want you to look at me when I fuck you. I want you to remember who you belong to. No one else is ever going to touch you again." He crouches over me and brings his knee up between my legs, spreading me open. "There's no one to stop me now, Lyra. No one to protect you." He leans down and runs his tongue across my mouth. "You filthy little bitch," he whispers in my ear and brings his knee up hard between my legs, stinging my core.

He walks out of the room, and just when I think he's going to leave me alone he returns with a lit candle stick. He pauses above me and lets the candle drip hot wax across my stomach. It burns and sizzles when it meets my flesh, but once again I can't react. This is the worst form of torture. I've never felt so exposed and defenseless in my life. I just want it to end, and if he's going to kill me I just want to get it over with. I can't take anything else.

I try to imagine being in the gardens with Chepi. I try to imagine being happy again. I try to imagine anything good and serene, but I fail as Samael continues making a trail of liquid fire across my stomach like he's a child drawing a picture.

"Should I fuck you with this candlestick? I bet it would feel better than that prick Lycan."

A sudden knock sounds at my door, drawing both of our attentions, only I can't even look at the door.

"Not now," Samael says in a sharp tone that would most definitely deter any of the servants.

The knock sounds again, but no one speaks.

"This better be good," Samael says while pulling the door open. I can't see who is at the door, but I hear commotion, and then Samael falls flat on his face next to me. He's completely limp.

Chepi runs up to my face and starts licking the tears off my cheeks, which only causes more tears to fall. I try to speak, but nothing comes out. I hear heavy footsteps, and a large blanket is placed over me. Nyx comes into view.

"It's going to be okay, Lyra," he says, but his jaw is set hard, and his face is stern.

He picks me up, cradling me in his arms as my head flops back, limp. He cups my neck with his hand and presses my face against his firm chest. Chepi flies up and lands on my chest, snuggling into the blanket I'm wrapped up in. I hear more footsteps and people talking. I think I hear Lili's voice at some point, but Nyx places his hand on my forehead, and it's the last thing I remember.

FOURTEEN

I wake to find I'm in bed, but I'm not in my bed. I don't think I'm in the castle at all. My body is cradled by pillows on either side of me, and smooth black silk sheets hug my skin. I'm naked and alone. I sit up and hiss through my teeth at the pain in my side.

The room is shrouded in darkness, except for the soft orange light of the crackling hearth beside the bed. The flames dance and flicker, casting ethereal shadows on the wall, making the gothic grandeur of the room come to life. The vaulted ceilings soar high above, decorated with intricate gold and cherry wood beams that seem to shimmer in the firelight. The floor is made of a magnificent cherry wood that glows in the dark, adorned with large black fur. A wooden table sits to my left, surrounded by black leather chairs, and a black and gold ornate chandelier hangs above it, twinkling like a thousand stars. Through the sheer black curtains that cover the windows, I sense the darkness outside, the stillness of the night, and the mystery that surrounds this place. The air smells of cedar with hints of sweet mango, the aroma wrapping me in a sense of tranquility and calmness. The only sound that echoes through the silence is the gentle crackle of the fire, whispering promises of warmth and comfort.

I hear heavy footsteps outside the door. I quickly settle back down into bed, pull the sheets up high, and close my eyes like I'm sleeping.

"She's been like this for three days." Nyx sounds stressed, like he actually cares what happens to me. I know it's him immediately because my nose smells his sweet musky scent.

"Her fever broke a few hours ago. I think she'll wake by morning," says a woman's voice.

I hear more footsteps enter the room, then another man speaks. "You need rest. You've barely slept the last few days. Flora is the best healer. Lyra is in the best hands."

"Thank you, Bim. He's right, Nyx, I've done all I can for her. I promise you she'll wake soon." Flora's voice comes out soft and soothing. It's silent for a moment, and then I hear footsteps leave and the bedroom door close again.

Relieved to be alone, I open my eyes to find Nyx is standing next to the bed looking down at me. Relief crosses his face, and he moves to sit next to me on the bed. I shrink away from him, afraid for a moment of what he might do.

"Don't touch me," I warn him.

His face quickly goes from relief to something different. Maybe sadness or pain. I'm not sure.

"I'd never harm you," he says softly.

"Forgive me, but I've been told that before, and that very same person did harm me."

"You mean Samael?"

"No." I don't give further explanation, and he just looks at me, studying me.

"How are you feeling?"

"I'm okay," I lie. I feel awful. My body is sore, and I feel broken. I feel hollow inside, and I don't know if I'll ever feel whole again.

"Would you eat something with me? Please?"

I am hungry, and I don't want to lie here feeling self-conscious under his gaze any longer.

"If you give me something to wear, then I could eat something."

He smiles and nods before going out of the room. He returns and places some clothes on the end of the bed.

"I'm not sure what you'd like to wear, but I assume you want something soft and comfortable, so I brought a few options. I'll leave you to change and return with some dinner in a few minutes." He smiles softly, nodding his head in assurance. I nod back once to acknowledge him. He steps out into the hallway and closes the door behind him.

I ease out of bed to find he did leave me an array of choices. There's a light-pink linen gown and a soft white floor-length chemise. I choose to slip on black silk pants with a black silk top. They're slightly baggy but nonetheless comfortable. I'm surprised he gave me options and didn't just leave out some revealing outfit for me to wear so he could gawk at me.

I wander into the bathroom to wash my hands, and I catch my reflection in the mirror. My hair is a tangled mess falling over my shoulders, but my face is not as bad as I thought it'd be. They said I was asleep for three days. There's no way I could've healed that quickly. I only have the light remnants of a black eye. I quickly look down at my chest where the snake bit me, and all I see are two little white dots. There are a few white splotches across my stomach as well from the candle, but they don't hurt. My ribs hurt, but the bruises on my side are light and faded. Flora, whoever she is, really must be a gifted healer. I'm grateful for that. I hear the bedroom door open and hurry out of the bathroom.

"Everything alright?" Nyx looks me up and down as if expecting to find me injured again.

"Yes, I think so," I say back quietly.

"Please come sit," he says while placing a large tray on the table and pulling a leather seat out for me. I sit in it, and he scoots me in before taking the seat across from me.

"Where's Chepi?" I ask, slightly alarmed.

"He's okay. He's been exploring the castle and making friends when he's not sleeping next to you."

I immediately relax a bit.

"I wasn't sure what you like, so I brought a little bit of everything I could find at this hour." He begins lifting lids off of plates, revealing a variety of dishes. "This here is silver bisque; it's a potato leek soup with mushrooms and cream. Very good and not too rich. I like to dip these honey-coated rolls in it." He points to another dish full of thin slices of white fish. "This is smoked cloud pepper fish. I like to spread a little bit of the creamed cheese on a roll with a piece of the smoked fish. It's quiet good." He points to the last dish on the table, a plate of round, white balls. "These are called travelers delights. They're basically sweet cookies rolled in sugar and drizzled with honey."

"Thank you." I take a honey roll and begin dipping pieces into the silver bisque like he suggested. My stomach is in knots, but even though I feel hungry I just can't bring myself to eat much. The food does taste delicious though. The soup is creamy and seasoned perfectly. The rolls are moist and fluffy with just a hint of sweetness to them.

"Where are we?" I probably should've asked that sooner, but my mind is still foggy.

"We're in my home. The Noble Vale of Nighthold," he says casually.

"I'm in the Faery Realm?"

"Yes, you're in the Faery Realm."

"And are you a Faery?" I almost don't believe it's possible. I've never met a Faery before, but I always thought they were evil and had a mouth full of sharp teeth.

"Yes, I am Fae, among other things. Are you alright?" he asked softly, lifting a hand to touch mine. I pull my hand back quickly, placing it in my lap.

"Yes," I try to assure him.

"Listen, it's late, past midnight. You look like you could still use some rest. How about I get Chepi and let you rest until morning? We can talk more then." His voice is calm and collected, but his eyes look concerned.

"I am still tired. That sounds good." I give a half smile and make my way to the bed.

Nyx returns a few minutes later with Chepi in his arms. Chepi jumps on the bed and gives me a few yelps and licks before nosing his way under the silky covers and lying down beside my leg. I settle into the pillows, and Nyx turns out the lights. The room is still dimly lit by the soft glow of the dying fire.

"Goodnight, Lyra," Nyx says quietly and closes the door before I have a chance to respond.

My mind is still spinning with everything that's happened. Is Samael dead? How did I get to the Faery Realm? Can I trust Nyx? Am I safe here? I've been alone my whole life, yet I've never felt as alone as I do right now. I tuck my arms into my chest as if to ease the hollow ache, and eventually, sleep finds me.

I wake alone, well mostly alone. Chepi is rolling around on

the bed. Someone must've left me fresh clothes, because there's a neat pile at the end of the bed and a note. I grab the note while giving Chepi some belly rubs.

Lyra,

Please make yourself at home. But don't go outside.

I will see you later.

Nyx

A man of few words, it seems. I step into the bathroom, and an ethereal sight greets me. A bath filled with a magical elixir, its pinkish hue illuminating the room, emanating an inviting warmth. Radiant hibiscus flowers with hot-pink petals dance on its surface. Despite my initial hesitation, I am drawn to its inviting aroma, as though it promises to wash away all my worries. I sink into the bath, and an instant sense of peace washes over me. The water seems to have a mystical quality, its gentle touch soothing my every muscle. I reach for the soap, its scent of fresh peaches and cream tantalizing my senses. I lather my skin and hair, letting the suds envelop me in its sweet fragrance. As I rinse, I feel myself becoming lighter, my worries washing away with the soapy water. I step out, my skin silken and refreshed, ready to face whatever the day may bring. I comb my hair and make a partial braid on each side then tie them together in the back to help hold my hair out of my face. I leave the rest of the wavy mess to hang behind my back.

I grab a few flowers from the bath and weave them into the braid as well. I start looking through the pile of clothes neatly left on the end of the bed. Once again Nyx left several options, which are all greatly different from one another. The clothes here are like nothing I've ever seen before. Everything seems so much more modern and whimsical than back in Cloudrum. There are no heavy gowns with overly tight bodices to choose from. Instead, I find two dresses, and neither of them reaches the ground like they would back home. Both look like they'd fall about to my knees. One is made of light green, iridescent chiffon. The other is drastically different. It's still short and lightweight, but it's all black with short sleeves. The bottom of the dress is draped in a V at the front and back but shorter on the sides. Lastly, there's a pair of dark tights and a pastel pink top with puffy sleeves. I get dressed in the black dress. The fabric is soft and airy. It's easy to move around in and not heavy like the clothes I've grown accustomed to. I like it, and the fabric smells fresh like spring.

A light pounding on the door makes me jump. I hurry over to open it just a crack to peek through. At first I don't see anyone, but then I hear someone clear their throat. I look down to find some kind of creature with a tray in his hand and gasp.

"Excuse me, miss. I didn't mean to frighten you. I've brought you breakfast. May I come in?" the creature says in a child-like voice.

It takes me a second to compose myself and find my manners, then I open the door wide. "Yes, please come in."

This creature is tiny—the top of his head only comes up to my knee—and he looks almost like a goblin but with a cuteness that's hard to deny. His pudgy belly and legs make him seem harmless, and his dark-purple skin contrasts with shoulder-length gray hair that partially covers his pointed ears. The creatures glowing green eyes are captivating, and his smile is warm and friendly, revealing straight white teeth that are only slightly pointed. As he approaches me, a citrus scent fills the air, instantly calming my nerves and soothing my senses.

"What are you?" I whisper, a bit awed by this little creature. He flies into the air to place the tray on the table, and I notice he has gorgeous delicate wings that are almost translucent purple with splashes of silver.

"I am a Twig Wisp. Have you never met one like me before?" He has a little voice, and he keeps his face lowered to the ground.

"No, I've never seen anything like you. Sorry. I'm being rude. I'm just curious . . . What is your name?" I feel slightly embarrassed.

"Everyone calls me Twig. You may call me Twig." He gives me a devilishly charming little smile.

"You may call me Lyra, and this is Chepi." I point to Chepi, who is already on the ground licking Twig's leg.

"Oh, we've met. We even went flying together yesterday." Twig pets Chepi's head and places a bowl full of sliced meat on the ground in front of him. "I brought breakfast for both of you."

"Would you like to join us?"

"I've already had breakfast, but I'll stay with you while you eat as company, if you'd like?"

I almost squeal because I am so delighted to learn more about Twig. "Yes, please. That'd be lovely." I smile. It feels like the first real smile I've had in a while.

Breakfast is a large tray full of tropical fruits and delicate, colorful pastries. I immediately grab a berry muffin with pink sugar sprinkles of top of it. My stomach seems delighted as I take in the mouth-watering aroma of everything.

"Do you live here?" I ask Twig between bites.

"I go wherever I'm needed by his majesty, but currently I live here, yes." His voice is slightly high-pitched like a young boy's would be.

"His majesty?"

"His majesty King Onyx, who brought you here. This is his home, and I serve him." He must notice the concerned look on my face, because he continues, "Have I done something to upset you, miss?"

"Lyra, please, and, no, you haven't. It's just that I was brought here by a man I thought was named Nyx. I never realized he was Fae, let alone a king. I feel a bit silly."

How did I not realize? Of course Nyx is short for Onyx? It suddenly all makes sense. This is why Mr. Drogo forced me to spend hours learning about the Faery Realm and the ways of the Fae before dinner the first night I met Nyx. How could I be so dense? But why did Samael not want me at that dinner? What happened after I left? I always thought the Fae were evil, malicious beings, but I'm slowly learning I know nothing about anything that goes on in the real world.

Twig reaches out and touches my hand with his pudgy purple fingers. He has black pointed nails, but he only brushes against the back of my hand for a second. "Don't worry Lyra, his majesty is a good man. I'm sure he'd have corrected the error when you spoke with him."

I suddenly feel a sense of calm again, and that hollow ache in my chest is less pronounced. I pick up another muffin and cut it in half, spreading some creamy butter across it.

"You're right, Twig. I'm sure I'll feel better after we speak today." I bite into the muffin, and it's a burst of flavor in my mouth—soft, creamy, sweet from the sugar, and tart from the berries. "The food here is delectable. I don't know why I'm so famished this morning."

I clear more than my fair share of food.

"Eh hem." Twig clears his throat looking a little guilty. "I'm sorry. I don't want to mislead you. I may be the cause of your appetite."

"What do you mean?" I'm curious. I've always had a good appetite, just not so much lately. Until this morning that is.

"It's the magic that I've been weaving since I arrived here. By letting out a trickle of my essence, I can manipulate emotions to some extent. I simply wanted to ease your burden. I sensed the anguish that weighed heavy in your chest, so I used my abilities to ease it a little. Perhaps the hunger you feel is a result of that emotional release. I only wished to bring you a measure of comfort, and I hope that you won't fault me for it," Twig explains, his words stumbling out in a near-stammer.

I don't feel upset he used his magic on me. I feel good. "I'm not upset. It's okay, really." I give him a soft smile before asking, "What else can you do?"

Twig's voice brims with excitement as he tells me about his abilities. "I can soar through the skies with ease and possess incredible strength, despite my petite stature. And while I may appear diminutive compared to you, I can lift you with no trouble at all," he says, grinning mischievously. "But that's not all. As a descendant of the Tree Wisps, I can also influence plant growth and promote healing in the natural world. Though my abilities may not be as potent as my ancestors', I take pride in carrying on their legacy. My ancestors helped form all the forests we see today."

I wish I knew what sort of magic I'll inherit. So much has happened lately that I've lost my sense of time. I can't believe it's already almost January. Ten more months until my birthday. Ten more months until I come into my magic. For so long I buried the thoughts of my powers because it always seemed so far off, but now as the date approaches I can't help but wonder how my powers will manifest when I turn nineteen. My father was the most powerful king in the history of Cloudrum. I can only hope my magic lives up to his. When it does, when I learn to wield my magic, I'll kill Samael and put an end to his tyranny once and for all. Twig must've noticed my mind went somewhere else for a moment. He reaches over and touches my hand again.

"Twig, you're amazing," I reply honestly and smile at him.

His purple cheeks darken a bit, and he gives me a shy smile back. "I must be going now. Please explore the castle. Chepi knows his way around already. Have him show you. I will see you again, Lyra." Twig flies over to the door. "Just don't go outside alone." With that, he disappears out the door.

CHAPTER
FIFTEEN

I spend the next couple hours chasing after Chepi through the castle; he runs down hall after hall like he already has this place memorized. I can barely keep up with him.

This castle is possibly the most magnificent place I've ever seen. I may not have been to very many places in my life, but I've read lots of books and seen many paintings, and nothing compares to the grandeur of this place. As I descend the grand spiral staircase, the gleaming cherrywood floors stretch out before me, aglow in the warm candlelight. Each step reveals new, intricate details of the golden wall sconces that illuminate the castle. Chepi, effortlessly darting across the grand foyer, comes to a sudden halt on one of the ornate black and gold rugs. I pause, taking in the breathtaking sight of the sweeping floor-to-ceiling windows draped in delicate black curtains. Overhead, grand chandeliers sway, their shimmering light reflecting off the crystals and casting a mesmerizing dance across the walls.

Through the windows I can see lush green vegetation everywhere. We are not in a forest but a jungle, and it's not winter here like back in Cloudrum. It appears to be summer. Dense undergrowth surrounds tall trees in a tangled mess of vines that crawl up the sides of the castle. Faint buzzing and pleasant chirping rings out in the distance. It is utterly beguiling. I've never seen anything like it. It's nothing like the barren pine forests of Tempest Moon. I wish to go outside and explore, but I remember Twig warning me not to go outside alone. I'm not sure if the warning was for my safety or because I'm a prisoner here.

The castle is eerily quiet. Only the faint sounds of the jungle fill the halls. I haven't run into a single person or creature while exploring. Seems a bit odd for such a grand castle to be so empty. At home I'd find servants, guards, and sometimes even visitors all over the castle grounds.

I don't know much about the jungle, only what Mr. Drogo taught me in our lessons. He always says the jungle was full of more venomous and poisonous creatures than I could count. That's why it was rarely mentioned in textbooks because it was rarely explored by anyone except the Fae who live here. I can't feel like I'm being held captive all over again. I can't bear to get away from Aidan and Samael just to have another man try to control me. I want fresh air. If it was really that dangerous outside, I'd think someone would be around to stop me from going out there. Since there are no guards, it can't hurt to explore the castle grounds a little.

"I'm just going to get some fresh air and take a look at the castle from outside. Come on. Let's go," I say to Chepi while heading over to the large double doors in the foyer. I don't know why I'm tiptoeing. I shouldn't have to be sneaking about, and Nyx never told me to stay in my room. I pull one of the doors open, and it makes a long loud screeching sound that echoes through the foyer. I close my eyes and cringe for a second, expecting someone to come running, but no one comes. I go outside and give Chepi a reassuring look before I close the door behind us.

I'm immediately hit by the stuffy, warm air. It smells sweet and damp like fruit and wet vegetation after fresh rain. It feels thick in my lungs. Nothing like the inside of the castle, which is surprisingly cool and drafty compared to this. The large stones making up the courtyard and path around the perimeter of the castle are all overgrown and covered with ivy. It doesn't look old and unkempt though. It looks beautiful and dreamy. The sky here is different. It's not the normal blue hue I'm used to. It looks angry and enchanted with dark swirls of purple and gray cutting through large cottony white clouds. The sounds are almost deafening. The buzzing, chirping, and humming coming from all directions remind me I'm not alone out here.

I follow the stone path around the castle then down a set of stone steps where the path begins to lead away from the castle and into the jungle terrain beyond.

"Stay close, boy," I whisper to Chepi as he silently walks beside me, his fluffy ears perked up and his tail wagging. We follow the path as it transitions from a smooth stone pavement to a rugged dirt trail. The pathway is still visible, but it's almost entirely overgrown with greenery, making each step a cautious one. My eyes have to remain fixed on the ground to avoid tripping over any protruding roots or vines. Suddenly, the sound of water catches my attention, and I glance up. Despite the thick vegetation that blankets the surroundings, there is a massive river that snakes through the terrain, cutting the earth in half. It appears to be as vast as a lake, and the current seems tranquil. I take off my shoes and tiptoe toward the water's edge to test the temperature with my toes.

"I wouldn't do that if I were you," Nyx says.

I jump, almost falling into the river, then he wraps his arm around my waist and pulls me back against him in an instant. Once on steady feet, he releases me immediately, and I step back.

"You scared me. Why shouldn't I dip my feet in?"

"This is Guri river. It's not safe to swim in. There are all sorts of creatures in here that would love to take a bite out of you. Didn't I tell you not to go outside?" Nyx raises an eyebrow, and I look away.

"This place is beautiful. I've never visited a place like this before. I only wanted to look around." I pause to take in the beauty of the river and jungle surrounding us. "I'm sorry I just couldn't stay inside," I say finally, and the pause between us stretches on so long that I don't think he's going to speak.

"Would you like a tour?"

"I would like that, yes, King Onyx." My mouth quirks up on one side.

"You must've met Twig. For such a little fellow, he sure does have a big mouth." He shakes his head but doesn't seem upset by Twig's forwardness.

"I like the little guy. He's sweet and super fascinating. Don't be hard on him. He didn't mean any harm in telling me," I say quickly, hoping I haven't gotten Twig into any trouble.

"Don't worry. I'm not upset. I would've told you. You were just hurt, and last night you were tired and upset. I wasn't trying to hide anything from you." His eyes are soft and kind. "So what do you say, Lyra? Are you up to a little tour before we head back?"

"Yes, I think I'd like that, but I'm not really wearing appropriate shoes for a hike. Maybe just a short tour." I smile but feel kind of funny for coming out here in these flimsy slippers, but I hadn't planned on leaving the castle today.

"Don't worry. We won't be walking." He smirks at me. "Are you afraid of heights?"

"No, I don't think so."

"Okay then, I'm going to give you the best kind of tour from above, but first I'll need to release my magic, revealing my true form. Second, you'll have to allow me to touch you and carry you. Alright?" He gives me a reassuring nod, then the moment his magic drops my breath catches. I thought he was handsome before, but now he's stunning. Undeniably beautiful. He has giant black and gray wings like a wyvern, slightly pointed ears, inhumanly flawless skin, and gray eyes. I thought his eyes were alluring before, but now they glow. I don't know what to say for a minute because I can't stop staring at him.

"I can understand why you might be hesitant to trust me. You've been hurt before, and I don't blame you for being cautious. But I want you to know that I will never hurt you," he says, holding out his hand to me.

Whatever essence Twig put on me today must still be working, because I take his hand and say, "I trust you."

He doesn't waste any time. Nyx takes my hand, pulling me close to him as he picks me up, cradles me to his chest, and lifts me up into the air. A rush of wind blows over us as we take flight, his arm behind my back and my face buried in this chest. I'm afraid to look out and afraid he may drop me.

"I can't give you a tour of my land if you just stare into my chest the entire time. It might be a nice view, but it's one you can see anytime."

I loosen my hold slightly, looking up at him. Glowing gray eyes meet mine and soften, tugging at something in my chest.

"Look." He nods toward an emerging vista. I don't want to look away from him, but for a moment I do. Oh my gods, the Noble Vale is gorgeous. We are high above the trees; the air feels cooler and lighter up here. Chepi looks way too happy flying alongside us with his tongue hanging out of his mouth. Poor guy has never had anyone to fly with him before. Now he has Twig and Nyx. The thought warms my heart.

The view below takes my breath away as I lay my eyes on a colossal waterfall that tumbles down from the Guri river. Majestic birds soar above, gracefully cutting through the billowing mists. Their wingspans are wider than my height, and their iridescent feathers shimmer in vibrant hues of blue, red, and green. As I peer into the forest, I catch sight of fiery red furry creatures effortlessly swinging through the vines from tree to tree, soaring through the air with lightning speed.

"What are those?" I point at the cute, furry creatures.

"Those are called Bearded Cheeks. I'm not sure why because their faces are hairless. They're mischievous little creatures that'll steal the jewelry right off your body if you're not careful," Nyx says.

I find my fingers grazing the bloodstone at my neck for a moment.

"That is Topaz Falls. It's the largest waterfall in the Faery Realm, and the giant birds circling above are called lyng-lyngs."

"They're beautiful," I say honestly, still a bit awed by my surroundings.

"That they are," he whispers into my ear before diving down closer to the falls. My stomach drops, and I let a little yelp sound come out of my throat. Nyx laughs but holds me tighter to him.

"All of this, this place I mean, it's lovely. Why didn't you want me to go outside?"

Nyx flies us further up the river. "It's not that I don't want you to enjoy being outside; I just don't want you going outside alone. This is the jungle, and it may seem lovely because the few creatures you've seen are beautiful, but dark creatures lurk in these jungles as well. Not all Faeries are charming like me either. Some would seek to harm you." Nyx circles around the castle, pointing out different plants and animals along the way before landing on my balcony back at the castle.

"So you think you're charming?" I say, turning in his arms to look at him.

"Oh, I know I'm charming, Lewis. It's why you're smiling at me like that now." I like the way my last name rolls off his tongue. He lowers me to my feet, and I step back, wiping the smile from my face. As soon as I look back at him, his wings disappear, and his appearance changes back to more human than Fae. His gray eyes no longer glow. He opens the door for me, and we head inside. The castle feels nice, not humid like outside. It's cool, and there's a fire going in the fireplace.

"How is it cool enough in here to have a fire going when it's so humid outside?"

"It's magic. I've always liked having a fire. It's something that relaxes me, so I keep the castle cool and comfortable."

I don't know how the day went by so fast, but when we landed on the balcony the sun was already descending the sky. My stomach was growling, causing me to wonder what might be for dinner. Nyx must've heard my stomach or sensed my train of thought.

"You need to eat. You can wash up if you'd like, and I'll fetch us some dinner."

I may have frowned a bit, causing him to pause.

"What's wrong? Are you not hungry?"

"No, I'm hungry. Nothing's wrong. That sounds great." I smile a bit so he'll believe me. It seems to do the trick, and he leaves.

I am hungry. I just can't help but wonder what I'm doing here. Is Samael alive? What's happening in Tempest Moon? What happened to my parents? Am I a prisoner here? My list of questions is long and exhausting. I also wonder why he's having me eat all my meals in my room. Does no one else live here? I may not have seen Flora and Bim, but I know they were here late last night. I wonder who they are and if they live here. I wonder if he'll introduce me to anyone. I don't want to escape one prison just to live in another. I hope he doesn't plan to have me stay in the room and not socialize with anyone else like how I lived back home. I don't get the feeling Nyx is like that. He let me roam the castle and grounds alone all day today. I didn't even see any guards watching me. I try not to make too many bad assumptions and wander into the bathroom to clean up. I'll file my questions away for later.

My hair is a little messy from the flying, and it's extra wavy today. I try to tame it a bit with my fingers and tuck it behind my ears. I wash my hands and wander over to the closet. I was planning on putting on the oversized black silk pants and top I wore last night, but it appears while I was gone today someone stocked my closet full of clothes. There are several dresses and an assortment of tops and tights. In the drawers I find several long and short chemises along with various other clothing options. I grab a black chemise and slip it over my head. It's silky and feels soft against my skin. It has tiny lace straps and falls just above the knee. It hugs my body perfectly, and I wonder how Nyx knew my size.

I go stand by the fire and wait for Nyx to return. The heat feels good on my back. I've always loved having a fire going too. It makes everything feel cozier. Before long Nyx knocks then comes in with a tray in hand. As soon as he sees me, his eyes trail up my body slowly from my feet. He smiles when he meets my eyes.

"You are so beautiful, Lyra." He places the tray on the table and walks over to the fire to stand in front of me.

I feel a strange sensation every time he's near me — my heart races, and my stomach fills with a nervous flutter. It's an odd feeling that I can't quite explain. His scent is alluring, and his eyes seem to peer into me. Unlike Aidan or Samael, he doesn't look at me as if I'm something to be possessed.

"Thank you." I can feel my cheeks flush from his words. "So what are we having tonight?" I ask, heading over to the table and taking a seat.

"I bring you fish curry and wild rice. Will this be ok? If not, I can ask the cook to make you something different." He sits across from me, lifting the lids off our plates.

"No, this is perfect. Thank you," I say before I start eating.

Everything tastes delicious, and I find myself almost devouring my plate when Nyx clears his throat. I remember he's across from me.

"I'm sorry. I have been really hungry today," I say, feeling a bit embarrassed.

"Don't be. It pleases me to see you have an appetite." He laughs, gesturing to my plate.

I feel my cheeks warm and try to change the subject. "Why did you call me Lewis earlier?"

"Lewis is your last name. Is it not?" He looks perplexed by my question. He's right that it is my last name, but most people who were friends with my mother and Silas would call me by my mother's maiden name, Moon, or Silas's last name, Sellar. I like hearing him call me Lewis. It makes me think of my father.

"Forget it. I assume it was just you trying to be charming." I realize I actually don't even know if Nyx was friends with my mother or Silas. He visited once for dinner, and there were plenty of reasons for his visit. I'm sure friendship was not one of them. Once I'm finished eating, Nyx snaps his fingers and our plates disappear. A bottle of wine with two glasses take their place on the table. He fills two glasses then extends one to me.

"May I offer you some wine?"

"Yes." I take the glass and go sit on the fur rug in front of the fireplace. I take a few sips. It tastes light and slightly sweet with hints of strawberry.

"Do you like wine?" Nyx asks, coming to sit beside me.

"I've never had it before now, but it tastes divine." I take another sip.

"How have you never tasted wine before now? You're a princess. You grew up in a castle. I'm sure you attended many dinner parties, did you not?"

"I only ever attended dinner when my parents wanted me to for appearances. I was never allowed to attend any parties. I was only allowed water, and I ate most meals in my room." What's the point in lying?

"Your parents don't sound very nice. I only met them a handful of times, but I could sense they were not good people."

"You can sense emotions?"

"Not exactly. I can sense emotions if what someone is feeling is really intense, but other than that I can see everyone's auras and get a good sense of what kind of person they are deep down."

"What do you see when you look at me?" I ask nervously, turning my head to meet his gaze.

"I see a girl who has been through so much pain and hurt. You carry the weight of the world on your shoulders, and you've been forced to suppress your true self. But I want you to know that you are so much more than what you've been made to believe. I see strength and beauty that shine from deep within you." Nyx's words are soft and gentle, and I feel a warmth spreading through me that I haven't felt in a long time. I take a sip of my wine, feeling a bit lightheaded, and turn to face him. His hand reaches up to touch my cheek, and for a moment I flinch. But as his fingers brush against my skin, I feel a sense of calm wash over me.

"What did Samael do to you?" he asks softly.

"Is he dead?"

"No . . . but he should be." His jaw tightens.

"What are you going to do to me?" I ask, finally getting a little bit of courage from the wine.

He looks at me furrowed brows. "I'm not going to do anything to you."

"I just mean, what now? You brought me here, and Samael is still alive. He'll want to get me back." My voice comes out smaller than I would like.

He places his hand on my cheek, gently coaxing me to turn to him.

"What do you want, Lyra?" He holds my gaze.

I look down self-consciously. "I don't want to go back, if that's what you're asking."

He places his hand under my chin until my eyes meet his. "Then I'll never let him have you." His voice comes out thick, and his eyes glow for the briefest moment. "I don't know everything you've been through, Lyra. Maybe one day you'll tell me, but I promise you'll always be safe with me."

Nyx's words are reassuring, and I can feel the sincerity in his voice. Despite my reservations and fears, I can't help but trust him. "Thank you," I whisper softly, my eyes meeting his. "I don't know if I'm ready to talk about everything yet, but I appreciate your kindness and understanding. It means more than you know."

I blink back tears. I don't know why I feel so emotional right now, but I believe him. I feel safe with him, and it's something I haven't felt for a long time. I always went to bed afraid, afraid Samael would visit my bedroom or my nightmares would haunt me in sleep, but right now I feel a warmth in my chest and something inside me telling me I'm going to be okay. Although deep down I know I'll never be truly safe until

Samael is dead. I watch the fire and let the silence stretch on between us. It doesn't feel uncomfortable though.

"There's a rumor that Samael killed your parents, that it wasn't an accident. He's broken all the laws of decency your parents swore to uphold. Worse, there are rumors he's collecting grimoires by any means necessary, searching for something. He's even tortured and killed entire bloodlines to take their grimoires," Nyx says, breaking the silence. A dark feeling inside me starts to take form. It's a feeling of rage.

"He must be stopped. With my parents gone, there's no one to leash him. I think I know what he's looking for in the grimoires. I spied on him in the castle that night I ran into you after dinner. He was speaking to someone, a woman. He was trying to find the *Moon Grimoire*. I've been racking my brain ever since trying to understand why he would want it." I get to my feet, feeling the need to move.

"What is he looking for?" Nyx asks.

"I believe he is looking for a way to make his magic dark permanently. You see, when we come into our powers on our nineteenth birthday, we either inherit light magic or dark magic. It has been over a hundred years since a Sorcerer has inherited dark magic. Samael can do dark spells with his light magic, but it'll never be as powerful as it would be if his core magic was dark." I swallow the rest of my wine and pace in front of the fireplace.

"So why would that make him want to find your mother's grimoire?"

"My mother has never confirmed it, but there have always been whispers that someone in her lineage used to have dark magic. I don't know who or if it's even true, but I do know if I heard the rumors then Samael has too."

"Do you believe it's possible for him to turn his magic dark permanently?" Nyx gets to his feet and touches my forearm, stopping me from pacing.

"I don't know if it's possible. I've never even seen my mother's grimoire." I run my hands through my hair and sigh loudly.

"Hey, we'll figure this out together. I'm going to help you."

Before I can respond, we hear scratching and yipping at the door. Nyx looks at me, brows raised, and I laugh.

"It's Chepi. He's ready for bed."

He laughs under his breath while heading to the door. He opens the door, and Chepi comes running in, doing circles around our feet before jumping onto the bed, rolling on his back. I give him a few belly rubs, and so does Nyx.

"I better let you get some sleep. Remember, you're safe here. Goodnight, Lyra." He gives me a gentle smile, but it doesn't meet his eyes. I wonder what's bothering him.

"Goodnight, Nyx." I crawl into bed and pull the covers up over me and Chepi. He turns out the lights and leaves without another word.

CHAPTER
SIXTEEN

I wake to Nyx on top of me, shaking me.

"Lyra, wake up!" His voice sounds panicked. I meet his eyes and push him off with both hands.

"Don't touch me," I hiss.

"You were having some kind of nightmare. I heard you yelling, and I couldn't wake you . . . I'm sorry." He sounds genuine, and I feel bad for my reaction.

"I'm sorry. I just . . . please don't take it personally." I relax a bit. My body is hot and damp with sweat. I was having a nightmare, but it's all jumbled in my head. I was reliving the night Aidan was on top of me and saw Luke's murder again. The thought makes me shiver.

"Okay, I'll leave you to go back to sleep now that I know you're well."

He starts toward the door, but I can't help grabbing his hand to stop him. "Wait."

He turns to me, a surprised look in his eye.

"Would you stay with me? Please?" My voice comes out wobbly. He stares at me as if he's having some inner debate.

Just when I think he's going to leave, he says, "Okay." He pulls a chair in front of the fire and takes a seat.

"What are you doing?"

"I'm staying with you so you can sleep." His voice is soft, but his eyes still look worried in the glow of the fire.

"I want you to sleep next to me."

He seems to mull it over for a minute then comes to the bed. I pull the covers back for him and slide over. He lies down on his back next to me, careful not to touch me in the process.

We both stare at the ceiling in awkward silence for a while until he asks, "What was your nightmare about?"

I can't bring myself to talk about Aidan. I feel too ashamed and just uncomfortable. I'm not ready for him to know what happened to me. I feel a lump forming in my throat, and I can't help the tears that run down my face. He turns onto his side so he's facing me now. "Tell me, Lyra, please?"

I do. I tell him about everything except Aidan forcing himself on me. I tell him about the ceremony and about Luke, the old Sorceress, the other Lycans who died because of me. I sob and tell him I don't know what any of it means and that I can't get their faces out of my head sometimes. He doesn't ask any questions. He just listens to me quietly, and every now and then I see his jaw tick. That's the only sign I get that tells me he's upset. He brings his hand up and wipes my tears.

"Is this okay? Can I touch you?" he asks softly.

I nod, and he pulls me to him. I curl my body against his and cry into his chest. He just holds me platonically and rubs the back of my head whispering into my hair. "You're okay now, Lyra. I'm not going anywhere."

It's the last thing I remember before I fall asleep.

I wake up some hours later still held by Nyx, my face pressed to his chest. I listen to the slow rise and fall of his chest as he breathes. I don't want him to wake. I don't want to leave this spot. I feel so oddly at home in his arms, and it warms my chest and sends nervous sensations through my stomach. His arms tighten around me, and I tilt my head back to look up at him, finding his gray eyes looking down at me.

"How long have you been awake?" I'm surprised to find him staring at me.

"Not long." He runs his fingers through my hair, playing with the curly pieces.

"I'm sorry for last night. I didn't mean to be so emotional and to sleep on you all night," I mutter into his chest, feeling a little shy.

"Don't be sorry. I slept well, and I like having you close to me." He moves his hand in slow circles on my lower back, but he never tries to grope me. "Lyra," he says quietly into my hair.

"Yes?" My voice is still heavy from sleep.

"I want us to talk about what happened to you, about the ceremony, about everything. Maybe after breakfast if you're feeling up to it," he says gently, still teasing my lower back with his fingers.

"Okay...but for now can you hold me a little while longer?" I ask, feeling vulnerable and in need of comfort. I nestle my face against his chest, breathing in his soothing scent. His arms encircle me tightly, and I feel a sense of safety wash over me. "I never want you to let me go." My voice is barely audible.

"As long as you need," he replies, his embrace growing even stronger. I must have drifted off to sleep again, because I awaken to the feeling of Chepi's wet tongue on my toes, causing me to laugh.

Nyx laughs too before saying, "What would you like to do this morning?"

"What are my options?"

"Well, we could get cleaned up and have breakfast here or have Twig pack us breakfast to go. We can have a bath in the hot springs not far from here." He smiles down at me, and something about him looks so happy and genuine.

"Um, definitely hot springs," I say, giggling a little. "Just let me brush my teeth quickly. Should I change?"

"You can wear whatever you'd like." He slides out of bed, holding his hand out to help me up. "I'll be back in a few minutes. Take your time. We'll leave when you're ready," he says before disappearing out the door.

He says I can wear whatever I'd like. I'm not used to someone not dictating my appearance. It's feels oddly empowering. I skim through the clothes in the closet and decide to slip on a light-pink dress with puffy off-the-shoulder sleeves and an extra-wide brown belt laced up the front.

When I'm done freshening up, Nyx appears back in my room. "Ready to go?"

"Yes," I answer, hopping off the bed.

"Would you like to fly or channel to the hot springs?"

"What does it mean to channel?"

"Well, it's like teleporting. It doesn't hurt or anything. I'll hold on to you and imagine where I want us to go, then we'll appear there in a few seconds." He says this like it's no big deal. I've heard the Fae are very powerful, but being able to travel places instantly seems crazy.

"Can you channel anywhere?" I have so many questions now.

"I can channel anywhere within my Realm so long as it's a place I've been before."

"Can all Fae channel?"

"Yes, we can, but how far we can channel greatly depends on how powerful we are. So naturally I can channel us far." He winks at me, and I can't help the smile that spreads across my face.

"You sure are full of yourself," I say before taking the hand he extends to me. He gives me a charming half smile.

"You may feel warm for a second, but it's just my magic surrounding you. Are you ready?"

"Yes," I say, hesitantly stepping close to him. He tightly embraces me, embracing me in darkness. His powerful magic pulsates, emanating a warm and familiar scent. The wind howls in my ear, intensifying his musky sweetness. I feel as though I'm being swept away in a vortex, tossed and turned until I'm suddenly lifted into the gentle warmth of the balmy air. Nyx steadies me, offering support as I open my eyes, the darkness fades away, and I feast upon the breathtaking view. We find ourselves in the lush jungle by the edge of a tranquil pool of water.

"Wow." I spin around, taking in the location. The water is pearlescent glowing-blue with clouds of steam rising off it. The hot spring is tucked back under a cliff shaded from the sun. It's not very warm out yet, so I can't wait to get in the hot water.

I haven't had much time to process what happened last night, and my thoughts are in a jumbled mess. Does Nyx harbor romantic feelings toward me, or is he merely looking out for me as he said? I can't stop thinking about how I feel when I'm with him, the fluttering of butterflies in my stomach, the quickening of my pulse. Being around him makes me feel both nervous and excited at the same time. But I have to be cautious because I don't know if I can trust him yet. I don't have anyone else to turn to, and there's nothing else for me to lose. When he held me in his arms, I felt safe and comfortable, an intimacy I've never experienced before. It's all so confusing, yet something about him makes me want to reveal everything to him. I want to trust him, and more than that I want him. It's a crazy thought, considering that all I know about him is that he's the Fae king of Nighthold.

"Go ahead and get in the water. I'll turn around while you get situated," Nyx says while turning away from me to face the trees.

I take off all my clothes and settle into the water. It's warm and feels delicious, soothing my body in all the right places.

"I'm settled. You may turn around," I call to him.

Nyx turns to me and starts to undress, without asking me to turn around. I feel flustered and unsure where to look. But I can't help stealing glances at him, and I'm struck by his sheer physical beauty. He's all broad shoulders, thick muscles, and a tall, commanding presence that makes me weak in the knees. My gaze wanders down his chiseled abs, and I can't help but notice the impressive size of his length. I bite my lip, my mind racing with desire and a hunger I've never felt before.

"Didn't anyone teach you it's not polite to stare?" he says while wading into the water.

I cough, surprised. "I wasn't staring." My face is on fire.

"Sure, you weren't, Princess. It's okay. You don't have to lie." His mouth quirks up on one side.

The water is just cloudy enough to hide my naked body beneath it, and I'm thankful because his eyes haven't left me since he entered the water. He moves close so we're both sitting on a ledge just deep enough to keep my body concealed.

"I want to talk about everything you told me last night." The tone of his voice snaps my attention back to him.

"What do you want to know?"

"Does Samael know what happened at the ceremony?"

"I'm not sure. I think he knows something by the way he was talking. He knew about the old Sorceress, and he knew things that happened while I was with the Lycans, but I don't know how. Maybe he had spies or did a spell. I can't be sure."

"Why was he torturing you that night after your parents' funeral?" His eyes never leave my face.

I look away. Suddenly, I feel self-conscious. "I don't know."

"What do you mean you don't know? He just came in and started torturing you and had a snake bite you?"

I know he wants a more detailed answer from me, but this isn't a conversation I want to have. "I don't know what you want me to say, Onyx. Samael is evil. He has never needed a reason for any of the malicious things he does. He's been abusing me for as long as I can remember. Is that what you want to hear?" My voice comes out high-pitched. His jaw clenches.

"What has he done to you, Lyra?" he asks through gritted teeth.

My chest feels tight, and that lump is beginning to form in my throat again, but I will not cry. I'm tired of crying all the time.

"I don't want to talk about this, Nyx, and it's not important." I try to steady my voice. "Why were you even at my parents' funeral? Why did you save me that night? How did you know what was happening?" When he doesn't respond and just stares at me, I feel my anger bubbling up to the surface. "Why don't you tell me anything? I didn't even know you were a king until Twig let it slip. Why haven't I met any of your friends or family? I heard you talking to people the night I woke up. Why are you hiding me here? What do you plan to do with me?"

Nyx's expression softens, his eyes meeting mine. "I never planned on doing anything with you, Lyra," he says, his voice low and earnest. "I just wanted to see you again after I left the castle. I'd been thinking of ways to find you, but then your

WHAT LIES BEYOND THE REALMS

parents died and I lost all hope. At the funeral, I searched for you but you were nowhere to be found. I thought you were grieving and wanted to be alone. I had no idea what Samael was doing to you, or I would have intervened years ago."

He pauses, his gaze drifting away briefly before returning to me. "The night Chepi led me to you, I had no idea what I would find. I didn't plan any of this. But I'm glad I took you away from that place, Lyra. You deserve so much better. And you're right - I do have friends and family here. I'm not hiding you."

Nyx reaches out to take my hand, his touch warm and reassuring. "You've been through something traumatic, and I wanted to give you time to heal. And, to be honest, I wanted to get to know you without any distractions. But I'll gladly introduce you to anyone you want. Tonight, we can have dinner with Bim and Flora."

I feel a warmth spreading through me at his words, the tension in my body easing. Despite everything that's happened, I can't help but feel a glimmer of hope that maybe, just maybe, things can be different with Nyx.

"Who are Bim and Flora?"

"Bim has been my best friend since we were kids, and Flora is my cousin but also a very close friend. The three of us grew up together."

"I'd love to have dinner with them tonight."

He smiles slightly, and I find myself smiling back in response. The atmosphere lightens as the unease dissipates.

My mind is racing, and I can't seem to calm it down. I feel lost, like I have no purpose or direction. I don't have a home or family to turn to, and I don't know what's going to happen next. I'm here with Nyx, but I don't know what his true intentions are. I don't have any way to defend myself or those around me.

I need to discover my true powers and abilities, and I hope it happens soon, but my nineteenth birthday is still many months away. The ceremony with the Lycans still haunts me, and I need to figure out what it all means. I want to understand what the Sorceress did to me, but I don't know how to find her.

Going back to Cloudrum seems like the only option, but I can't risk Samael finding me. That only leaves one option: I need to go back to the Cinder territory and find the Lycans there. I may even have to face Aidan again, but I'm not sure I'm ready for that.

I should probably tell Nyx about the page from my father's journal that explains the prophecy. He's Fae, so he might know something about it. I just don't know for sure if I can trust him yet. I need to take Chepi later to snoop around. I never went inside Nyx's personal chambers before. Maybe I need to.

"What are you thinking about?" Onyx tilts his head, studying my face.

"I'm not your prisoner here?" I ask to confirm what he said earlier.

His eyes darken for a moment, but he recovers quickly. "No, Lyra. I told you already I just wanted to get you somewhere safe. If you wish to leave, you may at any time." He watches me closely.

"So if I wanted you to take me somewhere, you would?"

"Just ask me, Lyra. I'm sensing a point to this line of questions."

"I want you to take me to the Cinder territory," I spit out finally.

"What, why?" he says, surprised.

"I've been denied information my whole life. I've always been told what to do and kept hidden away in the castle. I need to know what happened to me. I need answers, and the only person I know who can give me the answers I need right now is Aidan."

At the mention of his name, Nyx clenches his jaw even tighter. I think he might chip a tooth. I don't know the history there, but I get the impression Nyx doesn't like the Lycan.

"Aidan and the Sorceress made it seem like they were doing what my parents asked. I need to know why. Please, Onyx. I also don't want you just to take me there and drop me off. I don't wish to stay there. I want to stay here with you. I wish to return to Nighthold once I get answers . . . if you'll still have me." My voice trails off on the last part. I don't know what I'll do if he won't help me. I hold my breath waiting for him to respond.

Nyx smiles mischievously at me. "Okay, Lyra, I'll take you to see the Lycan. I'll help you get the answers you need, but it's going to cost you."

I raise an eyebrow, intrigued. "Oh? And what might that cost be?" I ask, a smile playing at the corners of my mouth.

He raises a hand and runs his fingers along my cheek. "You are so beautiful."

I lean into his touch, welcoming it on instinct. "What's it going to cost me?" I press.

"A kiss."

"Just a kiss?"

"You're welcome to give me more than a kiss, but just a kiss will do for now." He winks at me with a sarcastic smirk still on his face.

My face heats, and my body suddenly feels too hot. Gods, do I want to kiss him. More than I've ever wanted to kiss anyone. Aidan's the only man I've ever kissed, and that wasn't even something I wanted. The moon bread clouded my judgment. I also didn't know Aidan was a murdering rapist at the time. What if I'm a bad kisser? Panic surges through my chest for a moment, and Onyx must see it written on my face, because his hand comes up to my cheek, drawing my eyes to him.

"Don't get shy on me now, Lewis." I turn away from him, running my hand across my face. "I'm not shy I—"

"Have you kissed many men, Lyra?" he teases, cutting me off.

"No." My cheeks are on fire, and I hope he thinks it's just from the hot water and not me dying from embarrassment at my lack of experience. I look down.

He moves his hand under my chin, guiding my face up to meet his eyes. Once I meet his gaze, his eyes soften. "You have nothing to be shy about. It's adorable, but don't look down. Don't be embarrassed—ever. Not with me, okay?"

"Okay," I say softly. He releases my chin and runs his fingers gently down my neck. A thrill courses through my body. I want to kiss him, more than anything. Then his hand comes up to cradle my cheek, and I know that I'm ready. He leans in and never looks away from my eyes until the last second when I close mine.

As his lips brush against my eyelid, a jolt of electricity shoots through my body. His kisses trail down my face, sending tingles over my skin. When his lips meet mine, they're warm and soft, and my heart skips a beat. His kiss is gentle yet passionate, and I find myself opening my mouth to deepen it. His tongue caresses mine, and I feel a rush of heat throughout my body. I can't help but moan as his arms tighten around me, pulling me into his lap. I go willingly, and my legs wrap easily around his waist. His arm wraps around my back, holding my body close to him. I feel his arousal pressing into the soft parts of my stomach, and his touch sends shivers of pleasure through me. I find myself lost in the moment. Our kiss feels like a dance, each of us taking turns leading and following. I don't know how much time has passed, but I don't want it to end. Finally, we break apart, both of us gasping for air. Looking into his eyes, I know that I want to kiss him again and again.

I close my eyes, savoring the feeling of his touch and the warmth of the rain. The drops pelt against our skin, mingling with the wetness of our bodies. I never knew rain could be so comforting. Nyx's hand moves from my back to my face, wiping away a tear that I didn't even realize had fallen. His touch makes me tingle. I open my eyes and look up at him, captivated by the intensity in his gaze.

He leans down and presses his lips to mine once again. This kiss is different, more urgent, as if he's trying to convey something to me through it. Our bodies press together, and I feel the heat building between us. It's like a wildfire, burning out of control, and I never want it to end. I don't know how long we've been tangled together or when it started raining. I pull my face away from him for a moment, tipping my head back and letting the warm rain crash onto me, laughing. When I bring my face back, his eyes are glowing. He looks so incredibly sexy and breathtaking. His hair is wet and drooping slightly over his forehead, and his muscled chest and arms are glistening from the warm rain. How could this man ever want me, an inexperienced shy girl with no power? My face must betray me, because he runs one hand through my hair, tucking it behind my ear before asking, "What's wrong?"

"Nothing. Nothing's wrong." I smile at him, and he pulls my head down to rest on his chest. He holds me there, trailing his fingers through my hair and down my back in the rain. I rest my cheek on his chest and try to remember a time I felt this good. In his arms, I feel so safe, happy, and content, like I'm right where I belong. Does he feel the same?

"How old are you?" I ask. I know the Fae live longer than any other being and that some live to be well over a thousand years old. Nyx looks like he's in his early thirties at most, but that doesn't mean anything. He'll age a lot slower.

"I am three hundred and thirty years old," he says into the top of my hair.

Oh my gods, he has already lived more than three times my whole life span. He must've been with dozens, no probably hundreds of women in his life. I'll surely never be able to please him with all the experience he has. My heart starts to race a bit as my mind tries to wrap around this fact.

"I can hear your heart racing and sense your panic. Does my age bother you?" he says, leaning back so he can look at my face.

"No, not at all. It's just you have so much more experience than me in, well, everything. You've lived so much life, and I've never done anything. It's hard to comprehend. I'm just taking it all in. I'm not panicking or anything."

"You're perfect, Lyra, just as you are. Experience will come with time. Don't ever feel bad about who you are." He kisses my forehead, causing my heart to pound in my chest again, and this time I seek out his mouth. Our lips collide in a messy, wet kiss. Our fingers tangle in each other's hair. My breasts feel heavy and sensitive pressed against his chest. His hand trails down my back and cups my ass, squeezing slightly and holding me close to him. His other hand finds its way between us and cups my sensitive center. He pulls his head away from mine, both of us panting.

"Is this okay?" His eyes glow with passion.

"Yes," I whisper before his mouth descends on mine again. He parts my lips and slides a finger inside me. I hold my breath, waiting for the pain, but Flora really did heal all parts of my body. Instead of pain, a delicious thrill courses through my body. I moan, and the sound only makes him kiss me harder, working his finger in and out and rubbing his thumb in tantalizingly slow circles on my center. He wraps his other arm around my waist and starts coaxing me to move. I ride his hand, and the pleasure it's eliciting from me is almost too much to take. His lips leave mine, and he begins to lick and nibble on my earlobe.

"Come for me, Lyra." His breath teases my ear, and his words undo me. My body convulses against him, and my head falls to rest on his shoulder. My breathing is shallow as my insides tighten around his fingers in sweet release. He waits for my body to relax before he eases his fingers out of me, wrapping both arms around me and holding me close.

"Are you okay?" he asks, softly rubbing the back of my head with one hand.

"Yes." I smile. "Better than okay. I've never done that before. I mean . . . I've been touched like that before, but it didn't feel like that."

"Glad I was able to please you, Princess." Onyx kisses the tip of my nose. "Are you hungry?" he asks, and my stomach answers him by growling. "Let me get us somewhere dry, and we can see what Twig packed us to eat."

He raises a hand in the air, and our clothes levitate before dropping into the backpack he brought, then the backpack flies into his hand, and we disappear.

CHAPTER
SEVENTEEN

His sweet musky scent envelopes me with the wind, and we appear in a cave. I'm still wrapped around Onyx, and he's holding me to him. I let my legs drop to the ground, suddenly feeling flushed and a little self-conscious now that we're both naked without the water as camouflage. It's not exactly cold out—the air is humid—but my body still shivers from being wet. Onyx releases me and snaps his fingers, drying both of us instantly. I look down at myself and touch my hair in shock for a moment.

"How did you do that?"

"Magic," Onyx says. He smirks while pulling clothes out of the backpack. "I much prefer you like this, but I'm assuming you'll be more comfortable in these." He hands me my clothes, a mischievous smile playing on his lips as he does. His eyes linger on my body, but he must sense I'm uncomfortable, because he turns around and gives me privacy. Once we're both fully clothed, he pulls a couple of blankets from the pack and arranges them near the opening of the cave, then with the flick of his wrist a fire crackles to life.

As we sit there, wrapped in the warmth of the blankets and the glow of the fire, I can't help but feel like I'm in a dream. The rain beats a soothing rhythm on the cave entrance, and the jungle stretches out before us like a never-ending tapestry of green. Nyx's arms wrap around me, and I lean into his embrace. The scent of his skin mixed with the smell of the rain and the fire creates an intoxicating aroma that fills my senses. I feel at home with him.

He pulls out the containers, and my eyes widen. The pastries are like nothing I've ever seen before, with colors so vibrant they almost look like they belong in a painting. I pick one up, taking a bite and closing my eyes as the flavors burst in my mouth. They're sweet, with a hint of tanginess that's irresistible.

"These are amazing," I say, looking over at him with a smile.

"I'm glad you like them," he says, his eyes holding mine for a moment before he looks away. There's something in his gaze that I can't quite decipher, a hint of something deeper that I can't quite name. I take another bite of the pastry, hoping to chase away the sudden unease that's crept into my mind.

Nyx pulls out another container, uncovering it and placing it next to me. It looks like the sugary berry muffins I had before.

"Twig told me you like these," he says, handing me a berry muffin.

"Yes, I do, thank you." I take it from him, not wasting any time before biting into the delicious muffin. "What are these muffins called?"

"Pink Pixies," Nyx says before biting into one himself.

"Pink Pixies, really?"

"Yes, why?"

"My father, before he passed, he used to call me his little pixie. I've never heard anyone else say it."

"I don't know why the muffins are called that, but Pixies are tiny Faeries who live in the Dream Forest. They're cheerful, mischievous little Faeries no larger than your hand. I wonder if that's where he got the name from."

"Impossible, my father has never been to Nighthold. He always used to tell me the Faery Realm was a dangerous place."

"He wasn't wrong. It is dangerous. But all the realms have their dangers. My realm is no different."

"So far it doesn't seem very dangerous. Beautiful and enchanting come to mind, but not dangerous."

"You've only seen a very small part of Nighthold. The Faery Realm is vast."

"Where do all the Fae live? I haven't really seen anyone around the castle grounds."

"Well, the castle is my home, and I've always enjoyed my privacy. No one lives in the castle except me. All the staff have homes nearby. There's a little village not too far from the castle. I'll take you to see it soon, if you'd like."

"Yes, I'd love that." I gently lean back into his touch. "Aside from the village, where do the rest of the Fae live? What is the rest of Nighthold like?"

"Nighthold is very large. There are four main territories. We are in the Noble Vale, which as you know is humid and wet and made up of vast jungle. The Fate Fields north of us make up the tundra. It's quite the opposite of here. Huge mountains, barren terrain, freezing cold, and snow most of the year. To the south are the deserts of Vision Valley. Then just west of us is Onyx Land; it's the smallest territory of the four but holds the highest population of Fae. Onyx Land has beautiful coastlines, vast country plains, and one large city. It's the largest city of any territory in Nighthold and Cloudrum."

"Is Onyx Land named after you?"

"No, the opposite. My parents named me after Onyx Land. The city was my mother's favorite place to be, and that's where I grew up." He nips at my ear.

I laugh and ask, "What happened to them? Your parents? Where are they now?"

"They left this world a long time ago, and that, Princess, is a story for another time." He tries to sound stoic, but there's a sad undertone to his voice, so I drop the subject.

"Will you at least tell me their names?"

"My father's name was Callum, and my mother's name was Scarlett."

"Scarlett is a beautiful name."

"Yes. She was very beautiful and kind. I think you'd have liked her." He runs the tips of his fingers up and down my arm while we talk.

"I'm sure I would have. Do you have other homes or just the one here?"

"I have a home in all four main territories."

"I'd love to see them all someday." A smile spreads across my face as I turn my head to face him.

"Which one would you most like to visit?"

"I don't even have to think about it. I'd want to visit your home in Fate Fields. I love the cold, snowy weather; it makes me want to cuddle up inside by the fire with hot chocolate."

"That can be arranged." He tugs me closer to him. Little bolts of excitement shoot through my chest. "Where is Dream Forest?"

"It's an island off the coast of Vision Valley." We both continue eating in silence.

I whisper a soft thank you to Nyx, feeling a sense of gratitude and warmth inside me that I haven't felt in a long time. He leans in, his lips brushing against the top of my head before pulling away slightly to ask what he's done to deserve my appreciation. I take a deep breath, gathering the courage to speak my truth.

"For today," I say softly, "for being kind to me. No one has ever treated me this way before." Nyx's eyes soften at my words, and he draws closer to me, pressing his lips against my jawline and trailing soft kisses down my neck and collarbone. The touch of his lips sends shivers of excitement through me, and I can feel the heat rising in my cheeks as my body responds to him.

"What are Bim and Flora like?" I ask, leaning into his touch.

"Well, they're both sarcastic pains in my ass, to tell you the truth, but loyal to a fault, and I love them. Bim leads the Fae armies for me. He's a fierce fighter and strategist. Flora's specialty is healing. She's the one who healed you when I brought you home."

"Are you not able to heal?"

"Most Fae have basic healing abilities. I can heal minimal injuries, but I'm not very good with anything more serious. Things can go terribly wrong if you don't know what you're doing."

I try to steady my racing heart, but my thoughts keep spiraling out of control. What am I doing here with Onyx anyway? He's Fae and a king, and I'm a Sorceress, a mixed pairing that's frowned upon in both our worlds. I can't imagine he would ever want anything serious with me. Maybe he's just looking for a good time until he finds someone more suitable. The idea crushes me. But no, I can't let myself get caught up in this. I need to focus on my goals, on finding answers from the Lycans and figuring out how to stop Samael before he can do any more damage. My powers are still developing, but I can't let that stop me. I need to be strong and determined, no matter how distracting Onyx may be. I can't lose sight of what's important.

I clear my throat, straightening up. "Are you ready to head back?"

"Sure." He sounds distant, and for a moment I wonder what he senses from my emotions.

WE CHANNEL BACK to the castle, and Nyx leaves me in my room. He tells me to make myself at home, and he'll be back before dinner. I have a few hours before I have to get ready.

"Hey Chepi, you up for helping me snoop through his majesty's bed chamber?"

Chepi jumps off the bed so fast, wagging his tail. I open the door and wander down the hall and set out to find Nyx's bedroom.

"Stay close just in case we run into anyone. You might have to make us invisible."

Chepi rubs against my leg in understanding and then starts padding down the hall in front of me. "Do you know the way already?" He yips quietly at me then picks up the pace, winding through the maze of hallways. I hope he knows where he's taking us. I know Nyx will be gone for a while, so we have plenty of time. I can't help the guilt that creeps into my chest, but I quickly squelch it. He just seems too good to be true. I have to find out if he's hiding anything. I can't feel guilty for protecting myself, even if it involves invading his privacy.

Chepi doesn't take me to Nyx's bed chamber but to his office. It appears to be an office of sorts at least. It must be Nyx's office, because no one else lives here. It's dimly lit by the fireplace, and its black curtains are pulled closed, so it doesn't feel like day or night. A large desk sits in the center of the room, and the wall opposite the fireplace is one huge book-shelf filled with books. I carefully make my way to the desk and sit down, eyeing the papers and books on top of the desk. Everything looks harmless enough at first glance, but then I see something tucked under *A Tree Whisp's Guide to Herbology*, a deteriorated notebook. I pull it out. Scribbled across the cover it reads, "Lewis Lineage." Lewis is my last name and was my biological father's last name. Not many people speak the name Lewis anymore. My mother always used Silas's last name Sellar or her maiden name, Moon. She'd call me Lyra Moon even though my true name is Lyra Lewis. I think she wanted everyone to forget my father after he passed, but Onyx knows my last name is Lewis. Why would he have this and not share it with me?

The notebook is fragile and dusty. I slowly turn the pages, reading through what appears to be a family tree of sorts. Each person on the tree has their own page with a sketch of what they look like next to their name, details about their family, their bloodline, and their powers.

I'm only halfway through the notebook when I hear foot-steps coming down the hall.

"Shit," I mutter to myself and duck under the desk, tucking the notebook back where I found it first. Chepi runs over to me, hopping in my lap. I hold him close to my chest, and I know his magic will keep us hidden. The door opens, and I hold my breath wondering who could be coming in here. There's no way Nyx is back yet. It could be Twig, but whoever it is sounds too heavy footed. I want to peek, but I'm too afraid to move. I don't want to get caught, especially since I'm snooping through Nyx's office. The footsteps come close to the desk. Whoever it is stands only inches from me. I can hear them breathing. I bury my face into Chepi and try to take slow, quiet breaths. They rustle through some papers on the desk then leave the room, closing the door. I let out a loud breath and ease up to my feet, surveying the room. We're alone.

I look over the desk and everything seems to be in place except for a envelope that has "King Onyx" written across the top of it. I grab the envelope and look it over. I can't see through it, but it has my family's Sellar seal on the back. I wonder if this is from Samael, possibly negotiating for my return. I have the urge to open it, but maybe this will be a good test to see if Nyx tells me about it.

I go back to skimming through the notebook when I have to stop and do a double take because the name reads Euric Lewis, which is my father's name. I look at the sketch next to the name. It's old and faded, but it looks like a young version of my father. The page reads:

Euric Lewis
Son of Edward Lewis and Marian Time
Bloodline: Fae
Abilities:
    -Channeling
    -Telepathy
    -Pyrokinesis
    -Midnight Mind

This can't be right. I read it over multiple times. I cannot deny my father's name and picture, but my father was a Sorcerer. This says he was Fae, which doesn't make any sense. If he was Fae, how did he and my mother rule over the Sorcerer Realm as king and queen? Was he lying about his lineage? My mother had to have known, which also means she's been keeping the fact that I am part Fae from me my entire life. For all I know she was Fae too. Why does Onyx have a notebook about my father's lineage? My lineage? Why hasn't he shared any of this information with me? I knew he was too good to be true. I've been letting my feelings for him blind me.

He must have ulterior motives. At the very least, he's keeping secrets, and I need to figure out why. If this notebook is right, if my father was Fae, then the prophecy from his journal must be about me. A chill runs down my back at the thought.

I carefully make sure everything is the way I found it and hurry back to my chamber to clean up and get ready for dinner.

CHAPTER
EIGHTEEN

s I stand in the closet, browsing through the clothes, I'm torn between wanting to impress and wanting to remain comfortable. Eventually, I decide to go all-out, reasoning that it's better to be overdressed than under-dressed. I choose a slinky, all-black dress that sparkles, with a deep V neck that dips between my breasts, which bulge between the fabric. A slit goes up one side all the way to my hip, revealing the entirety of my leg when I walk. This dress should help me achieve my goal of distracting Onyx and making him regret deceiving me.

I take my time with my makeup, adding dramatic smokey eyes and rosy cheeks and lips. I let my hair flow in loose, tousled waves. The dress is form-fitting, and the fabric accentuates every curve. I feel self-conscious for a moment, but I shake off the feeling and slip into a pair of sparkling black heels to complete the look. When I catch a glimpse of myself in the mirror, I can hardly believe it's me. Chepi is already passed out on the bed, bored to death from watching me get ready.

As I wait for Nyx, I pace around the room, my nerves

getting the best of me. In an effort to calm myself down, I wander over to the drink cart and pour myself a glass of amber liquid from one of the decanters, hoping it will take the edge off. I take a sip, wincing at the taste, but the warmth that spreads through me is comforting. With each passing moment, I grow more anxious, wondering what tonight will bring and whether I'll finally learn the truth about my father.

Finally, there's a knock. I hurry to the door then pause to adjust myself before opening it. When I do open the door, Nyx is standing there in black pants and a long-sleeved black tunic. His messy hair falls a bit over his forehead. He looks so sexy, and I have to remind myself he's a liar. I will deny him. He looks me over closely, and when our eyes meet his are glowing slightly.

"You look incredibly beautiful, Lyra," he finally says, holding my gaze. His eyes trail down my body again. "Are you sure you're ready to be around other people? It's not too late to have dinner here."

"Yes, I'm ready," I reply, studying him. *Liar.* He extends his hand to me, and I take it, letting him pull me close. His arm wraps around my lower back, his fingers brushing my bare skin and sending a thrill through me. *Liar.* Then I hold my breath as the room goes dark and the wind picks up, swirling around us, and we channel.

We touch down, and I almost stumble over, but Nyx holds me close until I get my bearings. I turn away from him expecting to see—well I don't know what I was expecting to see, but it wasn't this. We stand before an enormous obsidian palace, the starry night reflecting off the ornate structure.

"Bim and Flora live here?" I ask quietly.

"Not exactly. Some of the Fae elders live here, and they throw the occasional dinner party. I need to speak with them, and Flora and Bim will be here for the party tonight, so what's that saying? Two birds, one stone?"

I'm glad I decided to go with the fancy dress tonight. I'm also a little nervous about having chosen something so revealing. I take in a breath, trying to calm my nerves, and continue up the steps with Nyx at my side.

"Stay close tonight," he says, and then we entered the palace.

We're greeted by servants immediately who usher us to the courtyard in the center of the palace. I thought Nyx had a large castle, but this place is huge. Where Nyx's home is more simplistic, this place is the opposite of that. The open-air courtyard in the center of the palace is surrounded by black and gold pillars. Ivy twists around them, stretching all the way to the ceiling. There must be at least a hundred people here, and I need to find a way to get away from Nyx. This could be the perfect opportunity for me to see if anyone at this party knew my father.

"Lyra, this is Granger. Granger this is Lyra," Nyx says to an older gentleman with a peculiar look to him.

"Pleasure to meet you," I say, giving him a slight smile.

"The pleasure is mine," the peculiar man says, eyeing me in a way that makes me uncomfortable. "Granger is one of the Fae elders. He's been around for over a thousand years. He was friends with my parents," Nyx says to me.

"I'll let you two catch up. I need to find the privy chamber." It's the only excuse I can come up with to step away.

"I'll take you," Nyx says.

"No. Please stay and visit. I can manage on my own." I don't give him a chance to protest, walking into the crowd.

I wander through the courtyard, taking in the breathtaking sights before me. Faeries flit and dance with their delicate wings on display, each one more stunning than the last. They remind me of Twig's, yet with a full-sized grace. The pastel attire they wear, paired with their shimmering, translucent wings, is a feast for the eyes. Meanwhile, I feel out of place, a solitary figure in my all-black attire. It seems I'm the only non-Faery present, surrounded by a sea of ethereal beauty.

"Stardust, miss?" says a woman dressed in an all-green suit with pink flowers in her hair. Startled, I turned to see she is carrying a large tray of drinks. I take one, slamming it back. I place the empty glass back on the tray and take a second to sip on.

"Thank you."

She gives me a bewildered look at first, then a smile spreads across her face, and she winks at me before walking away. I guess the Fae don't slam back liquor like the Lycans do. I look down at my glass, sipping the silvery, sparkling liquid. It's sweet and minty. The way it sparkles reminds me of starlight, and I finally understand why it's called stardust. It's not too strong, which is nice, but I'll probably need another one to rack up the courage to start questioning random Fae about my father.

"I don't think we've been introduced." A man's voice snaps me out of my reverie. I'm stunned I hadn't noticed him earlier, as I'd been so entranced by my surroundings. The centerpiece of the courtyard is a magnificent fountain, with water dancing high above the crowd in a dazzling display of purple and pink. As the pink and purple bubbles drift across the room, Faeries stop and pop them on their tongues. Finally, I turn my attention to the man who's addressing me. His appearance is undeniably striking with shoulder-length, messy, dirty blond hair and skin that exudes a golden-tan glow. It's as if this man's beauty is a result of his Faery heritage.

"No, we haven't. I'm Lyra." His emerald, green eyes glow at

the sound of my name. "Pleased to meet you, Lyra. My name is Colton. This is my home."

Oh shit. Is this guy an elder? He doesn't look older than Nyx. He must be an elder if this is his palace. I need to try to get information from him about my father.

"May I offer you a tour and another drink?" he asks, grabbing a glass of stardust off a platter going by. "Stardust seems to be your drink of choice this evening?"

I take the glass from him after finishing the last sip from the one in my hand. He takes my empty glass and tosses it over his shoulder. It disappears before my eyes.

"Thank you. Yes, a tour would be great."

He holds out an arm, and I take his elbow allowing him to guide me through a side door.

"So did you come here alone tonight?"

Shit. I can't tell him I came with Nyx. "I came with a friend of mine. Her name is Flora," I say, hoping he won't read into it. We travel up several flights of stairs. When we finally reach the top, it's a wide balcony set up like a cozy lounge. There's a bar on one side, and the other side looks over the party.

"The view of the party from up here is often much more enjoyable," he says, moving toward the railing.

I move closer and look over the ledge. It's a sea of color down below. "It's beautiful from up here." A pink bubble drifts toward me, and I lean forward, hoping to catch it with my mouth so I can see what all the fuss is about.

"I wouldn't do that if I were you," Colton warns.

"Why not?" I ask, stepping back, watching the bubble travel out of reach.

"The pink bubbles are hallucinogens, and the last time a guy mixed stardust with pink bubbles we caught him trying to have sex with a tree out back"

I nearly choke on my drink. "Poor guy."

Colton laughs. "More like poor tree," he says.

I put my drink down, suddenly realizing what he said about the stardust. "Wait, what is in this? Am I going to start hallucinating?"

"Hallucinating? No. You'll be fine. Come sit." He moves toward one of the large white settees next to the bar, taking a seat and patting the cushion for me to sit next to him.

"Where's your drink?" I ask.

He snaps his fingers, and two glasses full of amber liquid appear in his hands. "This is just whiskey. It's harmless. I promise." He hands me one of the glasses, and I take it.

"So, are you one of the elders?" I ask then take a drink from the glass. The whiskey is smooth and woodsy tasting in my mouth.

"I'm old, yes." He moves closer, sitting right next to me.

"Does the family name Lewis mean anything to you?"

"Why do you ask?"

"Never mind. It's not important." I feel uneasy, just realizing we're completely alone up here. The party down below is much too loud for me to scream for help if I need to. I try to rise to my feet and return to the party, but Colton's hand stays me, resting on my bare thigh with a scorching touch that sends unexpected ripples of warmth through me, eliciting feelings I wasn't expecting.

"No, stay. Finish your drink, and I'll tell you everything I know about the Lewis family name." His fingertips slowly circle the side of my thigh, which is visible thanks to the high slit in the gown. I gulp down the rest of the glass as fast as I can, placing it on the table in front of us.

"I finished it. Now tell me what you know."

"Euric Lewis was the last person I knew to carry the Lewis family name. He was an extremely powerful Faery. Why are you so interested in this?" Colton's finger travels down to my knee and slowly back up my thigh over and over again. The touch causes my toes to curl. I don't know what's wrong with me. I don't even like this man, but that finger pressing against my thigh and running lazy circles across my skin is making my flesh react.

I clear my throat, trying to regain my composure. "What happened to him?"

"He was banished from the Faery Realm many years ago. Some say he rules in Zomea now." Colton raises a hand to my face, tucking a piece of hair behind my ear. I feel his eyes linger on the side of my face, but I refuse to look at him.

"Can you tell me about him?" I ask just as Colton leans in close to my ear.

"What do you want to know?" he whispers. The words tickle my ear. I squirm away, but he places his hand back on my thigh. The touch of his hand is almost hot, and heat spreads through my body. I feel my face flush as arousal sinks into my core.

"What was in that drink?" I ask, but before Colton can answer Nyx comes through the door.

"I've been looking all over for you," Nyx says, extending a hand to me. His eyes go straight to the spot Colton was touching on my leg moments ago like he could see the imprint. I take his hand, instantly relieved when he pulls me to my feet.

"Nyx, my man. I didn't know you two knew each other," Colton says, getting to his feet. He extends his hand for Nyx to shake, but Nyx just looks down at him with his lips pressed in a hard line.

"Lyra, let's go." Nyx places his hand on the small of my back, ushering me back to the party. The callouses on his hand scrape my sensitive skin, causing me to clench my thighs together.

A man approaches us right away, smiling broadly at me.

"Lyra, this is Bim," Nyx says as he came to stand in front of us.

Bim is tall but shorter than Nyx, and he has a wide, muscular build with a bit of a pudgy belly, short light-brown hair that's slightly messy atop his head, and a trim brown beard to match his light-brown eyes.

"Pleasure to meet you," I say, returning a smile.

Bim takes my hand and places a kiss on the top of it.

"Oh, the pleasure is mine, Princess," Bim says. His breath on the back of my hand tickles in a way that shouldn't arouse me but does. Something is wrong with me. My body feels flush and . . . wet.

"Don't start," Nyx elbows him, but Bim just chuckles. Nyx still has his hand wrapped around me, and I press into him, touching my hand to his back. He feels so strong, and his back is firm. He keeps talking to Bim, but I can't focus on their conversation. I move in front of Nyx, burying my face in his chest and wrapping my arms around him. I tug his shirt up in the back. My hands find the warmth of his bare skin. My heart is racing, and I need to be closer to him.

"Lyra, are you alright?" Nyx places his hand under my chin, coaxing me to look up at him. The golden chandelier dazzles above his head. "Shit. Did you eat or drink anything?" he asks, brows furrowed.

"Maybe," I drag the word out slowly then bite my bottom lip. Nyx smiles at me, wrapping his arms around me.

"We'll talk later," I hear him say to Bim, then darkness surrounds me. The smell of him almost destroys me.

A moment later we're back in the quiet of Nyx's castle standing in the bed chamber. I push him back toward the bed, and he sits down. I crawl onto his lap, pushing on his chest until he falls back onto the bed.

"Lyra, wait. What did you have at the party?"

I can't think about anything else right now. I need him.

"Lyra, I need to know what you had," Nyx says while gently placing his hands on either side of my face, forcing me to meet his gaze.

"Stardust," I whisper then push his hands away. I start undressing him, pulling his shirt over his head. I'm going to eat him alive.

"Lyra, stop. I don't want you to do anything you're going to regret. You don't understand that stardust is a powerful aphrodisiac. It doesn't last long. You should be snapping out of it soon."

I don't know what he's saying. All I know is I need him. I need to taste him.

I lean down on top of him, finding his mouth and letting my hair fall around us, hiding our faces. I run my tongue across his bottom lip and bite down on it. He makes a guttural sound deep in his throat, and it lights me on fire. I can't stop groping him. I run my hands through his hair and across his chest, devouring his mouth with mine. I press my tongue against his, wanting to taste every part of him. I feel ravenous. I can't get enough of him. I start tugging at his pants, but he halts me, grabbing my wrists and tossing me back on the bed. He crawls on top of me, kissing me deeply.

"I'm not going to have sex with you when I know you'll surely regret it later."

"I won't." It's a plea as I move my hand, grasping his hard length pressed against his pants. He moans, and I take it as my chance. I start tugging his pants off, but again he stops me. He grabs my wrists, bringing them together over my head and pinning me there with one hand. I buck beneath him, wanting him to take me.

"Please," I cry out.

Nyx just smiles down at me, pinning me with his body. "So demanding."

I use my legs, wrapping them around him and pushing him over. The only reason it works is because he wasn't expecting it. Back on top of him, he chuckles loud beneath me. I get to work on his pants again, trying to fully undress him. I need him. He places a hand to my forehead, and it's the last thing I remember.

I OPEN MY EYES, blinking slowly, thankful for the dim light of the fire. My head is pounding, and I don't think I could handle any bright lights right now. I'm in bed, but this isn't my bed chamber. I sit up and see Nyx sitting in front of the fire, drink in hand. He must notice my movement because he moves to the bed, sitting next to me.

"How are you feeling?" he asks.

"My head is hurting. How long was I asleep?"

"Just a couple hours. It's not even midnight yet. I had to use a compulsion on you. I'm sorry for that."

Oh gods. I am starting to remember what happened before I fell asleep.

"Let me get this straight. I was basically trying to devour your body to the point of you having to force me to sleep it off." I cringe as I recount the night's events in my head.

"Did Colton give you stardust to drink?" Nyx asks, his lips pressed together.

"No, he didn't." I'm remembering what Colton told me now about my father. He confirmed that my father was a Faery. "Why was I the only non-Faery at the party?"

"It's not often people from other realms visit Nighthold. No one in Cloudrum really likes the Fae, especially the Sorcerer

Realm. Your people despise us." His words ignite something inside me.

"Funny how you say individuals in the Sorcerer Realm hold disdain for the Fae. They once had a Faery rule as their king."

Nyx looks at me, and his brows furrow. "What are you talking about?"

"Don't you dare lie to me, Onyx. Not now." I don't take my eyes off him.

"I don't think you know what you're talking about, Lyra," Nyx says, reaching out to touch me like he's trying to calm me. It has quite the opposite effect.

"I saw the notebook in your office today. I know about the Lewis lineage. You received mail from Samael too. I won't even ask what it says, because I'm sure you'll just lie about that too," I say between clenched teeth.

Nyx doesn't say anything. He just stares down at his drink.

"How could you keep that from me? Why wouldn't you tell me about my father? Am I part Fae? Why did you even have that notebook about my family?"

I push off the bed. I can't stand being next to him if he can't even tell me the truth.

"Lyra, please let me explain." He puts his hands up as if to calm me down.

"I trusted you. You're just like everyone else. You lie and just want to use me for your own benefit. I trusted you, Nyx." My voice breaks, and I feel my eyes swell with tears, but I won't let him see me cry.

Before he can say anything else, I move toward the door. He grabs my arm but not hard enough to stop me.

"Don't touch me." I swat his hand away and flee to my room before he can say anything else. I don't hear him follow me, and I'm thankful I know the way back to my bed chamber after exploring earlier today.

CHAPTER
NINETEEN

I step out of my dress, the fabric falling to the floor as I make my way to my bed. I let out a sob as I crawl under the covers, tears streaming down my face. My mind is a mess. I don't understand why I've been so emotional and unpredictable lately. It could be the lingering effects of stardust or the excessive drinking. Or maybe it's this place and its magic that's getting to me. I bury my face in my pillow, desperate for some kind of solace. The truth is, my chest aches because of my feelings for Nyx. Despite my best efforts, I can't deny the attraction I feel toward him. Something about him makes me feel happy and safe, like I'm exactly where I'm meant to be. And that's why this hurts so much. I thought I could trust him, but now I'm not so sure. He's been keeping secrets from me, and it feels like a betrayal. He doesn't know me well, but it hurts that he's been investigating my family history without my knowledge.

After speaking with Colton earlier, I can only assume that Nyx must have known my father. And it's possible that Nyx was even the one who banished him from the Faery Realm.

I probably shouldn't have blown up and left so dramatically. Maybe I can partially blame my heightened feelings on the stardust drinks. He'll never tell me the truth now after that scene I made. I don't know what he's going to do with me. Maybe he'll just start locking me in this room, or maybe he'll trade me back to Samael.

There's a knock at the door, and I know it has to be Nyx. I keep the pillow over my face and stay quiet. I don't know if I'm ready to talk to him. Of course, when I don't respond he comes inside anyway. I feel him sit on the end of the bed.

"Can I help you with something?" I say, muffled into the pillow.

"You can start by showing me your face." He grabs the pillow and tosses it aside. He looks stressed, and I feel bad for a minute, but then I remember he's the one hiding things. I scowl at him.

"I know you're upset. I was planning on talking to you. I was just waiting for the right time and didn't think you would go looking through my office while I was gone." He runs his hands through his hair, flustered.

"You can talk to me now," I say under my breath, looking away from him.

"Your father, Euric. He was Fae, and I knew him. We were friends once," he says, gravely looking at his hands in his lap. "When I was young, I used to look up to him. He was about a hundred years older than I was. When Bim and I'd get into trouble, he was usually the one to bail us out. He was very close with my father, Callum, and like a second father to me, then they had a falling out. My father never talked about it. Just one day Euric was gone. He'd never tell us what happened. I don't know if my own mother even knew what happened between them." He looks at me, sorrow in those gray eyes. "It was after my parents died when I took over as king. I went to Cloudrum to see the other territories and meet their leaders. My first stop was Tempest Moon to meet the king and queen of Cloudrum. You cannot imagine the shock I felt when I found out Euric was the king of Cloudrum. That he was not only king but pretending to be a Sorcerer as well."

"What happened? Did he tell you why he left?" I need to know the truth behind my father's actions. "Colton told me he was banished from Nighthold, and some now believe he rules in Zomea."

"He wouldn't tell me what happened between my father and him. Have you heard the term 'midnight mind' before?"

"No, but I saw it in the notebook as one of my father's abilities. What does it mean?"

"It can mean many things. It's a rare gift amongst the Fae. I don't know anyone alive today with the ability. He had the ability of foresight, and he could also visit Zomea in his dreams."

"Zomea as in the afterlife?" I ask, my heart practically beating out of my chest.

"Yes. Midnight mind is very dangerous. One of the reasons it's so rare is because many of the Fae with the ability go crazy and never have offspring to pass the gift along to.

Your father knew about you before you were born. He knew lots of things and kept many secrets."

"What did he tell you?" I sit up, holding the sheets to my chest and focusing on Nyx.

"He loved your mom dearly. She didn't know he was Fae, at least not at the time I was there. I didn't know your mother well, but I didn't like her. I got the sense she wasn't a good person. I think your father was blinded by love."

"Why are you telling me this? What did he tell you?"

"He told me he was going to have a daughter one day, and after you were born your mother would fall for another man and betray him. He told me you were important for the future of the realms, and I needed to protect you no matter what. He made me swear I'd protect you. You have to understand I thought I was protecting you by letting you grow up as a princess with your family. I attended your father's funeral. Then I saw you. You were so young and innocent. I thought I was doing the right thing. I had no idea how cruel Samael was."

"It's okay. I don't blame you for what happened to me." I place my hand on top of his, drawing his eyes back up to mine.

"I'd try to visit the castle over the years to check on you, but your mother was always trying to keep me away. I think she had her suspicions. When I finally saw you at dinner, I knew something wasn't right. I think Samael was becoming suspicious of me as well, because he caught me asking questions about you to some of the castle staff."

"That must be why he didn't want me at dinner that night. He's the reason I made an excuse to leave early. He was kicking me under the table and promised I'd pay for it later if I stayed at dinner that night."

Nyx's jaw ticks. "I will kill that fucker. I promise you his days are numbered."

"Why didn't you take me that night after dinner?"

"I didn't know for sure what your life was like. I barely spoke to you for more than a minute. I didn't want to take you away from a life you were happy with. Trust me, I thought about it, especially when I ran into you later that night in the hall. I also didn't want to cause a war with your parents. I went back home but then found out you were with Aidan in the Lycan Realm, and I began to worry for your safety. I started plotting with Bim how I would take you and bring you to Nighthold. Then I got news of your parents' deaths, and I knew I had to see you." He takes a deep breath, turning my hand over in his and rubbing his thumb along my palm. "When you weren't at your parents' funeral, I panicked a bit, but I knew you were near, and I could feel you. You were feeling really strong emotions, mostly dread. I was planning to look for you after the funeral when I ran into Chepi, and he led me to your room. You know the rest from there."

I look down at our hands, trying to process everything for a moment. "So you only brought me here to keep me safe because you promised my father before I was born that you would?"

"Yes and no. I was keeping an eye on you because your father asked me to, yes, but I can't help the way I feel when I'm near you. I want you, Lyra. I want to be close to you. I want to protect you, not just because your father asked me to but because I care about you. The more I'm around you, the more I feel this pull to be with you. It's been driving me crazy. Then when I couldn't find you tonight, I started to panic again. When I found you with that prick Colton, his hand touching you . . . it took everything in me not to declare you mine right then and incinerate that asshole. I know what he was doing. He saw you drinking the stardust and was trying to seize an opportunity. Please don't be upset with me, Lyra. I know you have a lot of questions, and I do too. I don't have all the answers. It's late, and I know you have to be tired. This is a lot to take in. Can we talk more about it tomorrow?" His eyes plead with me.

"Yes," I say slowly, watching him and processing his words. He wants to declare me his . . .

"Can I stay with you tonight?" he asks, and my chest tightens.

"Yes," I whisper again moving over to make room for

him. He snaps his fingers, and the lights go out. The fire still crackles just enough to where I can still see him.

He pulls back the sheets and slides into bed next to me, lying on his side to face me. I turn on my side to face him. My eyes find his in the dark. His glow slightly, and his hand touches my side, running his fingers down the length of me slowly.

"You're naked," he says, sounding a bit surprised.

"I was in a hurry to get into bed when I came in here. Plus, the sheets feel nice on my skin." I see him crack a smile for the first time since we started talking tonight.

"I'm not complaining." He pulls off his shirt then relaxes next to me again. This time when his hand finds me, he places it on the small of my back and pulls me to him. I suck in a breath when our bodies meet. He feels so warm and smells so good that my mind goes blank. I look up to meet his eyes, and the second I do he kisses me. His lips touch mine, warm and demanding. I open my mouth for his tongue and welcome his touch. He has one arm tucked underneath me. His hand at my back keeps me pressed close to him, but his other hand ventures to my breast and slightly squeezes and pinches at my peaked nipple. I moan into his mouth, and he groans, deepening the kiss. I can feel his arousal through his pants pressed against my stomach. I let my hand find it and slowly stroke him through his pants. He makes a guttural sound and pulls his head back to look at me.

"Fuck," he groans as I stroke his cock.

He unfastens his pants and pulls them off. This time when he comes back to me, he climbs on top of me. My legs open for him, and he holds his weight up on his arms, finding my mouth again. I lick his bottom lip and nibble on it, causing him to groan into my mouth. I can feel him press against my opening, and panic seizes me. I don't think I'm ready to do this with him. I don't want to ruin things, and after what happened with Aidan I just don't think I'm ready. I don't know how to tell him. I'm afraid for a moment Nyx will be upset with me. My breathing quickens, and I close my eyes trying to gather myself.

"What's wrong?" He kisses my forehead and runs his hand down my cheek, pushing my hair out of my face.

"Nothing," I say quickly, opening my eyes to look at him.

"It's okay. You can tell me anything," he assures me, not taking his eyes off mine.

"I'm just . . . I'm not sure I'm ready to have sex," I finally mutter under my breath, feeling embarrassed.

He pulls away from me, falling back onto his side and facing me.

"Are you upset with me?"

"No, Lyra, I don't want to do anything you're not ready to do. It's okay." He places his hand on my cheek, so I turn to face him. "I'm not upset. We'll move at whatever pace you want." He places another kiss on my forehead and pulls me close to him.

"We can do other things. I just want to wait a little while before we have sex."

"I like . . . other things. Let me make you feel good," he says in a low voice before pushing his lips to mine.

His kiss is ecstasy, and I could drink from him all night. He explores my mouth with his tongue, and his hand glides down my body, cupping my center. I feel the pressure building in my core. I seek out his cock once more, rubbing my fingers across the beaded liquid at the tip before stroking him slowly from root to tip. He groans at my touch and pushes a finger inside me. He moves his fingers in and out slowly while his thumb presses against the bundle of nerves at my center. I breathe heavily into his mouth. My mind goes blank as I stroke him faster, following his increasing pace as he moves in and out of me. My body is on fire. I ride his hand, moving my hips and twirling my tongue with his. Just when I think I'm going to explode from the pleasure, he curls his fingers inside me, hitting just the right spot. I find my release at the same time he does.

Both of us lie there looking at each other, panting. I release him, and he slowly eases his fingers out of me. He moves to get up.

"Please don't leave," I say quickly.

"Oh, Lewis, trust me, I'm not going anywhere," he says, getting out of bed.

I relax on my back, still recovering from what just happened. He goes into the bathroom to clean up, then brings a damp warm washcloth and cleans me as well. Once satisfied with my cleanliness, he tosses the washcloth and climbs back into bed. He pulls me to him, and I relax my back against his chest. I can feel his breath tickle the top of my head.

"Goodnight, Lyra." He kisses the top of my head and holds me close.

"Goodnight, Nyx." I relax my head on his arm and fall asleep surrounded by his warmth.

CHAPTER
TWENTY

The soft glow from the morning sun shimmers through the translucent curtains warming my face. Nyx is still tangled around me, and my chest warms. How can this feel so good being so close to him? I've never been in a relationship before, and I wonder if that's what this is. Is this what true intimacy is supposed to feel like?

He repositions behind me, and I feel his hard length pressed against my backside. I turn over in his arms to face him. He's awake, smiling at me.

"Good morning, my love," he says, and my breath catches when he says it.

"Good morning." I smile sleepily up at him. "Did you sleep well?"

"Very," he says, kissing the top of my head.

"Would you like to take a bath?" he asks while rubbing his stubbled jaw against my hair.

"A bath sounds good," I say quietly into his chest.

Before I have a chance to think about it, we appear in the

bathroom. Nyx holds me cradled to his chest. The bath is already full of warm water.

"That was unnecessary." I laugh as he lets my feet slowly drop to the floor.

"What good is having powers if I don't use them for important things like this?"

"Yes, baths are very important." I laugh as I turn to face him.

"When it comes to you, everything is important," he says matter-of-factly and taps my nose with the tip of his finger.

As I step into the bath, I feel Nyx's gaze following me, and I don't shy away this time. I take my time, letting him take in my body as I submerge myself in the water, surrounded by luxurious baby-blue bubbles. The water is warm, and the scent of blueberries fills the air. Nyx climbs into the bath behind me, positioning himself with my body between his legs.

"Do you think Bim dislikes me after last night?"

"No."

"I feel a bit ridiculous for ignoring him and practically molesting you in front of everyone at the party. Great first impression, huh." I grab the soap.

"Trust me, last night was nothing. I'm sure he found it amusing." He takes the soap from me and begins cleaning my back and lathering my hair.

"Still I'd like to apologize and have a second chance to get to know him a little bit. We left before I ever got a chance to meet Flora too."

I lean back and let him rinse my hair. He runs his fingers along my scalp, massaging the soap out. It's bliss. I could lie in this bath and let him massage me all day.

"You'll have a chance this morning. I said I would show you the village, and I figured we could stop by Bim's place after. I need to talk strategy with him if I'm going to take you into the

Lycan Realm. Flora is usually at Bim's place, so I'm sure you'll get to meet her."

I practically splash all the water out of the tub, swinging around to face him. "Yes, I'd love to see the village, and you're really going to take me to speak with Aidan?"

"I know you want answers, and I said I'd help you get them. If you think Aidan will help us find this old Sorceress you speak of, then we need to make a plan to go see him." He doesn't sound happy about it.

We finish getting cleaned up, and I quickly braid my hair to the side while Nyx gets dressed. He's in his usual black pants and black top. I go for something casual as well, putting on a pair of black tights and a light-green tunic.

"Shall we?" He extends a hand to me, and I take it.

In a flash of warm wind, what once was the bathroom is now a bustling little village.

As we arrive on the outskirts of town, the tree line greets us. We find ourselves standing before a group of small straw structures huddled together near the riverbank. A dirt path stretches ahead, leading us down to the back of these buildings. My eyes are immediately drawn to the water, where an array of boats and canoes are moored. People are bustling about, conducting trade and chatting with those on the decks. The smell of spices and freshly caught fish fills the air, carried on the warm breeze. It tickles my nose and adds to the lively atmosphere of the river.

"Come. I want you to try one of my favorite things to eat when I'm here." Nyx pulls me along the path until we duck inside one of the miniature huts. It's busy, and there are people everywhere sitting and standing along tall and short tables randomly spread out across a dirt floor. It's definitely nothing fancy. Everyone is dressed casually and would never know Nyx was their king. No one stares at us. No one even acknowledges us as we wind through the scattered tables to the deck outside.

"Hey Timmy, how's the family?" Nyx asks a chubby older man stopped at the dock in a boat.

"You know me. Can't complain," Timmy says while loading his boat with a container of what appears to be some type of slug. Gross.

"Have you seen Polly around this morning?" Nyx says, leaning on the wooden railing to peer into the boat.

"Yeah. I passed her a few minutes ago. She's making the rounds. Should be coming by you any minute," Timmy says and sits down, seemingly satisfied with how he's arranged everything in his boat. "Well, I'm off. Good day to you and your lady friend."

"I'm sorry. Yes, this is Lyra," Nyx says, turning back toward me.

"Good day, Lyra. Hope to see you around," Timmy says while pushing his boat off away from the deck.

"Likewise." I smile and wave.

"I wish you tight lines, my friend." Nyx nods, and Timmy paddles down the river, mixing with the cluster of boats ahead.

"What does that mean?"

"Timmy is a fisherman. Wishing him tight lines is like wishing him good luck. Timmy is also Fae, and most Faeries are superstitious, especially the ones who like to fish."

"I don't follow."

"Tight lines can mean the line is tight because there's a fish on the other end, which is ultimately what I am trying to wish him good luck with. But a tight line could also mean you're snagged in the moss or stuck in a tree stump. So by saying 'tight lines,' I can get away with saying good luck without the fishing gods knowing and denying the fisherman's luck all together. Make sense?"

"Not even remotely, but okay." I laugh. It makes sense in some twisted superstitious way.

"Is everyone here Fae?"

"Mostly, yes," he says but doesn't offer up any more details.

"Here she comes. See the boat with the little red flag on the front." He points up the river. In the distance I see a wide canoe with a small red flag attached to the front hanging high.

"Yes, I see it," I reply, standing next to him to peer over the railing.

"That's Polly. She makes the best Riffs you'll ever try. I promise." He sounds super excited, and I have no idea what a Riff is, but I'm excited now too. He waves her over, and she pulls up to the deck, tying onto a beam.

"I thought that was you, Onyx. Who's the pretty lady?" Polly says in a modulated voice. Polly is a voluptuous woman with skin chiseled by age and sun damage, as if from years spent out on a boat. Her dark hair falls just to her waist in braids woven with flowers and greenery. She looks quite a bit older than Nyx, and I wonder if she knew my father too.

"This is Lyra. Lyra this is Polly, my favorite chef in all the Realms." Nyx smiles at her and winks.

"Flattery will get you nowhere, boy. I know what you're after. And it's a pleasure to meet you, dear." She swats Nyx's hands away from her boxes and gives me a smile. Her teeth are white and straight but a little pointier than I expected. Definitely Fae. She reaches into a box and pulls out a small bag, handing it to Nyx.

"These are fresh. I just made them this morning."

Nyx takes the bag and gives her some coins. "Thank you, Polly. You spoil me." He waves her goodbye.

"Pleasure meeting you." I smile and wave.

"Stay out of trouble, boy. Lyra, make sure he shares with you," she yells after us, waving.

We head back inside, and Nyx finds a table in the corner with two chairs. He pulls one out for me, and I take a seat before he comes to sit next to me.

"Here. You must try it while it's still warm." He removes a rectangular dough piece from the bag and hands it to me.

"What is a Riff exactly?" I ask, turning it over in my hand to examine it.

"It's a fish hand pie. Polly's husband is the fisherman in the family, but Polly makes the fish pies. She uses the best spices. It's delicious. I promise."

I take a bite. It's an explosion of flavors in my mouth. It makes the meat pies back home seem bland. I taste lots of spices, cardamom, turmeric, ginger, and a hint of sweetness, maybe coconut and cinnamon. The dough is cooked just right, slightly soft inside but flakey and buttery on the outside. I shovel several more bites down my throat before I get a chance to tell Nyx I like it.

"You're right. This is delicious. The combination of flavors hitting my tongue is . . . invigorating. Where has this been all my life?"

His smile widens. "I'm glad you like it. I'll grab us some water."

He speaks to a woman at the counter before coming back with two tall glasses of water. I finish my hand pie and clear my palate with water.

"There's something I've been meaning to talk to you about. Since we're both being honest with each other now . . . I feel I should tell you." I need to ask him about the prophecy from the journal. He might know something.

"Come. Bim lives just outside the village, and it's a beautiful walk. You can talk to me about it away from prying eyes and ears." He finishes his water, and we make our way outside the small, crowded hut.

The sun is well overhead, and I can feel my face glistening with sweat beads. We continue down the dirt path past many huts that are all full of people eating and drinking. Some appear to be selling clothes and fishing gear. Once we get past the hustle and bustle of the fishing village, our path winds away from the water through the denser vegetation under the trees. Everything is so spread out here. We pass what appear to be pathways leading to houses, but I can't see most of the houses due to the trees and the vastness of the properties.

"Now, what would you like to tell me?" Nyx asks. There's no one around to hear me except the birds.

"Before you brought me here, Lili was searching the library in secret for answers about what happened at the Lycan ceremony. While she was searching, she found one of my father's old journals. I never actually got to see the whole journal, but she ripped a page from it to show me."

"What did it say?" Nyx comes to a stop, facing me.

"I can't remember exactly but something like this. 'I visited Zomea today and finally figured out how it'll work. All of my work hasn't been for nothing. What I thought was impossible has been hidden right before me this entire time. He shared the prophecy with me, and it's then I knew. I know it will be her.

"'One born of Fae and Sorcerer blood must consume blood of the Lycan and Lamia before their powers manifest. Blood of all the realms must live inside her. To successfully unlock the bridge to Zomea, three innocent Lycans must die at the hand of the one they trust before the first shift under the full moon. A single Lamia must choose to end her life prematurely, giving her blood willingly under the light of the blood moon. Only then may the key unlock the bridge.'" I recite the passage to him word for word as best I can remember it.

"Are you sure that's what it says. You remember it exactly?"

"Yes, I read it over so many times that the page is seared in my mind." I turn to start walking again.

"Where is the page now?"

"I left it tucked under the mattress in my bed chamber. I don't know if Samael will find it, or maybe he already knows about it. Do you know what it means?"

Nyx starts walking again, but his pace is slow.

"It must be about you. You're the only one I've ever known born of Fae and Sorcerer blood. As far as visiting Zomea, I told you your father had midnight mind. He could travel to Zomea in a way with his mind. The more concerning part is who told him about this prophecy and what unlocking the bridge might do . . ."

"So you believe I am the key—it's like she says in my dream?"

Nyx holds his arm out in front of me, stopping us abruptly, "What dream?"

Shit. I haven't really told him about my nightmares or premonitions, whatever they are. If I want Nyx to trust me, then I need to trust him too. I've never really shared them with anyone other than Lili. I guess that's only because I've never really had any other friends to share them with.

"Not a dream exactly. I have nightmares on occasion, and sometimes they're just that— nightmares. But sometimes they're something else, something more. Lili always called them premonitions because sometimes what haunts me in my sleep becomes a reality in the future."

"When did this start happening, the nightmares that were really premonitions?"

"Not long after my father died." I swallow hard because I

think I know where his thoughts are heading, and I don't want to accept it. I haven't let myself consider it.

"And this nightmare you've had before, someone has told you you're the key?" Nyx asks, rubbing his forehead.

"Yes, I think it was an old woman, but her face was hidden by a hood. I've seen her several times now. She tells me I'm the key and that I have all the power. I just need to unlock it. She also tells me I'm running out of time and I need to choose or it'll be decided for me, and I will destroy us all . . ."

"That's a bit ominous," Nyx says, and a laugh bursts out of me.

"You think?" I slap his shoulder. "What do you think it means?"

"What does it look like when you're in this dream? What are your surroundings?"

"I'm in a forest, only it doesn't look like any of the forests I've ever seen, and it's on fire. It's on fire, and the trees are black and—bleeding."

"Lyra, I don't know what your dream means, but I think I know where you're going and why it's happening." Nyx places his hand to my back, urging me to start walking with him again. "You have midnight mind."

"I thought you said midnight mind died out. You also said it made people go crazy." I start walking faster, feeling anxious now. I knew this was coming. It's the only thing that makes sense. It's the reason I didn't start having the premonitions until after my father passed. I just was hoping it wasn't the case.

"Your father had midnight mind. You're half Fae. It makes perfect sense that he'd pass it on to you. Your dream where you don't recognize the forest—I believe you're visiting Zomea." Nyx matches my pace. "Don't worry. It's not much further. Just around the bend ahead. We can finish discussing this when we get there. Bim and Flora may have some insight."

"I'm not worried."

"Glad to hear it. It just sounds like you're breathing heavily, so I thought you might be."

"No, it's just hot. And yes, I'm a little freaked out. I just learned I'm half Fae and visiting the afterlife in my nightmares."

Once around the bend, we stop outside a wooden gate. Nyx opens it, and we walk down a narrow path into a lovely little garden full of the most spectacular flowers.

"Does Bim garden?" I ask, a bit surprised.

"No, that'd be Flora. She grows different things for healing, and I think she just likes to garden. But I'll be sure to tell Bim you thought he planted all these flowers. He'll be impressed you think so highly of his horticulture skills." He laughs, plucking up a pink flower and tucking it behind my ear.

After zigzagging the gravel path through the gardens, we finally make it to Bim's house. It's a cute two-story cabin with white window panes and a red front door.

"Is he expecting us?" I ask as we climb up the steps to the front door.

"Nope. I thought after last night you'd like to surprise him." Nyx smiles at me and gives the door a firm knock.

CHAPTER
TWENTY-ONE

Before I can hit Nyx on the shoulder for not warning me, Bim opens the door.

"Hey, what are you guys up to?" Bim asks, pulling the door open and extending an arm to invite us in.

"Lyra wanted to see you," Nyx says, and I practically choke on my saliva.

"I bet she did." Bim winks at me and closes the door behind us.

"Um . . . Yes, I want to apologize for my behavior last night." I clear my throat.

"No need to apologize. I love feisty women." Bim laughs, and Nyx elbows him.

Bim's house is simple but cute, and there's definitely a woman's touch here. I assume that's Flora. We go into the kitchen and sit down on a couple of bar stools. Bim hands us each a glass of beer then sits down across from us. The sun is shining through the window and sky lights overhead, but it's nice and cool inside. It must be from magic as well.

"So other than Lyra wanting to see me, what brings you two here?" Bim asks.

"Well, I got to meet Timmy and Polly as well. I also learned what a Riff is today," I tell Bim gleefully.

"What the fuck, Nyx? You saw Polly and didn't bring me a Riff?" Bim laughs and takes a swig of beer.

"I came to talk to you about Cloudrum. I'm taking Lyra to the Lycan Realm," Nyx says, and Bim spits his drink out across the counter.

"What!? Why?" Bim asks.

"She needs answers, and I want to help her get them," Nyx says stoically.

Bim looks over at me before asking, "Answers?"

I start to tell him about the Lycan ceremony, but he already knows most of everything that happened because Nyx relayed it to him earlier. I tell him that I need to speak to Aidan and find the old Sorceress, because they're the only ones who might be able to give me insight into what the ceremony means. I tell him about the prophecy from my father's journal and the midnight mind.

"Samael will be looking for you the moment you set foot back in Cloudrum. It's dangerous." Bim runs his hands through his hair.

"They did something to me. I may feel like myself right now, but what happens when things start changing? I have no idea what they did to my body, what they put inside me. I need answers so I can be prepared before it's too late. I don't want this midnight mind to make me go crazy, and I need to know what being the key means. Is Zomea even something we want to unlock a bridge to?"

A look of understanding crosses his face. "I know, Lyra. I'm sorry. What they did to you—it's despicable. You have every right to know what it means. I just don't know if you'll get the answers you're looking for from Aidan of all people. That guy's a prick." Bim's voice comes out softer.

"I have to try," I tell him with a sense of urgency.

A woman comes into the room. She's beautiful with curly red hair falling over her shoulders as she strides straight toward me. Large chocolate eyes lock onto mine before she grabs me, embracing me in a tight hug.

"Lyra, I'm so glad you're better. We're going to be great friends," Flora says before releasing me.

I'm stunned for a moment but recover quickly. "Thank you, and thank you for healing me."

Flora just smiled and nods at me while pulling a stool over. She folds her deep red wings behind her, settling down next to Bim, whose wings are not out, and I wonder why some of the Fae choose to have them out and some don't. I'll have to remember to ask Nyx about it later. Bim quickly fills Flora in on what we're discussing. I take another drink from my beer, waiting for her to protest us going back to Cloudrum as well.

"Why don't I take Lyra with me to the elder's library today? We can try to find more information on Euric, Zomea, and this prophecy he talks about. If we do, then maybe you won't have to resort to speaking with Aidan at all. If we don't, then I agree you both need to go and find out what you can," Flora says.

"Have you ever exhibited any other unnatural abilities? Other than the premonitions?" Bim asks.

"I don't think so. Why?"

"It's because you're half Fae, and the Sorcerers may come into their magic when they turn nineteen, but the Fae are born with their magic. Not only are we born with magic, but when a parent dies we usually inherit pieces of their magic as well no matter what age we are when it happens," Nyx says.

"What they're both trying to say is if you have midnight mind and your nightmares started after your father's death, then that's something you inherited from him. But you should've been born with some Faery magic of your own as well," Flora says.

"I've never had any abilities as far as I know other than the dreams," I say, trying to think if I've ever felt any kind of magic in myself before.

"Interesting," Bim says, glancing at Nyx.

"There's somewhere I want to take you tonight, but I do have a few things I need to do. Would you like to go to the elder's library with Flora?" Nyx asks, looking at me.

"Yes, that sounds great. I appreciate the help," I say.

"Flora, channel her back to my place before sunset," Nyx says.

Flora gets to her feet and comes around the table to my side. "Are you okay to channel with me?"

I wonder if it feels the same to channel with all Fae. I guess I'm about to find out.

"Yes." I rise to my feet, taking Flora's offered hand. I cast a final glance over my shoulder toward Nyx and Bim before everything turns a brilliant shade of red. The sweet aroma of strawberries from Flora envelops me, and a warm gust of wind begins to lift my hair. Though I can't see anything, I don't feel the same darkness that I did with Nyx. Instead, the gentle red wind tickles my nose as I feel the soft grass beneath my feet. Flora holds onto my hand until I'm steady, and I look up to take in my surroundings. We've arrived at the stunning obsidian palace.

"The elder's library is here at the palace?" I ask quickly. Obviously it's here, because why else would she channel us here? An unusual feeling starts to settle into my stomach at the thought of running into Colton again.

"Yes, Granger has a huge library beneath the palace. It

extends three levels below the ground." Flora says, leading her way up the stairs to the front entrance.

"Do we need permission to go?" I ask.

"I was planning on coming to the library today to do some research on a type of healing magic, so Granger is already expecting me. He's rarely here anyways. I only ever see him when he's throwing a party." A servant answers the front door, and I recognize her right away as the Faery who was holding the tray of stardust with pink flowers in her hair. She's still wearing a green suit but has no flowers today. She and Flora talk quietly for a moment, then she guides us through the palace until we reach a grand black and gold door. She abandons us there without a word, leaving Flora to open the door and lead me down a long, winding staircase. The library's first level sprawls before us, with rows upon rows of towering bookshelves that stretch at least twenty feet high. I'm amazed by the sheer size of the place, and I can't fathom how anyone could reach the books at the top of the aisles without magic. It's overwhelming, and I have no idea where to begin searching for anything.

"How do you know where to start looking?" I ask.

"I don't, but Emmalina will know where we should get started. She oversees the library, and here she comes now."

A petite woman in dark-green robes approached us.

"Hello ladies, how may I be of service?" Emmalina asks. Flora quickly summarizes what we might be looking for and tells her we could split up to cover more ground. Emmalina takes us to the next floor down and shows Flora an aisle where she can get started researching all the different ceremonies held in all the realms. Emmalina leads me down to the bottom level of the library, and I can't help but feel a shiver run down my spine. The air is colder down here, and the lack of light makes it seem eerie. But despite the chill, there's a certain grandeur to the space that leaves me in awe.

The endless rows of towering bookshelves, the intricate carvings on the walls, and the faint scent of old parchment all create a sense of magic and wonder.

"Here we are," Emmalina says, breaking me out of my thoughts. "Take a seat at the table by the fire, and I'll bring you some books that might help with your search." I nod, grateful for the warmth of the fire, and take a seat at the table. As I wait for Emmalina, I can't help but feel a sense of excitement and nervousness. This could be my chance to finally learn about my family's history. After a few minutes, Emmalina returns with a stack of books and places them in front of me. "These are the ones I could find on the Lewis lineage. I hope they're helpful." I thank her, and she gives me a smile before turning to leave. As I open the first book, I can't help but feel a rush of anticipation. The weight of the pages and the smell of the ink only add to the magic of the library. I know this is going to take time, but I'm willing to do whatever it takes to uncover the truth.

It's cold and creepy down here, but I'm so determined to find out more about my family's lineage that I don't mind. After what feels like hours of reading, I'm still no closer to the answers I seek. I let out a frustrated sigh, running a hand through my hair, trying to alleviate some of the stress I'm feeling.

Suddenly, I hear someone clear their throat, causing me to look up from the book. To my surprise, it's Colton, standing on the other side of the table, his intense gaze fixed on me. I feel goosebumps spread across my skin. I still remember the way his hand felt on my thigh last night, but I refuse to let him know that.

"So we meet again," he says with a wink, and I can't help but roll my eyes.

"What are you doing here?" I ask, knowing how silly it sounds since I'm in his home after all.

"How was your night last night? I bet it played out in Nyx's favor. Am I right?" Colton says with a sly smile that only adds to my irritation.

"That's none of your business," I retort, trying to keep my voice steady. "And I'm not under the influence of anything right now, so it might be a little difficult for you to try to take advantage of me again. I'm also very busy, so if you'll excuse me..." I look back down at my book, hoping he'll go away if I ignore him.

To my surprise, Colton closes my book and sits on the table in front of me.

"What are you doing?" I ask in exasperation.

"Still trying to find out more about Euric Lewis?" he asks, ignoring my question and sifting through the stack of books in front of me.

"Don't worry about what I'm trying to do," I say, pushing my chair back to create some distance between us.

"Try this one." He tosses a book at me, the cover blank and unfamiliar.

"Why would you help me?" I ask, confused and wondering what his angle is.

"Let's just say we have a common interest," Colton says, hopping off the table and vanishing into thin air. The scents of citrus and spices linger, and I can't shake the feeling that something isn't right.

I open the book Colton threw at me and start to skim through the pages. It sounds like the rantings of a paranoid lunatic. This was definitely someone's personal journal, but whose? I come across an entry that's signed at the end— Callum. How in the world did Colton have one of Nyx's father's journals? Nyx never told me how his parents died, and I'm starting to wonder if his father went crazy, because his journal is mostly jumbled thoughts, and it's all a bit ominous. He sounds paranoid. I keep skimming the pages until I come across an entry that mentions my father's name. Callum goes on to talk about my father's obsession with Zomea and dark magic. That doesn't sound anything like my father. He'd never do dark magic. Callum sounds like the crazy one from the looks of this journal. Callum admits he banished my father from Nighthold after learning he was working to open some type of connection between Zomea and Eguina where people could pass freely between our world and the afterlife. That seems an awful lot like cheating death. I hear footsteps coming down the stairs, and I quickly tuck the journal into my tights and pull my tunic over it.

"Did you find anything useful?" Flora asks from across the table.

"No, nothing. But I was only able to get through a couple books. Did you find out anything?" I decide not to tell Flora about the journal. It's Nyx's fathers, and maybe he wouldn't want anyone else to see it. Especially if it makes his father come off a little mad.

"I found out a couple things that could be useful. Let me take you back home, and I'll tell you and Nyx about what I found at the same time." Flora extends her hand to me, and I take it, letting her sweet aroma kick up around me with the wind.

~

"Did you two find anything?" Nyx asks from the kitchen, where we find him packing a bag with Twig.

"I didn't find anything, but Flora may have some information. She wanted to wait and tell us both at the same time," I

191

say to Nyx, moving to stand beside him.

He wraps his arm around my shoulder, holding me close while we both look to Flora.

"Okay, I couldn't find anything about the prophecy or Zomea, but I did come across some other information that you two may want to know. I found references to what happens when you consume the blood of a Lycan," Flora says.

I feel my pulse pick up. *Please don't let me turn into a wolf.*

"It says you may start to exhibit some of the Lycan's secondary powers."

"What does that mean? I thought the Lycan didn't have any magic?"

"They don't necessarily have magic in the way a Sorcerer or Faery would, but they do have powers within them and within their lands. The main power within them allows them to have more keen eyesight and hearing than we do, along with their ability to shift into a wolf. But their secondary powers would be more specific to the individual Lycan," Flora says.

Nyx squeezed my shoulder gently. "Do you know what secondary powers the Lycan at the ceremony had? You said the pack leaders came up and talked about all of them during the ceremony. But we don't have to talk about it if you don't want to," Nyx says.

I thought of their faces. Luke, Yuri, and Dawn. There last breaths flashed in my mind, and I had to push the memory away, swallowing hard. "Yes, I remember them. Luke was an exceptional hunter. Yuri was a gifted healer. And Dawn was a skilled tracker."

"Yes, those are their secondary powers. You may start to inherit them to an extent. You may also start to notice you run a little warmer than before. But you shouldn't shift into a wolf," Flora says.

Well, I'm thankful for the last part, I guess.

WHAT LIES BEYOND THE REALMS

"Is there anything else I should know?" Nyx asks.

"Yes, the next blood moon is in two weeks' time," Flora says then bows her head slightly to Nyx and smiles widely at me before channeling.

"Tonight might be the last night I have you to myself for a while. I'm not going to waste it." Nyx just gives me a cocky smirk.

"Wait. Where did she go so abruptly? And what do you mean it may be the last night we're alone for a while?"

"Flora has things to attend to. She's not big on small talk either. Tomorrow night we'll meet Flora and Bim in Nitross, then the following morning you and I leave for Cloudrum."

"What is Nitross?"

"Nitross is the city I grew up in. It's the largest city in Nighthold. It's on the coast, so it'll be our last stop before we make the jump to Cloudrum. But we can talk about that later. Tonight I wanted to take you somewhere."

"What exactly did you have in mind?" My interest is piqued.

"Remember how you said you loved the snow and the mountains?"

"Yes . . ."

"I thought I could take you to stay the night with me at my home in the Fate Fields. Just the two of us."

He's so damn sexy when he's smiling at me like this. How can I deny him?

"Sounds good to me. What should I pack?"

"Nothing. I'll make sure we have everything we need. Let's go tell Twig he's on Chepi duty tonight, then we can leave." Nyx takes my hand and guides me out into the hall.

We find Chepi already with Twig, snacking on slices of meat. I tell Chepi I'll be back tomorrow, and he takes it fine. He's more interested in food than what I have to say at the moment. Should I bring Chepi with us to Nitross and back to Cloudrum? Or should I leave him here? I need to remember to talk to Nyx about that later. Nyx exchanges words with Twig before they both turn their attention back to me.

"Here. Change into these, and I'll pack a few things. Then we can leave," Nyx says, handing me a pile of clothes. I wander into the bathroom adjacent to the dining room and get dressed. I guess tights and a tunic isn't proper attire for the snow. I have on thick fur-lined leggings with a white sweater and white and black jacket on top of that. A black knit hat covers my ears, and I slip into black, fur-lined boots. Feels a bit ridiculous wearing all this in the heat of the jungle. I look in the mirror and laugh a bit, but I'm sure I'll be thankful for all the layers soon enough. I head back to the kitchen, and Nyx appears. He's donning warmer clothing as well, a large black coat and knit hat.

"I heard you like hot chocolate, so I took the liberty of making a special concoction for the two of you," Twig says, shaking a large thermos in front of me before stuffing it into the backpack Nyx holds.

"Yum, thank you, Twig." I wonder what special means. Did he put magic in it?

"Now my home in the Fate Fields is much too far for us to fly. We'll have to channel. It's further than I've ever channeled with you while you've been awake. I just want you to be prepared that it'll take slightly longer than the few seconds it takes to get around here." Nyx pulls the backpack onto his back.

"How long exactly? Will it feel the same?"

"Maybe a couple minutes. It'll be dark, but it'll feel the same as before. I'll be holding onto you the whole time."

"Okay, well, I'm ready when you are." I smile, stepping in close to him and giving Twig and Chepi a little wave.

WHAT LIES BEYOND THE REALMS

Nyx wraps his arms around me and pulls me close. I rest my head on his chest, tangling my hands in his jacket and closing my eyes. His scent envelopes me for a second, then everything goes dark. I hold on tight to Nyx for what feels like several minutes as the wind kicks up around us, wiping my hair in all different directions. I push my face into his chest and close my eyes, then suddenly I feel the brisk cold, and our feet crash into the snow. Nyx releases me but holds out an arm until I'm steady again.

When I look around we're completely secluded and high up in the mountains. White mountain peaks extend in the distance as far as I can see. Some are higher and some are lower than where I stand. It's barely dusk, and the sun has created a soft-orange and pink hue swirling through the sky above the mountaintops. The snow is dense, and all the trees are covered in pillowy white piles.

"It's breathtaking."

"Look up," Nyx says, then a broad smile spreads across his face, almost taking my breath away. Gods, I want him. I look up, and Nyx waves his arm. Candles burst to life above us.

"You have a tree house," I squeal.

There's a wood cabin above us built high into the trees. It's separated into two houses that are connected by a bridge that's covered in candles.

"How do we get up there?" I ask breathlessly.

"With magic," he whispers in my ear, his stubble brushing my cheek.

Nyx kisses my forehead while taking my hand, and we appear up on the bridge. The view is spectacular. Candles line the bridge tucked inside little lanterns. They're dotted in the trees surrounding us as well, creating a warm glow. The bridge is dusted with snow, and I run across it to the larger cabin with Nyx in tow.

As I step inside, I'm greeted by the warm glow of a fire in a cobblestone fireplace. The space is open-plan with a kitchen, living room, and dining area all seamlessly flowing together. The ceilings are high and arched with a spiral staircase leading up to a loft that I assume is the bedroom. In front of the fireplace, I spot a large L-shaped sofa, its cream upholstery dotted with fluffy cream furs. I hurry up the staircase and find a spacious four-poster bed surrounded by sheer white curtains. The bed is dressed in a white down comforter, inviting me in. Although the house isn't large, its coziness and romantic ambiance more than make up for its size.

"What's across the bridge?" I turn to Nyx, who's been following me as I "oooh" and "aaah" at everything.

"Let's go find out," he says, pointing for me to lead the way.

I sprint back across the bridge and into the smaller cabin. To my surprise, the entire cabin is made of glass with a ceiling like a giant sunroom. In the center of the room, I find a massive sunken-in tub surrounded by benches on all sides. The sight is breathtaking, and I can already feel myself unwinding in this serene space.

"It's a stargazing tub. Wait until you see it when it's completely dark out here," Nyx says.

"It's fantastic, and I cannot wait to use it."

"Are you hungry?" he asks, and my mouth starts to salivate because all I've eaten today was a Riff.

"I'm starving."

"Come on. Let's go eat in front of the fireplace, then we can take off a few layers of clothes." He flashes me a playful smile.

I follow him back across the bridge into the main cabin. He helps me out of my jacket, then I remove my boots, sweater, and hat.

"Much better," he says, walking over to the couch after having removed his boots and jacket as well.

"So what's for dinner?" I raise a brow, looking at the backpack in his hands.

"I wanted to keep it simple, so I had the chef whip up some sandwiches. I hope that's okay." He hands me a sandwich.

"It's perfect. Thank you." I take the sandwich and don't waste time biting into it.

We both eat relatively quickly, neither of us speaking much because we're both really hungry.

"And for dessert..." Nyx says, making two mugs appear in our hands. He fills them with the hot chocolate Twig made, rainbow sprinkles floating at the surface. I lean back into the cushions and tuck my feet underneath me, sipping the hot chocolate. It's delicious, and the warmth coats my stomach.

"When Twig said he made this hot chocolate special for us, was he implying he tampered with it somehow?"

"You know I wouldn't put it past him, but he just wants us to have a good time."

I'm not sure what that means. A part of me wishes I questioned Twig more about it before we left, but I keep drinking it anyway. It's delicious, and I could use a good time, especially knowing what the coming days hold.

"How do we get from Nighthold to Cloudrum? How do we cross the Feral Sea?" I ask, moving to angle my body toward him.

"Well there's a couple ways it can be done. There's a portal in Nitross that takes you straight into the black forest."

"Is that how you got me here when I was unconscious?"

"No. Only Fae can move through the portal. I didn't think it was safe for you, and I didn't want to risk it." He takes another drink of hot chocolate.

"But I am at least half Fae. I have Fae blood inside of me." I state this like he doesn't already know.

"Yes, your Fae blood should mean you can sense the portal. It may even be one of the reasons your mother kept you away from the black forest. If she was hiding the fact that you are half Fae, she wouldn't want to have to explain to you about the portal. If she even knew about the portal. I can't be sure," Nyx says.

Thinking about my mother makes a knot form in my chest. Deep down I love her, and a part of me may even miss her at times, but I also hate her for the way she treated me. I hate her for selling me out to Aidan. She wasn't a good person, and I worry that whatever darkness lingered inside her bloodline could manifest in me when I turn nineteen. As the date approaches, I can't help the uneasy feeling I get sometimes. What if I were to inherit dark magic? A Sorcerer hasn't inherited dark magic in so long this would be nearly impossible, but I can't help the lingering wariness in my chest.

"Hey, where did you go just now?" Nyx waves a hand in front of my face, drawing me from my thoughts.

"Nowhere. So how did we cross?" I asked, shaking my head.

"We flew, and we'll fly again this time."

"You flew all that way carrying me?"

"No, the Feral Sea is vast. I could probably do it in a pinch, but it would be draining, even for me. We rode on Quazie," he says.

"Who and what is Quazie?"

"He's a Quetzalcoatlus. They're very rare, and there are only about a dozen of them alive today."

"A Quetza what? What's that?"

"Think of him as a giant bird. His wingspan alone is the length of three horses standing head to tail."

"Wow, I can't wait to see him." I finish the last of my hot chocolate and mull over everything Nyx told me.

I can't believe all this time there was a portal to the Faery Realm practically in my backyard. I wonder if Samael knows it's there or if my mother knew about it. Maybe Nyx is right and that's one of the reasons she kept me from the black forest. My mother may have been strict with me my entire life and not exactly a loving mother, but I still want to know what her motives were. I need to know why she died. I wonder what Samael's investigation at the castle found out. Not that I can believe anything that comes out of his mouth. I know he had something to do with their deaths. If they didn't die by his hand, then he certainly orchestrated it.

"Did you ever learn anything about how my mother and Silas died? There was an investigation, or at least that's what I was told."

"Samael told everyone it was a carriage accident and that they were on their way back home from visiting the Lamia Realm. But we both know it wasn't an accident," Nyx says softly, like he's trying not to upset me. "Do you want to talk about it?" He places his hand in my lap on top of mine.

"No," I say quietly, looking down at our entwined hands.

The hot chocolate relaxes me. I have a little bit of the happy, feel-good feeling I remember from my first breakfast with Twig. I wonder if everything he makes has this effect.

"Can we go in the water?" I ask Nyx, pulling him out of whatever deep thoughts he's caught up in. His eyes look heavy, like he's worried or maybe just tired.

"Yes, of course. I've been thinking about getting you naked all day." He gives me a wicked grin, getting off the couch and pulling me up with him.

"Do you have any whiskey?" I look back at him as I walk toward the front door.

"Yes . . ." he says slowly, like he knows I'm up to no good.

"Great. Grab it and meet me across the bridge." I run out the door.

CHAPTER
TWENTY-TWO

I step out onto the bridge and quickly realize that I'm underdressed for the freezing weather. Despite the discomfort, I power through and run to the other side, my bare feet sinking into the snow. A sharp pain shoots up my ankles, but I push though it and make it inside. To my relief, I see that the water in the tub is already steaming hot with light-pink bubbles frothing across the surface. Nyx must have used magic to have it ready for me. I quickly strip off my clothes and lower myself into the water. The change in temperature is jarring, but as the needle-like sensation subsides, I sink into the water and sit on one of the benches. The water is pure bliss, and I can feel my body start to relax. The scent of fresh berries, citrus, and vanilla wafts up, and I can tell that the water has been infused with some kind of magical elixir. Whether it's the hot water or the hot chocolate, I feel more relaxed and at peace than I have in a long time.

Nyx rushes in with a bottle in hand and strips off his clothes. He rushes into the water so fast I don't even get a chance to enjoy his body.

"Too cold out there for the big strong Faery?" I giggle.

"Very funny. I told you I'm not a huge fan of the snow or the cold. That's why I like living in the jungle."

"Let's play a game," I say to him, grabbing the bottle of whiskey and bringing it over to the ledge next to us.

"What kind of game do you have in mind, Princess?" Nyx tugs me closer to him so I'm standing between his legs, and he's sitting on the bench.

"How about we take turns asking each other questions? If you choose to answer, you have to answer honestly. If you don't want to answer, you have to take a drink of whiskey."

I raise my brow and let my arms fall next to me, running my fingertips along his muscled thighs.

"It sounds like you're trying to get me drunk so you can have your way with me." He smirks.

"Who me? I'm just an innocent young girl. I'd never . . ." I can't help but laugh. "You'll only get drunk if you're not forthcoming." This time I wink at him, and he smiles.

"Okay, you're on, Lewis. Ladies first?" He takes the bait, and now I need to rack my brain. I know there's a million things I want to ask him, but I'm suddenly drawing a blank. I must make my questions count.

"Have you ever been in love?" I ask even though I'm afraid of the answer.

"No."

"Why not?" It seems odd for someone so old to have never been in love.

"Let's just say I've been waiting for the right person. Now that was two questions. I'll let it slide this time." Nyx flashes a furtive grin, and I can't help the fluttering feeling that starts in my chest.

"Have you ever been intimate with someone?" he asks.

I look away, not wanting to entertain his question or risk facing the onslaught of inquiries that could follow. I quickly seize the whiskey, offer him a sheepish grin, and down the fiery liquid. Thank the gods for the rules. He regards me with a doubtful expression but refrains from further interrogation. Now it's my turn to ask a question.

"How powerful are you exactly?"

"Well, I'm the most powerful Faery alive today," he tells me, and I instantly have multiple follow-up questions. But I just wait for him to take his turn, filing my questions away for later.

"What do you want out of life?"

For a moment, I'm caught off guard, and I'm not sure how to answer his question. It's not that I don't have dreams or desires, but they always seem so far out of reach, like wispy clouds on the horizon. The question of what I want out of life feels like an invitation to confess my deepest, most secret wishes.

I laugh nervously, feeling a bit foolish. But as I look into his eyes, something stirs inside of me. They are the kindest eyes I've ever seen, warm and gentle, with a playful glint to them and I can tell that he genuinely wants to know. He's listening to me so intently, as if what I have to say truly matters.

"I want to be free," I begin, my voice barely above a whisper. "I want to break free from the chains that bind me, the fears and doubts that hold me back. I want to experience life fully, to take risks and explore new things. I want to fall in love and start a family someday, to build a home and a life for myself."

As I speak, I feel a warmth spreading through my chest. These are the things that I've always longed for, but never dared to say out loud. But now, with him listening, I feel emboldened. "I dream of living on a farm, surrounded by animals, and taking care of those who cannot care for themselves. I want to help heal the world, in my own small way. I want to make a difference."

As the words spill out, I can feel my heart racing. This is the first time I've ever truly spoken about my deepest desires, the things that used to keep me up at night. But as I look at him, I know that I've found someone who understands. Someone who sees the world in the same way that I do.

"My turn," I exclaim before he can comment about what I divulged. "You say you're the most powerful Faery alive today. Who is more powerful than you if not a Fae? Also, have you always been this powerful? Were you born with all your power?"

He plants his lips in a flat line. "That's like ten questions, but I'll do my best to appease you." Nyx leans forward, his eyes focused and intense as he speaks. "I say I'm the most powerful Fae because it's not easy to gauge the power of the other realms," he explains. "Aidan, for example, is an older Lycan with pure brute strength. That alone may not make him the most powerful, but the force of all the packs behind him is not something to scoff at. Drew, on the other hand, is the leader of the Lamia, and the Lamia have always been a bit mysterious. I know she's powerful, but the extent of her power remains unknown to me, and honestly I hope I never have to find out. As for Samael, he could become incredibly powerful if he ever learns to harness his magic properly. He's always been known as a powerful Sorcerer, and if he does find the spell he's looking for in the grimoires to make his magic dark, I don't know what that would do to his powers."

Nyx pauses for a moment, his expression thoughtful. "He's also the only child of Silas, which means that when Silas

WHAT LIES BEYOND THE REALMS

passed Samael would have inherited some of his power," he continues. "When a parent passes, the power always goes to the oldest child, but not always all of it. It's just random what one gets." He leans back, his gaze never leaving mine.

"As for your other question," Nyx says, his voice softening, "I was born with my power. I was always very powerful growing up, but when my parents passed I inherited all of my father's power and a sliver of my mother's power, making me the strongest Fae alive today."

"What do you think will happen with my magic? I often wonder what my powers will look like when I turn nineteen. If I'm being honest, I'm also a bit afraid of what my magic will be like."

What if my magic is dark?

He takes pity on me. "You are a bit of a conundrum. You're half Fae, which means I would expect you to have been born with some magic inside you. Not to mention I would have expected some of your father's powers to have manifested inside of you after he died. We know you inherited midnight mind, but maybe the rest was such a small amount it went unnoticed. Since your mother was a Sorceress I imagine you'll gain some or all of her power when you turn nineteen and your magic comes to life. Now it's my turn. This time I'm just taking a drink because I'm thirsty," he says grabbing the bottle and taking a swig. "Has anyone other than Samael hurt you?"

The question puts a knot in my stomach. "Yes," I answer simply, and it looks like he clenches his jaw but doesn't press for more information.

"What are you afraid of?" I try to change the subject.

"War," he says. I want him to elaborate, but if I'm giving one-word answers I can't complain when he does. The only war I've ever heard of was the War of the Realms. I know very little about it, only that it was hundreds of years ago and is what separated the realms.

"Who else has hurt you?" Nyx pulls me from my train of thought. If I tell him it was Aidan, then he won't want to take me to the Lycan Realm. I have no choice but to grab the bottle and take a drink. I can tell by the look in his eye he's disappointed with my lack of response, but I just shrug my shoulders. That's the game.

"The War of the Realms was before you were born. Why are you afraid of war?" I hope he doesn't take a drink just to spite me.

"Did you learn anything about the War of the Realms growing up?" He answers my question with a question, but I play along.

"Not much. Just that it was a very long time before I was born, and it's what divided the Realms, causing everyone to segregate."

"My parents and your father fought in the War of the Realms. The war wasn't about segregation. That just happened to be one of the outcomes when things settled. Before the war there was no Nighthold or Cloudrum. The Feral Sea didn't split the land but surrounded it instead. All the Realms were connected, and the continent was called Eguina."

"What in all the realms has the power to split the earth like that?"

"It's what lies beyond the realms," Nyx says, and an uneasy feeling sparks to life in my chest.

"Zomea."

"But how?" I forget about the game for the moment.

"Zomea is not fully understood. It's hard to understand something we've never seen, hard to grasp the idea of an alternate universe let alone an afterlife. A group of Sorcerers wanted to unlock Zomea, but many of the Fae were against it, especially the ones with midnight mind. The Fae with midnight mind were the only ones who could see Zomea and probably understood it more than anyone else. The war went on for years, and it came to a head when Zomea was unlocked."

"Who unlocked it and how?"

"I don't know how it was unlocked, but a group of Sorcerers ultimately found a way to unlock it. The ground shook for days. Huge cracks formed in the earth and grew so large you could no longer see land on the other side. Fire erupted from volcanoes that had been silent for millennia, spewing molten lava that consumed everything in its path. The sky turned black as night, and ash rained down like a deadly snowstorm, choking the air and suffocating the land. Your father Euric is the one who was able to close Zomea for good. Then our fathers set out to kill everyone who knew how to unlock it, and most of the Fae with midnight mind were slaughtered in the process as well. Once the land was split and there was a big divide between the Fae and the Sorcerers, my parents claimed Nighthold and your ancestors claimed Cloudrum. Over the years, the realms were formed, and the Lycan and Lamia fell into place, having their own territories as well. To this day Zomea is rarely spoken about, and not much is taught about the war because most literature on it has since been destroyed in one of the largest cover-ups in history—orchestrated by our fathers."

I move to sit next to him. I need a moment to process.

"Come here." Nyx pulls me onto his lap, and my legs wrap comfortably around his back.

"I just don't understand why my father would fight so hard to close Zomea then put the very key that opens it inside me, his only daughter. Why was he trying to open it again if doing so hurt so many?"

His eyes wander away from me, and I can tell he's thinking of something else, but what?

"The difference is the prophecy Euric wrote about says you are the key to unlocking a bridge to Zomea, not unlocking Zomea itself. I spoke with Granger about this, and he believes by unlocking a bridge to Zomea it would be like a portal of sorts where you could travel there physically. Now you can go there in your dreams, and it's random. You don't have control. Unlocking a bridge would mean you or anyone else could practically walk into Zomea. At least that is the theory. Granger didn't know of there ever being a bridge or portal to Zomea before." Nyx takes a sip of whiskey, distracted. I wonder if he's not telling me everything.

"Are you sure you can trust Granger? I wish you'd have told me you were going to talk to him about me."

"Yes, we can trust him. And you're right. I'm sorry. Next time I'll include you."

"Do all the elders live in that palace together?"

Nyx picks up curly pieces of my hair playing with them. "No, they don't. The palace is Granger's home, just him and his family live there."

"When I met Colton, I assumed he was an elder because he told me that was his home."

"Colton didn't lie. I'm sure he just tried to manipulate the situation because that's what Colton does. Granger is Colton's father, so it's his home, but he's not an elder." Nyx runs his hand in slow circles down my back, and his touch feels so nice.

"That explains why I ran into him in the library earlier today." Nyx's hand is still on my back. "Why didn't you say anything earlier?"

"I'm saying something now. What's the deal with you two anyways. Is he a friend?"

His hand seems to relax, his fingertips drawing lazy circles on my skin. "He's not a friend. We have a complicated history —I don't trust him. What did he say to you in the library?"

I glance over at my pile of clothes. Nyx's father's journal is still tucked into my pants out of sight. I don't know why exactly, but I decide to keep it to myself. "He didn't say much, just asked what I was doing, and I gave him a vague answer. Then he left."

"Good. Enough talk of war and the past. We're here together right now. Let's enjoy tonight." He gently takes my chin in his hand and kisses me softly.

"Your fingers look like prunes. Are you ready to go up to bed?"

"Yes, I think so, although I'm not looking forward to running across the bridge again."

"Lucky for you I can help with that."

Nyx channels us to the bedroom, and we're immediately dry and warm. I'm still wrapped around him, and he carries me to the bed, pulling the comforter back and laying me down. I sink into the down blankets and revel in the soft white sheets. Nyx crawls into bed next to me, pulling me close to him. I turn onto my side to face him and look up, finding his eyes on me. He's seemed tense all night, and I wonder what might be bothering him, but I don't want to ask. Instead I kiss him.

I press my lips against his, savoring the taste of his mouth as our bodies entwine. The sensation of his bare skin against mine is electric, and I can feel his hardness against me. It's all I can think about, the desire to feel him inside of me. But a part of me is scared, scared of what this means, scared of moving too fast and ruining everything. I want to make him feel good, but I'm not sure if I'm capable, especially after all the other women he's been with. Despite my doubts, I try to relax and let myself take control. I push him gently onto his back, never breaking our embrace as I straddle him.

As I explore his body with my lips, his hands gently caress every inch of me. I can feel his fingers tracing along my lower back and squeezing my ass. I pull away from his mouth, kissing my way down his chest and across his collarbone then down his stomach. I pause just below his belly button, looking up at him with anticipation. His eyes are locked on mine, and I can see the lust burning within them. I take a deep breath and run my tongue along his waist, tracing the muscles there.

With one hand, I slowly stroke him from the base of his cock to the tip, savoring every inch of his length. A small bead of liquid gathers at the top, and I use my tongue to taste his salty pleasure. I let my tongue dance around the head of his cock, savoring the sensation of his skin against my lips. As I stroke him with my hand, I look up at him again and see the intensity in his gaze. I meet his stare and take him into my mouth, sucking hard as I explore every inch of him.

"Fuck, Lyra," comes out in a strangled whisper.

I suck, moving my mouth up and down, twirling my tongue around the tip and lightly massaging his balls with my hand. I pull away for a moment.

"Am I doing it right?" I ask, wanting to be sure it's what he likes.

"You couldn't do it wrong," he says, and I move my mouth over him again. This time he tangles his hands in my hair and gently guides me up and down while I suck him. Each time I go down I try to take him further into my mouth, gagging when the tip hits the back of my throat. I suck him harder and faster, letting his hands set the pace.

"Lyra, I'm going to come," he says, releasing my head, but I don't stop. I want to taste him. I want to feel his release. I twirl my tongue and suck until I feel him twitch in my mouth, and I swallow his warm pleasure. I lick him clean then relax next to him on my back, feeling proud of myself for making him come.

"Gods, I don't deserve you," Nyx says, rolling onto his side to face me.

I just smile at him, but then he pulls the covers back, exposing my body. I don't know why I feel self-conscious when his eyes linger over me slowly. He's seen me naked before. He kneels down between my legs, pushing them apart. Panic shoots through my chest like a thousand needle pricks.

"Wait, what are you doing?" I plead, trying to stop his face before he drops down any lower.

"I want to pleasure you. I let you taste me. Now it's my turn," he says, and my stomach knots.

"I've never...I mean, no one has ever gone down there like that before. I don't know," I mutter, tongue-tied.

Nyx whispers hotly against my skin, "Relax. It'll feel good. Just lie back and let me taste you." I try to comply, but my body is taut with anticipation. Nyx leans over me, his lips placing feather-light kisses along the inside of my thigh. The scratch of his stubble sends shivers down my spine. As he slowly spreads my lips with his tongue, I can't help but squirm. He steadies me with his arms, spreading me and pulling me closer to him.

His tongue finds its way inside me, causing me to gasp at the sensation. He trails his tongue back up to the bundle of nerves at my center and sucks gently, his tongue moving in tantalizing circles around my nub of flesh while he slips a finger inside me. My fingers fumble to grip the sheets beneath me, my body writhing beneath his touch.

"So wet for me, Lyra," Nyx murmurs. He pulls his finger all the way out and then pushes two back inside me, eliciting another moan from my mouth. He starts to move his fingers faster and deeper, each thrust sending waves of pleasure through my body.

As he fills and stretches me with his fingers, his tongue never stops, exploring every inch of me until it feels like I'm going to burst. "I want you to come for me, Lyra," he says, his words almost undoing me. "I want to taste you."

My heart is racing against my chest, my breathing quickening as I arch my back, consumed with pleasure. Nyx keeps licking and sucking, his tongue never relenting, until I finally find release, my body shaking with the force of my orgasm. He keeps licking me and thrusting inside of me, prolonging my pleasure until my breathing slows and my legs stop trembling. Only then does he slowly pull out his fingers, licking them clean, and pull the blankets back over us.

"So sweet you are, Lyra," he says, licking his lips and pulling me close. My body feels spent, like jelly, and I revel in the warmth of his embrace.

"Gods, I really don't deserve you," Nyx sighs, wrapping his arms around me.

"Stop saying that," I reply, running my fingers across his arm. "You do deserve me. You're a good man, Onyx. You're the only man to ever treat me like I matter."

"Well, that makes me want to kill all the men in your life," he says, squeezing me a little tighter. I turn to face him.

"I've never felt this way before," I admit.

"How do you feel?" he asks.

"I dunno. It's silly... I know I haven't known you for very long, but it feels like I've known you forever."

"I know what you mean," he says, his eyes intense. "I only just got you in my bed, but I already cannot bear the thought of another man touching you. I don't ever want to let you go." The possessiveness in his tone sends a thrill through me, turning me on even more.

"You won't have to. I don't plan on going anywhere." I place a kiss on his mouth and nestle my head into his chest. I savor the moment, feeling the warmth of his embrace and the beat of his heart against my cheek. His strong arms wrap around me, pulling me closer, as if he never wants to let me go.

I fall asleep in his arms listening to the storm outside, thinking that no night could be any more perfect than this.

CHAPTER
TWENTY-THREE

Something's burning! I'm crawling as fast as I can across the forest floor. My knees are stinging from plants stabbing and slicing at me. I'm trying to crawl away from the fire, but flames keep bursting to life in front of me, like they're coming for me. My skin is drenched in warm blood from the trees. It's hard to see where I'm going. A wolf runs past me, brushing against my side and causing me to fall over. I wonder if it's Luke. I jump back up, trying to regain my footing. I squint into the smoke, but my eyes are burning, and I can't see the wolf anymore. I run but don't make it far before I trip over something and go flying face-first into the ground. A set of arms grab me and pull me to my feet.

"Luke."

"He's looking for you, Lyra," he says.

"Who's looking for me? What do you mean?"

"He wants you for himself. You must stay away." He's shaking me, and I feel the heat of the fire surrounding us. "Go now, Lyra."

I GASP AWAKE, disoriented. Then I hear Nyx breathing next to me, and I place my hand over my chest to calm myself. I'm covered in sweat, and the sheets are soaked. Thank the gods Onyx is sleeping. I relax back into the pillows. What does it mean? I've had dreams like this before with Luke, but this one seemed so real. It has to be the midnight mind. I have to be visiting Zomea. What's going on there? Why is everything burning? Was he warning me to stay away from Samael? I need to figure out how to stay in the dream longer. If my father mastered it, then I know I can too. I wish there was someone else with midnight mind I could talk to who could help me. Maybe the elders remember what it was like for the Fae with midnight mind and have an idea of how to control it. I'm afraid if I don't learn how to control it, it's going to make me go crazy.

I listen to the slow breathing of Nyx next to me and stare out the window at the snowflakes collecting on the sill. Just when I think I'm never going to be able to fall back asleep, my eyes start to feel heavy. For a split second I think I've fallen into a dream again when a quick burst of light and a flash of purple appears in front of the window. Nyx sits up next to me, and I know I'm not dreaming. I sit up, blinking the heaviness out of my eyes. The purple figure comes into focus, and I realize it's Twig. Nyx waves a hand, bringing all the candles in the room back to life.

"Twig, what's wrong?" he asks.

A sudden sense of panic hits me.

"Is Chepi alright?" I ask quickly, pulling the sheets up to my neck.

"Yes, I'm sorry. I don't mean to alarm you. A letter arrived at the castle only moments ago, and it's spelled." Twig flies closer to the bed, hovering above our feet.

"Spelled how?" Nyx asks, studying Twig.

"It just appeared, and I don't know how to explain it, but I felt a sense of urgency to bring it to you when I touched it. It's addressed to Lyra." Twig pulls the envelope out of his pocket and offers it to me. Nyx takes it before I even think about moving.

"Enchanted mail is rare, old magic. It could be a trap from Samael. Do you recognize the writing or the seal?" Nyx asks, showing me the envelope.

I grab it, recognizing the writing immediately.

"It's from Lili. This is her handwriting." I turn it over in my hands. I had no idea she knew how to send enchanted mail, but I guess there's never been a reason for me to know that.

"If you won't be needing anything else, I'll take my leave." Twig tilts his head to Nyx, his beautiful translucent wings glowing in the candlelight.

"No. Thank you, Twig. You may go."

Twig disappears in a small burst of wind. Nyx moves closer to me, wrapping his arm around my shoulder.

"Are you alright? Do you want me to open it?" I've been so stressed hoping Lili is okay and wondering what is going on back home. My hands start to quiver. I can't imagine she'd be sending me good news. I tear the envelope open, pulling out the parchment and unfolding it slowly. I hold it between us so Nyx can read it with me.

My darling Lyra,

I wanted to write to you sooner, but things have been unpredictable at the castle of late. King Samael has been frantic since you left. Each day you are away I worry the castle grows colder, and a darkness has started to loom over Tempest Moon. I can feel it in my bones.

Samael disappears for days at a time, and no one knows where he goes. When he's here, he spends all of his time

locked in his chambers, and I can hear screams coming from his wing of the castle in the dead of night. I was able to sneak back into the library and read more of your father's journals. I found an alarming passage, and I knew I had to risk sending it to you as soon as possible. I don't know what it means exactly, but I fear for you, Lyra, and I fear for all of us if Samael isn't stopped.

I know what he did to you that night. I know what he did to you all those nights, and I am a coward for never speaking up, for never helping you. I live with the guilt every day. I was afraid to speak against the prince, and I tried to turn a blind eye to it. It wasn't fair to you, Lyra, and I do not blame you if you never forgive me for not sticking up for you. I know I can never make up for it, but I promise I will do everything in my power to help you now. I will keep researching your father's journals and send you anything I find that may be helpful. I know you are safer with King Onyx than you ever were here. Don't ever come back. I don't know what Samael will do if he gets a hold of you. May the gods save us all.

Lili

Tears stain my cheeks, and Nyx leans in, wiping them away softly with his fingers. He places a kiss to my damp temple. "I'm with you now, Lyra, and I won't let anything happen to you. I'll handle Samael. His days are numbered."

"I want to be the one to end him. He must be stopped before he hurts anyone else. Who knows what horrible things he's planning."

"We'll end him together then." Nyx brushes my hair out of my face, and I reach into the envelope pulling out the tattered piece of folded-up parchment, the piece that must be from my father's journal. I hold my breath, unfolding the weathered page gently.

It's too late now. I've already placed the key inside her. I

didn't know it could destroy her. I cannot let Macy get wind of this. I will keep visiting Zomea until I find a way to fix this. I don't care about the risks. If I cannot find a way to fix the key, I can only pray to the gods she unlocks the bridge before the key consumes her. I will resurrect Athalda to start planting failsafes now. I feel it...my time is running out. Someday the bridge will be the only way I can get her back.

I drop the page onto the bed. A wave of shock crashes into me, and I feel my chest tighten, and my heart starts racing. I don't want any of this. What is this key inside me? And if my father never found a way to fix whatever he did—the key will consume her—me. I suddenly feel I might be ill. Nyx picks up the page, reading it over again.

"Fuck Euric, and fuck leaving fate to the gods. Lyra, I can feel your heart racing. It's going to be alright. I promise. We'll figure this out together." His hand comes up to my cheek, coaxing me to face him. I turn, meeting his gaze, those gray eyes glowing slightly.

"Breathe." He places a kiss on my forehead, and I focus on the touch of his warm lips.

"Nyx, this means I have no choice but to unlock the bridge to Zomea. If not, I could die. I must find Aidan soon. I need to know what he knows about everything, and I need to know who Athalda is."

"Hey, come here, Princess." Nyx pulls me into his lap, brushing my hair out of my damp face. "Remember, you're so unbelievably strong. You've been through so much, Lyra, and you didn't let anything break you. And now, now you have me, and we'll get through this together."

I relax against his chest, letting his touch calm me. He's right. I will not let this break me. "If only I had my magic, I'd feel less helpless at least. I'm still months away from getting any real power of my own." I sigh, readjusting.

"There's something I want to talk to you about. I've been waiting to tell you because I didn't want to give you any false hopes." Nyx sits up straighter.

"What is it?" I ask, lifting my head to look at him.

"We might be able to help you get your magic before you turn nineteen. Not your Sorceress magic, which will have to wait until your birthday, but your Fae magic is a different story."

"What do you mean? I thought you said it's possible I only have midnight mind."

"You said you didn't start having these vivid nightmares until after your father passed, right?"

"Right," I say, turning in his lap to fully face him now.

"I believe Euric found a way to suppress your Fae magic when you were born to protect your identity and his. I think when he died, his magic did probably go to you, at least a portion of it, but I wouldn't be surprised if even in death he found a way to suppress that too. The midnight mind is different. Maybe he wanted you to have it so he could eventually communicate with you, or maybe he couldn't control it, because Zomea is powerful and a bit of a mystery to us all."

I feel the unease start to slice through my chest again.

"What does this mean?" I ask.

"At the party, I told you I needed to talk to Granger. He might have a way to restore your powers. I asked him to investigate it for me first thing in the morning. I want to take you to the palace to meet with him but only if you want to."

"Of course, I want to," I exclaim. The thought of possibly getting my magic, and not just my magic but a piece of my father—gods, I'm just getting used to the idea that my father was Fae and I am half Fae, and now to know I could have had magic inside me this whole time.

"Are you alright?" Nyx asks, pulling me from my spiral of thoughts.

"Yes, just anxious. When do we leave?"

Nyx tucks a piece of my hair behind my ear. "It's still a couple hours until dawn, but if you can't go back to sleep we can take a bath and get ready now."

There's absolutely no way I can go back to sleep after the letter from Lili, the piece of my father's journal and now the possibility of having magic.

"A bath would be great."

"Wait here." Nyx goes into the bathroom. I hear the bath start to fill and let my head fall back on the pillows. I cannot believe I might have actual magic in just a few short hours.

"Lyra, this is my wife, Elspeth. I believe she can help you," Granger says from across the room where his wife sits at a table.

"Pleasure to meet you," I say, moving closer to the table. His wife isn't as frail-looking as I thought she'd be given she's well over a thousand years old. She doesn't even have gray hairs yet like her husband. Instead, chestnut-brown waves hug her heart-shaped face. But it isn't her youthful appearance that catches me off guard. It's her eyes, which shimmer a yellow, gold color that's quite mesmerizing.

"I'd like to speak with Lyra alone," Elspeth says, looking to Nyx then to Granger. Nyx's hand came up just then, touching the small of my back.

"I don't think that's a good idea," he says.

I appreciate him wanting to stay with me, and his touch brings me more comfort than he knows, but I need to know what Elspeth has to say and if she can help me.

"I'm alright," I say, moving just out of his reach. My body feels colder and misses his touch already. He looks at me like he's about to protest again.

"Really," I say quickly.

"Come, let us go find a couple drinks downstairs," Granger says to Nyx, waving him toward the door.

He quickly kisses my temple. "I'll be right downstairs if you need anything," he says quietly, then they were gone.

"Please come sit next to me," Elspeth says while pulling out the chair at her side. I hesitantly approached the table and take the seat she offers.

"The daughter of Euric Lewis in the flesh," she muses.

I'm not quite sure what to say to that, so I stay silent.

"You have his eyes you know. The cerulean and emerald eddied against each other like two seas not meant to mix. I'd recognize those eyes anywhere."

"Thank you." I clear my throat, feeling a bit uncomfortable under her gaze.

"Did Onyx tell you why he brought you here today?"

"He says you may know a way to help me get my Fae magic, that my father may have suppressed it inside me to hide my identity."

"Euric always was ahead of his time. Always scheming and never quite satisfied with what he had." She turns her body so our knees met. "Did Onyx tell you how I may be able to release your magic?"

"No, he didn't," I say finally.

"Your father was an expert telepath. I believe this is how he was able to hide your magic without you having knowledge of it. I have a similar gift, a form of telepathy if you will. It's called mind walking."

"Yes. I remember reading in the Lewis Lineage that one of

his abilities was telepathy. "What is mind walking and how do you think it can help me?"

"If you'll allow it, I can enter your mind. I'll have to go deep into your memories and your childhood to try to find what Euric buried. By recovering these memories, I believe I can restore your Fae magic."

"Will it be painful?"

"It will not be pleasant, which is why I asked to speak with you alone. I don't think Onyx would let you follow through with it if he knew the risks. But I believe it should be your choice and your choice alone."

A chill works its way up my spine. No matter how unpleasant this process may be, I have to try.

"I want you to do it. See if you can recover my magic." I sit up straighter.

"Let me first explain the risks—"

"I don't want to know them. It'll make no difference in my decision," I say, interrupting her.

"Very well. Then let's get started. I'd like you to lie down for me," Elspeth says, getting to her feet and walking over to a chaise lounge in the corner of the room. I situate myself by lying down on my back, and Elspeth pulls a chair over, sitting directly to my left.

"I want you to find a spot on the ceiling and try to focus on that spot while clearing your mind. Take this pillow and feel free to squeeze it."

I take the pillow from her and hold it to my chest, tangling my fingers in the tassels hanging off the corners. I find a small crack in the ceiling and let my eyes lock onto it. I'm not sure how to clear my mind, so I just try to think about my breathing. I take a long, slow inhale through my nose and pause before letting the air slowly leave my lungs. I don't know what to expect. I wonder if maybe she'll place a hand on my forehead like Nyx did when he forced me to sleep. Then it hits me.

My nails dig into the pillow as I feel her push into my head, but not physically. Physically she doesn't touch me at all, but I feel her presence brush against the inside walls of my mind. Mental shields I didn't know I had seem to fight back as she tries to find an opening. I stare at the chipped paint around the crack in the ceiling. *Breathe in.* I feel the moment she gets past my shield because I have a moment of reprieve. *Breathe out.* A sharp pain slices through my skull as I feel her dig deeper into my mind, peeling back layers of memories.

It feels like time has slowed, and I don't know how much more of this I can take. Memories I didn't even know I had fly across my thoughts like I'm viewing them through a moving window. It's a window that moves too fast for me to focus and make sense of anything. I hold the pillow tighter to my chest. I don't blink as wet tears stain my cheeks. Suddenly the images slow, and what were blurry scrambles of faces and places now become clearer. I see my father and the image is so real, so vivid. I know this is my memory, but it's like he's here in front of me. *Breathe.*

"Euric, are you sure this is a good idea?" a woman says. It's not just any woman. I recognize the scars across her face—it's the old Sorceress. How have I never remembered this before? How could I forget her scarred face and black eyes? Before my father can respond, Elspeth pushes past the memory. She digs her claws in deeper, and a scream dies in my throat as I try to cope with the pain. Now I see my father pacing in front of me. A dark shadow of some type of creature is behind him. I can't see clearly, but a terrible, cold feeling presses into my chest, and I squeeze the pillow tighter to me.

"Hold on, Lyra. I'm almost there," Elspeth says, but it sounds like she's very far away, her voice barely a whisper.

"I'm sorry, my little pixie. One day you'll understand," my father says before pressing a kiss to my forehead.

A fire erupts inside my chest, the heat spreading through my body. It feels like I'm burning alive from the inside out and I swear the bloodstone at my neck starts to vibrate. This time I know a scream leaves my lips. I clutch the pillow panting. I feel Elspeth's grasp on my mind recede, and I blink at the blurry crack in the ceiling above me. The heat subsides, and Nyx's face comes into focus over me.

"Lyra, are you alright? Lyra?"

He picks me up, and the moment he touches me I gasp, snapping back to reality and suddenly finding my voice. Nyx sits down on the chaise, holding me in his lap. I touch my temples and my forehead, almost surprised to find they're intact after the pain I just experienced.

"I think I'm okay. I felt it. I felt my magic. My father, he apologized and kissed my forehead and heat radiated through me, then it was gone." I sit up in his lap, finding Elspeth still sitting in the chair next to us. "Did it work?" I ask quickly, looking down at my arms and hands, expecting something to be different.

"We'll know in time," says Elspeth.

"What the fuck did you do? We could hear Lyra screaming from downstairs," Nyx says while looking me over for injuries.

"I'm okay. I told Elspeth I wanted her to try to dig through my memories and release my magic." I move, feeling the need to stand. "What does 'in time' mean exactly? How will I know?" I look down at my body, still expecting to see something different, like somehow the magic changed my appearance. I still look the same, and I let out the breath I hadn't realized I was holding.

"I found the exact moment Euric buried your magic, and I released it. But, Lyra, you are half Fae and half Sorceress. I've never met another like you, and our history books on the subject are weak. As Fae, we are born with our magic, but we learn to wield it slowly over time. I imagine something similar will happen with you now. You'll feel it soon enough," Elspeth says, getting to her feet. "Now I'm feeling rather drained. You must excuse me while I retire." She hurries out of the room, her husband extending an arm for her to hold onto. I'm still in shock by the whole experience, and by the time I realize I should thank her she's out of the room.

"Come, let me take you home. We can talk about this there. You should rest." Nyx scoops me up in his arms, and we channel to the castle. I don't feel tired, and I don't need him to carry me, but it feels nice, so I let him. We appear in my bed chamber moments later, and he gently sits me on the end of the bed before sitting next to me.

"Are you sure you feel alright?"

"Yes, I'm fine. I promise." I move to cross my legs and face him on the bed. "When do you think I'll be able to use my magic? Do you think what Elspeth did really worked?"

"If she says it worked, then I am inclined to trust her. Fae magic is a fickle thing, especially when it is so new. Fae magic differs from Sorcerer magic. It almost has a mind of its own. We must learn how to control it and trust it."

"What do you mean it has a mind of its own?"

"It's different for me now because I'm older and have spent many years learning to control my magic. For example, if you're in a dangerous situation, your magic will want to be released. It will want to protect you. If I get really upset, I can feel my magic pulse under my skin, trying to work its way to the surface. Our magic is heightened with our feelings. It'll want to protect you and respond to any extreme emotions you may feel."

"That sounds kind of—alarming. What if I can't control it?

We don't even know what powers I may have. What if I hurt someone?"

"I won't let that happen. It's a learning curve, but one I'm certain I can help you with. Just tell me the minute you start to feel anything unusual. Your magic may feel cold or warm. It's possible it may have a tingling sensation. It's different for everyone. Either way, you'll know when you feel it. It's nothing to be afraid of." Nyx leans in, kissing my forehead and running his hand down the back of my hair.

"I know it's already been a really long day for you, and you must be exhausted, but if we want to leave for Cloudrum in the morning we should still meet Flora and Bim in Nitross tonight. If you want to wait, I completely understand, but the blood moon is in less than two weeks' time. If you're to unlock the bridge to Zomea, we need answers fast."

I sit up, meeting his gaze.

"No, I understand. I want to go. I need to go. I've also decided I want to bring Chepi with us. I know it might be dangerous, but we normally do everything together, and it just doesn't sit right with me leaving him here."

Nyx smiles at me. "As you wish, Princess," he says, getting to his feet.

"There should be a pack in your closet. I'll leave you to gather what you need. I have to take care of a few things before we leave. Come find me when you're ready." Then he vanishes.

Now that I finally have a moment to myself, I grab my bag of clothes from last night, shuffling through it until I find Callum's journal still tucked safely inside my pants. I start skimming through the pages. Why would Colton give this to me? There must be something in here he wanted me to find. Or maybe he just wanted to create some kind of rift between Nyx and me. I pause on the last line of one of the pages. An uneasy feeling settles over me as I read it over again. *Euric's offspring will be born for darkness.* I slam the book shut and hide it in the pack I'm bringing to Cloudrum. What does "born for darkness" even mean? How could Nyx's father know anything? He sounds crazy.

As I pack my bags for Cloudrum, I try to occupy my mind with mundane tasks, but the gnawing sense of unease in my gut won't dissipate. My thoughts are consumed with questions about my mother's past and the possibility of dark magic being passed down through her bloodline. I know Fae magic is neither dark nor light, but the idea of something sinister lurking within me is unsettling. The journal I discovered was written long before my parents even met, so how could Callum have known about the dark magic that may run through my veins? Will I be cursed with it when I come of age? The thought sends a chill down my spine, and my stomach churns with anxiety. I shake my head, trying to dispel the negative thoughts, and focus on the task at hand. With my packing complete, I decide to seek out Chepi and head to Nyx's chambers.

"I figured you'd like to see this," Nyx says, coming up behind me from where I now sit in his study. He drops the envelope I found the other day into my lap. It's the one with my family's seal on the back. I carefully open it and unravel the paper folded up inside.

Onyx,

You have something that belongs to me. It would be wise for you to return her or you will soon face more than just my wrath.

King Samael

"Are you going to return me?" I ask, looking up.

"Of course not. Don't even ask that," he says, taking the letter back from me and tossing it into the fire. "Samael can get fucked. You don't belong to anyone. Are you ready to go? Did you pack some clothes?"

"Yes, I'm ready," I tell him, standing up from the chair and pulling my pack over my shoulder.

"Don't look so worried. I'd never let anything bad happen to you," Nyx says before taking my pack and tossing it over his shoulder. I gather Chepi in my arms, and Nyx pulls us close, then we vanish.

CHAPTER
TWENTY-FOUR

"I was beginning to worry you love birds wouldn't come back down from the mountains," Bim says.

"Pleasure to see you again, Lyra dear. Don't mind him," Flora says, brushing past Bim and giving me a hug. I hug her back, and it feels nice. I think we could actually be friends. I've never really had any friends before other than Lili, so the concept is new to me.

I sit Chepi on the ground and take in our new surroundings. We're in a giant manor home. I can tell right away it's one of Nyx's homes by the simplistic grandeur of the place. It's so similar to the castle in the Noble Vale. Chepi rubs against my leg then takes off down the hall, already itching to get a lay of the land.

"I had Bim meet me here because most of our armies are stationed in Onyx territory. I need to speak with some of the commanders and make sure everything runs smoothly while we are away. Flora will keep you company while we're gone. Should only take a couple hours," Nyx says.

I nod to him as he and Bim vanish in unison.

"Would you like to go for a walk of the grounds? The gardens around here are extraordinary," Flora says.

"Sure. That'd be nice," I say, then yell, "Chepi, let's go outside."

He comes flying around the corner, panting. Flora and I both laugh, then we step outside into the gardens. I'm immediately struck by the beauty of the scenery. The lush green grass underfoot and the large square beds overflowing with the most exquisite flowers, their colorful petals like a rainbow blooming in front of me. Everywhere I look, there are enormous fruit trees providing shade, and the air is thick with the sweet, heady scent of blooming flowers.

The manor is situated atop a hill, and from here I can see the landscape extending for miles, the rolling hills and endless sky stretching out before me. Off in the distance, past the edge of the property, I can make out a village. The village appears to be thriving, with hundreds of rooftops visible, and the sound of people bustling about their daily lives reaches my ears.

Nyx told me that Onyx territory was the most populated in all of Nighthold, and now I can see why. The abundance of life here is almost overwhelming, and I find myself wanting to explore the town to see what else Nighthold has to offer.

But today I have more pressing matters on my mind. I share with Flora everything that happened with Elspeth at the palace this morning, and she listens carefully, her brows furrowed in concentration. For a moment, she doesn't say anything, and her expression is inscrutable, making it difficult for me to discern her thoughts.

"That's...concerning," she says, her voice low and measured. "Elspeth is powerful, and if she's digging around in your mind like that you need to be careful around her, Lyra."

I nod, taking her advice to heart. "I know. I don't trust her, but I don't have much of a choice right now. I need her help if I'm going to figure out what's happening with my magic."

Flora nods in understanding, and we continue walking through the gardens, discussing my situation and what our next steps should be. Despite my worries, being in the gardens with Flora is a welcome respite, and I feel a sense of calm wash over me in the midst of the natural beauty surrounding us.

"I want you to teach me how to channel," I say, causing her eyes to flash back to me.

"Lyra, I'd love to, but I have no idea if you're even capable of channeling."

"Well, will you at least try? Please," I press. Her eyes soften.

"Yes, of course I will."

She leads me to a more open area. There's a large grass plot with a fountain at its center. She has me walk with her to the fountain then about thirty feet away to the edge of the grass.

"Now I'm going to go sit by the fountain, and once I do I want you to imagine being there with me. Close your eyes and visualize where you just stood next to the fountain and will it to be," she says.

I watch her walk over and take a seat on the edge of the fountain. Chepi jumps up beside her, and both of them watch me. I close my eyes, focusing on my breathing then on the fountain. I try to visualize the fountain in my mind, the gray statue of a woman at its center, the smell of the water being stirred up. When I don't feel anything, I open my eyes in frustration. I find both of them still focused on me, only Chepi now lies in Flora's lap.

"Nothing's happening," I say, clenching my fists at my sides.

"Fae magic is heavily based on emotions. Try to think of something that elicits a strong emotional response from you then imagine moving to the spot next to me again," Flora says.

I try to think about different little things that upset me or make me happy. This goes on for over an hour, and I haven't so much as stirred the grass at my feet. Flora and Chepi both lie sprawled out in the grass at the base of the fountain. I know what I need to do. I just haven't wanted to try it yet. I need to think about something more extreme to get a larger emotional response. It's just all of those things bring up bad emotions that I've worked so hard to bury.

"Nyx and Bim should be back soon. Let's head back inside and open some wine before it gets dark. I'm famished," Flora says. Chepi perks up. I'm sure he's hungry too.

"Okay, let me just try one last time then we can go." I take a deep breath in, and with each passing second my heart races faster. The images that flood my mind are haunting, but I can't stop them. I envision Samael's footsteps as he creeps over to my bed in the dark of night, and I recall the last night I saw him and the snake bite. It's as if my mind is a projector and the scenes of that fateful night flash before me. The Lycan ceremony fills my thoughts next, and I can hear Aidan's paws hit the ground, his nails tapping against the old wooden stage. I look at the crowd and see the pain and devastation in their eyes, as if they're living through the terror once again.

And then I see Luke. I see his piercing light-blue eyes staring back at me, full of terror, and my breath hitches in my throat as I watch the life drain from his eyes once more. The emotions are too much, and I feel the warm sensation in my chest grow. I close my eyes, focusing on the sensation, and let the wind start to stir around me. The sweet smell of honeysuckle tickles my nose, and I realize that it's my scent, my magic. The gusts of wind toss strands of my hair as I stand in the eye of the storm. I can feel the earth darken around me, and I realize that I am channeling.

My eyes remain closed, but I know the world has gone

even darker. When I open my eyes, a rush of warm honeyed wind drops it all, and the soft sunset light stings my eyes. I look down at my feet then over at Flora and Chepi, who are both standing up and watching me intently. I can feel the sweat beading on my forehead, and I let out a shuddering breath.

"It didn't work," I say, feeling slightly defeated.

Flora approaches me with a smile. "Lyra, that was incredible. You did it! You channeled your magic. We felt it. You may not have actually moved, but I could smell your magic, your essence. The earth darkened around you, and the wind picked up. You'll be a natural in no time with some practice. You should be proud of yourself." Chepi barks in agreement, and I can't help but feel a sense of pride wash over me.

"Thanks. I think I'm ready to go inside now," I say, starting to walk back toward the manor. I don't know if I can channel if I have to relive some of my darkest memories every time I want to. We walk back in silence, and I stop in the lounge, dropping down on the couch. Chepi curls up next to me, and Flora heads into the kitchen to open a bottle of wine, bringing me a glass. Nyx and Bim appear in the sitting room with bags in tow.

"Perfect timing, boys. Wine?"

"Yes, please," Bim says, and Nyx comes over to sit next to me on the couch.

"I missed you," he says, pulling me in for a kiss.

"It was only two hours, my gods," Bim says, grabbing his wine and downing half the glass.

"We missed you too, Bim," I say, smiling at him.

"I bet you did." He gives me a wink and a wicked smirk.

I just laugh, leaning into Nyx and handing him my glass to have a drink.

"We must leave first thing in the morning right before the

sun comes up. Only about seven hours from now," Nyx tells me while tucking my hair behind my ear.

"I'd like to go to bed then, if that's okay? I'm exhausted, and I want to be ready for tomorrow." I stand up from the couch.

"Yes, of course. I need to talk to Bim and Flora for a few minutes, but I'll join you shortly. Our room is the last room on the left."

"Goodnight." I wave to Bim and Flora.

"Goodnight, darling," Flora says.

"Yeah, goodnight darling," Bim mimics her yelling down the hall, and I laugh.

Once in the bedroom I take off my clothes, wash my face, and climb into bed. I sink into the pillows, snuggling Chepi and falling asleep before Onyx can join me.

"It's time to wake up, my little Pixie." I hear the words and jolt awake.

"What did you say?"

Nyx stands over me. "I said it's time to wake up, Lyra."

I swear I heard him say "my little Pixie." Only it didn't sound like him exactly. I swear I heard my father's voice. It sends a chill through me. I must've been partly dreaming when Nyx tried to wake me. I brush off the feeling and stretch before sitting up. It's still dark outside, and when Nyx turns the lights on I have to cover my face for a moment.

"It's so bright," I say, collecting myself. "What time did you come to bed last night?" I slide out of bed and wash up in the bathroom.

"I didn't. I had a lot to do, and I can work well off little sleep."

"Oh . . . Okay, well what should I wear today for the flight?" I try to tame my hair into a braid.

"Just make sure you wear pants to protect your legs and something warm. We need to leave in ten minutes. I'll leave you to get ready. Come to the kitchen when you're done." He kisses me on the top of my head and leaves.

As I dress, my mind continues to spiral, weighed down by the heavy burden of my worries. The dream about Luke still lingers in my mind, haunting me with the memory of his sharp blue eyes. And then the sound of my father's voice echoes in my head, taunting me with the possibility that I might be losing my mind. I take a deep breath, trying to steady myself, but the unease in my chest remains.

The thought of seeing Aidan again only intensifies my anxiety. I'm scared of the emotions that will resurface and the memories that will flood back. *Is going back to Cloudrum the right decision?* I ask myself, uncertain of what the future holds. The tightness in my chest persists, a reminder of the weight of my choices.

I resolve to find the old Sorceress, even more so after seeing her in my memories with my father. I need to unlock the bridge to Zomea by the blood moon...or face my death.

As I rub my chest, trying to alleviate the pressure, I finish getting dressed in layers, donning fur-lined leggings, a black tunic, gray sweater, and jacket. Chepi remains tucked deep under the covers, and I gather him in my arms, feeling the warmth of his little body against mine.

"Come on, squish. It's time to go." I kiss the top of his head, and he nestles in close to my chest, still sleepy. I grab my pack and head for the kitchen to meet Nyx.

The manor is dark and quiet with no sign of Bim or Flora anywhere.

"I made some eggs and toast. You should try to eat something before we leave." Nyx brings me a plate.

"You cooked for me?" I'm more shocked that he can actually cook something.

"Don't get too excited. It's just eggs and bread." He laughs, shoveling down a piece of toast himself.

"Where's Bim and Flora?" I ask between bites of egg.

"They're not coming with us to Cloudrum," he says, and a piece of egg falls out of my mouth.

"What? Why not?"

"Well, for one, they both hate leaving Nighthold. But I have things I need them to do here while we are away. I don't know how long we will be gone, and I need them to hold things together here. That's why Bim and I met with the commanders yesterday to make sure things run smoothly while we're gone."

I nod in understanding, although I would've felt better if they were coming with us.

"Ready?" he asks me while coming to stand next to my chair.

I take a drink of water and let Chepi finish the rest of my eggs then slide off the chair. I kind of wish I had something stronger to drink.

"Ready." I pick up Chepi and take Nyx's hand.

Darkness slowly falls over us as the wind picks up and we channel. I find us standing atop what I think is a rocky cliff. "Where are we?"

"These are the Ebony Cliffs on the coast of Onyx land. It's a haven for sea birds and is where Quazie lives."

It's gorgeous. The sun hasn't risen yet, and the light-blue hue illuminates the landscape. As far as I can see, steep rocky cliffs extend into the mist and drop into the Feral Sea below. The salty breeze sticks to my face and collects in my hair. Nyx throws his arms up in the air, and at first I don't know what he's doing, but then I realize he's using magic to call Quazie to us.

A few minutes pass, and I start to wonder what we'll do if he doesn't come, then I hear a loud screech in the distance. A huge head with a long beak breaks through the mist. He soars high above us, circling, then lands next to Nyx, practically shaking the ground. My gods, his beak alone is longer than I'm tall. I swallow hard, imagining that beak devouring me whole. Nyx pats him on the side.

"Lyra, meet Quazie. Good boy," he says, stroking his neck.

"Hello . . . Quazie," I stutter, causing Nyx to glance back at me, a broad smile spreading across his face.

"Remind me again why we can't just channel to Cloudrum?" I ask, my voice stuttering.

"I know he looks terrifying, but he's just a big softy. Cloudrum is too far for me to channel with you, and once we reach Cloudrum I can't use my magic. I'm sure Samael will be tracking any large traces of magic in his territories. We need to stay hidden from him for as long as possible . . . Come and give Quazie a pat."

I slowly creep toward him, cowering down a bit, afraid I'm going to spook the creature and cause his beak to impale me. Nyx just laughs, and once I'm close enough he grabs me, pulling me close to him and Quazie. I hold my hand out and let him guide me to the large bird. He feels softer than I expected and makes a low cooing sound as I run my fingers down the side of his neck.

"See, he likes you." Nyx nudges my shoulder with his elbow. "Are you ready for this?"

I take a slow breath in. *Stay calm.*

"As ready as I'll ever be." I pinch my eyes closed as Nyx places his hands on my waist, and we move with his magic, landing softly on Quazie's back. Nyx waves his arm, and reins appear around Quazie's neck. Nyx grabs hold of them, and I wrap both my arms around Chepi, squeezing him tight to my chest, even though he doesn't seem fazed at all by this.

"Let's go, boy," Nyx says, tapping his legs on Quazie's sides.

We shoot into the air, and my body falls back between Nyx's legs. I let my back burrow into his chest. He wraps one arm around my waist, and I close my eyes tight. The cold wind causes tears to stream down my face as we whip through the clouds. It feels like we're going straight up for far too long, and if Nyx wasn't behind me I'd surely have flown right off the back of Quazie by now. Finally, we level out, and I feel the warmth of the sun on my face. I slowly open my eyes to find we're high above the clouds, and it's lighter up here. We fly through the first part of the sky to be touched by the morning sun. I can see Quazie more clearly. He really is magnificent, and his wingspan is enormous. His feathers are different shades of blue and purple while his beak is bright orange. His beak is terrifying, but still he's a jaw-droppingly beautiful creature.

"Doing okay?" Nyx asks, squeezing me tighter around the waist.

"Yes, I'm good. How long will it take to get there? And where are we landing exactly?"

"It'll take most of the day. We should land on the coast of Cinder Territory just before nightfall. I can't risk landing inland. I don't want anyone seeing Quazie, or us for that matter."

I shake my head to acknowledge him rather than yelling over the wind.

"You should try to sleep some more if you can. I won't let you fall. Once we get to Cloudrum, remember I won't be able to channel us. We'll have a bit of hiking to do before we find Aidan. You could use all the rest you can get."

I try to settle into his chest and rest my eyes.

At some point I fell asleep, but it isn't very restful. It's a fitful tangle of images and voices digging into my mind. Even now I feel the claws of unease sinking in and souring my stomach.

"Sleep well?"

I feel Nyx's breath on my ear. "Er yes," I mutter. I don't know when I became such a liar, but I don't want to worry him. I need to keep my own thoughts under control.

"Hungry?"

I nod, and he wrestles through his pack and hands me a bite-sized square purple cake.

"Thank you," I say, biting into it without question. He gives Chepi a piece of meat, and Chepi scarfs it down. "What kind of cake is this?" I ask, finishing it off.

"It's called a plum cake. Twig made them for us. It should help calm your nerves for the flight."

Interesting. I can't tell what time it is or how long I was asleep for. "Are we getting close?"

"Little more than halfway there."

My stomach sinks at the thought. My legs are sore, and as much as I appreciate Quazie flying with us I can't wait to have my feet back on solid ground. "Do you know how to find Aidan once we land?"

"I've been to his place once before, many years ago. I'm pretty confident I can find it again. Bim has spies everywhere, and he got word yesterday that Aidan's been there all week, so I'm hoping he's still there when we arrive."

Bim has spies everywhere. I wonder who else has spies everywhere. Surely Samael probably has spies too. Let's hope we stay ahead of them. I'll not let him take me back to the castle, not until I'm ready to finish him once and for all. Nyx still doesn't know my history with Aidan, and I play with the idea of confiding in him, but I just can't bring myself to do it. I don't want Nyx to know Aidan forced himself on me. I don't want him to see me differently, and I don't want him to kill Aidan, at least not until after we get any useful information out of him that we can. Then I'll happily kill him myself.

"Why are you so quiet?"

I don't answer him for a minute, then finally I say, "I'm just ... afraid."

"I told you I won't let anything happen to you."

"I know you did, and I'm not just afraid for me. I'm afraid for you. For us." My voice breaks a bit.

His hand slides under the warmth of my sweater, his skin meeting mine in a rush of heat that spreads through my body. As his fingers press against my tummy, I can't help but tense up with fear. He notices and his voice, filled with understanding, cuts through the air. "It's okay to be afraid," he reassures me. "After what you've been through, I'd be surprised if you weren't afraid coming back here, but it's going to be okay, Lyra. Nothing would keep me away from you."

As he continues tracing lazy circles across my stomach, I try to will myself to relax, to let go of the fear that has taken hold of me. I focus on the comforting warmth of his touch, wishing his fingers would trail lower and sink into my flesh.

We fly on in silence for a long while until the sun starts to make its descent from the sky and the air around us changes. Quazie dives lower, and the familiar scent of Cloudrum's pine trees rush toward us—it smells sweet, sharp, and a bit like chimney smoke. A chill creeps up my spine, and I have to hold back a shiver. It's full winter now in Cloudrum. I know it's going to be a cold trek through the snow.

"Hold on tight. We're about to make our descent." Nyx

wraps his arms tightly around me while holding onto the reins, and I grab Chepi once again, holding him close.

Quazie dives, and so does my stomach. I don't know what was worse, the takeoff or the landing. There're no high cliffs here, and Quazie brings us down onto a little rocky beach dusted with snow. Nyx grabs me, and we hop off Quazie, whose magic makes our landing slow and easy on the knees. Once we hit the ground, everything happens so fast. The reins disappear, and Quazie takes off straight into the sky, disappearing into the clouds like he was never here at all.

CHAPTER

TWENTY-FIVE

As I hike through the woods, I can feel the chill of the night settling in. The sun has long set, and even the moon is obscured by the thick fog, making it difficult to see ahead. Despite the snow not being too deep, it has covered the ground, making it easier to walk, but tripping hazards like tree stumps, roots, and rocks are scattered everywhere. This is no paved path, and I'm sure Nyx thinks I'm the clumsiest person alive. I constantly stumble, and he has to reach out to steady me. If we were trying to be stealthy, I fear I've failed us. My clumsiness has certainly alerted every creature within earshot of my clunky approach.

"How much further to Aidan's village?"

Nyx has been quiet the last couple hours, although I don't know why because his whispering can't be any louder than me falling all over the forest.

"We'll make it there around midday tomorrow."

My heart sinks. I can't hike the rest of the night. Gods, I need to work on getting in better shape.

"Will we be walking all through the night?" I whisper back.

"No, I have a place for us to stay the night not too much further. Maybe another hour. Can you make it?"

"Yeah. No problem," I pant back. I'm breathing heavier than I'm proud of, and I make a mental note to work on that once we get back to Nighthold. I wonder where exactly we're going to stay the night. It doesn't look like Nyx's backpack is large enough to be carrying a tent. Maybe he'll use magic to make us one, if that's possible. He doesn't seem to want to talk while we're out here, so I just keep my questions to myself. I need to start thinking about what I'm going to say to Aidan when I see him. The thought of speaking to him makes my stomach knot. Once I learn to use my Fae magic and come into my Sorceress powers, Aidan is going to be toward the top of people I want to kill, right after Samael.

I don't know how we're going to convince Aidan to take us to the old Sorceress, assuming he even knows how to find her. I didn't really think that far ahead. I just know I need to find her. Using my sexuality to manipulate him is out of the question. I refuse to resort to such a cheap tactic. Nyx could use brute force to extract the information from him, but I'm not sure that would be wise if he's trying to keep a low profile. That leaves me with few options, but I can't dwell on it right now. My mind is racing, unable to focus, consumed by the bitter cold that gnaws at my bones. I'm exhausted, and every step is a struggle to keep my balance. Chepi flits by our side, his fur a warm cocoon against the icy winds.

Finally, Nyx halts beside a massive tree, and he begins to circle it, studying the ground intently. It doesn't appear any different from the other trees we've passed, but I trust Nyx's instincts.

With a graceful motion, he drops down onto his hands and knees and presses his palms into the dirt and snow. The snow immediately begins to melt, revealing a glowing green circle beneath his touch. The circle extends out to about five feet, and with a clicking sound, a section of the ground transforms into a door-like opening. Although the entrance is large enough for a person to pass through, the sight of the dark, bottomless hole sends shivers down my spine, tapping into my fear of tight spaces.

"Please tell me we're not climbing into that hole?" I whisper in a voice that's a little more tense than I'd like it to be.

"Yes, Princess, we're doing just that." He chuckles, pushing some dirt and leaves aside.

My palms are growing slick from the thought of crawling down there. I hope there are no bugs. Nyx waves his hand, and a small, white, glowing orb appears. It slowly descends into the hole, illuminating it for us.

"There's a ladder. I need you to climb down, and I have to cover our tracks and close the hatch. I'll be right behind you. I promise it's nice down there."

With a deep breath, I step onto the ladder, the orb providing just enough light to see the walls and rungs beneath me. The walls appear to be made of concrete, smoother and cleaner than I expected. I quickly make my way down, Chepi flying next to me, and once my feet touch the ground I wait for Nyx to join me. He takes my hand and leads us down a narrow hallway illuminated by the orb. We reach the end of the hall, and the orb brightens, revealing a spacious room filled with two sets of bunk beds and a few crates. Beyond that is a stand-alone bed, larger than the bunks, with a shelf next to it stocked with supplies. Although the room is hidden underground, it's larger than I anticipated, and I try to shake off the feeling of confinement by imagining we're above ground.

"What is this place?" I ask while surveying the supplies.

"It's an underground bunker. I have one hidden in every

realm. Only someone with Fae blood can unlock it," he tells me nonchalantly.

"What for? Do you use them often?"

"You can never be too careful. I don't use them often, no, but they've come in handy a handful of times. Like right now." He smiles, pulling me close to him and planting a kiss on the top of my head.

"Are you smelling my hair?" I laugh, as I feel his nose nuzzle against my hair.

"Yes. I can't help myself. You smell delicious. Sweet like honeysuckle." He chuckles softly, running his hands down my body.

"I want to make it to Aidan's village tomorrow if we can, so we should try to get some sleep. We'll have a lot of walking to do," Nyx says while removing some of his clothes.

"Why can't you just fly us to the village?"

"I could, but I'm trying to refrain from using large amounts of magic. I don't want to risk Samael being able to track us. This small orb of light is one thing, but anything more could put us at risk."

"Right, no magic, but Samael doesn't even know we're here? How would he track your magic?" I start removing my boots and some of my clothes so I can climb into bed.

"Samael is going to be on high alert. I don't think he'd expect us to come back to Cloudrum, so we have that on our side. But I'm sure he has a spell set to alert him of anyone using large amounts of magic. I want to try to avoid magic at all costs," he says, climbing into bed and pulling me under the covers with him.

"What about when you opened the door to get us down here and covered our tracks?" I'm concerned about the magic now and hoping Samael hasn't already been alerted of our presence.

"That was a very minuscule amount of magic. It wouldn't be enough to set off a spell."

I relax a bit, cuddling close to Nyx. The orb slowly dims out, and we lie in the dark for some time. I listen to the sounds of Nyx's breathing and close my eyes, hoping sleep will find me soon. Just when I think Onyx is asleep, his voice scares me, and my eyes fly open at the sound.

"Can I ask you something, Lyra?"

"Sure, go ahead."

"Why didn't you want to answer most of my questions the other night in the Fate Fields?"

My heart sinks into my stomach as I struggle to come up with a response. Which questions did I sidestep? Did I avoid telling him about Aidan's abuse or if I was still a virgin? I had been truthful about everything else, but now those unspoken questions weigh on me, leaving me unsure how to proceed. If I reveal too much, it could change our approach with Aidan, and I'm not sure I'm ready for that yet. Before I can form a reply, he breaks the silence.

"It's okay. You don't have to say anything. I didn't mean to make you uncomfortable. I just hope one day we can talk about it. I hope one day you'll feel safe being open with me."

His tone breaks my heart, because I do feel safe with him and don't want him to think otherwise.

"I do feel safe talking to you. I'm just still getting used to having someone like you in my life. I've never really had someone to talk to and share things with. Someone I could trust growing up. Forgive me if I'm not as open as I'd like to be. Just give me time."

"Take all the time you need," he says gently, kissing the top of my head. His voice sounds slightly somber though, and I feel bad for not telling him everything.

"I'm not a virgin," I say then snap my eyes closed, bracing myself for what his response will be.

"Oh . . . I assumed that you were. I just thought you didn't want to answer that question because you were embarrassed." Nyx moves onto his side so he's facing me, but I keep my eyes closed.

I can feel my cheeks flush, and I don't know why talking about it makes me uncomfortable.

"Was it someone you had a relationship with back at the castle?" he asks, and I can feel his eyes on me.

I don't want to reveal Aidan's name, and I don't want to tell him exactly what happened. I try to think of what to say but decide a vague truth is the best route.

"No, I've never been in a relationship before. It was a friend of my parents. I was drunk. It was a mistake."

I turn onto my side, facing him, and let my eyes look up into his. He stares at me, his lips set in a flat line. I feel like I've upset him, but he just pulls me tighter to him, and I relax into his chest. He wraps his arms around me to comfort me and runs lazy circles up and down my back until I fall asleep.

CHAPTER

TWENTY-SIX

I awake to the sound of—nothing. I sit up quickly, and the unnatural silence of the room sends a sharp pang of worry through my chest. It's pitch black in here, the orb no longer illuminating the bunker. I blink in the darkness, but my eyes don't adjust. There's not even a hint of light for them to latch onto. I start feeling around the bed, and I don't feel Nyx anywhere. Maybe he went to the bathroom. I throw the blankets back, feeling for Chepi. He's usually snuggled under the covers at the foot of the bed. I can't find him either. That pang of worry in my chest starts to expand.

"Chepi? Where are you, boy?" I whisper into the dark. I don't know why I'm whispering, but it feels wrong to yell. I stay silent for a moment waiting to hear Chepi, but nothing . . . just silence. I fumble to my feet and start feeling for the wall. Once I find it, I start going around the room.

"Chepi," I call, a little bit louder this time. I pause and then hear Chepi yip. I'm relieved that he's okay and still down here with me. It sounds like he came from down the hall by where we entered the bunker. I keep my hands stretched out in front of me and make my way toward Chepi. Once I reach the ladder, I find Chepi pacing at the base of it.

"What's wrong, boy?" I pick him up, petting his head. He lifts his head, looks to the entrance in the ceiling, and yips again. Nyx must've gone outside. It's incredibly disorienting being in complete darkness underground. I have no idea if it's morning yet or not. I'm barefoot and in nothing but Nyx's tunic. It's not exactly the best choice to wear outside in the snow. But what if he's in trouble? What if he went outside to relieve himself and was attacked? It's going to take too long for me to go find more clothes and shoes if Nyx really is in trouble. *Shit.*

"Chepi, stay here. I'll be right back," I say while placing him back on the ground. He yipped and pawed at my legs in disapproval. "I'm sorry, but I can't risk you getting hurt too." I feel for the ladder in the dark. Once I grab hold, I start to climb the long narrow path to the surface.

As I get closer to the surface, I start to hear noise from outside. I can't quite tell what it is, but I hear thumping. The sound sends a wisp of panic through me, and I pick up my pace. I reach the hatch door and stop and listen for a moment before I can reconsider. I push the hatch open as hard as I can. Bright morning light blinds me momentarily, and chunks of snow and ice fall in on me. I climb out of the hatch, looking down at Chepi then close it behind me. I get to my feet quickly and look around. At first all I see are pine trees covered in snow. Then I come face to face with an utterly horrific creature.

I feel frozen in my tracks, holding my breath as I take in the sight before me. Standing tall at around six feet, the creatures body resembles that of a skeleton with abnormally long arms and chunks of rotting flesh hanging from them. Its forehead is adorned with two giant S-shaped horns in the darkest shade of obsidian extending a foot above its head. My gaze travels down the grooves of its horns, eventually resting on its face. The face of this demonic being is half-skeleton, half-something that may have once been human with red slits for eyes and no nose. I lock onto the creature's eyes, slowly starting to back away as it opens its mouth. A dark black hole reveals no teeth, but a reedy sound echoes out of its throat. I cover my ears on instinct as the loud, piercing call sends shivers down my spine.

I turn to run as the unnerving sound snaps me out of my shocked state. I take a few steps when Nyx appears, covered in black blood. His eyes glow as they meet mine, and he grins.

"How can you smile right now when that thing with red slits for eyes and rotting flesh is coming after us?" I exclaim.

He moves past me, sword in hand, and begins battling the creature. He quickly cuts off the horrific sound it was making by kicking it in the chest, causing it to stumble back a step. The monster is surprisingly agile for a rotting skeleton, but Nyx is faster. He slices off an arm, black blood splattering his face, but the creature keeps coming for him, undeterred by the missing limb. Nyx dances around, popping up behind the thing and cutting its head clean off with one swift swipe of his sword. Black blood mists into the air, staining the snow, and the creature's head lands right next to me, its horns glinting in the snow.

"What was that thing?" I ask, panting.

"A Monstrauth," Nyx replies. I want to ask for a further explanation, but two more Monstrauths I hadn't noticed before start heading our way. "You're very distracting when you're wearing nothing but my tunic. We should really go back down the hatch before you freeze to death."

Nyx moves toward the Monstrauths, and I know I should head back into the bunker, but I find myself strangely aroused watching him fight. Gods, his body and the way he moves. I can't take my eyes off him. The Monstrauths are fast, but he's

WHAT LIES BEYOND THE REALMS

always faster, ducking and swinging his sword, slicing the monsters to pieces. Nyx stabs one deep in the chest, its frail bones cracking as he pulls the sword back out. He swings his arm backward and beheads the other, and before I know it both Monstauths are lying in a pile of crumbled bone and flesh, staining the snow.

Perhaps it's my return to this place and my closeness to the Lycan Realm, but I have a feeling that my body temperature has gone up, like Flora predicted. She said that I might start to manifest some of the secondary Lycan abilities and feel warmer. I've been standing barefoot on the snow all this time and still feel cold. However, it's not as uncomfortable as it would have been before, which is odd.

"Quickly go back down the hatch. I need to cover this up, and I'll be right down behind you," Nyx says while pulling the hatch door open.

I nod, quickly fumbling down the ladder, my feet slick and frozen. Once the door slams shut, I'm left in utter darkness again. I finally reach the bottom and sit down on the ground, pulling Chepi into my lap. He sniffs me frantically then licks my face. His warm tongue makes me laugh despite what just happened. Only a few minutes of silence pass, then Nyx opens the hatch door and hurries down the ladder. He waves a hand, tossing the small orb of light out, which illuminates the bunker once again.

"What is a Monstrauth? Where did those things come from?" I ask, getting to my feet. I look him over head to toe. He doesn't seem to be hurt.

"I haven't seen one in years. It's a type of demon, conjured by—I can only guess, Samael." Nyx starts walking back toward the main room of the bunker, unstrapping his sword and removing his sullied clothes.

251

"Why would Samael conjure such a demon? What do they do?"

His clothes are covered in black splatters of blood that smell like rotting flesh, causing my nose to wrinkle. He ties them in a bag, tossing them into a crate on the other side of the room.

"Monstrauths are hunters. I can only assume he has them searching for you or me or anything else he may want. The sound it was making, it was calling more to it. I got rid of all the evidence and covered our tracks, but we should probably lie low for a few hours, remain in the bunker until nightfall. Monstrauths have terrible vision at night, and it could give us the upper hand if we run into more of them on our way to Aidan's village," Nyx says while slipping on a clean tunic and shorts.

"Well, that's disturbing. Samael has to be working with some really dark magic to be conjuring up demons like that. No way would that be in his family's grimoire. I've seen him do some pretty bad stuff, but I've never seen him do something like this," I say. It's possible it'd be in mine though, but I don't say that out loud. I don't want to accept that such a demon would come from something he found in the *Moon Grimoire*, from one of my dark ancestors.

"You have to be freezing. Let me help you get cleaned up." Nyx moves, looking me over closely for injuries and bending down to run his hands along my legs and feet.

"I'm okay, really. Those things never touched me. What were you doing outside anyways?" I ask while following Nyx into the bathroom hidden behind a stack of crates.

"I could hear them moving around above us. I could sense it was something evil. I didn't know it'd be a demon, but I had to check to be sure. I'm sorry I didn't want to worry you by waking you up."

"Well, I was worried. Please wake me next time."

"Okay, I will." Nyx places a kiss to the top of my head then starts to fill a bucket with water and fetch a towel and bar of soap for us. We both wash our hands and faces. The fresh lemon scent of the soap is a welcome smell after that rotting stench wafting off the Monstrauths. Nyx leaves the bathroom after I tell him I need a couple minutes to finish cleaning up.

I undo my braid and let my hair fall down my back in a mess of waves. I clean my mouth and pinch my cheeks. I think I'm ready to sleep with Nyx. There's really no reason to keep him waiting. I don't think he's only after sex, because if that was the case he could get sex from anyone. He's a king after all. I don't want to deny myself anymore. I want him more than I've wanted anything. Gods, especially after watching him fight. I stare at myself in the mirror wishing I had something sexy to wear instead of an oversized tunic. I pinch my cheeks one last time until they turn light pink, then I push my hair behind my back and head out of the bathroom.

Nyx is lying in bed watching me. The orb is dim, and the lighting should be forgiving. At least that's what I tell myself as I take off the tunic and let it fall to the ground, pooling at my feet. Nyx just watches me silently, a slight glow in his gray eyes. Once I'm completely nude in front of him, I stand there for a moment and watch him. His eyes slowly travel my body and seem to glow slightly brighter as he lingers over certain areas.

He stands, coming in front of me. I tug at his shirt, and he pulls it off, dropping it to the floor. I run my hands slowly across his chest and stomach, tracing the bulge of his muscles. He still has shorts on, but I can see his arousal pressed against them, ready to be released. I place my hand on his cock and rub against it over his shorts.

"What are you doing, Lyra?" he says in a seductive whisper.

"I want you," I whisper back in a breathy tone.

He doesn't question me. He pushes his shorts off revealing his swollen cock. I wrap my hand around the thickness, slightly stroking it.

"Fuck," he gasps before picking me up and carrying me to the bed.

He gently places me on my back and crawls on top of me. His lips find mine. He kisses me gently. His tongue twists and tangles with mine, and his hand comes up to my jaw, deepening the kiss. My core is hot, and it feels damp between my thighs. All I can think about is wanting to feel him inside me.

He continues kissing me until finally he pulls away and takes a breath. He slowly trails kisses down my neck and sucks on my skin, gently pressing it with his teeth. I moan, and my body arches against him, asking for him to enter me. He continues moving down my body, pausing over the tiny white scars on my chest where Samael's snake bit me. His eyes look up to me for a second, and I don't know what I see in them. Passion, maybe anger, either way it's the flash of a fierce animalistic look that causes my breath to catch. He kisses my scar and begins caressing my left breast with his hand while sucking on the right one. His tongue twirls around my nipple, and his teeth graze my perked flesh, causing my thighs to dampen further with excitement.

I don't know how he makes my body respond to him this way. I feel a deep need inside of me. I need him to fill me. I want to be as close to him as I possibly can. He moves slowly across my body like he's studying it, taking it in for the first time. He nibbles and kisses my stomach before settling between my legs and pressing his tongue to my center. I buck up at him and squirm under his touch. He steadies me with one arm and uses the other to press a finger inside of me.

"You're so wet for me, baby," he whispers before licking me

again. He moves his finger in and out while he twirls his tongue around my clit until this pressure inside me builds, and I feel like I'm going to explode.

I moan and sigh and push my hips up against his hand and mouth, wanting more, wanting release.

"Not yet," he whispers, pulling his mouth away and looking up at me. He slowly eases his finger out, and his mouth finds mine again. I can taste the salty sweetness of my sex on his tongue. I feel him press at my center, and I reach down to grasp him, stroking slightly. He makes a guttural sound into my mouth at the contact. Our kiss isn't gentle this time. It's sloppy and wet. Teeth hit together slightly. We are both about to tip over the edge with anticipation. Suddenly he stops, pulling away from me and finding my eyes.

"Are you sure this is what you want?"

"Yes, I'm sure," I tell him, lifting my hips in answer.

"Thank fuck." His voice comes out hoarse.

I move my hands around his neck and tangle my fingers in his hair, pulling him back to my mouth. He kisses me, deep and demanding. He slows when I feel his tip press inside of me slightly. He moves his head back, placing a hand at my jaw so my eyes focus on his. He runs a thumb over my bottom lip and I open my mouth, pulling his finger in and sucking hard. His eyes are glowing full of passion. He holds my gaze as he slowly pushes into me as far as he will go then stops. My breath catches, and my body stretches. He gives me a moment to adjust to him inside me, all while not taking his eyes off mine. Just when I think I can't take it any further, he slowly eases the rest of the way inside me, and I suck in a quick breath at the feeling. He's huge, and my body goes tense for a minute at the slight sting of pain. Then my body relaxes and starts to enjoy the fullness of him.

"Are you okay?" he asks while not taking his eyes off mine.

"Yes," I say, breathless.

I move my hips a bit, letting him know I'm ready and wanting him to take me. I tug on his neck with my hands until he comes down to find my lips. He kisses me softly then starts moving inside of me, slow and gentle, eliciting all sorts of pleasurable feelings. I had no idea sex could feel this way.

I feel him pull all the way out then slowly push all the way back in, taking my breath away when he hits something inside of me. Breathy moans escape my mouth, uncontrolled. He devours my moans with his lips and tongue, eating them up. I can't help but think how perfect this is. How perfect he feels inside of me. I've never felt so close to anyone as I do right in this moment, and I never want it to end.

I tangle my hands in the pillows above my head, and he moves to gently grasp them with one hand while his other hand massages my breasts and squeezes my nipples, sending sparks through my core. He begins thrusting faster and pushing inside of me harder, deeper, leaving me breathless. I can't focus on anything else.

"Is this okay?" he whispers, slowing for a moment and meeting my eyes.

"Yes, don't stop, ever," I spit out between delicate moans, causing him to smirk at me before thrusting into me again. He leans back, bringing his hands to my hips. I open wider for him and let my legs intertwine behind him. He holds my hips in place, thrusting hard and fast. One hand traces across my waist then starts massaging my clit. I arch into him, head falling back into the pillows. My heart is racing, and my insides are going to explode from the pleasure he's extracting from my body.

"Come for me, baby." His words undo me, and my body answers his command. I convulse and moan, finding my release at the same time he finds his.

He relaxes on top of me but stays pressed inside me until my legs stop quivering. He tucks my hair behind my ear and kisses me again, long and slow, before slowly pulling out of me and falling onto his back next to me.

My body is already missing his presence filling me. My breathing slowly recovers. Nyx wraps one arm around me, pulling me close to his body. I softly whimper and turn on my side, resting my head on his arm, watching his face. Both of us glisten with sweat. My body feels exhausted all over again, and I have no idea what time it is, but sleep finds me.

I don't know how long we fell back asleep for, but I wake to find Nyx running his hand up and down my thigh, which is draped over his body. I must've sought him out in my sleep.

"Did you have a nice nap, lover?" he says, placing his finger under my chin so I look at him.

"Yes, I did. My body was exhausted. What time is it anyways? It's really disorienting being down here in the dark."

"It's just past noon," he says, turning to face me. He's rock hard again, and my eyes shoot from his hard length back to his face.

"Ready again?" I smile up at him.

"I'll always be ready for you. I don't think I'll ever get enough of you."

I know the feeling. I already feel wet at the sight of his hard cock and his words. I press my body against his and lean up to kiss his mouth. His tongue is warm, and I love the way he tastes. I pull away slightly, nibbling on his bottom lip, then draw my tongue across it. I reach down and wrap my hand around his length, squeezing gently and stroking him slowly. He breathes heavily into my mouth.

"I want you to ride me baby," he says, sounding slightly breathless. I feel my cheeks flush at the thought, and he doesn't miss a thing. "What's wrong?" His hand caresses the side of my face.

"It's just . . . I don't know how." I look away.

"It's okay. I'll show you. You can't do it wrong. I promise."

I lock onto his eyes, nodding in agreement.

He kisses me again, and this time when his tongue meets mine he pulls my body on top of his so I'm lying against his chest. I continue exploring his mouth and his lips, breathing him in while his hand slides down my body caressing and squeezing my ass, then sliding between us to cup my sex. His finger slides between my lips, rubbing lightly then pressing deep into my flesh. I moan into his mouth, and he eats it up before the sound can escape me.

"You're ready for me," he whispers onto my lips, slowly bringing his fingers out and showing me the wetness there. He turns his fingers to the side, examining them before taking them into his mouth and slowly sucking my moisture off each finger. "I love how your body responds to me. I love the taste of you, the feel of you around my cock."

His words make me flush, and watching him suck my wetness from his fingers makes my body heat all over, especially my core. He moves my legs so I'm straddling him properly. I lift my body up and use my hand to guide him to my entrance.

"That's it. Now lower yourself slowly so I don't hurt you." He places his hands on my hips to help guide me down.

My body was longing for him and the feel of him. I slowly lower onto his cock. It's complete ecstasy. I slowly drop down as far as I can go until we're pressed together. I can feel him so deep inside of me that it causes a rush of sensations to spread across my body, eliciting a whole new feeling of pleasure inside me. I didn't think he could go any deeper, but this new position has proven me wrong.

"What do I do now?"

"Just move your body. Listen to your body. Do what feels good," he says while using his hands to move my hips so that I lift off him slowly then press back down to the base. I press my hands to his chest to steady myself while I slowly ride him. At first the motion is slightly erratic, but once I get the hang of it he releases my hips, letting me take control.

Just when I don't think he can reach any deeper inside of me, he does. My insides coil at this newfound pleasure. I rock back and forth, staring into his eyes and letting him take in my body. He explores my chest and caresses my nipples. He trails his hands down my body. One holds my hip, and the other finds my center. He moves his thumb on my clit, and an embarrassing sound escapes my mouth.

He sits up suddenly, staying inside of me but pressing our bodies together tighter. He reaches around and grabs my ass, helping to push and pull me toward him so he hits deep inside of me. My breathing is erratic, and I can't help the noises of pleasure that keep coming out of my mouth. He collects my hair behind my head, pulling it out of my face.

"Gods, you are beautiful," he tells me, and I feel delirious. I look away, but his hands find my face, forcing me to look at him. "You're mine, Lyra, and I'll never let anyone hurt you again. Do you understand?" The dominance in his voice almost puts me over the edge. I like him like this. I want to be his. "Tell me you understand." He releases my face and runs those hands back down my body.

"I understand," I mutter breathlessly.

His thumb finds my clit again, pressing and teasing while I rock faster on top of him.

"Tell me you're mine," he demands, lifting his hips to meet me and thrusting deeper inside me. I suck in a breath, and my head falls back. He feels so good, and I'm not going to last. His cock is hitting just the right spot, and his thumb is doing things to me that make my eyes roll back and my legs shiver.

"Tell me," he says again.

I whip my head up, finding his eyes on me glowing with lust.

"I'm yours," I spit out between moans, not taking my eyes off his.

He makes a guttural sound, and our mouths collide. His thumb works my center and with his cock pushed deep inside me I find my release coming in waves. I shake and cry out into his mouth, feeling his cock twitch inside me with his own release. He holds me tight against him until my body steadies, and my head falls to the hollow of his shoulder.

"Gods, I don't deserve you," he says while stroking my hair that's slick and damp with our sweat.

"You do. You do deserve me, Nyx." I kiss his collarbone and then his neck. I don't want this day to end. I want to stay in bed with Nyx buried inside me. I can't get enough of him and the feelings he elicits from my body.

"Would you like to take a bath and have something to eat?" he asks while lazily stroking my hair and back.

"Yes, that'd be nice." I make no effort to move. He lifts me up, and I let my legs wrap around his waist. He carries me into the bathroom, waving a hand to fill the bath with warm water, then slowly slides me off of him and lowers us both into the tub.

"Careful. You're using magic again."

"Don't worry. I won't put you at risk. Filling a tub is nothing, just like the orb of light." He turns me around so my back is to him. He grabs a bar of soap and starts washing my hair. The scent of citrus fills my nose. I let him massage me and wash me all over until he's satisfied with my cleanliness.

"Now turn around and let me wash you," I say, moving to face him and holding my hand out for the bar of soap.

He doesn't say anything. He just grins at me before handing me the soap and turns to give me his back. I lather the soap in my hands and massage it gently into his scalp and neck. Then I lather it up some more and begin cleaning his body, starting with his back and shoulders. His shoulders are so broad, and the hard, thick muscles on his arms feel nice. Once I'm satisfied with his cleanliness, I lean forward and kiss his head. I stand to find a couple of towels, and we take turns drying each other.

He places a kiss on my forehead then grabs our packs, handing me mine and rummaging through his. We both get dressed, and I braid my hair in two braids one down either side of my head.

"Next time you ride me, I want to hold onto those braids," Nyx says, giving me a devilish smile.

I smile back and plop down on the bed. "So what do we have to eat?"

"I have some dried meat, cubes of cheese, and dried fruit. Oh, and some travelers delights and honey-coated rolls." He pulls out a couple of containers and places them between us. Then places another container full of meat on the ground in front of Chepi.

We eat our fill, and my nerves start to stir up in my chest, shooting down to my stomach as I imagine leaving the place I've grown so fond of in the last few hours. I don't want to think about what may lie ahead of us as we hike across the Cinder Territory tonight.

"What type of things should I be worried about tonight?"

"What do you mean exactly?" Nyx lies on his elbow across from me.

"Like what kind of creatures are out there? Should I be

worried about more Monstrauths attacking us? And you can't fight with magic . . . " My words trail off, but he understands my point.

"Well, for starters, I'll fight with magic if I absolutely have to, but I don't think it will come to that. I'm an excellent swordsman and a trained fighter all around. As for what creatures are out there . . . the Lycans are out there for one. I wouldn't put it past them to attack us if they think we're sneaking through their territory unannounced. There are other things that live in these woods, but nothing compared to the Shifting Forest on the other side of the Lycan Realm. That's where most of the dangerous creatures live. I don't think anything will attack us tonight. It's possible we could run into more Monstrauths depending upon how many are out there, but like I told you before they can't see well at night. I'm more worried about you tripping and hurting yourself than I am a creature hurting you."

That makes me laugh and flush. "I can't help that I have poor balance." I cover my face with my hands, giggling. "There's something else I should probably have mentioned before."

"What is it? There's no need to be shy, especially after what we just did." Nyx smirks at me, causing my face to heat.

"I'm not taking anything for protection." My voice dies off.

"It's okay. I take a tincture once a month to prevent pregnancy."

Of course he does. Who knows how often he's having sex with other women? The idea makes my chest feel tight, and I start to accept I have much deeper feelings for Nyx than I've been allowing myself to believe. I never had this conversation with Aidan, and that makes my stomach churn. I hope Aidan takes a tincture too.

"What's wrong?" he asks, drawing my eyes back to him.

"Nothing, why do you ask?"

"Your face always gives you away. You looked disturbed for a moment."

"Oh, it's nothing. I'm fine."

"Lyra, tell me please."

I don't want to lie to him, and I can't tell him about Aidan.

"I was just thinking about how many women you must spend time with."

His lips press into a flat line, and I mentally brace myself for his response.

"I have been with other women in the past, and I know that must be hard for you to hear. I know you've been with one other man, and the thought makes me want to disembowel whoever it was. But know this, Lyra, I've never felt the way I feel for you with another. I only have eyes for you." He takes my hand in his and places a kiss atop it, easing the tightness in my chest.

"I want you to teach me how to defend myself. I know I'll never be a great fighter or anything, but it'd be nice to at least be able to defend myself. I was foolish before. Growing up, I never wanted to learn physical combat."

"As soon as we get back to Nighthold, I'll teach you how to do more than just defend yourself. Your Fae magic will help you. You'll start feeling it more in time. And when your birthday comes and you have your Sorceress magic, I know you'll be powerful. But one should always know the basics of physical combat. You never know when you might need it."

The time passes fast, and before I know it Onyx is going through our bags and leaving some stuff here so he can combine our things into one large backpack he can wear. Once he has everything arranged to his liking, he pulls on his boots, lacing them up tight, and I do the same. Once I stand and survey the room one last time to make sure we're not forgetting anything, I file this place away in my memory. This is the place where I felt the intimacy grow between us. This place I gave a piece of myself to him.

He pulls me close, kissing me long and hard. "Are you ready to face the forest, Lewis?"

I nod, breathless from his kiss. We walk back down the hall, crawl up the ladder, and Nyx helps me to my feet. Chepi flies beside me. My eyes adjust to the moonlight as I look around. Nyx seals the door to the bunker and takes my hand. All I can hear in the distance is the hoot of an owl and the crush of snow under our feet as we leave behind our serenity.

CHAPTER
TWENTY-SEVEN

"So how long has it been since you trekked through the Lycan Realm at night with a girl?" I ask to break the silence.

Nyx laughs. "I'd have to say this is a first for me. I've been through this territory before, but not like this and not with a woman."

"Are you cold?" He rubs my shoulders while we walk.

"No, I feel okay right now. All the walking is keeping me warm. Well, except for my nose." I bring my hands to my face and blow out warm air to warm my nose.

"I've traveled through here once before, but it was on horseback and along the river. Nothing looks familiar now. Maybe it's being in the dark." I try to keep my pace up with his.

"With Aidan?" he asks.

"Yes, with him. When he brought me to the ceremony. I plan to kill him." My voice is stoic, and Nyx pauses for a moment to look at me.

"You plan to kill Aidan?"

"Yes." I continue walking ahead.

"He'd deserve it, after the ceremony and everything he put you through." He walks up behind me.

"Not today, but once I have all of my powers. Once I'm strong, I will kill him." I open my mouth to speak again, but Nyx places his hand over my mouth, motioning me to be quiet.

My heart starts to race, and my eyes widen. He can see or sense something out here in the woods. He points to his ears then points to our left. I guess that means he heard something over there. I try to hold my breath and listen intently, but I don't hear or see anything. Chepi is silent next to me but is also staring in the same direction, like he may have heard something too.

"I thought I heard something. Let's keep going. Try to stay quiet for a bit and keep close to me." Nyx reaches for my hand, but before he can take it something large slams into his back, knocking him to the ground.

I scream as a large black figure tumbles with Nyx down the hill. My body is frozen for a second. My heart's about to beat out of my chest, then my mind catches up, and I start running down that hill after them. Chepi flies in front of me, growling. The echo of an animal's snarl rings out into the cold air, and as I get closer I see a large black wolf circling Onyx in the dark. I grab Chepi and hold him close to me.

"Easy wolf, do you know who I am? I don't want to have to kill you," Onyx says in a calm voice, and the wolf just snarls louder. His eyes glow light blue, and his maw is dripping with frothy saliva. I take another step, and a branch cracks under my foot, causing both the wolf and Nyx to shoot their attention in my direction. Once the wolf's eyes meet mine, he tilts his head and softens his face for a moment.

"Rhett?" I whisper with a hand held out in front of me.

In a split second, he's in his human form, charging toward me. He pulls me into a hug, lifting me off the ground. Chepi squeals between us, and I let him go so I can fully embrace Rhett's hug.

"Lyra! I thought I'd never see you again." He squeezes me tight.

Nyx is there next to me in a split second. He doesn't look pleased by this encounter.

"I didn't think I'd see you again either. I'm so sorry for Luke and for everything that happened." Tears fall down my face.

He sets me back down, taking my face in his hands and wiping my tears away.

"It's okay, Lyra. None of it was your fault. I'm sorry for what happened to you. That prick Aidan needs to be stopped. I told you it wasn't safe for you to be alone with him."

Nyx's face goes from mine to his as if he's piecing together what happened.

"You're naked," I say, stepping back because Rhett has no clothes on.

"Yeah, sorry . . . turn around." He laughs.

Nyx and I both turn around and exchange a look. Something rustles behind us, then Rhett taps my shoulder. I turn back around to find him in torn pants and a black tunic.

"This is Nyx . . . Onyx, I mean. This is King Onyx from Nighthold. Nyx this is Rhett . . . a friend." I stutter, looking between the two of them and just now realizing how awkward this whole encounter has been.

"Yes, we've met," Nyx says between gritted teeth.

"Sorry, man. I'm in charge of patrolling this area. I didn't know who you were or that you were with Lyra. I just smelled an outsider."

Rhett extends his hand to Nyx, who takes it and gives him a nod and firm shake. I laugh.

"What's so funny?" they both say, turning to face me.

"Er, nothing. Sorry." I giggle.

"And who's this little guy?" Rhett asks, looking to where Chepi hovers next to me.

"Oh, this is Chepi," I say.

"I've never seen a flying dog before."

"Chepi isn't a dog. He's a Glyphie," I say, rubbing Chepi's head. He yips at Rhett, his tongue falling out of his mouth. Rhett laughs.

"So what are you guys doing here?"

"We're going to find Aidan. I need him to tell me how to find the old Sorceress who was there at the ceremony."

"Did you know what the ceremony meant?" Nyx asks Rhett while placing a hand on my lower back.

"No, none of us knew anything. Lyra, I swear. I was devastated after seeing—well you know. By the time I tried to look for you, it was too late. I found out later from Larc that Aidan threw you in the back of a carriage and took off. I'm sorry, Lyra. I should've come after you. I should have tracked the carriage. You must understand I—we all were in a bad place after the ceremony."

"I don't blame you at all, Rhett. I didn't expect you to come after me. I know Luke was like a brother to you, and I'm so, so sorry. I'm just glad to see you're okay," I say, touching his arm gently.

"Thanks, Lyra. It's been rough. Tensions have been high among the packs, and most of us have left the village to patrol our territories," Rhett says.

"Have you noticed anything different? Seen an increase in activity from some of the darker creatures that inhabit this place?" Nyx asks.

"As a matter of fact, yes, we have. Things in the Lycan Realm have felt off. It's like a darkness is growing here. We have had to patrol more than ever lately. Zog's pack has seen an increase in spider wraiths in the Shifting Forest, and here we have been dealing with a type of demonic creature. I'd never seen one before until about a week ago when they started showing up in small packs all over the Lycan Realm." Rhett's features harden, and I can feel his concern.

"Did they have red slits for eyes?" I ask.

"How did you know? Have you guys seen them?" Rhett asks.

"Yeah, that's a Monstrauth. Nasty demons conjured to hunt what the conjurer desires," Nyx explains. "We suspect Samael is behind their appearance."

"That wouldn't surprise me. There's been talk that he's gone crazy since taking the throne. I haven't been to the Sorcerer Realm, but whispers are growing that Samael is unstable, murdering entire families and stealing grimoires," Rhett says.

Nyx and I both looked at each other.

"Yeah. We've heard the same rumors, only I don't think they're just rumors. We believe Samael may be trying to find a way to make his magic permanently dark, but it's just a theory I have," I say.

"It sounds like a plausible theory. Are you sure you want to find Aidan? If I was you, I'd go straight back to Nighthold. Cloudrum is growing more dangerous by the day, and just wait until you see Aidan's place, wait until you see the entire village," Rhett says.

"What do you mean? What's happened to the village?" Nyx asks before I can.

"At the ceremony he said he was doing what was best for all the packs, but really he was just looking for money. I don't know why he did what he did to you or who ordered it, but whoever it was paid him handsomely. The entire village has been transformed. You'll understand when you see it," Rhett says.

I trust Rhett, but now doesn't feel like the right time to tell him about my father and the prophecy. I don't even want to tell him my own parents ordered the ceremony to take place. The thought causes my stomach to feel sick.

"We don't want anyone to know we're here. Can you keep it a secret for now please?" I ask.

Rhett nods. "Of course, Lyra. I won't tell anyone. Are you trying to make it to Aidan's place by morning?"

I look at Nyx, who nods.

"In that case, I'll go with you guys. It's dangerous out here, and I'll make sure no one else in my pack stumbles upon us."

I look to Nyx for his answer or approval.

"We better get going then," Onyx says and looks at Rhett, his eyes hardening for a moment before he leads the way back up the hill.

All of us walk on in silence for a long while. Nyx leads the way. Rhett tugs on my arm for me to slow down, and I do. I know Nyx can sense us and probably realizes our pace has slowed behind him, but he keeps his pace and doesn't act like anything's wrong. Rhett nudges my arm with his elbow.

"So, what's the deal with you and the Faery King?"

"Oh . . ." My face flushes, and I'm not sure how to answer for a moment. I don't know what the deal is exactly. Are we together? It feels like we are, but nothing has really been declared. He did say I was his, but that was in the heat of passion. Did he mean it? Did I mean it?

"I can smell him all over you," Rhett whispers with a playful glint in his eye. My face flushes with embarrassment.

"We're just old friends," I tell him and immediately regret it. I hear Nyx's steps slow for the briefest moment, and I know he must be listening to us. Fae hear everything. I don't want to hurt his feelings by saying we are just friends, but it's not like he's asked me to be anything more than that. My chest hurts slightly. There's a strange tugging feeling where my heart is, and I don't know what it means, but I try to push it out of my mind.

"Old friends . . . right." Rhett laughs. "All I have to say is he better treat you right. If he doesn't, he'll have to answer to me." He smiles in my direction.

"Yes, he does. I promise."

"And if things don't work out with you and the Faery king, you know where to find me." We pick up our pace to catch up to Nyx.

My feet ache with every step, and the silence between us is suffocating. I try to break it a few times, but my attempts fall flat, and we're back to awkwardness. The longer we walk, the more I stumble, and I can feel Rhett and Nyx's eyes on me. They're both walking on either side of me, as if they're afraid I'll fall off the cliff. It's irritating but also somewhat comforting.

Finally, my body gives in to the exhaustion, and I stumble over a slick rock. My ankle twists, and I cry out in pain. I brace myself for impact, but Nyx's strong arms catch me before I hit the ground. It's a relief, but I still can't help but feel embarrassed by my clumsiness.

"Shit," Rhett exclaims, looking at both of us.

"Are you okay?" Nyx sits me down on a large rock.

I try to stand up, but the pain in my ankle makes me wince. "I think I just sprained my ankle," I admit. "It hurts, but I don't think it's broken or anything. I can keep walking." I try to put weight on it to prove my point, but Nyx and Rhett don't look convinced.

"You can climb on my back. I'll carry you," Rhett offers. "It's not too much further. Maybe a couple hours max. Plus, we can probably go faster without you walking anyway."

I consider his offer for a moment before Nyx speaks up.

"I'm going to carry you, baby. You can climb on my back." His voice is soft and reassuring, and I can't help but nod in agreement.

Nyx sets down his pack before kneeling in front of me. I climb on his back, wrapping my legs and arms around him. His muscles ripple under my grip, and I feel safe pressed up against him. Rhett winks at me and mouths "baby" as I settle into place. I roll my eyes but can't help the smile that tugs at my lips.

"Are you sure this is okay?" I ask, worried about being a burden.

"Yes," Nyx responds, "I like your body pressed against mine, and you're hurt. But as Rhett said, we'll go faster this way. No offense." I can see how it amuses him, and I relax as we continue our journey.

I press my cheek against his back, letting my head rest. I don't like slowing the group down, but it's true they're both in much better shape than I am. Now I've gone and screwed things up by hurting my ankle.

"I'm going to heal you once we get to Aidan."

"No, you can't risk the magic. I'll be fine. I just need a day to rest."

"Lyra, have you always been this clumsy? I don't remember you tripping once when we went hiking to the swimming hole?" Rhett asks, and I feel flushed with embarrassment. Now that he brings it up though, I do feel kind of off. It's hard to see out here at night, but something has felt strange. That unsettled feeling festering in my chest has grown since touching down in Cloudrum.

"Why do you ask?"

"It's just—at the ceremony you drank a lot of Lycan blood. Have you noticed anything different?"

"I'm not sure. I guess since we've been back in the Lycan Realm I've been warmer."

"Warmer?" Nyx asks.

"Yeah. I was going to mention it this morning, but we got distracted. When I was barefoot in the snow, it was cold but oddly tolerable." I turn my head to meet Rhett's gaze. "Our friend Flora back in Nighthold said I may run warmer, so I just assumed that was it."

"It can yes, but it can also make you go crazy, lose coordination, become sick," Rhett says, and I feel Nyx tense.

"She hasn't exhibited anything negative yet. Wouldn't that have happened a long time ago?"

"I'm not sure. It's not a common occurrence for one to drink Lycan blood. It could be affecting you more now that you're back in the Lycan Realm, or it could be nothing. Just be aware of it," Rhett says.

"Tell me if you feel anything out of the ordinary. I don't care how distracted we are, okay?" Nyx says.

"Okay."

We do seem to make good time now that I'm not walking, and Nyx goes even faster with me on his back, which is crazy to me because I'm not dainty by any means. We walk along a half-frozen creek for a long time, then eventually the boys hop on rocks to cross it. Rhett finally stops at the top on an embankment, and Nyx slowly lowers me to the ground, keeping one arm out for me to brace myself.

"What's up? Why'd we stop?" I ask Rhett.

"We're close now. Just follow this hill down and keep going straight until you see a narrow dirt road. It'll take you partly through the village, then you'll see Aidan's driveway. You remember what it looks like, right?"

"Uh, yes, I do."

"Okay this is where I'll leave you two. I don't really care to

273

see Aidan. But I wish you guys the best. I hope you find what you're looking for. And if you start feeling weird, get as far away from the Lycan Realm as possible, fast."

I embrace him in a hug. I don't know when I'll see him again, so I hug him tight. "It was really good seeing you, Rhett. I'm going to miss you."

"It was good seeing you too, blondie. Don't be a stranger. Onyx, you better take good care of her, and don't leave her alone with that prick Aidan no matter what."

"Don't worry. She's in good hands." Nyx extends his hand for Rhett to shake.

"Good meeting you too," Rhett says, petting Chepi on the head. Chepi flies in close, licking his face, and Rhett chuckles.

I watch Rhett walk away, feeling a bit sad to see him go. He shifts into his wolf form, looking back at us one more time, then takes off running into the forest until he blends into the night.

"I think I can manage walking the rest of the way, so long as we take our time," I tell Nyx, shifting on my feet.

"Not a chance, hop on," he says, kneeling in front of me.

I hesitate for a moment then hop on his back again. Nyx and I continue walking in silence for a few minutes after our conversation about Rhett. I feel awkward and unsure of what to say, but Nyx breaks the silence, his voice soft and gentle.

"So 'old friends,' huh?" he says, and I can hear the teasing undertone in his voice.

I cringe at my own awkwardness. "I knew you heard that," I murmur, mentally berating myself for my lack of composure.

"Is that what you want, Lyra, to be friends?" Nyx asks, his voice gentle but probing. "I didn't get that feeling in bed earlier."

I feel my cheeks flush, embarrassed by my own words. "I didn't know what to say. Rhett caught me off guard."

"And you like him? Is he the boy you slept with?" Nyx asks, his voice betraying a hint of jealousy.

"Oh gods, no. Yes, I like him as a friend, but nothing more. Nothing sexual has ever happened between us."

"I just watched him hold you while he was nude," Nyx says, his voice tense.

"I think nudity is just normal for the Lycans. Honestly, there's nothing between us other than friendship. I haven't even known him for very long." I adjust my grip around Nyx's neck as we continue walking.

"It's not like you ever asked me to be something more than a friend. I didn't want to assume anything just because we slept together. I'm sure you've slept with many girls before me without it meaning anything," I say, trying to hide the vulnerability in my voice.

Nyx sighs, and I brace myself for his response, feeling exposed and raw on his back.

"Throughout my life, I've been with many women, Lyra. But none of them can compare to how I feel about you. I don't just want a friendship with you. I want to be yours in every way – body, mind, and soul. I have no desire to possess you like others might. My only goal is to cherish and adore you, give you everything you could ever want and more. I just want you, Lyra, in every sense of the word."

My heart pounds in my chest at his words, and I feel tears prick at the corners of my eyes. "I want to be yours, Nyx," I whisper, my voice filled with emotion.

He grips my thighs and twists me around, holding me in front of him, and kisses me deeply. I open for him immediately, wanting his tongue in my mouth, wanting anything to feel closer to him.

"Good. Because I wanted to kill Rhett when he kept

hugging you," he says, and I know by the hardened look in his eyes he's not joking.

"Well, I'm glad you practiced good restraint," I tell him, pulling him in for another kiss.

"Goddamn snow, you have way too many clothes on," he mutters, trying to rustle under my layers of sweaters to touch my skin. His hands finally slip under my shirt, stroking the skin on my back. I moan into his mouth.

"I can't wait to be alone with you in bed again," I whisper between kisses.

"Soon, my love," he says, placing a kiss on my nose then continuing to walk toward Aidan's village. The rest of the walk, all I can think about are Nyx's hands on my body. I should be thinking about how I'm going to face Aidan and what I'm going to say to him, but my mind keeps betraying me, replaying the hours I spend with Nyx inside of me.

"When was the last time you saw Aidan?" I ask, breaking the silence.

"At your parents' funeral."

"How do the two of you know each other? Are you friendly with one another?"

"He knows me because I am the king of Nighthold, and I know him because he's the leader of the Lycan Realm. Neither of us has ever considered the other a friend. An acquaintance would be a better word for it. We've had our fair share of run-ins over the years, but Aidan's always been a bit of a prick. I've never liked how he treats women or how he treats his packs. Why do you ask?"

"Just curious."

We finally make it to the village, and the sky is a light-blue hue, like the sun is only a couple hours from rising. The village is eerily quiet. Everyone must still be asleep, or it's mostly deserted. All the packs must be patrolling their territories. I don't know what's normal for this village since I was only here at its busiest time of year for the ceremony, but it feels as though it's devoid of life. The only sound that breaks the eerie silence is the crunching of gravel and snow under Nyx's feet.

When we reach the start of Aidan's driveway, I point to it with a trembling hand, and Nyx starts walking down it. With every step, my anxiety grows. Memories of my last visit to this place flood my mind, and I can't help but feel sick to my stomach. I know I have to face Aidan, but the thought of being back in that house, where he abused and hurt me, is almost unbearable.

As we approach the barn, memories of Luke bubble up, and I can feel a lump forming in my throat. The thought of him coming out to greet us with his floppy hair and innocent smile brings both happiness and sadness.

The cabin comes into view, and I can barely recognize it. What used to be a rustic, cozy log cabin is now a foreboding fortress of black stone and iron. It's as if someone had taken a snapshot of my nightmares and brought them to life. The black stone walls loom over us, adorned with fierce wolf carvings that look almost alive in the dim light of the dawn. I shudder as we approach the tall iron fence at the front, and Nyx pulls the gate open.

As we walk toward the main house, my heart is racing, and my palms are slick with sweat. The once-humble cabin has been transformed into a grand palace made of gleaming, petrified wood and is now two stories high. The wooden door that used to welcome guests is now an enormous set of unbreakable obsidian doors that match the surrounding walls.

"Are you alright?" Nyx asks, and I know he must be picking up on the strong wave of emotions rolling through my body.

"Yes, but this is different. The wall and the cabin, it was

basic farmland last time I was here and now..." I whisper, trying to collect myself. *Calm. Just keep calm.*

We reach the top of the steps, and my breath catches in my throat as Nyx knocks on the door. The sound reverberates through the eerie silence of the village, and I can't help but feel like we're disturbing the peace. The anticipation is making my head spin, and my heart feels like it's about to burst out of my chest. I grab Chepi and wrap my arms tightly around him, drawing comfort from his warm, furry body. The unease that has become a permanent fixture in my chest rears its ugly head, causing my palms to sweat and my stomach to knot. Chepi comforts me with a lick on my cheek and a snuggle into my neck, slowly easing the anxiety in my chest. I take a deep breath and let it out slowly. *Calm.*

No one answers, and after another minute Nyx knocks even harder, kicking the door a bit.

"This better be fucking good." Aidan pulls the door open.

I see his face the moment he sees Nyx and the surprise that crosses it. But then his eyes lock on mine, and that's when he smirks. His ugly, sarcastic smirk. I want to jump down and slap off his face.

"Back for more, Cheeks," Aidan says, winking.

"Don't fucking speak to her," Nyx says, and Chepi starts to growl. I worry for a moment Nyx is going to use his magic, but I feel the tension leave his body as he loosens his grip on me a bit.

Nyx's voice takes on a commanding tone, and I can feel the power in his words. "We have important matters to discuss with you, Aidan. It's imperative that we speak with you immediately."

Aidan greets us with a sly smile, and my skin starts to crawl. Memories of his rough hands and unwelcome touch flood my mind, and I can barely stand to be in his presence. I cling to Nyx's back for support and comfort, feeling the warmth of his body seeping through my skin.

"Of course, King Onyx. Please, come inside," Aidan says, holding the door open wider for us to enter. I can see the glint in his eye as he looks at me, and I feel sick to my stomach. How could he have done those things to me?

I try to steady my breathing and focus on the task at hand. With Nyx by my side, I can do this. I just need to stay strong and keep my emotions in check.

CHAPTER

TWENTY-EIGHT

N yx sits me down on the couch in front of the fire, kneeling on the ground in front of me to examine my ankle. Chepi plops down next to me, cuddling close to my side. Thank the gods this is no longer the couch where I actually asked Aidan to kiss me. I try to push the thought from my mind and focus on the pain in my foot. This room is unrecognizable except for the giant fireplace in the same spot. Instead of being built out of cobblestone, it's been turned into shiny black stone. The ground beneath me was once half-rotted, unfinished wood, but now petrified wood sparkles in the firelight.

"You got yourself hurt there, Cheeks?" Aidan says, coming to kneel next to Onyx.

"Stop calling me that. Yes, I twisted my ankle." I scowl at him.

"Here, just elevate your foot," Aidan says, moving some cushions and motioning for me to turn sideways on the couch.

I furrow my brows at him, wondering why he's acting so normal. I do as he says and place my foot on the pillows. Nyx takes a seat on the mantle across from me next to the fire, and Aidan pulls over a chair to face us. I don't know why, but sitting here looking at these two men who couldn't be more opposite is just weird. I have so much I want to say, yet my words don't come out. I feel tongue tied for a moment. Nyx must notice, because he starts the conversation for me.

"We want to know what the Lycan ceremony did to Lyra." Nyx looks directly at Aidan.

I don't know which male looks broodier. Nyx is taller and more serious and orderly, while Aidan just looks like a sarcastic ass who's full of himself.

"Of course, you do." Aidan chuckles. "Let me get us a few drinks before we get down to business." Aidan moves into the newly remodeled kitchen across from us.

We wait in silence, and Nyx gives me a reassuring smile while reaching over to rub my shoulder with one hand. The touch calms my nerves.

"This should put some hair on your chest, Cheeks," Aidan says, dropping a glass of potato piss in my hands then handing one to Nyx. He takes his seat and holds up his own glass.

"What, no moon bread this time?" I ask Aidan, giving him a dirty look, but he just ignores me.

"To . . . old friends," he says with that ugly smirk on his face. When neither of us say anything, he just shrugs his shoulders and takes a long gulp.

I smell my glass and wrinkle my nose at the scent. I forgot how strong the Lycans like their whiskey. But I have a feeling I'm going to need whiskey to make it through this conversation, so I look at Nyx and give him a nervous smile and take a drink. I don't see Nyx drink from his glass. Instead, he places it next to him on the mantle. I guess it's smart for one of us to stay sober for this.

"We're not here to be friends, Aidan. Now cut the shit and

tell us what we need to know before I'm forced to no longer be a gentleman," Nyx says

"Oh, but we are friends, intimate friends. Aren't we, Lyra?"

I feel my stomach squeeze. Nyx doesn't know I slept with Aidan, the most repulsive, despicable fucking male other than Samael. I don't want Nyx to know what happened. I can't bare the idea of him looking at me differently.

"You sure do talk a lot of shit, Aidan. Now tell me where we can find the old Sorceress from the ceremony and what it did to Lyra." Nyx gets to his feet, and I can feel the tension rising in the room.

"The old Sorceress you speak of is named Athalda, and you can find that old bitch in the Shifting Forest. As for the ceremony, I don't know what it did to Lyra, nor do I care. I got what I wanted," Aidan says, moving his foot to rest on his knee.

"What did you get out of it? You said you were only doing what my parents wanted. What did you mean?" I ask.

"As you can see, Cheeks, things have changed around here. Your parents may have died, but they still made sure I got my payment. They paid me handsomely to make you drink that Lycan blood," Aidan says, and I can feel my magic again. My body is suddenly feeling too hot, like something is crawling under my skin.

"How could you kill them! You killed Luke for money? That's all his life was worth to you?" Disgust fills me as I stare at Aidan and his hollow blue eyes.

"That little shit didn't mean anything to me. The pack is better off without him. We didn't need a weak link patrolling the Shifting Forest. He would've gotten himself killed sooner or later. At least this way I got a nice payday out of it. That money will be of more use to the pack than any of those adolescents," Aidan says.

I'm so angry that my blood is going to burn me alive. It's

going to boil me from the inside out. The rage I feel for this man. Nyx sits on the edge of the couch next to me and places an arm around me. His fingers brush against my arm, cooling the heat building inside me. I know Chepi can sense it too because he starts nudging my hand with his nose.

"Where in the Shifting Forest can we find Athalda?" Nyx asks, changing the subject.

"She has a home built into the mountainside deep in the Shifting Forest. Not a place either of you want to go venturing," Aidan tells us, and I grow more irritated.

"Well, I need answers, Aidan, so either you're going to give me some or you're going to tell us how to find Athalda." I try to keep my voice calm and collected. *Breathe.*

"I don't know why your parents ordered what I did to you at the ceremony. Honest, Lyra, you can think I'm despicable or whatever you want—I don't give a shit—but I'm telling the truth about that. Athalda arranged everything, and that sneaky bitch has her secrets. Good luck getting her to tell the two of you," Aidan says.

I look over at Nyx and he nods at me, somehow knowing what I was asking of him. I want him to tell me if Aidan's telling the truth. I don't know how he does it, but usually he can sense when someone's lying. I think he knows when I'm lying, but he usually lets me get away with it. I don't want to tell Aidan anything about the prophecy in my father's journal, because if he truly doesn't know anything it's pointless sharing that information. If he really is just a pawn in all of this...we need to find Athalda.

"I'm waiting," Nyx says, his lips pressed in a flat line. Aidan is testing his patience too.

"I'll find you a map of the Shifting Forest and tell you how to get to Athalda's place. I'll try to get word to 'Zog's pack too that you'll be coming through there. All sorts of shit has been sprouting up since Samael became king," Aidan says, moving to the kitchen.

"What do you know of Samael? What's he playing at with all of this?" Nyx asks.

"Samael, that prick." Aidan chuckles to himself and rejoins us with his glass refilled. "I know he's power hungry; I know he's been plotting. I wouldn't put it past him that he's the one who killed your parents. Carriage accident is what he told everyone. I don't believe that shit. I think he got word of what your parents were planning, and he took things into his own hands. Even I could tell your parents were planning something. I could feel it in the castle in Tempest Moon. And now that Samael is king, spider wraith attacks have tripled in the Shifting Forest. More are breaking through the borders each day. Monstrauths have been hunting the cinder territory for the first time in over a hundred years. A darkness is settling over Cloudrum. All the creatures can feel it. I don't give a shit what that prick does as long as he leaves Lycans out of it. I've heard the whispers of him making animals his test subjects. If I ever get word he's using a Lycan—war is going to start in these parts a lot sooner than I'd like." Aidan runs his hands through his hair, and the first signs of worry cross his features for a moment, but he's quick to control it.

"I can't heal Lyra's ankle because I risk Samael tracking my magic. Do you have a healer here and a place we can rest until tomorrow? Then we need to find this Athalda."

"I have a guest house on the property you can use as long as you'd like. Most of the village is cleared out this time of year, but Marth's wife is a good healer. I'll ask her to come check on you."

"And I'll be back later to collect this map you speak of," Nyx says.

It's nice of him to offer us a place to stay and a healer, but no way am I thanking him for it after what he's done to me. Aidan only ever does what serves Aidan. He can only be helping us for selfish reasons, and the thought makes my chest tighten with worry.

I move to get up, but Nyx bends over and cradles me in his arms, carrying me to the door. Chepi's wings materialize, and he quickly flies over, landing on my chest. We follow Aidan around the back of the large, newly remodeled cabin and down a dirt path obscured by trees that leads further back on the property.

"Marth's wife's name is Hilda. I'll ask her to bring you guys a little bit of whatever Marth's got cooking for dinner later too. I'll be around if you need anything else." Aidan points to the cabin up ahead then turns back, disappearing down the path. Surprisingly, the guest house is clean and kind of nice. It's set up similarly to Aidan's house before the remodel, but this place has more of a woman's touch to it. The sofa is faded red with white flower designs on it and large fluffy pillows. I wonder what woman would ever want to be with Aidan.

I get comfortable, and Nyx gets to work lighting a fire in the fireplace. He finds a cream-colored quilt to throw over me, tucking it gently around me and Chepi.

"Comfortable? Warm?" he asks.

"Yes, thank you." I smile while pulling on his arm so he'll sit with me.

He sits behind me, pulling me back to lean against him. I tilt my head back to see his face, and he kisses my forehead.

"What do you think about everything Aidan says?" I rest my head on his chest. "Can we trust him?"

"I think Aidan's an opportunistic asshole. He's always going to do what's best for himself, but I don't think he's who we need to be worried about right now. I didn't get the sense he was lying about anything he said back there, and I don't think he wants Samael sniffing around. We don't need to worry about him giving up our location. As much as I hate to say it, if war does come it'd be nice to have the Lycans as allies. I think Aidan would need us more than we'd need him."

"Yeah," I say, sighing deeply.

"I'm interested in finding Athalda. I'm hoping she'll be able to fill in more pieces of the story than Aidan was," he says, pulling my messy braid free and running his hands through my hair.

"Why does Aidan call you 'Cheeks?'" Nyx asks, and I feel my pulse quicken.

"I don't know why Aidan does anything. That man is repulsive."

"Please don't."

"Please don't what?" I ask, turning to meet his face.

"Don't lie to me about this. What is the deal with you two? I know you hate him because of what he did to you at the ceremony, because he killed your friend. He's despicable, and you're right to hate him—it just felt like there was something else going on between you two back there," Nyx says, holding my gaze. I can't help but look away as a sense of shame washes over me.

"I don't want to talk about Aidan anymore," I say, pulling him in closer and placing a kiss on his mouth.

"You really think we can wait until tomorrow to go after Athalda?" I ask, knowing Nyx may have dropped the subject of Aidan for right now but won't forget it.

"Yes. You're hurt, and we just spent all night hiking. The Shifting Forest is dangerous, and we need to be well rested. I promise we'll find her and get answers, Lyra. I'm not going to let you die. We still have plenty of time before the blood moon if you need to complete the ceremony. I'm still not convinced you do. I'm not going to let anything happen to you. We'll get to the bottom of all this, together."

I feel the sincerity in his voice. He pulls me into him, deepening the kiss. Gods, I would let this man do anything he wanted. I pull away, breathless. My lips are already puffy from our embrace.

"Thank you," I whisper, letting some tension leave my body and relaxing my head against his chest.

We sit like that for a while, just resting in silence. Both of us are deep in thought. Nyx runs his hand through my hair, playing with the wavy bits. I listen to the rise and fall of his chest. I wish my father was here. I wish I could just ask him what all of this means and why he made me the key to unlocking a bridge to Zomea. Why did he even want a bridge to Zomea? What greater purpose does all of this serve?

"I'm going to go speak with Aidan. I want to make sure I get that map from him and find out what we can expect to come across in the Shifting Forest," Nyx says, moving behind me and pulling me from my thoughts.

"I'll go with you."

"No, you need to rest. I'll ask when we can expect the healer, Hilda, to be by as well. Do you want me to move you to the bed?"

I see no point in fighting him. I am tired, and I don't really want to see Aidan again.

"No, I'm fine here by the fire . . . be careful." I move some pillows and lie back.

"I'm always careful. I'll be back soon, lover," he says, placing a kiss on my forehead and patting Chepi on the head before disappearing out the front door.

I wait a couple minutes to make sure Nyx is gone then grab my pack and rummage through it for Callum's journal. I may be afraid for what's in it, but I need to know. I flip through the pages quickly, looking for the last line I read. Once I see it again, I read it over—*Euric's offspring will be born for darkness.* That uneasy feeling returns to my chest, and I hesitantly turn the page to read the final page in the journal.

Born for darkness and destined to be with my son. Scarlett was right in questioning me. I banished Euric only to avoid the inevitable. Do I save my people or do I save my son? Why can't they be one in the same? Can his light save her, or will her darkness destroy him—destroy us all?

I drop the journal, and it lands with a heavy thud at my feet. Chepi stirs next to me, sensing my distress, and nudges my arm with his nose. My heart squeezes, and I try to make sense of the jumbled mess of emotions within me. It's as if the ground beneath me has shifted, and I'm left reeling. Destiny, darkness, and magic swirl around my mind, suffocating me with their weight.

I stare down at the journal, its leather cover gleaming in the dim light. Was I truly destined to be with Nyx? Or was I meant to destroy him, to be the harbinger of his downfall? The weight of the revelation crashes over me, and I can't help but feel overwhelmed by the magnitude of it all. How could Callum have known about my dark magic inheritance? I don't even know if it's true myself. Did he write anything more about it in another journal?

Questions pile on top of questions, and I realize just how much I don't know. Why did Colton give me this journal, and does he have the next one? Did Callum get a chance to write another before he died? Scarlett, Nyx's mother, is mentioned in the journal too. Does she have a journal of her own?

A sick feeling churns in my stomach as I imagine showing the journal to Nyx. What if he's afraid of me, afraid that I'll do as his father wrote and destroy him? I wrap my arms around Chepi, pulling him close to my chest as I stroke his soft fur. The thought of losing him, of losing Nyx, is unbearable. But can I keep this secret from him forever? I don't know, and the uncertainty is suffocating.

"I don't know what to do, boy," I say into the top of his head as tears run down my cheeks. I touch the bloodstone at my neck and try to think about what my father was trying to do with all of this.

Chepi licks my tears away and snuggles close to my neck, comforting me until we both fall asleep.

CHAPTER
TWENTY-NINE

I'm jolted awake when a knock sounds on the door. Gods, how long have I been asleep? It looks like it's dark outside. Where is Nyx? Nyx wouldn't be knocking. I stumble off the couch and hobble over to the door. Chepi hovers over my shoulder. My ankle seems to be hurting worse now than this morning. Maybe it's just because I've been off it all day. I need to stretch it out a bit.

"Who is it?" I call through the door. Can never be too careful.

"It's Hilda, ma'am. I've brought you some food and come to check on your ankle."

I open the door, offering a gentle smile and extending my arm to invite her in. She's a short, boisterous woman with gray hair pulled up in a messy bun. She has on a long-sleeve black gown, and I wonder how she's not freezing walking outside like that. I close the door and hobble back to the couch. She places some bowls on the table then comes to sit next to me.

"Marth's been making clipper stew all day. I brought you and King Onyx each a nice large bowl of it and some fresh towarra buns, still hot for dipping," she says cheerfully with a smile.

"Thank you so much." I smile back at her.

"Now let me see this ankle of yours." She motions for me to put my foot in her lap. Once I do, she feels all around my foot and ankle, causing me to wince when she turns it to the side.

"It's not broken, but it is a nasty sprain." She reaches into a bag she has next to her.

"When will I be able to hike on it?" I'm worried. I may slow us down even more if I can't use my feet properly.

"Don't worry. I'll make sure you can walk soon enough. Now, I need you to come with me out to the woods," Hilda says after placing the food on the table.

"What? Why?" I ask quickly.

"If you want me to heal you, then stop asking questions and come with me. He can come to if you'd like," she says, waving in Chepi's direction.

"Come on. Wrap your arm around me, and I'll help you. We don't have to go far, but we need to get under the moonlight."

I drape one arm over her shoulder, and she wraps an arm around my waist as I hobble out the door reluctantly. Chepi stays in the air flying next to us.

"I heard the king and Aidan speaking about the Shifting Forest on my way over here. Is that where you are headed tomorrow?" Hilda asks while we make our way around the back of the cabin into the forest.

"Yes . . . we are. Have you been there before? Can you tell me what to expect?" I ask her, and she purses her lips together in thought while scanning the forest. I hadn't realized I slept for so long. I have no idea what time it is, but the moon is bright overhead.

"I've never been personally, but I've tended to Zog's pack

when they've come back wounded. Spider wraiths are what you need to look out for. Nasty buggers."

I can't place her accent, but Hilda speaks differently than the other Lycans around here. I remember Zog talking to me about spider wraiths and the Shifting Forest, but I was too creeped out by him to pay much attention. I wish I could remember everything he was saying. I had no idea the information would ever come in handy.

"Sit cross legged on the ground. Right over here." Hilda helps me down, and Chepi collapses into my lap. She opens up her bag and starts placing crescent-moon-shaped, light-blue rocks around me in a circle.

"What are you doing? How is this going to heal me?" I ask, examining the rocks.

"I may be a healer, but I'm no Faery or Sorceress. All of my magic comes from the moon. Just like magic that runs through these lands and the magic that allows us to shift into wolves, it all comes from the moon. These rocks will channel the moonlight to you, and it will heal your ankle," she says.

As I sit here with Chepi in my lap, I can't help but feel a hint of disbelief. Is it really possible that the moon's light could heal me? I've heard of stranger things though, and I'm willing to give it a try. I watch in awe as Hilda carefully rubs each of the stones together before placing them around me in a perfect circle, ensuring that each stone touches the next.

As the final stone is placed, a cool white light shines down upon me. It's as if the moon itself has cast a spotlight directly on me. The light sparkles and swirls with ethereal blues and dark midnight hues, creating a mesmerizing tunnel that connects the moon high above with where I sit. I'm completely captivated by the sight and can't look away. Chepi falls asleep in my lap, his light snores filling the silence, but I remain captivated by the moon's light.

Before I know it, the tunnel of light slowly dissipates and is gone. The moon seems lackluster now compared to the stunning display it put on just moments before. I turn to Hilda, still feeling a sense of wonder, and realize that the moon has truly worked its magic on me.

"That was amazing," I whisper.

Hilda just chuckles and starts collecting all the stones, carefully rubbing them together in her hands again before placing them back in the bag. I sit patiently watching her, still a bit awestruck by what just happened. Once she was done, I stand and find my ankle is already feeling considerably better. It's still sore, but I can walk now without having to hop or get assistance from someone else.

"Thank you," I say, looking over at Hilda. Somehow "thank you" doesn't seem like enough, but I have nothing to offer her.

"It was my pleasure, Princess. Now let me walk you back," she says, starting to lead us back in the direction of the cabin.

"What are spider wraiths exactly?"

"Legends tell us they're evil spirits that never passed on to Zomea because they have unfinished business in our realms."

The thought sends a shiver up my spine. "What do they look like?"

She makes eye contact with me for the first time, and her light-blue eyes glow. "They can appear nearly invisible, ghost-like, just a faint trace of smoke outlining what remains of their bodies."

"What do you mean what remains of their bodies? Why are they called spider wraiths if they used to be people?"

"Once they refuse to pass to Zomea, their souls split apart, deforming their bodies. They're said to appear as a giant spider with eight legs, but they carry the same head they did when they were alive."

"So you're telling me giant ghost spiders with human

heads are actually evil spirits that live in the Shifting Forest?" I choke in disbelief.

"That's exactly what I'm tellin' ya. They don't know friend from foe. They'll seek to harm whoever they encounter, no matter what your motivations are. They're the embodiment of evil alive on earth. The packs assigned along the borders keep them inside the Shifting Forest."

We finally reach the cabin, and Hilda follows me inside. I sit down on the couch and motion for her to sit with me.

"Please sit. Tell me more," I say.

She takes a seat, and Chepi plops down between us, rolling on his back. Hilda rubs his plump belly, and his tongue hangs out of his mouth as he soaks up the free belly rubs.

"Spider wraiths are the only creatures the Lycans are afraid of. Lycans may fear death, as all creatures do, but we accept it. We accept that when it is our time we'll go to Zomea. But if you die at the hand of a spider wraith—that's it. They tear your actual soul into pieces. Nothing lives on, not even in Zomea,"

The door swings open, causing both of us to jump.

"Sorry, I didn't mean to scare you ladies. Hilda, what do you think of Lyra's ankle?" Nyx asks, coming to kneel next to the couch.

"Oh, King Onyx, her ankle will be good as new by morning," Hilda says, getting to her feet.

"Thank you, Hilda, and please just call me Onyx," Nyx says, smiling at her.

She blushes and gathers her bag quickly. "I better be going. Eat your dinner before it gets cold. I brought an extra-large bowl for you, Onyx." She places a hand on my shoulder as she walks by and whispers, "Be careful, dear." Then she leaves.

Once we're alone, I spin around to look at Nyx.

"Where have you been all day?" I say a little too loud. "I

woke up to Hilda knocking on the door and realized it was practically dark out, and I was worried you weren't back."

"I'm sorry. I came back like I said I would, but you were sleeping, so I went and gathered some supplies for tomorrow. I knew Hilda was coming by, and I wanted to make sure you got the rest you needed. I didn't mean to worry you . . . although you do look rather cute all frazzled and worried about my well-being," Nyx says, moving to sit next to me.

"I'm not trying to look cute. Please don't leave me alone again, not here," I say. His face grows more concerned, but he nods in agreement.

"Let's get some food in you, and we can talk about the plan for tomorrow," Nyx says, getting to his feet.

"Wait, sit down. I need to talk to you about something," I say, reaching for his hand.

"Now I'm really intrigued. What is it?" Nyx says, moving to sit back down next to me. I pull Chepi into my lap, petting him, trying to calm my nerves.

"When I was at the library the other day, and I ran into Colton," I say. Nyx presses his lips into a hard line. I'm stalling, dragging out what needs to be said. My palms feel sticky, and I rub them on the blanket, clearing my throat.

"He gave me a journal. I don't know why he had it or why he gave it to me, but it's one of your father's journals," I say finally.

"Why are you just now telling me about this? Did you read it?" he asks, turning to face me fully now.

"I don't know why I didn't tell you before. There's been a lot going on lately. Yes, I read it." I swallow hard, feeling the tension radiating off him.

"Well, what did it say?"

"I have it here. I just finished reading it today while you were gone." I reach into my pack and pull the journal out. I hand it to Nyx before continuing, "Go to the last two pages and read them." I watch as he skims through the journal and slowly reads over the final pages. His eyebrows furrow.

"Well..." I wave my arms in front of me, waiting for him to say something.

"What do you want me to say, Lyra?"

"I want you to tell me what this means? What did your father tell you about me? Why did you keep this all a secret?" I can't help raising my voice.

"I've never seen this journal before, Lyra. My father never told me anything about you, and I have no idea why Colton would give this to you other than to cause trouble between us."

"How can I believe you? This wouldn't be the first time you've withheld information from me," I say, pushing my hair out of my face.

"Slow down, Princess. Here it says you'll destroy me. I have no reason to lie about this. I should be the one afraid of you right now."

I narrow my eyes at him. "I don't want you keeping anymore secrets from me because you think you're protecting me," I say, getting to my feet.

"It's funny you speak of secrets. I'm an open book. Ask me anything. You on the other hand always find a way to dodge my questions. You want to talk about keeping secrets, you need to look in the mirror."

I swallow uncomfortably.

"Yeah, why don't we get all the secrets out on the table?"

Nyx moves to stand right in front of me, and I can't help the frustration building in my chest. He's right. I am keeping secrets, but I don't want to be called on it, and I just don't believe him. How could he not know about Callum's journal?

"Stop," I say, looking up to meet his gaze.

"Stop what, Lyra? You don't want to talk anymore now that

it's about what information you're withholding? Don't play coy with me."

Gods, I knew dodging his questions was going to come back and haunt me. I put my hands on his chest, pushing him back, but he doesn't budge. He just grabs my hands, holding them there.

"Now you're going to shove me away instead of talking to me. We played the question game, and you drank instead of answering me. Earlier you blatantly lied to me, and before you tried to distract me by kissing me instead of talking to me. Now you're going to resort to shoving me away. What are you hiding, Lyra? Why won't you just talk to me?"

"Fuck you, Nyx." I turn to leave, but he grabs my arm. It's not hard, but it's firm enough to stop me. When I turn back to scowl at him, he's smiling. He has a wicked grin on his face.

"Why are you smiling like that?" I feel my temper rising.

"I've never seen you so hot and bothered like this. Such a dirty mouth."

"Oh, you're turned on now that I said the word 'fuck.'" I turn to hit him away, and he grabs both my wrists, holding them above my head and moving in so close I can feel his breath on my lips.

"Oh, I'm very turned on by you. Your temper, your flushed cheeks, and your naughty mouth."

I've backed up as far as I can go now. I suck in a breath as Nyx leans into me, my back firm against the wall.

"I'd follow you into darkness any day, Princess."

I look down, eyes wide as Nyx presses into me. He's not lying. I can see his arousal in his pants. It causes my face to heat for a totally different reason. I meet his eyes, and they're glowing now. I lean in like I'm going to whisper something in his ear, but instead I run my tongue up the side of his neck and bite his earlobe.

"Fuck, that's it." Nyx gathers me up in his arms so quick, carrying me toward the bedroom.

"I can walk."

"I've grown rather fond of carrying you around like this." He drapes me over his shoulder and gently slaps my butt, eliciting a yelp.

"I've been thinking about getting you in this bed all day," he says, sitting me down on the edge of the bed.

The bed in here is intimate and cozy with lots of furs piled on top of it. I start to undo my jacket, but Nyx grabs my hands stopping me.

As I sit here, my heart racing with anticipation, Nyx steps closer to me. His eyes are filled with hunger, and his hands are reaching for me. He takes his time unbuttoning the large buttons on the front of my jacket and gently slides each arm free. I feel the cool air hit my skin, and a shiver runs through me.

He pulls my sweater off over my head, and I feel his fingers trail along my skin. I close my eyes and let out a soft moan as he runs his hands up and down my arms before guiding them up and pulling my shirt off over my head, exposing my breasts. He tosses the shirt with the rest of my clothes on the dresser. Nyx walks in front of me, looking me over with a hungry expression.

"Lie back," he says, and I fall back on my elbows, watching him as he moves to grip my leggings around my hips and gently tugs them off one leg at a time. He kneels down on the ground, lifting my ankle and pressing kisses along it, then moving further up my leg. He licks and nibbles at my thigh, causing me to squirm. He stands to look me over as I lie completely bare in front of him.

I can feel the heat rising between us, and my body is humming with need. My eyes are locked onto his, and I can see the desire burning within them. "Your turn," I tell him, nodding at his clothes.

I watch him as he removes his shirt, revealing his muscled chest and arms. He kicks off his boots and slides off his pants, releasing his hard length. I can't stop staring, my eyes transfixed on his body. He walks over to me, and I feel his hands tracing up my legs.

"If you keep looking at me like that, I won't be able to control myself," Nyx says, and I smile seductively, biting my lip.

"I can't help it. I want you."

"How do you want me, Lyra?" he asks, pushing my legs apart with his knee.

I shudder with anticipation. "Filling me...now please," I whisper as he kneels down and pushes a finger inside me.

I run my hands through his hair, and a gasp escapes my lips as his face drops to my center, his tongue twirling around my clit. I can barely take it, the way his tongue and fingers undo me. He works me over with his tongue until my body is shaking with pleasure. Only then does he lift his head up to look at me, his lips glistening with my moisture. He slowly removes his fingers and works his way up my body.

"Now you're ready for me to fill you," he says as he thrusts his cock inside me in one swift motion, causing me to gasp. I wrap my legs around him, pulling him close to me so I can explore his mouth with my tongue. I bite down on his bottom lip just enough to make him groan and thrust into me harder.

He palms my breasts and takes one into his mouth, nibbling on my nipple just enough to make me inhale sharply beneath him. He thrusts inside me hard and stops there, not moving. He moves his hands to my face and wraps his arms around me.

"Look at me, Lyra," he says, his voice low and husky.

I meet his glowing gray eyes, and he starts to move inside me again. This time he goes much slower. He pulls all the way out then slowly thrusts all the way back in until my body is coiled tight with pleasure. I stare into his eyes as he moves inside me. I wrap my legs around his waist and arch my back, giving him full access. Every inch of him fills me, and I can feel the intensity building inside me again. I run my hands over his muscular back, pulling him closer to me. I can feel the sweat on his skin as we move together, and it only heightens my desire for him.

He kisses my neck, leaving trails of heat in its wake. I can feel my body responding to his touch, and I moan in pleasure. He takes my breasts in his hands and pinches my nipples, sending jolts of electricity throughout my body. The coiling heat inside me is unbearable, and I can barely catch my breath.

As he picks up the pace, I dig my nails into his back, arching my hips to meet his every thrust. He's hitting all the right spots inside me, and I can feel myself on the edge of a precipice. The tension is unbearable, and I need release.

"Nyx, harder," I gasp, unable to form a proper sentence.

He grunts in response and drives into me with even more force, sending me over the edge. I cry out in ecstasy as my body convulses around him, and he follows soon after, his release pulsing through him as he collapses on top of me.

We lie there in a heap, breathing heavily, the only sound in the room the thumping of our hearts. Our skin is slick with sweat, and the air is heavy with the scent of sex.

After a few moments, Nyx rolls off me and pulls me to his side, tucking me under his arm. I snuggle into his chest, feeling content and sated. The world around us fades away, and all that exists is the two of us, wrapped in each other's arms.

It's moments like these that I cherish the most — the moments where I can forget about the world and just be with

Nyx. I feel calm and at ease in his arms, and I never want to leave.

"I thought of something I needed to ask you today," I say, moving to pull the blankets over us.

"Oh yeah? What's that?" he asks, rolling on his side so we're facing each other.

"What's your last name? I don't know how I don't know it already."

Nyx laughs and trails his fingers down my face, pulling all the stray hairs away and tucking them behind my ear.

"That is incredibly random, but my last name is Cadeerie."

"Onyx Cadeerie. Nyx Cadeerie . . . I like the way it sounds." I smile at him, letting the name roll off my tongue.

"I'm glad you like it," he says, pulling me close.

"This was a nice distraction, but we need to finish our conversation from earlier," he says while trailing his fingers up and down my side.

"Are you afraid of me?" I ask, and Nyx chuckles.

"Do I look like I'm afraid of you, Princess?"

"No, but what your father says—I'm going to destroy you — destroy everyone. What does it mean? Do you think I'm going to inherit dark magic on my birthday?" I rest my head on his chest and listen to the sound of his heartbeat. The sound is soothing and helps calm the growing anxiety in my chest.

"Lyra, my father was paranoid. He was always obsessing over the future. I don't know if there is any truth to what's in the journal, but when we get back to Nighthold I'm going to have words with Colton. I'm also going to find out if there's another journal after this one that may shed some light on what he's talking about."

"Remember I told you I thought Samael was looking for the *Moon Grimoire* because there's always been whispers that someone in my lineage used to have dark magic?"

"Yes."

"What if it's true? What if I'm to be the first Sorceress in over a hundred years to inherit dark magic? Is it even possible? I get excited about my magic, and a part of me can't wait for my birthday, but then Nyx—there's a part of me that's afraid. What if this uneasy feeling festering in my chest is a sign." I sit up, pulling the blankets up to my chin.

"Lyra, there's not a dark bone in your body." Nyx sits up, touching the bare skin on my back. His cool fingers trail down my skin, causing a chill to work its way up my spine.

"That's where you're wrong. I do have dark thoughts. I want to kill Samael. I don't just want to kill Samael. I want him to suffer."

"Lyra, that's understandable. Samael is an evil piece of shit, and I'd think something was wrong with you if you didn't want to make him suffer. That doesn't make you bad. That doesn't mean you are destined to inherit dark magic, and even if you do you can use your dark magic for good, just like Samael uses his light magic to do bad things."

"I don't know if that's how it works. Not enough is known about dark magic because it's so rarely seen."

"We have a lot going on right now. Let's just focus on finding Athalda and figuring out if we need to open a bridge to Zomea or not. Your life is more important than stressing about what kind of magic you are going to inherit months from now." Nyx pulls me back down, and I let myself relax next to him again.

"You're right. One thing at a time." I take in a deep breath and tell myself I'll worry about Callum's journal and my magic later . . . if there is a later. For all I know we could fail at completing the ceremony, and the key could kill me in a matter of days. *Calm. Breathe.*

"Chepi!" I yell, and he comes running down the hall fast,

302

jumping on the bed. I know he was just lying out there on the couch waiting for us to be done doing our thing in here. He crawls under the covers and cuddles up next to my feet. I relax up against Nyx's body, breathing in his scent and stealing his warmth.

"Are you tired, Onyx Cadeerie?"

"Yes, I'm very tired, Lyra Lewis," he whispers back, and I laugh.

It is late, and I'm afraid of the challenges we'll have to face tomorrow. I don't know if I'll be able to shut off my mind especially after napping most of the day. Sometimes I think Nyx can read my mind because he starts trailing soft circles across my skin and says, "Sleep, Lyra. Don't worry about tomorrow. Just enjoy this moment we have together right now."

He kisses my temple gently, calming me until sleep does find me again, and the last thing I remember is his touch.

CHAPTER

THIRTY

S omething's burning! Blood from the trees is raining down on me. I try to wipe away the warm, viscous fluid from my face. I start running as fast as I can, heat from the fire steering my direction. A wolf comes out of nowhere, running in front of me and causing me to stumble and fall. Warm mud coats my hands. I try to get to my feet, but someone grabs me from behind. I twist around as a scream escapes me.

"Shh. He knows you're here," says Luke, placing a finger to my lips.

"Who knows I'm here? What are you talking about?" A branch cracks and falls next to us, the sound crackling across the forest like lightning.

"Luke! What are you talking about?" I yell, getting to my feet.

"Don't come back," Luke whispers then shifts back into a wolf and disappears into the flames.

"Luke!" I scream. I can't see anything beyond the smoke and the fire. I try to walk in the direction Luke went, but the fire is too powerful. The wind picks up, and the flames fan out around me.

My mother is suddenly in front of me, her body being swallowed up by smoke. She reaches for me, but my hand is slick with blood and mud. Her eyes widen for a moment, and then she's gone. I reach into the smoke again trying to find her, but my hands just swipe through the air.

"I was wrong about him." My mother's voice echoes in the distance, just a whisper in the wind.

I wake up in a panic, drenched in sweat. Nyx is still sleeping next to me. My mother—how? My mother of course is in Zomea, but she had fear in her eyes and her words—wrong about who? Samael? I need to get some fresh air. I quietly slide out of bed, careful not to wake Nyx or Chepi. I slip on my boots and grab the large quilt off the couch, wrapping it around myself.

Once outside the front door I feel like I can breathe again. I now know I must be going to Zomea. It's the only thing that makes sense. Why is Luke there and now my mother? I don't know who he's talking about and why he's so vague every time I see him. He has to be talking about Samael. It's the only thing I can think of, and Luke did appear to me in my dream right before Samael attacked me in my bedroom. But how would Samael know I have midnight mind? How would he know I was in Zomea? The cold air washes away the remnants of the dream, and I try to shake off the uneasy feeling coating my skin. It's eerily quiet out, but I guess it has to be late after midnight for sure. I take a few steps down the path toward Aidan's house. I'm not sure why. I'm just curious if I'll see any activity. Once the house comes into view, everything appears normal. There are no lights on. Aidan must be asleep for the night. I keep walking and find myself down by the barn. I wander inside and give the horses a few pets. I come over to

Aidan's horse, Geri. I recognize him because of the white spot on his face.

"He better be treating you right, boy," I whisper to him, rubbing his muzzle.

"Who are you talking to, Cheeks?" Aidan's voice startles me from behind, causing me to freeze up.

"None of your business . . . I was just going back to bed," I say, turning around to leave. He comes up right behind me.

"Not so fast, Cheeks. We barely got to talk earlier," Aidan says, putting his arm up to lean on the wall in front of me.

"We don't have anything to talk about." I scowl at him.

"I'd say now that your boyfriend is not around, we have a lot to talk about," Aidan says while lifting a hand up to tug on my blanket. I pull it tighter around me, shrugging him off.

"Let me by, Aidan."

"Or what, Cheeks?" He smirks at me like this is a fucking game to him. He likes getting a rise out of me.

"Or I'll scream." I could probably wake Nyx from here.

"Go ahead. Your boyfriend won't save you. I made sure Hilda put something special in his dinner. He won't be awake for hours."

A sense of panic takes over me, but what Aidan doesn't know is Nyx and I got distracted and never ate our dinner. I knew we couldn't trust Aidan. I look around the barn, quickly assessing for anything I can use to protect myself. What the hell was I thinking coming out here in nothing but shoes and a blanket?

"If Nyx wakes up and you've done anything to me, he'll kill you," I say to him through gritted teeth, trying to hide my panic with anger.

"Cheeks, you wound me. I thought you enjoyed our encounter last time. I've been thinking about that tight pussy of yours," Aidan says, placing his hand over his heart.

"You're despicable. I'd rather die than—" My words are cut off as Aidan slams me back against the barn wall, his hand gripping my throat. I gasp for air, clawing at his hand to no avail.

"You'd rather die than have me fuck you again? Is that what you were going to say?" He smirks, his hot breath fanning over my face. "Lucky for you, that's not what I have planned for tonight. Although I have a feeling that by the end of the night you might be wishing you were in my bed instead of where you're going."

"What's that supposed to mean? I'm not going anywhere with you," I hiss, trying to push him away. But his grip on my throat tightens, cutting off my breath.

Now's my chance. I kick Aidan in the groin, and he doubles over in pain. I try to make a run for the door, but he grabs me by the hair and pulls me back onto the hay-covered ground. I feel a sharp pain in my scalp and a wave of dizziness washes over me. I'm helpless under his weight, pinned to the ground as he climbs on top of me.

"On second thought, it looks like you need to be reminded who's in charge," he growls, his hands holding mine down. "What are you going to do? There was no one to stop me last time, and there's no one to stop me this time."

I struggle, but he's too strong. My mind races as I try to think of a way out of this, but nothing comes to mind. I'm trapped, helpless, at his mercy.

"Besides, Cheeks," he sneers, "even if your boyfriend wasn't drugged, do you really think he'd risk killing me? You think he really loves you that much that he'd start a war with the Lycans over you?"

"Fuck you, Aidan. You're not in charge. No one will ever respect you. Not even the Lycans respect you. Your own kind can't stand you. Haven't you noticed this village you rule over is deserted? The packs would rather be out fighting horrible creatures in the forest than inhabiting this place with you. I bet most of the Lycans would celebrate your death."

I spit in his face, and for a moment I feel a flicker of satisfaction. But it's short-lived. Aidan wipes the spit away and lifts his hand like he's going to strike me. I close my eyes and brace myself, waiting for the blow to fall. But nothing happens.

We both startle when the barn door blows open, falling to the ground with a loud crash. Its hinges are broken off, and its wood splinters into the air.

"What the fuck?" Aidan says, trying to get to his feet, but he doesn't get far. Nyx is there, and he doesn't move. He just looks at Aidan, who collapses to his knees, his hands flying behind his back like they've been bound. Chepi flies over to me, and I sit up, grabbing him and pulling him to my chest, covering us both in the blanket. I don't get up though. I'm too frozen to my spot, staring at Nyx. I've never seen him like this. His giant wyvern wings are out, and his ears are slightly pointed. His gray eyes glow bright, but they're somehow darker than normal. His jaw is set in a hard line.

"I thought we were old friends, Aidan? Then you think you have the right to touch what's mine." Nyx's voice comes out full and rich.

Aidan turns his head toward me, but his eyes don't reach me before Nyx forces his head to face him again. He never physically touches him, just uses his magic, treating Aidan like a puppet.

"Don't look at her." It's an order, and I can see the fury in Aidan's face at

"Fuck you, Onyx. I don't need to look at her. I've already seen everything there is to see. Did Lyra tell you how she practically begged me to fuck her last time she was here?" I recoil at his words, and I clench my jaw with anger and embarrassment.

"You drugged me! You drugged me and raped me. You're pathetic!" I yell, my voice trembling as I struggle to keep my emotions in check. I cling to Chepi and the blanket, trying to find comfort in their warmth. For the first time since entering the barn, Nyx's eyes flicker toward me, and I feel exposed under his gaze. In that moment, I see a flicker of understanding in his eyes, a recognition of the pain I'm trying to hide. I drop my gaze, my cheeks burn with shame as I struggle to keep my composure. The distraction is all Aidan needs. He's old, and he's fast. Nyx must've loosened the grip on his magic for a brief moment when he looked at me in shock after what I revealed, and Aidan seizes the opportunity to shift.

He stands before Nyx as a giant white wolf. His hollow eyes focus on Nyx, and his maw froths. Nyx doesn't look afraid though, and I have no idea why because I'm terrified out of my mind. I cover Chepi's face with the blanket to protect him, and I freeze. I can't bring myself to move. The two men stare at each other. Aidan in his wolf form, and Nyx in his full Fae form. I hold my breath and wait for one of them to strike. Aidan makes the first move. He leans his head back as an ear-piercing howl echoes through the barn. Nyx waves his hand, and the howl is cut off when Aidan's jaw breaks. I stare in stunned silence as the upper part of his muzzle cracks open, peeling back over his head. His head breaks clean in half, and his skin —gods, his skin—peels back from his body. Aidan is now reduced to two bloody piles in front of me. One is a pile of inside-out fur and skin, and the other pile is a twisted mess of flesh and bones. My throat spasms, and I think I might throw up. The bloody piles ignite in blue flames. In a matter of seconds, all that's left of Aidan is a pile of ash. Aidan's—dead.

I freeze, staring in disbelief at the pile of ash where Aidan had stood only moments before. My mind is racing, trying to make sense of what just happened. Nyx turns to me, his face softening with concern. He takes a step forward, but I flinch away from him, pressing myself against the wall.

"Lyra, are you okay?"

I don't know what to say. I don't know if I'm okay. The memory of what Aidan did to me floods my mind, and my throat tightens. I try to push it down, to keep it from over-whelming me, but it's no use. I start to shake, and tears spill down my cheeks.

Nyx takes another step closer, and I flinch again. He stops, holding up his hands in a gesture of surrender. "Lyra, I'm not going to hurt you. I promise."

I look up at him, searching his face I think I'm in shock at what just happened. I thought Aidan would've been more of a threat. I thought there was going to be a fight. I actually feared for Nyx for a moment, but Aidan never even touched him. I look into Nyx's eyes now, which are no longer glowing. His wings are gone, and he kneels in front of me, looking the same way he did when I left him in bed. I open my mouth to say something, but howls break out in the distance. Dozens of them. Bone-chilling howls echo across the lands, and a chill so strong creeps up my spine that I start to shiver. Nyx waves a hand, my blanket is gone, and my clothes are back on.

"We need to leave. Now." His voice is stern, and it snaps me back to the here and now.

I get to my feet, and Chepi's wings materialize as he hovers next to me. Nyx saddles up Geri and grips my hips, lifting me onto the horse, then he climbs on behind me. I grab Chepi and hold him close to my chest with one arm and grab the pommel with the other to steady myself. Nyx brings one hand around my waist and takes the reins with his other hand, then we take off into the night.

WE'VE BEEN RIDING for over an hour without saying anything. I don't even know where we're going, but Geri has been galloping this entire time, making it too hard to have a conversation or focus on anything other than holding on. The howls that broke out back in the barn went on for only a couple of minutes before silence settled over the Lycan Realm. It's been silent ever since. We haven't come across so much as another creature, and the only sound around us is that of Geri's hooves hitting the ground. It's eerily quiet, and I can't shake the anxiety in my chest.

I can't believe Aidan is dead. I don't have one ounce of empathy for him. The thought of Aidan being gone feels like the dark claw that dug its way into my heart has been eradicated. A part of me does worry I might see Aidan in Zomea like I see Luke. What if he's able to hurt me there in my dreams? I don't know enough about Zomea or midnight mind to know what is even possible. I try to bury the thought for now and think about the present.

Nyx used a lot of magic back there. Samael must be aware of it. Gods, I always knew Nyx was powerful, but he never even touched Aidan. He never touched him and was somehow able to peel his skin from his flesh and reduce him to ash. Geri's steps slow and his gallop turns into a slow trot.

"What's happening?" I ask in the first words spoken in over an hour.

"We are getting close to the Shifting Forest. We will proceed with caution. I don't want either of us getting bucked off by Geri here. Horses refuse to enter the Shifting Forest, so once we reach the outskirts we'll be forced to walk," Nyx says.

"How did you do that back there? How did you kill Aidan so easily? Are the other Lycans going to come after us?"

311

"I told you. I'm the most powerful Faery alive today. Aidan was no match for me, and the coward knew it too. That's why he howled like that. He was calling the others to him. Remember when we were in the tub in the Fate Fields? I told you Aidan had pure brute strength but not magic like you or I have? It never would have been a fair fight between us. The only reason he carried any power was because he had the strength of all the packs behind him. But you saw his village. There's unrest amongst the Lycans since he killed the three innocents in the ceremony. Normally I'd have stayed out of the Lycan politics and let nature runs its course, but hearing him... hearing he touched you—forced himself on you. Lyra, I may have lost control a little, but I had to end him. I'm sorry you had to witness that."

"Don't be sorry. I'm glad you did it. I just worry about what repercussions you'll have to face now. What will the Lycans do?"

"Well, you heard the howls break out. They know Aidan is dead. I'm sure it was felt across the Lycan Realm. Most of the Lycan will be pleased, but some will be upset. What they do next will all depend on who takes over as leader of the Lycans."

"How is that decided? Who do you think will take over?"

"The moon magic that runs through the lands in the Lycan Realm will choose two Lycan. I don't know all the logistics behind it, but I know the two chosen will feel it. Then one of them can choose to become the leader, while the other submits peacefully, or they fight until one submits or dies."

"How do you think the moon magic picks?"

"Like all magic, there's always a balance. The lands will probably choose a Lycan with a pure heart and a Lycan with a more corrupted heart. Then they'll let fate decide the rest."

"Were you around when Aidan became pack leader?"

"No, I wasn't, but I bet you can guess where his heart fell." I swallow hard, thinking about the Lycans and Rhett.

"I hope a Lycan pure of heart takes over as pack leader."

"So do I, Princess. If they don't and we find ourselves caught in a war with Samael, a war with Cloudrum, we may have just lost the Lycans as allies."

"I'm sorry," I say, feeling responsible for the fallout of all this.

"No, Lyra, I'm sorry. I'm sorry for not realizing sooner what that prick did to you. How could you even stand to be near him? Why didn't you just tell me?"

"I couldn't. I was afraid you'd look at me differently, afraid what you might do if you knew," I murmur.

"I wish I had midnight mind so I could go to Zomea and kill that fucker all over again. Slower next time. I'll never look at you differently, Lyra. Please never be afraid to tell me anything ever again, and once we get out of this mess we're going to talk more about this." His words send a warm feeling through my chest, and I lean back into him, wanting to feel closer to him.

"Okay," is all I say.

"Samael will for sure have felt the magic I used to kill Aidan. The Monstrauths will have felt it to and are probably already trailing us. Once in the Shifting Forest, I'll try not to use anymore magic than necessary to make us more difficult to track. We need to find Athalda and speak to her before Samael has a chance to find us. Then we need to either get the hell out of here and go back to Nighthold or plan a visit to the Lamia Realm to open the bridge and finish this before the key can harm you."

"Do you think Athalda will have the answers we are looking for? Do you think she will even tell us?"

"She knew Euric, and by the sounds of it she orchestrated the ceremony that put all of this into motion. She knows about you and the key. If she doesn't give us answers willingly, I'll force them out of her."

Geri comes to an abrupt stop, rearing up slightly. Nyx hops off and reaches up to help me down. I release Chepi so he can fly next to us.

"Will Geri be alright?" I ask, petting the horse.

"Yeah, he knows his way home," Nyx says patting Geri before he starts trotting away. "How's your ankle feeling?"

"Good, practically back to normal. Whatever Hilda and the moon magic running through the Lycan Realm did, it worked."

"Good. Take my hand. Stay close." I grip his hand, letting my fingers intertwine with his. Stepping into the Shifting Forest brings about an unusual feeling. It feels colder than the rest of the Lycan Realm, and something about it feels more magical, eerily so. It makes my skin crawl.

CHAPTER
THIRTY-ONE

As I trudge through the frigid, snow-covered earth, I struggle to keep my body warm. The only thing keeping me from freezing is the heat of the Lycan blood coursing through my veins. I huddle close, attempting to warm my nose with my breath as it billows out in puffs of smoke. The thick, low-lying fog permeates the air, carrying with it the noxious scent of rotting earth. I gingerly step around the spiky plants that litter the ground. The towering trees that surround us are some of the tallest I've ever laid eyes on. Their skinny, barren trunks only come to life up high, where midnight-blue leaves cling to branches that hang low, creating a creepy tunnel around us.

"Do you know where we're going?" I ask quietly.

"Yes, I looked at the map Aidan had, and I don't believe he was lying when he showed me how to find Athalda's place." Nyx pulls me close to him, wrapping an arm around me to warm me. "If we run into anything dangerous in this forest, I want you to grab Chepi and use his power to make both of you invisible for as long as you can then hide. Do you understand?"

315

I stop suddenly, turning to face Nyx. "How did you know Chepi could make me invisible? I don't recall ever telling you that."

"Chepi is a Glyphie from the dream forest, which is in the Faery Realm where I'm the king. Of course I know what he is and what he can do. Maybe most in Cloudrum don't, but most of all the Fae will know," Nyx says then chuckles softly, pulling me back to his side. I guess it never really crossed my mind that the Fae would know what Chepi can do, but it makes sense.

"I'm not leaving you. If something comes, I want to help. I've felt my magic now several different times, and maybe if I'm put in a situation where I really need it, I could fight. I could help you."

"Lyra, I know you want to help, but I'd rather know you're safe. It'll be easier for me to fight if I know you and Chepi are okay. So please, just this time, will you listen to me? When we get back to Nighthold, I promise I'll teach you to fight and help you wield your magic, but until then I need you to stay out of danger. That means hiding if we get attacked."

"Fine," I say, looking over at Chepi, who yips at me. I'm sure he wants me to hide too. Suddenly I feel a soft rumble underneath me, and my eyes shoot up to Nyx then to the trees up ahead. It sounds like something big is moving in the forest, causing the ground to tremble. I tense up, ready to run when I see the trees moving in the distance. The ground shifts. Suddenly, the group of trees that used to be in front of us disappear and are replaced by new trees that look the same, but I can tell they are different. I never thought this place was called the Shifting Forest because it actually shifts. I have a whole newfound sense of terror. Where did the trees go that were originally here? And how do we keep from disappearing next time the ground starts to rumble?

"What the hell was that?" I ask, loosening my grip on Nyx.

"I thought you knew why this place was called the Shifting Forest." Nyx laughs.

"It's not funny. It's kind of terrifying. I heard the plants here can have minds of their own, but I never really understood what that meant. What if we get caught in a shift?"

"It's okay. The shift wouldn't hurt us. It'd feel similar to channeling. It'd be annoying not knowing where the forest drops us, but it wouldn't be painful or anything. Just stay close to me."

He rubs his hand up and down on my shoulder, and the touch calms my nerves a bit. We keep trudging through the mud. The air smells crisp, and blankets of fog keep rolling in, dampening the air. I keep getting the feeling we're being watched. I can feel the hair on the back of my neck stand up.

"What should I be looking for? Do you know what Athalda's house looks like?" I ask.

"I wouldn't call it a house. Aidan says she lives in a giant cave that's been made into a house. We're heading toward Crater Mountain. It's hard to see it now in the dark with the fog, but we should start noticing the terrain become more mountainous and less swamp-like as we get closer. The cave she resides in can be found at the base of the mountain," Nyx says.

"I'm so anxious to talk to her. If she truly was friends with my father, and she's the one who orchestrated the Lycan Ceremony to take place with me, then she has to—" I suck in a sharp breath as my head starts pounding.

"What's wrong?" Nyx moves to stand in front of me.

"It's nothing. Let's keep going."

"It's not nothing. What's wrong, Lyra?" Nyx kneels down, looking into my face and examining me closely.

"It's just my head. I have a headache. I'll be fine." He scrunches his eyebrows.

"Really. I'm fine. It was a sharp pain for a moment, but it's not as bad now." I never get headaches, and the pain is worrisome, but I wasn't lying when I said it was starting to get better. The pain is slightly less now. Nyx seems unsatisfied by my answer, but we start walking again. I wonder if the headache has anything to do with being in the Lycan Realm like Rhett mentioned. I can't remember what he said exactly, but I don't think he said anything about headaches specifically. With my luck, it's probably this key inside me starting to eat away at my insides or something horrific like that.

"How long until the blood moon exactly?" I ask.

"Seven days."

"That's not very much time, especially if you can't channel us there."

"It's three days ride to the edge of the Sorcerer Realm, then we'd need to travel by boat or fly the rest of the way. There's supposed to be a portal in the Dark Lunar Reach past the Black Forest, but I don't know if we can trust it." Nyx sounds calm, and I'm glad one of us is because I'm already feeling anxious that we're not going to have enough time.

"That means it could take us up to four days to get to the Lamia Realm from here, and that's assuming we don't run into trouble along the way. Gods, I am going to die. I don't know how we are going to figure this out and make it in time."

"Lyra, I am not going to let you die. I told you I don't even know if I believe all of that. We'll speak to Athalda soon, and if we need to open a bridge to Zomea, then I'll get you to the Lamia Realm. I won't let anything bad happen to you. I promise."

I know Nyx cares about me, and I don't think he'd let anything bad happen to me, but I can't deny the unease that's made its home in my chest. I just want all of this to be resolved. I want to put an end to Samael and all of his madness, and I want to get whatever this key is out of me. I want to open the bridge to Zomea and be done with all of it. The ground starts to tremble again, and I clutch Nyx's hand and grab Chepi out of the air, holding him close to me.

"Lyra, that's not the forest shifting. Take Chepi and hide now."

"What could be causing the ground to shake if it's not a shift happening?"

Nyx squeezes my hand, forcing me to run with him behind several thick bushes.

"Stay here. Stay out of sight no matter what, Lyra. What-ever comes, I'm going to have to fight it without magic if we want any chance at finding Athalda before Samael finds us. If anything gets close to you, then you make her invisible, Chepi." Nyx looks to Chepi then looks back at me. I want to protest, but he releases my hand, dropping a dagger into it, and steps back out into the clearing before I can say anything else.

I know Nyx can handle himself. I mean I saw him with Aidan earlier, but he was using his magic then. I'm sure if he had to, he'd use his magic now too. I grasp the dagger in my hand and keep Chepi tight to my chest with my other arm. I stay crouched down but move over slightly until I can see Nyx through a hole in the branches. Small leaves start to tremble, and I freeze when a spider wraith appears out of the trees only a handful of feet in front of Nyx.

It's a monster spider that stands much taller than Nyx. It's translucent and ghost-like with huge furry legs that fade in and out with the fog. My eyes trail up its legs, taking in its horrifying body. When I reach its face, I hold Chepi tighter as spikes of terror squeeze my chest and extend throughout my body. The head is that of a person, only it's translucent. It appears to be an older male with five huge eyes that glow white. When I meet its giant eyes, I can almost see Nyx's reflection in them from here, then I realize this creature has two giant fangs, each one the size of my leg.

There's no way Nyx can outrun this beast with eight legs. I don't have much time to think, then it lunges at him with its fangs. I manage to stifle the scream that tries to fight its way up my throat. Nyx has his sword out, and he lunges for the monster's legs, but he passes right through it and falls into the mud. I drop the dagger, throwing a hand over my mouth as panic starts to set in. He crawls backward, barely missing its fangs as it lunges for him again. He rolls onto his side then jumps to his feet and slowly circles the beast. I notice at the last second that when it attacks it briefly takes on solid form. Nyx just needs to strike it at the right moment when he can hit solid flesh. I'm sure he realizes this, but I still have to fight the urge to scream it across the forest at him. Chepi starts to paw at me and wrestles free of my grip. I reach for him, but he flies over the bushes and toward the battle before I can grab him.

I get to my feet and run after him when he starts barking and growling, flying around the spider wraith's head. He's distracting it and helping Nyx. He gives Nyx the seconds he needs to gain the upper hand. The spider wraith lunges for Chepi, but Chepi's fast and just flies higher out of its reach. The wraith lunges for Chepi, and its body fully materializes. Nyx swings his sword and cuts two of the legs clean off. I place my hand over my chest, trying to calm my racing heart. I grip my bloodstone. *They are okay. They can handle this.*

I kneel again but keep my eyes plastered to Chepi. The ground starts to tremble beneath my knees, and I hold my breath, waiting for another spider wraith to appear out of the trees.

I shiver in the frigid air, struggling to keep my balance as the earth beneath me convulses with violent tremors. The forest must me shifting again. The tall trees around me sway and bend as if alive and writhing in pain. Suddenly, I'm lifted into the air, engulfed in a raging whirlwind that buffets me from all sides, blinding me with its ferocity.

With a thud, I land on my hands and knees in a shallow marsh, surrounded by tall grass and murky pools of water. The marsh stretches out endlessly, obscured by a dense fog that makes it impossible to determine its true extent. My boots are filled with water, making it difficult to move as I wade through the mire.

Desperate for higher ground, I crawl up onto a small hill, taking deep breaths and surveying my new surroundings. I'm lost in this unfamiliar part of the forest, completely alone. The thought sends a shiver down my spine, but I square my shoulders, determined to keep moving forward.

It's eerie here. The water is incredibly still, but the fog seems to have a mind of its own. It swirls and collects at random even though there's no breeze to cause such movement. I hope the forest didn't take me far. I hope I can find my way back to Nyx and Chepi. I see a flash of movement out of the corner of my eyes. I jump to my feet and whip around, but nothing's there. I grab the dagger Nyx gave me out of my boot, trying to hold it firm in my quivering hand. I see movement again, and I turn to the side but—nothing. Something brushes past me this time, and I feel a chill down my back as something whooshes past it. I spin to face it and freeze when I come face to face with a group of Monstrauths.

I count five of them as I start to back up slowly. How has Samael had the strength to conjure up so many of these demons? One alone should be draining on his power. A wave of nausea washes over me. He'll conjure up a whole army if we don't stop him. I start to worry for all the innocent lives that will be lost because of these vile demons roaming the realms, then I'm snapped back to reality when the one in the front of the pack tilts its head to the side. Streams of black saliva drip from its mouth as it steps toward me. There's the sound of bones cracking as it moves. I freeze as the leader approaches me alone. The other four remain frozen. Their red slits for eyes make it hard to tell if they're even looking at me. I grip the dagger in my hand. The smell of rotting flesh works its way up my nose as the demon reaches for me. I duck under its arms and slam my blade into its side. Blood squirts out, and I feel bone crack when I make contact, but the dagger gets stuck. I try to pull it free, and I'm forced to leave it in the Monstrauth's side. The demon isn't even fazed by my attack and moves fast, reaching for me again. I stumble back on the grassy hill, falling into the marsh water.

I am going to die.

I dig my hands into the dirt, pushing up and getting to my feet. I start to run, and it nails me in the leg, knocking me to the ground. I choke on water, gasping for air and crawling and scrambling to my feet. The demon hits me again, and I land hard on my knees. I roll back onto my butt as it strikes again. Its long black nails come right at my chest. I'm not fast enough this time. I can't move in the mud. My eyes widen, and my breath catches as I watch in slow motion as the demon swings its head toward me. One of its horns makes contact with my side, slicing me open. Tears burn my eyes, and I scream, afraid to touch my side and afraid of what damage has been done. One of the other demons makes a loud screeching sound, and they all start moving toward me. I get to my feet and run. I'm stomping through the mud and water and trudging over small hills of grass. I hear splashing gaining behind me, and I know the demons are in pursuit. Something slams into me from behind, and I go flying into the grass, hitting the ground hard. Wet, ugly sobs escape me.

I move to turn around when one of the demons lashes my right side, cutting deep with its nails. I stumble back, bringing my hands to my side as blood slowly pours down and soaks through the tears in my shirt. I don't feel any pain. My adrenaline is too high for that. These monsters are going to die. I look around quickly, trying to find anything to defend myself with while running away. I grab a long branch and whip around, lunging at the Monstrauths with the branch. The branch just whooshes through the air as they all dodge my attack. One of the demons jumps at me again, and I stumble back as it grabs my leg, slicing my thigh open. I scream as my flesh rips and blood gushes from my leg.

My body feels like it's on fire. I wonder for a brief moment if this is what it feels like when you die. Maybe this is poison from the demons coursing through my body. My throat swells, and my body feels weak from the blood loss. The heat begins to build, and I feel like my heart is going to explode out of my chest. I bring my hands up in front of me, turning my palms over to examine them. Something bad is happening. I look down at my mangled flesh then up to the demons approaching, the demons Samael sent after me. Rage fills my body to its core. It's an energy and feeling I've never felt before. My blood is boiling. My chest is tight, and a tingling sensation starts to spread over my skin.

And then it happens . . .

CHAPTER
THIRTY-TWO

I feel the power of my ancestors pulsing through my veins, calling for me to unleash it. I let out a guttural scream and lunge forward, ready to face the Monstrauths head-on. With every fiber of my being, I channel the energy and unleash it in a fiery blast. Heat bursts out of me. Not just heat but fire. I look down to see my skin is glowing. I'm glowing, and this is magic. This is my magic.

The Monstrauths circle around me, pulling me back to the here and now. I stand, panting, sweating, and feeling a mixture of exhilaration and fear at the realization of the power that lies within me. I know that I must use it wisely and control it, or it will control me. I look down at my hands and the liquid fire pooling there. I turn my hands to the demons and visualize Samael's face. I remember all that rage I felt a moment ago. All the rage that's been building inside of me all these years, and I feel the tingling spread from my chest to my hands. The liquid fire pulsing beneath my skin explodes out of me in a waterfall of flames headed straight toward the Monstrauths. I scream as my magic flows out of my body and crashes into the demons.

All the heat and pain building in my body flies out toward them, encircling and suffocating these vile monsters, melting them into nothing.

My magic pulses inside me, and a shockwave of fire and magic leaves my body, decimating everything around me. The grass turns to ash. I see the wave of power in slow motion as it spreads across the land, flattening trees and changing the landscape. In the distance I can see trees on fire. I look down at my hands, and the fire is still spilling out of me. It's not just coming out of my hands; it's radiating off my body like I am on fire. I don't feel like it's hurting me, but panic starts to set in. I don't know how to control it. I don't know what I'm doing. The magic senses my unease and seems to take on a mind of its own, pulsing down my body. The flames dance around me. How am I supposed to trust my magic when it does this?

"Stop," I yell at myself, at my magic, but it flares to life even brighter and hotter like it's taunting me.

"Stop!" I scream, falling to my hands and knees and burying my hands in the mud. The ground gets hot, and the hill I'm on begins to crack. The marsh around me starts to boil. I'm boiling the earth. I pull my hands free as blue and orange flames shoot out around me like I'm a fountain of fire. I start to panic, but that rage inside me has died off, and I'm beginning to feel weak. Nyx says the magic will feed off my emotions. I need to relax. I look down at my side, and the mud and sludge hides my wound. I know I've lost a lot of blood, and the thought doesn't help to calm my racing mind.

"Stop." My voice comes out as a whisper.

I fall back on my head, hitting the ground. I'm weak, and the tingling sensation under my skin has subsided. It feels like years' worth of pent-up rage just ran through my body and exploded all around me. My body has stopped emitting fire, but now I'm realizing it's hot. The forest is burning, and the heat is radiating toward me, threatening to melt my skin and choke me. It's so hot it makes it hard to catch my breath. I don't have the strength to move. I lie here staring up at the sky. The sun has started to rise, and the sky is full of smoke. It's dark black and gray and billows all around me, dispersing into the sky.

What just happened to me? How did that happen? That fire . . . it came out of me. I don't know how it's possible. I cough and choke. It's too hot. I roll onto my stomach, but I feel so weak. I don't know if it's from magic or from the loss of blood. I start to crawl, but I don't know where to go. The smoke is burning my eyes, and I can't see anything past the fire, the fire that's surrounding me. I want to cry. This is the end. But I don't even have the strength to muster tears. I push myself to keep crawling. I make it down one tiny hill and sink into the muddy water, which offers some relief from the heat.

My heart is racing, and my skin is no longer burning. I feel as though I might fall asleep. My eyes are heavy, and I no longer feel the pain from my wounds. I sway on my hands and knees in the water, trying to gather strength or willpower to get myself out of here. That's when I smell him, Nyx. I must be dreaming now. Wings crash down around me, shielding my body and darkening the world.

"I've got you." Nyx gathers me up in his arms, cradles me to his chest, and leaps into the sky.

"You found me."

"I'll always find you, Princess," Nyx says, squeezing me a little tighter.

"Wait. You're flying. Samael." My thoughts come out jumbled and breathless.

"My flying is the least of our worries after the magic you just unloaded back there. It was felt for miles. Samael will have sensed it for sure. Now I need to get to Athalda's." Nyx stoops down lower now that we're away from the smoke. "How injured are you?"

A moment ago I thought I was on the brink of death, but now that I'm in Nyx's arms and safe in the sky I think I may be okay.

"I'm okay. Nothing too bad. Where's Chepi?"

"He's here flying with us. He's safe. I found Athalda's cave while searching for you. Just hang on. We're close, and when we get there I'll do a thorough exam. We're going to get you fixed up. I don't trust the old Sorceress, but I know she wants you alive. She wants you to unlock the bridge to Zomea, and she won't do anything to jeopardize your life."

"Okay." It takes all the energy I have to say that. I relax and set my head against his chest.

"We're close. I promise," he says again into my hair, kissing the top of my head.

I must have dozed off, because I'm jolted awake when Nyx's feet slam into the ground, and he starts banging on a door. The door is built into a large tree that seems to grow into the side of the mountain.

"It's about time," says Athalda's hoarse voice, pulling Nyx inside. I feel a whoosh of wind, and his wings disappear as he carries me into the tree.

The inside of the tree opens up and extends deep into the mountainside. It's decorated almost like a normal house here but filled with the strange smells of pungent herbs. I'm not sure what I expected, but I didn't expect this. I thought maybe she'd have some big cauldron smoking on a table.

"Quickly. Lay her down over here," Athalda says from somewhere behind me.

Nyx carries me closer to her voice and lays me down on a large wooden table. It's not exactly comfortable, and a moan escapes my mouth as I try to reposition but can't. I have no strength; I hadn't realized I can't even lift my head up much on my own. Athalda's face comes into view as she leans over me. Those jagged scars and deep black eyes are unmistakable. "I told you I'd come find you after the funeral, girl. Then you disappear and show up here like this." She starts grabbing glass jars and placing them around the table. I can't see her, but I hear lots of clinging and rummaging.

"The whole damn Lycan Realm had to have felt that blast of magic. I will set a spell to camouflage my home and confuse anyone that comes looking for you two, but I can only buy you a day or two at most, then you need to leave," Athalda says.

"Yes, I understand. Can you help heal her?" Nyx asks Athalda, and his voice sounds strained. My heart hurts for him, but I can't raise my head to look up.

"Get her undressed so we can assess her wounds. I'll be back after I set the spell." Athalda's voice is gruff as she grumbles in the distance.

"I'm going to get you cleaned up. I need to remove your clothes so we can heal you. Just rest, okay?"

Nyx soothes me by rubbing my hair out of my face, and Chepi lies down next to my head, the tip of his wet nose tickling my cheek. Nyx unties and pulls my boots off one by one. Luckily, I don't have much clothes on. They've all been shredded and burned. He grabs the top of my shirt under my neck and pulls with both hands, ripping it in two all the way down my front until he reaches the end near my thigh. He lifts me up slowly, tucking one arm under my shoulders and pulls the torn shirt free, then rests me back onto the table.

I hear him fumbling around in what must be the old Sorceress's kitchen, because I hear lots of clinging and clanging of dishes. He comes back with a large bowl of warm, soapy water that smells amazing after the stench of rotting flesh and mud all night.

"This may sting, but I need to get all this mud off you so I can see where you're hurt. Athalda is hiding us, so I'm going to try to avoid using magic," Nyx tells me softly as he starts pressing a warm towel to my body.

He lathers it with soap and warm water then gently dabs and brushes my body with it, ridding my skin of the nightmare I endured. He repeats this process over and over again. Every now and then I hear him sigh or hiss, which leads me to believe I must look bad. The water stings when it gets near a wound, but it's nothing I can't take. I have no energy to react anyways.

"Lyra, you said you weren't hurt that badly. This wound on your side is deep." He starts pacing, and it makes me uneasy.

"I'm sorry."

"Don't be sorry. It's just I wish this didn't happened. I'm going to fucking kill Samael," Nyx says through gritted teeth.

"Move over. Let me get a look at her," Athalda says, coming up into the room. "Girl, that side is going to need to be stitched up." She pokes and prods me.

If I wasn't so drained, I'd probably feel embarrassed. I don't like lying here naked. Nyx seems to sense my train of thought and drapes a towel over my waist.

"Your other wounds are not so bad," she says more to herself.

"Now, boy, I'm going to need you to hold her down while I stitch her side. Think you can manage?" Athalda says to Nyx while moving around supplies. I don't much like where this is going.

"What can we give her for the pain?"

"I have a tincture I can mix with alcohol," Athalda says.

"Why the long pause? What's the catch?"

"It'll help with the pain but will also cause hallucinations. Should only last a couple hours," she says, mixing some liquids in a glass. She hands it to Nyx, and he brings it over, lifting my head for me to drink.

"Wait. I don't want to hallucinate . . . I'm afraid."

"It's okay, lover. I'll be here the whole time. Once she starts threading through your wound, trust me, you'll want this." Nyx brings the glass to my lips, and I do my best to gulp it all down.

It's a bold and complex blend of flavors with a tangy, almost savory quality that mingles with a subtle alcohol kick. I wish I had more alcohol, but I don't say so aloud.

"How will we know it's working?" I hear Nyx ask.

"We'll know. It should only take a few minutes," Athalda tells him, and she already sounds so far away.

My body feels heavy, and my chest feels tight. A sense of dread creeps in. My vision seems to be a little distorted. I try to find Nyx and Athalda in the room, but I can't lift my head. It feels like a boulder, and it's too heavy to do anything but drop.

"Nyx," I yell, but it could've just been a whisper. I'm not sure if I formed the word properly, but I must've made a sound because he appears over me. At first, I see his lips move, but my auditory functions seem to be delayed now too, because it takes a minute for me to realize what he's saying.

"How are you feeling?"

"Euphoric . . . yet grief stricken," I tell him, and his eyebrows furrow. Maybe I didn't tell him. I can't be sure.

"It's working. Hold her down and don't let her move no matter what she says."

I think Athalda is speaking, but it sounds scary and distorted, like she's a monster.

Nyx's arms come down on me, and his body presses against mine. It feels nice. A burning sensation breaks out across my side, and I think I'm on fire again. I think I scream.

"It's okay. It'll all be over soon."

The room is spinning, and my vision is starting to tunnel, then I focus on my dad.

"You're one step closer, my little pixie," he whispers then places a kiss on my forehead. He starts to fade and wobble out of existence.

"Dad, wait, don't go!" I yell at him, willing him to appear again, but he's gone and my vision darkens again. The pain in my side fades into the background, and I start thinking about my childhood. I think about my father. All of a sudden I realize I can recall memories with perfect clarity, things I shouldn't be able to remember start popping in my head and flashing across my mind like I'm right there again.

I'm four years old again and running around my dad's study.

"What's that, Daddy?" I ask as he turns over an object in his hands.

He looks troubled, and I press my hand on his knee.

"It's okay, Daddy. Don't be sad."

He pulls me into his lap and places the object over his face.

"Boo," he says through the mask. It's a brown and red mask made of some type of stone, and it has hallowed eyes and a hollow mouth.

"Ahh." I jump then laugh. The mask is creepy.

"This . . . Lyra, is something very special," he says, taking it off his face and handing it to me. It's heavy and cold in my hands.

"Can I have it?" I ask, holding it to my face. It's too big, and I can only see through one eye hole at a time.

Before he can answer me, the room starts spinning, and I look down again. I'm older, but not by much.

"Come on, pixie. It's not much further," Dad says, holding my hand.

We're walking, but I don't recognize this place. It's dark, and I think I hear the sea. We're in a cave.

"I'm scared," I tell him, and he picks me up but keeps walking.

"Never be afraid, pixie. Remember, you hold all the power in here," he tells me, pointing at my heart. Then he's gone.

"Lyra?" Nyx calls to me, and I blink, trying to focus on his face.

"What?" I ask, but it comes out garbled.

He says something else, but I just see his lips move. I don't hear anything, and he fades out of my vision again.

I'm back in the castle in Tempest Moon. I'm on my hands and knees outside my mom and dad's bedroom door, peeking through a crack. My mother looks so young, and my dad looks so troubled. They're arguing.

"Euric, you need to stop this. She's just a little girl," says Mom.

"Damnit, Macy, she's never been just a little girl, and she never will be. The sooner you accept that, the better it will be for everyone involved."

"Eavesdropping is not becoming of a princess, Lyra," Lili says, picking me up from behind and pulling my parents' door closed. The smell of lavender and vanilla fills my nose, then a hole forms in the ground, and Lili drops me into it. I'm falling into complete darkness. There's nothing and no one. I'm flailing and screaming, bracing to land somewhere. But the darkness takes over, and I get lost in it.

THIRTY-THREE

I wake up feeling disoriented. My body is sore, and I reach down to feel my side. It's all bandaged up.

"How are you feeling?"

Startled by Nyx's voice, I whip my head around to find him sitting in a chair across from the bed, watching me intently. His face is etched with lines of exhaustion and worry. How long have I been out? I also vaguely remember the strange visions I was having from the tincture they gave me.

"I feel okay. A little fuzzy in the head I guess." I smile at him, hoping to ease the tension in his features. "How long have I been asleep?"

"You blacked out while Athalda was stitching you up. Once she finished, I moved you to the bed in here, and you've been asleep for maybe three hours."

Not too bad. Feels like I was hit over the head with something, but other than that my body surprisingly feels okay.

"My side . . . is it okay? It doesn't hurt."

"It'll be okay. She did a good job and put a salve on it to

333

make sure it doesn't fester or cause you much pain," he says, moving to sit next to me on the bed.

"Where is Athalda now?" I ask, slowly sitting up. Nyx helps me lean against the headboard next to him.

"Somewhere in the house. This place is pretty big considering it's built into a mountain." He moves his hand under my jaw to turn my head to face him. "Are you sure you're feeling okay? You lost a lot of blood, and you expelled a lot of magic."

That's when I remember my magic.

The events of the night are a haze. I blink a few times, like it will help clear my head.

"I have fire inside me," I tell him, a bit awed myself. "Everything is a bit of a blur. I'm trying to remember everything that happened."

"It's the tincture Athalda gave you. Your head should clear up soon. Pyrokinesis was one of your dad's abilities that came from him."

"I know. I can't explain it exactly, but I felt it. I felt him like he was there with me when my magic came to life." I don't know how to put into words what I was feeling. He seems to understand, nodding at me.

"How will we know what other abilities I have?"

"Like Elspeth said, they'll show in time."

Nyx seems to be deep in thought, but I continue telling him about the Monstrauths and how my magic manifested, at least what I can remember. Once I finish, we sit in silence for a few minutes.

"Did you learn anything from Athalda? Can we trust her?" I finally ask, breaking the silence.

"I don't trust anyone in Cloudrum. But she did help you, and she's hiding us for the time being. I haven't talked to her about anything yet. I wanted to stay with you and wait until you felt up to it to start questioning her."

"Okay, I'm feeling up to it now, but let's wait just a few more minutes." I give him a shy smile, and he carefully pulls me to him so I'm sitting in his lap.

"I need some clothes," I say realizing I'm still naked and covered in bandages.

"I prefer you like this." Nyx gives me a playful smile while running his hand through my hair and guiding my face to his. He kisses the tip of my nose, my forehead, and my cheek. He trails soft kisses all over my face until the anticipation is killing me, and I reach up, gripping each side of his jaw with my hands, and take his mouth. He laughs into my mouth for a moment then deepens the kiss, taking my mouth like it belongs to him.

My core is heating with need. I feel his excitement pressed against me, and I fumble my fingers on his pants, trying to undo them to release his hard cock.

"Lyra, you're hurt," he breaks off the kiss, finding my eyes.

"I don't care. I need to feel you. I need you inside me, Nyx," I tell him breathlessly, and he pulls his pants down.

My eyes find his thick length, and I move to get on top of it.

"Easy, don't hurt yourself," he says, placing his hands on my hips to slow me.

I ease down on top of him, letting him stretch me. Once he's fully inside me, I find his mouth again moaning softly and slowly moving on top of him. I can't get enough of this feeling . . . of him, of needing to be close to him. He wraps his arms around me, holding me close while kissing me. He feels so warm and strong. I wrap my hands around his neck and ride him slowly, savoring the feeling of him inside me.

He leaves my mouth to kiss and suck his way down my neck. He massages my breasts and takes his time, taking each one is his mouth and twirling his tongue and nibbling at my peaked flesh there. I let my head fall back, gasping when I feel his teeth on my nipple. He wraps his arms around my ass, holding me to him, and stands, carefully laying me down on my back and climbing on top of me. He makes sure to hold his weight up so not to hurt my side. His gray eyes are glowing when he slowly thrust back inside me, holding my legs apart.

"I thought I was going to lose you before." His voice is stressed.

"I'm here. I'm okay." I breathe, pulling him closer to me.

Every time he hits inside me, the feeling is ecstasy. I wrap my legs around him, trying to pull him closer to me but he resists.

"I don't want to hurt you," he whispers.

"You won't. Come closer. Kiss me," I tell him while pulling on his arms and squeezing him with my legs. He obeys and finds my lips. I open for him, and my tongue finds his. I breathe him in and drink him up. I want all of him.

"Harder," I plead, pulling away to catch my breath.

He fucks me harder, pulling all the way out and thrusting all the way back in. He goes harder and faster until I cry out, losing all control and finding my release. I tremble underneath him, holding onto his arms. He thrusts inside me again, deep, and finds his release with my name on his tongue. He stays inside me while we both stare at each other and catch our breaths.

"I can't lose you, Lyra. You could've died," he tells me, his gray eyes glowing with something different than lust.

"I'm okay. You're not going to lose me."

He leans down and kisses me, and it's like he's kissing me for the first time. He's devouring me, and I love it. Before I know it, he's moving inside me again until we both find release a second time. This time he pulls out of me and lies next to me on the bed. We're both covered in sweat, and my skin prickles with warmth. My body already misses his presence inside me.

"I'll never get enough of this. I can't get enough of you," Nyx says, facing me and tucking my hair behind my ear.

"Me neither," I murmur, a smile playing at the corners of my lips.

A loud knock on the door makes us both jolt up.

"Time to get up, lovebirds. There are clothes outside the door. Get ready and come out here," says Athalda.

We both look at each other and laugh. I'm full of embarrassment. Were we loud? What did the old woman hear? Oh well, I just giggle as Nyx gets to his feet and gets dressed, then he goes to the door and retrieves a small pile of clothes for me. I can't complain because they're clean and warm, but the clothes Athalda provides for me are not the most attractive. I put on the gray sweatpants and colorful knitted shirt with a sigh.

"Ready for this?" Nyx asks, holding out his hand.

"Yes," I say with a sigh, taking his hand. I look down to see Chepi curled up in some pillows on the floor. He's had a rough night too, and I decide I should leave him to sleep it off as I follow Nyx out of the room.

As I gain more clarity, I take a closer look at my surroundings. Nyx guides me through the winding maze of narrow hallways. This place is truly unique with a mix of rooms that range from seeming like a typical house to others that appear to be carved directly into stone. The hallways themselves all have a cave-like feel with rough stone walls enclosing us on every side.

Finally, we step into a room that resembles a study or library, with floor-to-ceiling shelves lining the walls and filled with ancient tomes. A potbelly stove stands in the center of the room, providing both warmth and cozy ambiance. A comfortable couch and two chairs are arranged in front of the stove, with a small wooden table completing the inviting scene.

"About time," Athalda says, gesturing for us to sit on the couch while she takes a seat in one of the chairs. "Drink some tea. It'll help clear your head, and both of you eat something."

I hesitate, but nothing can be worse than the tincture she already gave me. Why poison me now after healing me? I grab a cup of tea and take a sip. It warms my belly and helps me feel relaxed. I settle into the couch with Nyx's arm around me holding me close.

Athalda doesn't speak until we both have our fill of soup and tea. Once we finish everything on the table, she clears her throat.

"Let me start from the beginning."

"What are you?" I interrupt.

"I'm a kind of Sorceress, but not the same as you or the other Sorcerers alive today. My name is Athalda Time, and your father Euric was my cousin," she says, and my head swivels from her to Nyx and back to her.

"How is that possible? I don't understand?"

"Marian Time was your dad's mother, your grandmother. My father, Gabriel Time, was Marian's older brother. My father was Fae like yours. My mother's name was Athena Black, and she was a Sorceress."

My mind is spinning. "I thought I was the only half-Fae half-Sorceress we know of alive today."

"You are other than myself. It was not common even back then, but it did happen on rare occasions." She takes a sip of tea, leaning back in her chair.

"How have I never seen or heard of you before?" Nyx asks, and I feel ridiculous for not thinking of that myself.

"I grew up with Euric, but we didn't age the same. My Sorcerer blood was dominant, and I aged as a Sorceress would. I died long before you were born." Athalda's voice is hoarse.

"Wait. What?" I look from her to Nyx again, confused.

"Then how? How are you here now?" Nyx asks, holding me a little tighter.

"Your father brought me back. Your father brought me back from Zomea. That's why even now you can probably sense something about me that feels off, but you can't quite put your finger on it. That's why my eyes are always black. I was in Zomea for many years. A soul does not come back to this world unchanged when they've been there for so long."

"Why would my father bring you back? How is this even possible?"

"To serve a purpose." Her black eyes focus on me.

"That's right. In his journal, he says he was going to resurrect you to start planting fail-safes. What fail-safes?"

"We do not want to unlock Zomea—that'd lead to an inexorable set of events. We do not want a repeat of the War of the Realms. But opening a bridge with the key would allow you to travel to Zomea at will. It'd allow you to go to Zomea in a controlled way. Not in a dream where things are unpredictable and you're only going there in your mind. A bridge would create a portal where one could travel back and forth physically. Euric brought me back to make sure I'd set things in motion for you to unlock the bridge when the time came if he failed."

"But why would I want to go to Zomea? Why did my father do this? Why does he want a bridge to be opened?"

"A bridge would allow people to visit their loved ones. It'd be a safe way to pass into Zomea without destroying the realms. It's something the Sorcerers all those years ago tried to do when they unlocked Zomea and Eguina was torn apart. They just didn't do it correctly. Your father knew he was going to die an early death, and he wanted a way back to you, to his family."

"How did he know he was going to die an early death?"

"Moirati is a Gholioth in Zomea your father grew close to. Gholioths are known to have precognition, and this is how Euric learned he'd die before his time. He became obsessed with finding ways to change the future, to cheat death. Then he learned of a prophecy, one that'd unlock a bridge to Zomea, allowing someone to ultimately cheat death by being able to travel freely from Zomea to the realms," Athalda says, her voice hoarse. She bends to pour herself some more tea.

"I think I know the prophecy you speak of. I read it in my father's journal."

"He just had to make sure that a Sorcerer, before reaching the age of being able to wield magic, carried the blood of all realms within them. And with you he was already halfway there. You carry the blood of the Faery Realm and Sorcerer Realm within you. The leader of the Gholioths—Moirati, well Euric stole some of his blood when you were little and gave it to you, making you the key."

"Wait, how would giving Lyra Gholioth blood make her the key?" Nyx says from beside me.

"Gholioths are the very essence of Zomea. They're the oldest creatures to ever exist in Zomea. They have never been a part of this world, have never entered these realms. It connected Lyra to Zomea in a way midnight mind alone could not. It connects her even now on a cellular level."

"Will Lyra be harmed if she doesn't open the bridge? Euric's notes say the key could destroy her. What did he mean?" Nyx asks.

"Like I said, Gholioths have never lived in the realms. They've never been of this world. He didn't know it at the time, but by removing that piece of Zomea, he made it unstable. Zomea demands the blood of Moirati back, and as you come closer to nineteen if the ceremonies are not complete and the bridge is not unlocked the key will slowly destroy you. The Gholioth blood with eat away at your organs. The blood wants to be reunited with its owner, and it'll kill you if you don't unlock the bridge and return it."

"Why now? Why before I turn nineteen? If I've had this blood inside me all these years, why didn't it kill me a long time ago?" I rub my clammy palms across my pants, trying to wrap my mind around everything.

"I don't know why the prophecy is what it is, but I'll tell you when Euric stole that blood from Moirati he didn't know what he was doing. From the moment that blood left Zomea, things have been slowly becoming unstable there. You have midnight mind...you must've seen the state it's in. Have you not?"

"The fires."

"Yes. The forest is on fire, and that's not the worst of it. It has taken years for it to get this bad, but Zomea has been suffering. If you do not unlock the bridge and return the blood to Zomea, the stability of its very existence could be threatened, not to mention what could happen to your life."

Nyx moves next to me, wrapping an arm around me and holding me tighter to him.

"If Lyra goes through with this and unlocks the bridge, how will Moirati's blood be returned to him without harming Lyra?"

"I don't have all the answers. But I do know Euric would never harm his daughter, and I know he was able to take the blood from Moirati without him knowing. He must have a way to return it to him safely. He wouldn't have brought me back to make sure the key doesn't destroy Lyra just for her to unlock the bridge and die anyway. He'll have a way. I'm sure of it."

"What about my mother and Silas? Aidan said he was doing their biding at the ceremony. Did you put them up to it?"

"Yes, I did."

"But how? My mother didn't even act like she missed my father. She wouldn't have wanted a bridge unlocked for him to come back, and she wouldn't care if the key destroyed me."

"The only way I knew how. The promise of power."

"Power?" Nyx says, leaning forward.

"There's an artifact hidden inside Zomea. This artifact is extremely powerful, and whoever possesses it has the power to control Zomea itself, ultimately controlling life and death. Your father used to possess this artifact, but he knew it was too much power for one person to have and eventually hid it where it belongs in Zomea.

"I made sure your mother and Silas learned about this artifact. They wanted to retrieve it for themselves. Your mother ordered Aidan to take you and complete the shifting ceremony. I was never fond of your mother, but I made her believe I was loyal to her so one day I'd be able to stop her when she made a move for power. I didn't anticipate Samael. You must understand I never meant for them to die. I was only pushing them to complete the ceremony and making them think it was their idea."

"What do you mean you didn't anticipate Samael? Why would my mother and Silas want the artifact? Why wait all these years before trying to get it?"

"They just learned about it recently when I pushed them in the right direction. I told your mother about you being the key and Euric's plan, but I knew that would not be reason enough for her to have you go through with the ceremony. I needed a reason that would drive her to want to go to Zomea, and that reason was power. I don't know how Samael learned of the artifact, but I know he killed your parents. I can only assume he tortured them for information before they died. Samael is blinded by his need for power."

"You think this is why Samael is after Lyra? He wants to use her to retrieve this artifact in Zomea?"

"I don't know what Samael knows, but I do know he is deranged and power hungry."

"Just to be clear, did you make up this story about an artifact with power to convince Lyra's parents to unlock the bridge to Zomea? Or was it really because you want to save Lyra before the key destroys her and completes Euric's plan of creating a way to pass between Zomea and the realms?" Nyx asks.

"That's correct, but I didn't make up anything about the artifact. The artifact is real and is hidden within Zomea."

"And you're not afraid if Lyra unlocks the bridge Samael will try to get it? You said it yourself...he's deranged and power hungry."

"Samael may try, but I'm sure it's hidden and protected. It's a risk we must take," Athalda says, crossing her legs.

I get up from the couch, feeling the need to move. Nyx gets up after me, jarred by my sudden movement.

"What's wrong?" he touches the small of my back.

"I just need a moment to think, to process. I need to move." My head is hurting again, and the stress of all this is weighing on me.

"Go lie down in your room. You have a lot to digest. I'll be here when you're ready to talk. Think about what you want to do," Athalda says.

I turn, heading back toward the room I was resting in before.

Once inside the privacy of our room, I throw myself down in one of the chairs and bury my face.

"Come lie next to me," Nyx says, kicking off his shoes and lying down on his back.

"I don't want to lie down, Nyx. I want to talk about this. All of this." I emphasize my point with my hands.

"I know that was a lot. Come sit down next to me at least, please." He pats the bed next to him, and I take a seat cross-legged on the bed.

I make sure he's looking at me when I ask him, "How much of this did you know? How much of this have you been keeping from me?"

"Lyra, I'm not keeping anything from you."

"I don't believe you. You're hundreds of years old. You're the Fae king of Nighthold. You knew my father. You expect me to believe you didn't know any of this?" My voice comes out high pitched.

"I promise I didn't know, Lyra. I suspected some things, but I wasn't in on all this."

"You suspected some things? Nyx, you say you care about me, but you don't even let me in your head. Stop treating me like a child and treat me like your equal. You need to tell me things. I want to know what you suspect. If you want to be with me, then we need to be a team."

"You are awfully cute when you get upset. Has anyone ever told you that?" Nyx is smirking at me now, and I feel like he's not taking what I'm saying to heart.

"Nyx, I'm trying to be serious. I could be dead in a few days for all we know."

"Stop. I will not let anything happen to you. I'm sorry. You're right. I was trying to lighten the mood." He tugs on my hand, pulling me closer to him, and I move to face him, letting my fingers intertwine with his.

"What do you think we should do?" I say, letting out a sigh.

"I think we need to go to the Lamia Realm and finish this.

Open the bridge to Zomea then get the hell out of here and go back to Nighthold. We can't risk not opening the bridge now. Not only do I not want to risk anything bad happening to you, but with Zomea being unstable—"

"What would happen if there was no more Zomea? I know it's unstable, but could it ever just be gone? What would happen to everyone there?" I never really let myself think about it before, but without Zomea there would be no afterlife.

"I don't know what will happen to Zomea if you don't return the blood to Moirati. You said it's on fire . . . it's possible it could reach a point of total destruction, but it's also unthinkable. Nothing like this has ever happened before. Euric messed with things he shouldn't have messed with. Without Zomea, when someone dies, they'd ultimately be stuck in Limbo forever. No one would find peace."

I roll onto my back next to Nyx and stare up at the ceiling. A part of me is upset with my father. How could he do this? What was he thinking? I understand what he was trying to do, I think, but what a mess he made.

"What do you want to do? I'll do whatever you want. This is all ultimately your decision." Nyx rolls onto his side to face me.

I can feel his eyes on me. I don't know what to do, and there's just so much to worry about right now. I still want to deal with Samael before Lili is hurt or anyone else in my realm. Who knows what he's been planning this entire time? I don't know if he ever found the grimoire he's looking for or if he found a way to make his magic dark permanently. How powerful would he be if that happened? I mean, Nyx is extremely powerful. There's just no way Samael could hurt Nyx . . . at least I don't think so. I'm afraid for— everyone. I don't care what happens to me anymore I just want to make sure Chepi is okay and Nyx is alright and all the people of

Cloudrum who are suffering under Samael's rule are freed. I can't deal with Samael right now, not with Zomea being unstable and the blood moon fast approaching.

I let out a loud huff. "We have to go to the Lamia Realm before the blood moon, and I need to unlock the bridge by whatever means necessary. I want us to deal with Samael. We need to come up with a plan to stop him. Who knows how many innocents have been harmed since he's come into power? But first—you're right—we need to deal with Zomea."

"I know Samael needs to be dealt with, but let's just focus on one thing at a time. We will unlock the bridge then go back to Nighthold. I want you somewhere safe to practice your Fae magic and become stronger. Not to mention we need to be prepared for your nineteenth birthday and whatever dark or light magic that brings you. When we take on Samael, we'll need a plan and reinforcements. My armies have been training off the coast of Nitross, and they know a time may be coming when we find ourselves in a war with Cloudrum."

"Is that what you were doing when you and Bim left me and Flora at the manor?"

"Yeah. I had a meeting with all the commanders, and I left Bim in charge while we are away. I hope it doesn't come to a war, but if it does we'll be ready for it. Now with Aidan being gone the Lycan may or may not be allies, but either way we'll figure it out."

"I'm sorry."

"Sorry for what?"

"You wouldn't be dealing with all of this if it wasn't for me. I'm the reason all of this is happening, and you killed Aidan because of me and—"

"I'm going to stop you there. You need to quit apologizing for things that are out of your control. You didn't cause any of this, and the only regret I have about killing that fucker is the fact that I didn't do it slower. Don't be sorry about that—ever."

I turn to face him, finally meeting his gaze. His eyes soften when they meet mine, and he pulls me to his chest, kissing the top of my head.

"Everything's going to be okay. I promise."

CHAPTER
THIRTY-FOUR

"Just because you're king of the Faery Realm doesn't mean you know everything. I'm sure there are many things the Sorcerers have kept secret from your kind," Athalda says, giving Nyx a stern look.

Athalda and Nyx have been arguing about how we should get to the Lamia Realm. I just sit back on the couch watching this unfold, stroking Chepi, who's awake now and sitting in my lap.

"If there are hidden portals in Cloudrum planted by the Sorcerers, I don't trust them. It's too risky putting Lyra through a portal right now. She doesn't even have her Sorcerer magic," Nyx argues back.

"It'll take you too long to get to the Lamia Realm without using a portal. Not to mention you'll have to travel across the entire Sorcerer Realm to get there. Who knows what traps Samael may have set or what monsters you'll have to battle along the way. Look at her. She's still injured. You'll never make it in time," Athalda scoffs.

Nyx growls. "I want to let Lyra decide. It should be her choice."

They both turn and focus on me. I've never traveled through a portal before, but I don't like the idea of spending the next three days traveling through my realm not knowing what we might have to face. I have no idea how many more of those Monstrauths are out there, and the thought sends goosebumps down my arms.

"I want us to go through the portal. Where is it and where will it take us?"

Nyx lets out a sigh. I think he was hoping I wouldn't choose the portal.

Athalda smirks. "The portal's not too far from here, a short hike. It'll take us to the edge of the Sorcerer Realm past the black forest. Then we can take a boat the rest of the way."

I've never had the opportunity to visit the Lamia Realm. My knowledge of this place is limited to what I've read in books and seen in paintings of the Mad Territories. Despite my concerns, I must admit that a small part of me is eager to finally see the Lamia Realm with my own eyes. It's always been depicted as a dark and somewhat ominous place, where the sun never shines and the atmosphere is always moody. This has always piqued my interest.

According to what I've heard, there's a castle there, but it's only for show, and below it the floors stretch on endlessly into the underground realm where the Lamias reside. The idea of exploring such a mysterious and intriguing place is truly exhilarating.

"We leave at first light," Nyx says, getting to his feet and extending his hand for me to take.

"That's in just a few hours. You'll have barely any time to rest," Athalda says.

"We'll be ready, so if you're sure you wish to come with us, make sure you're ready. Or you can tell me how to get to this portal and we'll make our way without you." I take Nyx's hand and let him lead me back to our room. Once inside, I sit in one of the chairs and watch him pace. I don't think I've seen him so flustered before, and I can't help the feeling he's not telling me everything. He can't be this upset just because we're going to use a portal to travel.

"I don't like this. Something just doesn't feel right." Nyx pauses, running his hands through his hair.

"What do you mean?"

"It's odd. I've never heard of there being portals in Cloudrum for the Sorcerers to use, and I don't know if I really trust Athalda. This whole plan just feels rushed, and I don't like it."

"Hey, try to relax. We only have a few hours until morning, and your pacing is making me anxious. I'm already stressed out about all of this. I need you to keep it together. You're always the calm one."

Nyx stops pacing, and he dons a mischievous smile. He moves around the chairs, coming up behind me.

"Where are you going?"

"I want to make you feel good and take your mind off things. You're right. I don't want you to stress. I just want to enjoy being with you right now."

He moves behind me and starts massaging my shoulders. I moan and turn my neck, giving him more access as he works the muscles in my back. I love the way he touches me. My body burns to feel him inside me again. He takes his time rubbing my shoulders and bends to place kisses up and down my neck. He nibbles on my earlobe, and I squirm.

"Feeling less stressed?" he asks while moving around the chair and kneeling in front of me.

"A little." I smile at him shyly.

350

"Sounds like I need to try harder at relieving your stress," he says, his voice thick. He starts pulling off my pants.

"What are you doing?" I ask, tipping my butt up so he can pull my pants all the way down.

"Tasting you." His voice is ruff, and his eyes are glowing slightly now.

He's looking at me like he wants to devour me. I clench my thighs together in anticipation. He places his warm hands on my legs, and the callouses tickle my skin as he strokes me up and down before gently tugging my legs apart. Once he spreads my legs, he looks me over thoroughly, licking his lips. My face turns a million shades of red, and a shiver spreads through my body.

He runs his hands back up my legs and between my thighs. He rubs my center, and a soft sigh escapes my mouth. He replaces his fingers with his mouth, then his tongue, eliciting sounds from me that make me momentarily wonder how thick the walls are. I hope Athalda can't hear us. I dig my hands into the cushions of the chair, my heart racing. The way he works his tongue sends sensations shattering through my body. It's almost too much to take. I throw my head back and tangle my hands in his hair, writhing from his touch. His mouth. His tongue.

"Stop, wait," I breathe.

"What's wrong?" His eyes shoot up to mine.

"Take me to the bed," I demand.

He doesn't ask any more questions. He scoops me up, pulling the blankets back and laying me down on the pillows. I pull my sweater off over my head and lie back, letting him take in my body. He doesn't take his eyes off me while he takes off his clothes and slowly climbs on top of me. I trail my hands down his body, feeling his chest and his racing heart, then I lower my fingers to the taut muscles of his stomach. He

351

watches me as I explore his body. I take his thick length in my hand and begin stroking him, sending a shudder through him. I continue exploring his body, feeling his arms and the muscles. I want them wrapped around me.

Gods, I can't get enough of this man. I don't know what I did to deserve him. I don't know how he can look at me with those glowing eyes like I mean the world to him. I wish I never slept with Aidan. I wish I'd saved myself. I wish my first time had been with someone I love—with Nyx. I can't help thinking about it, and I wonder if it bothers him that I've been with another. Surely he's had plenty of women in his bed before me. Gods, am I just realizing that I think I love Nyx? I think I'm in love with him.

He watches me silently as I work my hands across his body and then back to his face, caressing his jaw and pulling him to me. He kisses the tip of my nose then my lips. His kiss is warm and gentle as he uses his tongue to coax my mouth to open for him. I wonder if he can sense what I'm feeling or what I'm thinking. I wonder if Nyx loves me. He nibbles on my bottom lip, and I can't focus on anything else. I feel the tip of his cock press against my slick warmth, causing the muscles in my stomach to coil with anticipation. Once his tongue finds mine, he thrusts inside me, causing my breath to get lost in his. He wraps one arm around me and holds my hip in place with the other. I move my hips up to meet his thrusts and let my body move off instinct as I get lost in him.

His hand finds its way back to my center, and he starts to rub my flesh there while thrusting slow and deep inside me. I moan and cry out, squirming beneath him and digging my nails into his back.

"Come for me, baby. I want to feel you," Nyx whispers, and my body responds.

I squeeze my eyes shut and bite down on my lower lip as

release finds me. My body shatters beneath him in waves of pleasure. I slowly ease my hands from his back and open my eyes to find Nyx staring down at me. Once I meet his gaze, he starts thrusting inside me again fast and hard, losing himself in me. He lets out a moan, and I feel his release twitch deep inside me.

He lowers himself back down close to me, holding his weight with his arms and rests his forehead to mine. We stay like that for a few minutes with him seated inside me while we both catch our breaths and our bodies stop shuddering.

"Less stressed now?" he teases.

"Yes." I giggle as he pulls out of me and falls onto his back, pulling me close to him.

THIRTY-FIVE

"Are we going to wait for Athalda?"

Nyx sweeps me up into his arms and leaps into the sky. Chepi yips, flying along besides us.

"No. She told me how to find the portal and will meet us there."

Flying above the Shifting Forest in daylight is a little creepy. Every now and then I can see the ground shift and change below us.

"Do you think it's odd that Samael hasn't tried to find us yet? I mean he must know we're in Cloudrum by now."

"Yes, I do think it's worrisome. All the more reason to get the hell out of here. Athalda had her place spelled to hide us, so it's possible he assumed we fled to Nighthold after your magic was unleashed. He also has no way of knowing whose magic it was. He'd just know someone was using massive amounts of magic and roughly the location it was coming from." His face looks stressed. I trace my fingers along his jaw while watching him speak.

He continues, "When we get close to the portal, I want to

see if you can sense it and see if it'll reveal itself to you. That's why I asked Athalda to let us get there first. If it truly is a Sorcerer portal, you should be able to sense it once we get close enough."

"How do I sense it?"

"You listen. It should call to your Sorcerer blood. You should feel a gentle pull inside, guiding you toward it. Once you're close enough, it'll reveal itself," Nyx tells me, and I hope it works. I hope I can sense it. That uneasy feeling starts to fester in my chest again, and I tell myself to relax.

"We are getting close. I'm going to bring us down early to see how you track it," Nyx tells me, and I don't know how he sounds so sure. I'm not convinced I'll be able to track anything.

After a few minutes, he starts swooping down in a gentle zigzag through the trees. He touches down softly on the forest floor and holds me while my feet hit the ground and I get my bearings.

"Okay, what should I do?" I ask while looking around. I don't notice anything unusual.

"I want you to be still. Close your eyes and focus on slowing your breathing. Listen to your heartbeat. Imagine your blood pumping through your heart and out to your body. Your magic is inside you. Inside your blood. Be open to it," he says softly then goes quiet behind me, taking a step back.

"But I don't have any Sorcerer magic yet. What makes you think this'll work?"

"I don't know for sure it will, but hypothetically it should because you have Sorceress blood. The portal will recognize you."

I start taking long, slow breaths in through my nose, holding it for a second then releasing it slowly out of my mouth. I place my hand over my chest and feel my heart beating. I try to imagine my heart and my blood like he told me. I imagine the thick warm viscous liquid pulsing through my body, reaching my toes and my fingertips. I think about my blood traveling back to my heart, and that's when I feel it. I wouldn't have noticed it if I wasn't looking for it, but right there in the center of my chest under my hand where my heart is pounding I feel a slight tug.

"I can feel it," I whisper to Nyx.

"When you're ready, try to follow it," he tells me quietly.

The tugging sensation is constant. It's not a repeated tug or pulsing feeling. I step in the direction of the pull, and the feeling lessons a bit, but once I stop it returns. I try stepping to the side away from the pull to see what will happen, and I feel the tug become slightly stronger, like it's telling me I'm going the wrong way. Interesting. I open my eyes but keep my hand over my chest and focus on my heart and that small feeling inside me. I take it one step at a time, pausing to make sure I'm going in the right direction, and the direction it's pulling me. We weave through the forest a couple hundred feet, then all of a sudden the pull disappears, and I don't feel anything for a moment. I don't know why, but I take my hand off my chest and put both hands out in front of me, feeling the air around me. A shimmer appears. It's small at first then slowly expands until the shimmer is the size of a large door. I turn my head to the side, looking at it, then walk a circle around it, examining it. When I reach the other side, I can see Nyx's distorted body through the shimmer.

"I can't believe I did it."

"Don't touch it. We have to wait for Athalda. Portals can be unpredictable at times," Nyx cautions me.

"It's beautiful," I say aloud, taking a step closer and staring into the translucent shimmer. Nyx must be nervous by my proximity to the portal, because he comes over, wrapping an arm around me.

"It is." He kisses the top of my head. "Athalda should be here soon. Come sit with me," Nyx says, sitting down and leaning his back against a tree and pulling me into his lap.

"I can't wait to be back home, far away from this place." He tangles his hand in my hair, playing with the curly pieces.

"Me too. I can't wait to be back at your home. Away from here..."

"It can be our home too you know," Nyx whispers into the top of my head, and I lean into his chest.

"I like the idea of that," I say softly.

We sit in silence for a while, just enjoying sitting with one another. Chepi lies sprawled out in the dirt next to us. The birds are chirping, and the forest seems oddly peaceful at this moment.

"I need to tell you something." Nyx clears his throat, sitting up straighter.

I turn in his lap facing him, "What is it?"

"You're so perfect. I'm so lucky." He breathes into my ear then nibbles my neck.

I just giggle, feeling a bit shy by his compliment.

"What I need to tell you, Lyra, I—"

"Are you two ready to go?" Athalda says, coming up behind me.

"Yes, we're ready to get out of here," I say, getting to my feet. I look down at Nyx and catch a somber look in his eyes for a moment, but he recovers quickly, getting to his feet and smiling at me. I can see it in his eyes though. There's a sadness lingering there. I want to know what he was going to tell me, but now Athalda's here. He must just be worried about going through the portal.

"Are you sure you want to do this?" Nyx asks.

"Yes, I'm sure. I'll be fine. We're seconds away from being on the edge of the Lamia Realm." I give him a reassuring smile and place a kiss on his cheek. I bend down and pick up Chepi, holding him tight to my chest.

"Alright then it's decided. Let's get going," Athalda says, waving us closer to the portal.

She moves to stand right in front of it then looks back at me for a moment. When she does, I get the oddest feeling in my chest, but it disappears when she steps through the shimmering veil without another word. My breath catches in my throat when I see her body vanish.

"What does it feel like? Will it hurt?" I ask, turning to face Nyx.

"No, it shouldn't hurt. It'll feel like the wind is being stirred up around you for a brief moment, and then you'll be there. It's like stepping through a windy doorway. No worse than when we channel," he says calmly, but his eyes look troubled.

I turn back to face the portal but hesitate for a minute.

"Damnit, Lyra, I don't like this. I have a bad feeling," Nyx says, taking my hand.

I turn around and give him a long kiss, letting his tongue explore my mouth.

"Don't worry. I'll see you on the other side, lover," I say, breathless from our embrace. I turn, let go of his hand, and step into the portal.

THIRTY-SIX

My hair lifts around my shoulders, blowing in my face and making it hard to see. I close my eyes to protect them from the battering of my hair, and then my foot hits solid ground. I bring my free hand up to brush away the strands in my face when my face slams into a chest, and someone's arms wrap around me.

Immediately I know it's not Athalda's chest. I'm much taller than the old woman. This is a man. My eyes shoot open, and I try to push off his chest. I look up to see who it is, but I know. Deep down, I know who holds me. The smell of smoke and liquor heavy is on his clothes.

"Oh, how I've missed you, my sweet sister." Samael's shrill voice makes my heart sink into my gut. "And you have your sweet little pet with you."

Chepi growls, and I throw my hands out, hitting him in the chest and pushing him away, but he's too strong. He grabs my chin, lifting my face and forcing me to look at him.

"I don't like how feisty you've become. We'll need to rectify it immediately." His voice is toneless, and I brace myself for the hit I know is coming.

He strikes my face with the back of his hand, causing my head to snap to the side. A searing pain shoots through my cheek, and I can tell it's going to bruise. I grit my teeth, refusing to give him the satisfaction of seeing me flinch.

"Let me go!" I shout, thrashing my legs and arms. Chepi growls at Samael, but I shake my head, silently pleading with him not to attack. I can't bear the thought of Samael hurting Chepi.

"Citlali, restrain her," Samael commands, and I feel a strong grip around my chest.

I struggle against the hold, but it's no use. The person behind me tightens their grip as a rope is wrapped around me, binding my arms tightly to my sides.

"Now take her over there, but keep her close. I want her to see what happens next." Samael gives me a wicked smile, and panic sets in my chest.

I finally take a second to look around. It's cold and dimly lit. It looks like we're in the dungeons below the castle in Tempest Moon. I see now where I came through the portal inside a small open cell. It smells of death down here, and there are puddles of stagnant water and blood on the ground. Citlali pulls the rope at my back, dragging me to the back of the room until I'm pressed against the cold, stone wall.

"Try anything and Ill rip your fucking throat out," Citlali whispers in my ear then finally comes into view.

She smiles, revealing two sharp fangs coming out of the top of her mouth.

She is Lamia.

The candlelight flickers across the woman's red eyes, illuminating her features. Her jet-black hair contrasts sharply against her pale skin, and I can't help but feel a sense of revulsion mixed with a twisted sense of beauty. A wave of anxiety washes over me as I look around the hallway, taking in the sight of the guards and cells lining the walls. I don't see Athalda anywhere, and I'm relieved. Maybe that means the portal didn't bring her here, and Nyx won't end up here either. I know he'll come for me; he'll find me. I just need to keep it together until then. I try to take a deep breath. I can feel my heart racing in my chest. Chepi presses between my legs, rubbing his head against my ankle.

Samael closes the cell door and locks it, then he trails his hands across the bars, whispering an incantation under his breath. The bars illuminate for a moment then return to normal. I wonder why he's doing this and why all the guards are still facing the cell. Then my stomach turns sour, and I realize they're waiting for Onyx to come through the portal. I pray to the gods silently that he doesn't. I hear the whistle of a light wind, and he appears in a flash, standing in the cell.

Nyx recovers much faster than I did. His eyes glow bright immediately, and the dungeon fills with his scent as his magic comes to life. I know he's going to finally kill Samael, and it brings a wan smile to my face. Blinding light and fire burst out of him, slamming into the bars. I turn my face bracing for the heat.

Only it never comes. I turn back to the cell, and Nyx's magic doesn't get past the bars. It doesn't even shake them. He slams his hands into the bars, and a wave of power sweeps through the cell, but nothing happens. The bars don't budge.

"Your magic is no good as long as you're in that cell. You have no idea what it took to find the spell that would hold you," Samael says, trailing his fingers along the bars.

"Fuck you," Nyx says, voice taut.

"Now, now, play nice." Samael clicks his tongue. "I gave

you a chance to return what is mine. You chose to ignore my letters, forcing me to act."

"Where's Lyra? If you hurt her, I'll fucking kill you," Nyx grits out, jaw clenched.

Citlali has me pressed against the wall with her hand over my mouth just out of sight of Nyx. I squirm against the wall and bite down on her hand. She slaps me hard, leaving my cheek stinging and hot.

"Citlali . . ." Samael calls.

"Yes, my king," Citlali responds, repulsing me.

"Why don't you put my dear sister in the cell next to King Onyx? I want him to watch when I punish her. Throw that rat of hers in the cell with her too."

Samael's cold stare sends shivers down my spine, but I hold his gaze without flinching. I refuse to let him see my fear. As Citlali nudges me forward towards the cells, the guards part, making way for us. My eyes flicker to Nyx, and the sight of him sitting helplessly, his eyes burning with rage, brings tears to my eyes. I bite down hard on my lip, determined not to show any weakness in front of Samael. I focus on my feet, my heart beating like a drum in my chest. The lump in my throat grows larger, threatening to choke me. But I push the feelings down, not wanting to give them the satisfaction of seeing me break. I can't bear to look at Nyx, even knowing that I may never see him again. I repeat my silent mantra, *I won't let them see me cry*, over and over in my head until we reach the cell. With a rough shove, I stumble into the small, dark space, and the guard slams the door shut, the sound of the lock echoing through the cell.

I don't look over at Nyx. I just stare at my feet, blinking away my tears.

"Come now. Everyone, out. They won't be going anywhere. Oh, and Citlali, see to it that my sister has something more appropriate to wear," Samael sneers before he heads down the hall followed by Citlali and the guards.

I don't look at Nyx until I can no longer hear their footsteps traveling up the stairs. Once we're alone, I turn to find him facing me pressed against the bars. The bars are packed tightly together, but he fits a finger through the crack. I wrap my finger around his and sob.

"Lyra, baby . . . I'm sorry." His voice breaks, and his finger tightens around mine. "Don't cry. I'm going to get us out of this."

He rubs his finger along mine. I try to catch my breath and pull myself together. I need to think and stop being so emotional if we have any chance at breaking free. It takes me a few minutes, but I eventually slow my breathing and wipe my face. Chepi climbs into my lap and licks my cheek.

"Have you ever heard of a spell like this that blocks your magic?" I ask him, clearing my throat.

"Unfortunately, yes, I have. It's dark magic, which hasn't been used in hundreds of years. Samael would've had to give up something important to get such a spell," he says, furrowing his brows.

We hear the slow screech of a heavy door then the clink of footsteps coming down the stairs. Citlali walks down the hall with a red slip in hand.

"Put this on," she says, throwing a red silk slip at me.

"I'm not putting that on," I tell her in disgust as I hold it up. I'm not wearing this for Samael, that sick bastard, and I'll freeze to death in that down here.

"Put it on now, or I'll come in there and make you."

I just stare at her without moving.

"Better yet I'll go next door and play in your boyfriend's cell. Would you like that? I bet I could make him hard for me real quick," she says, pursing her lips in a cocky smile.

"You're repulsive," Nyx says under his breath.

Citlali ignores him and just continues to stare at me, tapping her foot. I don't want to wear this, but I don't want her to go into Nyx's cell. I don't want her touching him.

"Fine," I mutter through clenched teeth.

I quickly take off my clothes and put the slip on. I was planning on pulling my sweater back on once she left, but she takes my clothes and leaves without saying anything else.

As soon as she's gone, Nyx quickly removes his shirt and feeds it to me through the bars. I put it on over my slip, and his shirt actually falls lower on my legs then the slip does, warming me slightly. I pull my arms inside the shirt and hold them close to my chest, wrapping them around myself. It's cold down here, and it's only going to get colder as night approaches.

Nyx's hands are shaking with rage as he paces back and forth in his cell, his eyes blazing. Every now and then, he kicks his metal bars with a loud clang, sending sparks flying in all directions. I watch him, feeling a pang of helplessness in my chest. I wish there was something I could do to calm him down.

"It's no use," I say softly, trying to reason with him. "Stop exhausting yourself."

Nyx stops his pacing and turns to face me, his eyes still ablaze with anger. He opens his mouth to speak but then seems to think better of it and takes a seat next to the bars. I do the same, and we intertwine our fingers, leaning our heads together against the cold metal. Chepi curls up in my lap, nuzzling his head against my hand.

For a few moments, we sit in silence, lost in our own thoughts. The only sounds are the gentle shifting of Chepi's body and the distant murmur of voices from the guards patrolling the hallway. Then, Nyx leans his head against mine, his breath warm against my ear. "We'll get out of here, Lyra. I promise."

I close my eyes, feeling a surge of warmth in my chest. Even in this dark, cramped cell, Nyx's words give me hope. We'll get out of here, and we'll find a way to stop Samael.

"Why do you think the portal brought us here?"

"The portal had to have been spelled. Athalda must've betrayed us. Did you see her after you came through the portal?"

"No. I never saw her. I really thought she was on our side. I thought we could trust her. Was everything she told us a lie? Is she even related to me?"

"I don't know. When we get out of here, we'll find her, and I'll question her in my dungeon," Nyx says, repositioning next to me.

"That's if we get out of here," I mutter under my breath.

"Hey. Look at me."

I turn my head to meet his gaze. His gray eyes glow slightly.

"We will get out of here, Lyra. We'll have a life together, me and you. Maybe one day we'll even start a family and adopt all the injured animals you want." He smiles at me, and my heart squeezes.

"Yes. I'd love that," I whisper, smiling back at him.

I don't know how long we sit here shivering in silence. Finally, the sound of the door screeching followed by several footsteps rouses us both to our feet. Samael comes down the hall with that disgusting smile on his face. He's got two guards in tow.

"You're looking much better, my sweet." His shrill voice makes bile rise to the back of my throat. "Although I don't think that's the outfit I picked out for you."

He waves for a guard to unlock my cell, then he comes in. I

back up to the wall, but there's nowhere to go to escape him. He grabs hold of my wrist and pulls Nyx's shirt off over my head, throwing it to the ground.

"It wasn't enough for you to go fuck the Lycan. You had to let this Faery filth fuck you too." Samael spits in my face.

"Get away from her, you sick fuck," Nyx growls from his cell, but it doesn't faze Samael.

"You know what? Go get the old Sorceress bitch. I think it's time we have a word with her," Samael says to the two guards behind him, and they both nod simultaneously then leave.

So Athalda is here. She couldn't have done this. I don't want to believe it. I thought since she knew my father, I could trust her. What was I thinking?

"What do you want from me?" I yell, my voice cracking.

"Let me guess. I bet you think I want to use you to open the bridge to Zomea?" he says out of one side of his mouth. "I bet that old hag fed you all kinds of nasty lies. You see, sweet sister, I do want to use you to get to Zomea, but that's not all I want from you."

He moves closer, pinning me to the wall with his body. I squirm to get free but only succeed at cutting my skin open on the jagged stone wall behind me.

"You think I murdered my father and your mother for power? I have plenty of power without my father's pathetic magic. I had to get them out of the way so we could meet our true potential . . . together." He grabs my hair, jerking my head to the side. He runs his hot tongue across my neck, and I pull my head back, spitting in his face.

"You're disgusting."

He grabs my throat, pressing me against the wall. I hear Nyx's magic wreaking havoc in the cell next to me, and I wish I could call to my magic right now. I try to think about it. I try to imagine it pulsing under my skin but nothing comes.

"I told my father my plans, and when he wouldn't hear it, when he called Aidan to come train you, I knew he had to be dealt with. You see, I plan to make you my wife. You were always going to be mine."

"I'll never marry you," I mutter, my voice restrained by his grip on my throat.

"Oh, I think you'll change your mind. I can be quite persuasive, dear sister, especially if I start killing those you care about." He tightens his grip on my throat, and I gasp, trying to get more air. He moves his other hand under my slip, and a choked scream leaves my throat when he touches between my legs.

"You think I care about your virginity? Aidan did me a favor when he fucked you. Now you're broken in, and you can enjoy it."

I kick out, thrashing against the wall to get away from his touch. He finally releases me. I fall to the ground gasping.

"Get up," Samael yells while kicking me in the side. His foot hits my stitches, and I cry out. Chepi lunges for him, and I grab his scruff, pulling him back.

"Get away from her, you sick fuck! You can't even find a woman of your own. You have to molest your sister. You're sick in the head, Samael. Deranged." Nyx thrashes against the bars next to us, but it does nothing. Samael moves his leg back to kick me again, but the loud screech of the door stops him.

"Ahh, finally." He steps out of my cell as the two guards return. There's one on either side of Athalda.

THIRTY-SEVEN

"Perfect timing. My sweet Lyra, this is who you have to thank for our lovely reunion." Samael winks at me and nods his head to Athalda.

"How could you?" I spit out, getting to my feet. My voice is full of disdain.

"You don't understand. I didn't know, Lyra. Everything I told you is true. I promise," Athalda says quickly before Samael cuts her off.

"Enough." He waves his hand, and the guards hit Athalda over the back, knocking her onto her hands and knees.

"Stop! Leave her alone," I holler at Samael. I may hate Athalda right now for getting us into this mess, but she's the only family I have left, and I don't like seeing her being beaten on the ground.

"Oh, dear sister, that heart of yours. This woman betrayed you, and you wish to defend her?"

"Yes, I do." I stand up a little taller and face him.

Samael lets out a loud laugh. It sounds more like a cackle. "Get up."

Athalda slowly gets to her feet, and I see her knees are bloody.

"All she has to do is drink Lamia blood and the bridge will be opened?" Samael asks, facing Athalda.

"Yes," Athalda mutters.

"Why are you doing this? Why are you helping him?"

She looks at me, finally meeting my gaze, and I get that strange feeling again. It's the same one I had when she looked at me right before going through the portal. What does it mean? Is it my magic? Is she trying to tell me something . . .

"Are you starting all the fun without me, my king?" Citlali's voice pulls me from my trance. I don't even remember hearing her come down here.

"You're the star of the show. How could we start without you?" Samael's honeyed tone makes me sick. I wonder what the relationship is between these two. I've never seen Citlali before today, but her voice— she has to be the one I heard in Samael's chambers before, the one helping him hunt grimoires. I wonder if she's acting alone or if all the Lamia are aligned with Samael.

"Now for the main attraction . . . Lyra, my sweet." Samael comes back into my cell, and I back up to the wall, bracing myself.

"Don't make this any harder on yourself. If you're a good girl, I'll bring you to my bed chamber tonight." He reaches to touch my jaw, and I spit on his hand.

"Don't touch me. You're sick."

His eye twitches, and his jaw ticks. It's the only give away that he's upset. His voice remains honeyed as usual.

"Tsk, tsk, baby sister, your Faery has been a bad influence on you. That mouth of yours is going to get you in trouble." Samael clicks his tongue then punches me hard. Everything goes black.

I come to, gasping when one of the guards pours cold water over my head.

"Ah, so glad you're back," Samael coos.

I'm in a different room now. I whip my head side to side, but I don't see Nyx or Chepi. They must still be in the cells. My wrists and ankles are restrained against the wall, forcing my hands to dangle over my head. This room looks like the other parts of the dungeon, but this must be where he brings prisoners to torture . . . *great*. There's a wall full of weapons to my right. Athalda stands next to a guard toward the back of the room across from me, and Samael and Citlali are whispering in the corner. I find Athalda's black eyes and stare daggers back at her.

My wrists are rubbed raw from scraping against the bristly rope. My head is pounding, and I can only imagine what damage that punch did to my face earlier.

"Now, Lyra, you'll drink from Citlali, or I'll make things very difficult for you," Samael tells me as he and Citlali move closer.

I squeeze my eyes shut, searching within myself for the fire I know is there. I focus on the heat building in my core, trying to call my magic forth. But it's no use. My body feels heavy and unresponsive.

Suddenly, I feel a sharp pain in my cheek, and my eyes snap open. Citlali has gripped my face, her nails digging into my skin. I try to scream, but the pressure on my cheeks silences me. My body is trapped, unable to move more than a few inches. I buck against the wall, feeling my wrists and ankles start to bleed. Distorted screams leave my mouth as I try to shake my head and will this all away.

Citlali squeezes my face harder, digging her nails into both cheeks, and my eyes fly open, meeting her gaze. Her red eyes glow into mine, and all I see in her expression is hatred. I've never done anything to this woman. Never met her before today. Why is she so full of hate?

She brings her hand that's not holding my face up to her mouth and bites into her wrist, tearing the flesh open. I try to squirm and buck, but she presses in against my body. Her grip on my mouth never falters as she shoves her warm, bleeding wrist between my lips. Hot blood spills out, tainting my mouth with a copper metallic taste and filling my nose with the smell of rust. I cough and gargle, refusing to swallow and flopping my tongue around. I try to push the blood back out of my mouth through the cracks between her wrist and my lips. She presses my back into the stone wall so hard I think she's going to crack one of my ribs. She squeezes my mouth harder and uses her bleeding wrist to shove my head back. The warm fluid starts to spill down my throat, and there's nothing I can do to stop it. I'm choking, and I can't breathe through my nose with my face smashed like this. Her blood just keeps pooling in my throat. I force myself to swallow, trying to get a breath in, but her blood just keeps coming.

"I think that's enough." I hear Samael's voice, and Citlali lets go of my face and steps back.

I throw my head forward, spitting out the remaining blood left in my mouth and gasping for air. Blood spills all down my face and chest, and I can even feel it dripping down my legs. I gag as my stomach roils.

My heart feels like it's going to beat out of my chest. I hold my breath, waiting for the ground to shake or the earth to crack open and swallow me. I have no idea what opening the bridge even means, but a part of me expects something dramatic to happen. When a few moments pass and nothing seems to be happening, I let out my breath in relief. I know the prophecy says I have to be given Lamia blood at a ceremony under the blood moon, but a part of me thinks maybe the bridge would open right now. Athalda didn't tell Samael the truth, and he doesn't know anything about the blood moon.

Everyone is silent, but Athalda's eyes are still on me, and for a moment I swear she smirks at me. What's she up to? Samael steals my attention away when he starts to throw a tantrum, stomping his feet and pulling at his hair.

"Why isn't it working?" He breaks his usual composure. No one speaks. "What did you do?" he screams at Athalda's face.

"Maybe she isn't the key after all," Athalda says in her usual hoarse voice.

"Impossible," he hisses, turning to look at me. "You," Samael mutters, moving toward me. I brace myself for whatever he's going to do next. "What do you know? What did that old bitch tell you?" He grabs my face between his fingers.

"Nothing. She didn't tell me anything. I don't know anything, Samael," I plead with him.

He releases my jaw, shoving my head to the side in the process. He starts to pace, circling the room. Everyone is silent, and I know I'm not the only one feeling the tension. Citlali stands in the corner with her red eyes fixed on me.

Before I realize what's happening, Samael pulls a blade from his waist in a fit of rage and thrusts it into Athalda's chest. I hear her sternum crack when the knife pierces the bone. The room is silent, and Athalda's hands come up to the blade protruding out of her chest as she falls to her knees. A scream leaves my throat, and I choke out a sob as tears run down my cheeks.

"If she isn't going to tell us anything useful, then I have no use for her," Samael scoffs, turning back to come toward me.

I don't take my eyes off Athalda's as she chokes to get air and blood gurgles out of her mouth.

"Find me," she whispers, spewing a mist of blood as she

speaks Then she grabs the blade, pulling it free from her chest. Blood gushes out, and she falls forward in slow motion. She makes a wet slapping sound when she hits the stone floor.

I cannot believe my eyes. My brain is still trying to catch up to what's happening. I can't believe he killed her. I mean, technically she was already dead, I think. She said to find her. I can find her in Zomea? That has to be what she means. If only I knew how.

"Why did she say that? Tell me what you know, Lyra," Samael spits at me, but I just glare at him. "Sweet sister, I'm losing my patience." He taps his foot in front of me.

"I don't know anything, Samael, and even if I did, I'd rather die than tell you," I cry at him, speckling his top with redness.

"This is the last time I'm going to ask you nicely, Lyra. What do you know about unlocking the bridge to Zomea?" Samael speaks slowly and sternly, annunciating all of his words.

I stare right at him and say slowly and sternly, "Go. Fuck. Yourself." Then I smile big, flashing all my teeth.

Samael's jaw ticks, and a small giggle escapes my throat.

"Citlali." He says her name like it's an order.

She grabs a rod from the wall, and the last thing I see is her swinging it at my head.

THIRTY-EIGHT

"Time to wake up, my sweet," Samael whispers in my ear, and my eyes shoot open. "Aw, nice of you to join us."

I'm in my father's old throne room by the looks of it, but everything is different. The queen's chair is gone. Only the king's throne sits elevated at the far end of the room. He seems to have remodeled the throne room to be his very own private torture chamber. The dungeon down below had old rusty devices, but this room has shiny new toys for him to humiliate people with.

I'm positioned in the middle of the room facing the throne. My arms are strung up above my head tied with rope and strung around a beam. There's a table in front of me with chains at the top and bottom. It appears to be a swivel table with a large tub underneath. I've read about these before, and they're barbaric. You chain someone to the table, and when you tire of torturing them, you can flip the table and force their head into the tub of water for them to drown. I think I'm going to throw up. At least I didn't wake up attached to the table. It's what's next to the table that sends a tight feeling through my chest and down to my stomach. There's a table full of tools. I see a large sharp knife, several small, dull blades, needles and thread, a gag, a wrench, and several other things I don't recognize but want nothing to do with.

"You think you're going to torture me into telling you something? You forget you've been torturing me my whole life. I won't tell you anything, Samael," I scream at him as he sits down on the throne facing me. I hate seeing him sitting in that chair, the one my father used to sit in.

He looks so full of himself it makes me sick. "Oh no, my sweet little bird. That table isn't for you. But I promise you'll be squawking before I'm through," Samael says, tapping his fingers on his knee.

My heart starts to pound wildly in my chest again. I may be able to take whatever Samael does to me, but I don't think I can take watching him do it to Nyx. They can't take Nyx out of that cell though, or he'll be able to destroy them with his magic. Then I realize, oh gods, they're going to torture Lili. She must still be here, and Samael knows she was like a second mother to me growing up. I cannot bear that either. I don't have much time to contemplate the what if's because the doors kick open and in comes three guards followed by . . . oh gods.

Citlali and two guards have Nyx and they're dragging him in. Oh my gods, it must've taken all six of them to restrain him. He has iron cuffs around his wrists, ankles, and neck.

He sees me in the room, and when our eyes meet, his glow with fury. "Lyra, are you okay?"

"Yes. Yes, I'm okay, but Nyx . . . ." My voice breaks off, and I feel tears running down my face. I don't have the words.

"Oh, you two, this warms my heart." Samael chuckles as he walks over toward me. "Strap him to the table."

The guards and Citlali force Nyx down on the table. He puts up quite a fight, landing a kick in Citlali's face. I see blood drip from her lip, and it makes me smile. That bitch deserves to die when this is over.

"It's no use fighting, Onyx. The iron cuffs were made special for Fae like you. You have Lyra's father to thank for that. Your magic will do you no good here." Samael's honeyed voice is back.

"My father would never make something so cruel."

"Your father had lots of interesting artifacts your mother kept hidden away while she was alive," Samael says as he comes closer to me.

They finally get Nyx strapped to the table. At each corner of the table, a chain connects to the iron cuffs, and there's even one that attaches to his neck.

Samael rubs my hair out of my face, tucking it behind my ears. "I want to make sure you enjoy the show," he says, smirking at me.

"Everyone, out," Samael demands, and all the guards leave. Citlali remains lingering by the door.

"Ooouuutttt." He draws out the word slowly, and Citlali bows her head then disappears out the door.

"Now, where were we? Ah yes, Lyra, feel free to speak up at any time," Samael says, putting on his sweet voice that makes me want to rip off my ears.

"Lyra, don't tell this piece of shit anything. No matter what happens. Promise me?" Nyx says in a tight voice.

"I promise."

"I think we've heard enough from you for the night," Samael says while placing a gag in Nyx's mouth and strapping it around his head. His eyes are still on me, and they're glowing brighter than I've ever seen.

Samael moves to the table full of weapons and begins

picking things up and examining them. He slowly puts them back down as if he can't decide how to torture us. As if it's all a fun game to him.

"You love my little sister so much. Maybe I should carve her name into your chest." Samael grabs a blunt knife off the table.

Panic takes over my body. I feel like my heart is going to explode out of my chest when Samael brings the knife down on Nyx's torso. Nyx doesn't even flinch when Samael begins tracing my name across his chest. The room is silent, and all I can hear is the wet sound of the blade tearing his flesh. The smell of blood fills the air. Blood seeps out onto the metal table creating small pools that slowly drip onto the floor.

Nyx is still staring at me as if he's trying to tell me it's okay. I shake my head side to side as the tears fall silently down my face uncontrollably. I try to hold in my emotion, but a garbled sob makes its way out of my throat, drawing Samael's attention.

"Is my little bird feeling left out?"

Nyx's eyes are blazing into mine now, and he looks terrified. Samael was just drawing on his skin with a knife, and he looked unfazed, but now that he's coming toward me with the knife Nyx looks how I felt moments ago.

"Do you want a little something to remember your lover by?" Samael asks, getting to his knees in front of me.

I don't speak, don't even look at him. I just focus on Nyx as Samael digs the blade into my thigh. I feel my skin rip and tear with every ragged movement of the blade. I can't tell if he's drawing on me or just cutting me open. All I feel is fire. My leg feels like it's on fire. I refuse to look down, and I refuse to give him the satisfaction of seeing me squirm. I just stare into Nyx's eyes as he fades in and out with the blur from my tears.

Nyx starts making muffled grunting sounds through the

gag, drawing Samael's attention. He gets to his feet and tries to place a kiss on my mouth. I gag and rear my head back.

"You'll learn to be obedient, Lyra. If you're to be my wife, you'll learn to obey me," he says, moving to the wall behind me.

"I'll never be anything to you. When I get out of here, I am going to kill you, Samael. Mark my words," I howl.

He just laughs from behind me. I hear the swish of the whip before I feel it hit my back. It makes contact with my left shoulder, and heat radiates across my body. Nyx is shaking the table, grunting and bucking as much as he can for being strapped down.

"Fuck you, Samael. You might as well kill me, because I'll never be yours."

The look Nyx gives me is utter disapproval. I know he doesn't want to see me hurt, but I can't bear seeing him hurt either. And I cannot let Samael get the best of me. I can't let him break me.

"Look around you. You already are mine, Lyra."

Samael unleashes the whip with a frenzy, each lash sending a searing pain across my back, as if branding me with his fury. The agony becomes unbearable as he continues to strike me relentlessly, each blow stealing a piece of my strength. I struggle to stay upright, my legs trembling, and my grip on consciousness slipping away. Then, as if the torture wasn't enough, a cold blade slices into my skin, tracing the path of the whip's marks. My breath hitches, and I choke on a sob. I feel like I'm being consumed by the pain. Finally, Samael stops, and I gasp for air, barely conscious. He steps in front of me, his hand gripping my chin, forcing me to meet his eyes.

"What do you have to say now my sweet?" he says breathlessly.

I just spit blood out across his face. He pulls off his shirt, wiping away my blood, then grabs a rusty bar off the wall and shoves it in the fire. Oh gods, he's going to burn me. I'm so exhausted I don't think I even have the strength in me to be terrified, but my heart squeezes. Tiny needles spread across my body as anxiety and fear consume me.

Samael strides over, and I squeeze my eyes shut, holding my breath and waiting for the pain to begin. When it doesn't, a new fear shoots through my chest, and I open my eyes to find the rusty metal rod pressed against Nyx's stomach. A wicked grin spread across Samael's face. Nyx groans through his gag, and the smell of burnt flesh stings my nose, souring my stomach.

"Stop. Please."

"Does my little bird have something to say now?" Samael says, removing the glowing hot rod from his stomach.

"What do you want to know?"

Nyx grunts and starts trying to shake his head, but his neck is restrained. His eyes are piercing through me, and I have to look away. I don't want to betray him, but I can't bare to see him tortured like this.

"Why didn't the Lamia blood unlock the bridge?" Samael asks.

"Fuck you."

"You know what, Onyx? I don't think my sister here cares about you as much as I thought. She may let me go on torturing you forever without ever telling me what I need to know." Samael runs his fingers through Nyx's hair, toying with him. Samael looks up, his eyes meeting mine and widening slightly as a cruel smile curves across his face. "Lucky for you, my sweet, I have just the thing to get you talking." Samael strolls out of the room, and Nyx and I are left alone to stare at each other.

"I'm sorry," I whisper, feeling responsible again for all of this.

Why can't I get my magic to work? I could save us both right now if I could just get what happened in the Shifting Forest to happen again. I stare up at my bound wrists, willing fire to appear in my hands. I strain my gut, trying to push out any hint of magic. Nothing. I don't even feel a tingle under my skin. Nyx stares at me, unable to talk. He starts making a noise, but I can't make out what he's trying to tell me. I let my head fall forward, feeling defeated. I try to rack my brain for a way out of this. The door slams shut, and I jump at the sound, not having heard anyone come back in.

What I see makes my eyes widen and knees buckle. Samael has Chepi.

"No," I whisper to myself.

"What's that, my little bird? I can't quiet hear you." Samael moves closer, holding Chepi by his scruff and dangling him next to Nyx.

"Who would you save, Lyra, if you had to choose just one?" I try to blink away my tears and get control of my emotions. *Magic.* I scream internally. *Please, magic, I need you.* Suddenly a loud squeal echoes across the room as Samael breaks one of Chepi's wings. I scream and sob as I buck against my restraints.

"Let him go!" I scream.

Samael laughs, releasing Chepi's scruff. I watch in horror as Chepi falls directly into the tub of water next to Nyx's table. He quickly swims to the surface, choking and coughing. His tiny paws comes up to the side of the bucket, trying to pull himself out. He needs help. He can't get out, and he's going to get tired.

"Please," I cry out. Chepi pants, trying to stay afloat and pawing at the edge of the bucket. Samael leans down, turning his head sideways and smiling as he watches Chepi struggle.

"Please what, little sister?"

"Please help him. I'll tell you anything. Just please help him."

"I'll think about it after you've answered a few questions." Samael walks around the bucket, coming right up in front of me.

"Why didn't the Lamia blood unlock the bridge after you drank it?"

"It has to be given to me in the Lamia Realm during a ceremony under the blood moon." I strain to look over Samael's shoulder to see Chepi. He's struggling, getting weaker.

"Now help him please!" I scream, thrashing my body. I can feel blood dripping down my arms as I push and rub against my restraints. I need to get Chepi.

"I'm not finished talking to you." Samael grabs my face, squeezing my cheeks hard between his thumb and forefinger. "What do you know about the artifact?"

I shake my head side to side. My chest burns with panic. "Nothing. I know nothing about it."

"Lies!" He releases my face, shoving my head to the side. He moves so fast, lifting his leg and kicking the bucket over. Water spreads out across the floor, and Chepi's wet body coughs, choking on water as he starts to crawl toward me. His wing dangles, dragging on the ground.

"Chepi!" I cry out. Samael walks forward, pressing one foot down on top of Chepi's back. Chepi growls and squirms beneath him, but he's no match for Samael.

"Please. I've told you everything I know. The artifact is hidden in Zomea. I don't know where or anything else about it. I promise, Samael. Please don't hurt him," I blurt out in choked sobs.

"Too bad that's not good enough, my little bird."

His head whips to the door as a loud knock echoes across the room.

"Come in," Samael shouts, his voice full of irritation.

My heart falters as Lili steps into the room. Her eyes widen for a brief moment, then her face returns to the perfect picture of calm.

"Your majesty, there's a situation that needs your attention," Lili says. Her voice doesn't give away any emotion.

"Can't you see I'm busy," Samael growls.

"Yes, but, your majesty, some of the creatures from your wing of the castle have managed to get out and—"

"How did this happen? Which ones are loose? Move."

Samael pushes past Lili, releasing his hold on Chepi, and moves toward the double doors. Lili's eyes meet mine as she turns to follow Samael out of the room. She gives me a small nod, and I don't know what it means. She must be creating some kind of distraction for us.

"No one enters this room until I get back," Samael orders to the guards, and the doors slam closed. We are left alone in the throne room. Chepi crawls the rest of the way to my feet and starts gnawing at the rope around my ankles. I look at Nyx and wish he could speak to me right now.

"Lili's on our side. I know it. We need to get out of here and quick," I tell Nyx and Chepi.

Chepi keeps working the rope at my ankles, but he can't fly, and I know I need to take care of the ones wrapped around my wrists. I twist and pull at the ropes as blood drips down my arms. Movement catches the corner of my eye. The bookshelf starts to shake slightly. Fuck, there are many secret passages throughout the castle, and Samael must be using this one to get back to us quicker. I pull at my wrists harder, biting my lip as I cringe through the pain of the rope eating away at my flesh.

The bookshelf swings open suddenly, and I gasp as Mr. Drogo breaks into the room, panting.

"Princess Lyra, we don't have much time," he says breathlessly, making his way toward me and getting to work on the bindings at my wrists. "Things are not as they seem, Princess. Samael is not always in control of himself. You need to get far away from here fast."

My hands fall to my sides, limp, finally free from my bindings, but my wrists are past rubbed raw and the muscles in my arms feel like jelly. I drop to the ground to help Chepi get my feet free, and Mr. Drogo moves to Nyx. He takes the gag off from around his head. I get my feet free and grab Chepi, clutching him to my chest. I kiss the top of his head frantically as my heart swells with relief.

"It's going to be okay, boy." I sit him back on the ground and come to help Mr. Drogo break Nyx free.

We all freeze in unison as Samael's voice is heard through the door, speaking to one of the guards. *Fuck.*

"Hurry, get out of here. Thank you for helping us, but please go. I don't want you getting caught too," I say to Mr. Drogo. His eyes look like he wants to tell me something, but there is no time. He bows his head quickly, going back through the bookshelf and closing it behind him. I just have to get Nyx free, and then Samael will be no match for us. I try to undo the iron chain from one of his arms, but it's clamped in several spots. It's taking me too long. I just need to get one of his hands free.

The double doors swing open, and a charge of magic spreads across the room like static in the air. I'm pushed back to the wall in a wave of shocked air as Samael's eyes meet mine, their bottomless darkness staring into me.

"Looks like someone's been up to no good."

He's alone, and my heart sinks that Lili isn't with him to save us somehow.

"Fuck you, Samael. What do you think you're going to do? You think my entire realm won't destroy you and wipe this place off the map if you kill their king." Nyx thrashes on the table, and Samael shoves the gag back down his throat.

"I didn't miss hearing your voice. Now, my darling Lyra, I don't want to keep punishing you, but you leave me no choice. You won't tell me what I need to know, and every chance you get you disobey me. Others will have to pay for your disobedience."

My eyes quickly go to Chepi, who is still slumped over next to Nyx's table. *No.* I break out in a run, ready to dive over Chepi.

Time stops. Time does not slow down. It stops. A shrill cry escapes my lips, echoing through the castle. Terror seizes my gut as Samael whispers under his breath, and a wave of power shoots into Chepi. His body falls limp. My entire body heats as I burst into flames. I scream as magic rushes out of me, slamming into Samael and throwing him back toward the wall. A look of pure shock is plastered on his face. I drop to the ground.

"No, no, no, no, no . . ." I repeat over and over again, cradling Chepi's head.

His body is limp, and there's no life in his eyes.

"No. It's okay. You're going to be okay. It's not that bad." My voice comes out strangled, and the tears running down my face are drowning me. I shake Chepi gently, trying to wake him.

"No! Stay with me. Come back to me." I scream, shaking him, cradling him to my chest.

Samael gets to his feet. "That little rat is dead, you stupid bitch."

I let out a belligerent scream, my body convulsing. *I can't breathe. I can't breathe.* Chepi's body goes up in a burst of violet flames, leaving only a pile of ash. I'm rocking back and forth panting, in shock. He can't be gone. This can't be it. I hear Samael start laughing in the back of the room. I bury my sorrow for a moment, quickly building a barricade up around my heart. The pain threatens to consume me entirely. I take a breath, letting my chest fill with rage, with vengeance.

I stand, turning toward Samael. I see him standing in the back of the room. A circle of flames keeps him in place. The moment my eyes lock onto his, I feel it. I feel my magic, and for once I'm in control. I walk toward him, not taking my eyes off his as I slowly move through the flames. The fire spreads for me at my will.

"Well, this is certainly a surprising change of events," Samael says, choking on smoke. "You think you're going to fight me little sister?"

"No, I'm going to kill you," I force out between clenched teeth.

Samael throws his head back, and a deep chuckle echoes in his chest. But he's fast, and before I can attack him he steps to the side and lands a blow to my cheekbone. I call fire to my palms and send liquid flames at him, forcing him to the ground. Once he's down, I kick him in the side, hard. I kick him again and again as I scream at the top of my lungs. I pause for a moment, and he sits up, wiping the blood from his face.

"Do you know how your father died, Lyra? You were so young, so your mother told you it was a riding accident. Your father who was so powerful, the king of Cloudrum, you really think he died falling off a horse?" Samael spits blood onto the ground.

"What are you saying? Why are you talking?" Why am I even listening to this? I raise my hand ready to send a killing blow of flames down his throat.

"Onyx killed your father, little bird, and I'm sure that's not the only secret he's keeping from you." Samael smiles, blood and ash coating his teeth.

My hands drop as I turn my head to look toward Nyx, who is still strapped to the table and unable to speak.

"No. You're a liar. I don't believe anything that comes out of your mouth." I start to turn back to Samael, but he's up, and the distraction cost me. He grabs me by the hair, pressing his other hand to my chest. He whispers a spell under his breath that sends me flying across the room. My back slams into the bookshelf, and I cough up blood on impact, slumping to the ground. I look up as Samael starts walking toward me, his eyes narrowed and zeroed in on his prey. I meet Nyx's eyes one last time then turn, pushing through the door hidden behind the bookshelf. I don't want to leave Nyx, but I know Samael is after me anyway. Maybe if I lure Samael away, someone will help Nyx. It's a long shot, but if Lili is still around...

I stumble into darkness, frantically running down the stairs trying to remember where this passage leads. Once I reach the bottom of the staircase, a long, dark hallway branches out in front of me. This must be adjacent to the hallways passing by the kitchens and dining hall. I try to run down it as quietly as I can. I push on the stone wall along the way, hoping for a hidden door to open.

"Come out, come out, wherever you are." Samael's voice stretches across the cold stone hall, and panic seizes in my chest. I hit the end of the hallway, and I know I must've missed a door somewhere, but it's so dark down here. I can barely make out my hands in front of my face. I grab the bloodstone at my neck, running my fingers across it. *Calm. Breathe.* I'm not afraid of him. I have Fae magic, and I am the daughter of Euric Lewis. I am a powerful woman, and I will not cower away from this evil monster. I stalk silently back down the hall in the

WHAT LIES BEYOND THE REALMS

direction Samael is coming from. I listen for his footsteps, keeping my body crouched tight against the wall. Once I hear him approaching, I jump up and call my magic to my palms. I feel it pulse under my skin as liquid fire pools in my hands. I throw my arms up, directing my fire at him. He dodges my blow, rolling on the ground and popping up right in front of me, he grabs the top of my hair, pulling my back to his chest and wrapping his other arm around my waist.

"I told you already, Lyra, you belong to me. Now let's go finish things with your boyfriend. I'm growing bored of these games already."

I struggle against him as he hauls me back up the stairs. My scalp is on fire. Once back in the throne room, Samael releases me and throws me down on the ground hard. I bite my cheek and absorb the impact, flipping around fast and calling fire to my palms. Samael's there already with his hand on my forehead. I can't move, and debilitating pain shoots through my head.

"I'm really getting quite tired of this, my sweet. I don't want to keep hurting you, but you give me no choice. Where is the artifact being kept?" His eyes sear into mine, and I feel my nose start to bleed as pain explodes inside me. My body starts to combust, and I know it's my magic reacting to his invasion. *My magic will help me.* I just need to trust it like Nyx says. My head feels like it's going to burst as heat pulses under my skin. Samael pulls his hand away, his eyes widening as my forehead burns his fingers. Magic seeps out of me like an inferno ready to annihilate everything in its path.

"What the—" Samael looks down at his hand, and I jump.

I throw all my weight into him like a boulder crashing down a mountainside. I crash into his body, grabbing onto him wherever I can, singing his skin on contact.

He falls back on the ground, and I go down with him. I

press my hand to his face. His skin bubbles up under the press of my fiery fingers. I grab Samael around the neck, leaning in close to his face. I feel his skin sizzle under my touch, and I lock eyes with him. It's the first time I see a look of fear cross his face, and my lips curl.

I have him right where I want him.

He starts convulsing, and his eyes roll back in his head. His mouth starts frothing, and all I can see are the whites of his eyes, which are glazed over and milky. Did I kill him? Did he have some kind of a seizure from my magic? I release his neck and sit back for a moment.

"Pixie."

I suck in a breath, my hand flying to my chest as my father's voice comes out of Samael. How is this possible? What the fuck kind of magic is this?

"Open the bridge, honey. I'm here for you. Chepi is here waiting for you too. You know what you need to do. Unlock the bridge to Zomea, and all will be well. I promise. We are here for you." Samael's eyes close and his body slumps over, hitting the ground, lifeless.

Chepi is in Zomea with my father. I can bring him back. If I unlock the bridge, I can bring Chepi back. My heart starts to pound wildly in my chest, and I get to my feet. I turn toward Nyx, touching a hand to the spelled chains restraining him. I feel my magic pulse under my skin, and I call it forward, melting the chains and the whole goddamn table. Nyx pulls his gag off and reaches for me. I move out of his embrace.

"Tell me it isn't true, Nyx." I say while he stares at me. His eyes are soft and full of sympathy. "You killed my father?"

"Lyra, you must understand. I tried to tell you before we came through the portal. I've tried to tell you so many times. I just couldn't find the right words to explain."

"You killed him?" My hand automatically reaches for my

chest. My heart is racing, and I don't know how much more it can take. I need to build the walls up around it again. I grab the bloodstone at my neck, running my fingers across its cool surface. This stone has always helped calm me, but nothing is going to calm me right now. My heart feels like it's shattering into a million pieces, and I'll never be able to put it back together properly. I close my eyes tight. *Breathe.*

"I had to kill him, Lyra. You don't understand. Let me explain."

"No. Stop. You're a liar. You've always been a liar. How could you?" I start stepping back. I need to get out of here. I can't do this right now.

"Lyra, you're right. You are destined to inherit dark magic. My father's journal was right, and I was supposed to kill you. Euric killed my parents, and when I killed him, I was supposed to kill you too. But you were just a child, and I thought I would wait, give you time to live, to have a life. I came back once you turned eighteen, knowing I had to kill you before your nineteenth birthday before you inherit your dark magic—but . . ."

"No. You're lying. My father was friends with your father. He would never do that. I can't believe anything that comes out of your mouth. You probably just want to get the artifact for yourself. You're power hungry just like everyone else. Using me just like everyone else has."

I keep backing away, squeezing my bloodstone so tight I'm surprised it doesn't crack open. I need to get to the Lamia Realm. I need to get away from Nyx. I can't trust him. I can't trust anyone. I need to get Chepi back. I can channel. I know I can do it. I'm a Sorceress just as much as I'm Fae, and I'm not restricted by the realms like Nyx. I should be able to channel here in Cloudrum.

"Lyra, there's so much to tell you, to explain. Just stop,

please, and listen to me for a moment. Stop backing away. Euric isn't who you think he is."

Nyx's eyes glow into mine. I shake my head. No. No. No. I can't do this right now. I think back to Mr. Drogo and to his book on the Lamia Realm. I rack my brain until I see it clear as day. The lake in the mad territories on the edge of the Lamia Realm. I take in a deep breath, and I trust my magic. I trust it to take me there. I will it so, and the wind starts to pick up around me. Warm gusts of honeysuckle tear at my face.

"No, Lyra. Don't."

Nyx takes a step toward me, but it's too late. He's not fast enough, and he can't channel here.

"Liar," I whisper, and darkness envelopes me.

"I love you, Lyra Lewis." Nyx's words are just a whisper lost on the wind as I channel to the Lamia Realm.

MY FEET HIT the ground first, then my knees follow. I slam into the grass. I stand up, brushing myself off and taking in my new location. I stand on the edge of the tree line. I can see the lake in the distance. It's the one from the book. It's dark out, but I know that beyond the lake lies Drew's castle. I take a step in that direction, and a whoosh from the forest jars me back. I snap my head side to side, but I don't see anything. I turn back around, and red eyes glow into mine.

"I've been expecting you," she says, then she strikes, clobbering me over the head, darkness pulling me under.

SOMETHINGS BURNING! I choke on the smoke and start to run. I know this place. I don't let the flames slow me down. I push through the heat and the smoke, and I run like I've never run before. Tree branches hit and slice at my skin and my face, but I don't stop. I don't stop until a wolf lunges for me, grabbing my clothes in his mouth and halting my steps. I turn to confront the wolf, and it's Luke. I immediately wrap my arms around his neck, squeezing him so tight.

"I told you to stay away. I told you he's looking for you," he says quietly.

"Who are you talking about, Luke?"

He presses a finger to my mouth to silence me and crouches down, pointing beyond the trees. I peer through the branches and see—my father. My father and Athalda are speaking. No. They're arguing. I crawl in closer until their voices carry loud enough for me to hear.

"He was in your house, and you didn't kill that piece of shit? He killed me, your own family, and you could have ended him," my father says.

"You murdered his entire family. Did you expect him not to retaliate? It's not my vendetta. It's yours," Athalda says.

Nyx wasn't lying about that. My father killed his family— but why? How could he do that? Kill his own friends?

"It's ruined."

"Relax. Nothing's ruined. She's going to unlock the bridge, and you can finish what you started," Athalda says as my father paces.

"Yes, everything is falling into place and soon—"

I suck in a sharp breath as his head suddenly swivels to where I'm crouched in the bushes. His blue-green eyes glow as they lock onto mine.

Ashley R. O'Donovan is an emerging author of fantasy romance currently working on her next novel. Drawing inspiration from her love of travel, Ashley enjoys exploring new cultures and experiences, particularly in Kenya and Uganda, where she finds endless inspiration for her stories.

Born and raised in Monterey, California, Ashley loves spending time with her friends and family, and when she's not writing, you can almost always find her cuddled up with one of her three dogs reading a book, or catching the latest horror movie with her husband.

If you enjoyed this book, please consider leaving a review on Amazon and keeping in touch with Ashley on social media. She loves hearing from readers and is excited to share more of her stories with the world.

www.AuthorARO.com

instagram.com/ashleyrodonovan
tiktok.com/@authoraro

Made in the USA
Middletown, DE
11 September 2024

60218022R00239